ARMOR OF DUSK

By Jess Galaxie

feathersofdawn.com

ISBN 979-8-9889118-5-2 (eBook Edition)
ISBN 979-8-9889118-3-8 (Paperback Edition)
ISBN 979-8-9889118-4-5 (Hardcover Edition)

Cover Illustrator: Kaylie Leon
Graphic Designer: Rachel Nugent
Sensitivity Reader: Emeric Davis

I care far more about your safety than your reading this book. Please take the time to consider whether you are in the right headspace to read Armor of Dusk.

Adoption
Amputation
Anxiety
Arranged Marriage Mentions
Blood
Child Abuse Mentions
Corpse
Decapitation
Domestic Violence
Enslavement
Erectile Dysfunction
Food Insecurity
Gore
Graphic Depictions of Violence
Grief
Imprisonment
Incarceration
Kidnapping
Loss
Loss of a Loved One
Misogyny
Murder
Near Death Experiences
Neglect
Patriarchy
Pregnancy Mentions
PTSD
The Realities of War
Trauma
Vomiting
War Crimes

DEDICATION

To everyone who needs queer art right now
and everyone who refuses to stop making that art.

THE GRAVEYARD TREES
Traveling Trees Forest
North Cairn
Brittlebell
Martivin
HIGH CAIRN
Cairn
Dwindling Peaks
Climbing Thicket
Barren Rise Mountains
The Zotia Coast
The Wacot Empire
South Cairn
the Withered Woods
Froiland
The Cheybury Dynasty

CHAPTER 1

Year 570 with Vitiope
3rd of Asdel
129 Days

Asith woke in a small room that still felt strange to him. But that time, his heart remained calm and his breath steady at the sight of the unfamiliar ceiling. He sat up, rubbing the back of his head and combing his fingers through his hair. It was getting long, and even though he usually would have cut it to his chin again, he hadn't felt like doing that lately. He braided it as he'd seen Dradevai do with their own hair many times to get it out of their face. Asith didn't have nearly as much hair, but it held better than just tying it back. Then he could close his eyes each morning and imagine Dradevai's slim fingers threading through their silky black hair, easing the early waking hours where Asith had to acknowledge they were apart and they were not simply awake before him.

He had lost a lot of his clothes since they left South Cairn, which meant he didn't have to think rather hard about what to wear. He only had to choose from one of three tunics and one of two pairs of leggings. The trade and barter system in the Graveyard Trees reduced the value of his gold, which made it hard for Asith to get new clothes or shoes or anything other than food. Asith didn't mind having so few clothes, but his old boots had large holes and he had to trade away some of Dradevai's romance novels to get them. He had held out for as long as he could, but by the time he had read all the books twice, the heel of his left boot had completely broken off. Asith kept the last book in the series, though, under his pillow at night, rereading it when his limbs trembled uncontrollably at the thought of how alone he'd been.

As he laced up his heavy boots, Asith lost himself to thoughts of Dradevai's warm skin and soft feathers, his mind lingering on the memory of their weight in his arms. Asith shook his head and stood. The fast movement made him dizzy briefly, but at least it brought back the surroundings of the small room in which he slept. If he let his thoughts linger on Dradevai for too long, he would never leave the room and forget to eat that day, thus having to cook most of the food in his home just to satisfy his empty stomach. And he had things to do; he'd promised his aunt that morning.

When he stepped out of his house, the wide boardwalk swayed gently underneath him. On the upper boardwalks, which were built into the sides of the trees, snow lingered on their edges and along the bridges that swayed between them. Many houses were on his level, including the small house his father and mother had made their home, each painted with bright blues, reds, and purples. The mines provided pigments at a low cost, allowing people with the least to trade the ability to paint their home their favorite colors. He passed by a rainbow of homes but stopped by the little robin's egg blue house where his mother and father lived. It was his mother's favorite color.

Asith was already late to his aunt's, and he shouldn't bother them that early in the morning. His shoulders drew up as he approached their door, slowing down almost to a stop, and then he ran until he reached the stairs. A few people on the boardwalk stared. He swallowed hard and forced himself to slow down once he reached the top of the steep steps. His home was on the fifth level, among the smaller residences that were built into the sides of the massive trees that made up the walls. Each tree that made the walls of the city was once a dragon; their final act of defiance after the war was to lay down their life to create a wall for the few dragons who had fled with them. Currently, they protected a bustling city of dragons who were either born there or had found their way to the Graveyard Trees for safety. The yews, elms, and cedars all stood tall and strong against the yellow light of dawn, and new planks in the boardwalk shined like beacons against the older graying wood around them. The smell of snow mingled with the scent of freshly cut wood; like birchwood, which he had only realized Dradevai smelled like once he had arrived in the Graveyard Trees. He was still learning to distinguish the difference.

A copper dragon fluttered onto the boardwalk ahead, a guard just behind them, causing Asith to stop. They had just come from over the trees, both reverting to their smaller forms so the copper dragon could hold up their left hand and touch their thumb to their pinky. The sign was a holdover from when the city was first established; Lestash and his father had taught the gesture to Asith and his mother when they first arrived. It was not taught outside the Graveyard Trees, making it a strong way for dragons to prove their residency to the guards.

The guard returned to their larger form, showing off a bright orange band around one of their front paws. Their pewter wings stretched double

Asith's height, with a body about the size of a cow, and they ascended to the treetops with the other guards on lookout. The copper dragon picked up their basket, threw their hair over their shoulder, and walked toward a home. Above, dragons were flying over bridges, peacefully making their way through the city, their feathers splayed out as they easily glided underneath the protection of trees. Without the heavy winds of the mountains, they appeared almost like kites slowly drifting to the ground.

He needed to keep moving; otherwise, he would be caught there for hours, thinking of how the yellow light of the second sun would shine on Dradevai's feathers each morning in their hoard. Otherwise, everything would look gray. Even the brightly colored houses tinged darker when he thought about his loneliness for too long.

As he descended, he passed food vendors readying small carts, each with a metal rod curving over the top from one side to another. Each had rope and fabric tied around the middle, providing an easier grip for the back paws of nearly any dragon, and thus allowing vendors to easily transport their carts to any level. Many moved near the mines during the daytime to sell food to workers, then moved to the upper levels in the evening to draw in families who didn't have time to cook. Many dragons smiled and waved at Asith as he walked past. According to his neighbors, newcomers were rare, but they tried their best to always be welcoming. After all, they were seeking refuge from dragon hunters by staying there.

Two traders bickered at the bottom of the stairs, their argument loud enough to make Asith cringe. Thankfully, the two men stopped when they saw him, forcing smiles and waving. Asith waved back, taking a breath as he rubbed his ear. Once his feet touched the cobblestones of the streets, he quickly made his way through the area to reach the center of town, which had even more bustling people at that time of day than the boardwalks. In the very middle and oldest part of the town stood a temple built for Phela. On the highest spire, a shimmering golden statue held a bell that rang on the hour, and in her other hand, a rabbit peered over the city.

The bell rang, Asith's feet rooted in place as it swung back and forth. His attention was held entirely on a statue in the middle of a wide fountain with a depiction of Viteus taking Sula's hand and lifting them from the water; a representation of their ascension to godhood as Viteus's right hand and counterbalance. The bell shook Asith, his bones vibrating with the sound that suddenly seemed impossibly loud. It was all he could hear, all he could think about, but from the corner of his eye, Asith saw the slightest movement. He followed it, and the rabbit in Phela's hand was peering at him, its ears turned forward.

The ringing stopped, and Asith leaned down and scooped some water. It was crisp, the spring that filled it from underneath also drinkable. Asith pressed his wet hands to his face and shook his head before looking back at the rabbit. It was still, its ears back at a place of rest. His stomach lurched, but Asith walked towards the temple of Viteus, which rested near the central square in front of the temple to Phela. He ran his hands over his leggings to dry them. Asith needed to sleep more, obviously.

His aunt Lestash lived with her wife, Thistin, in a building just behind the temples where many other devout religious leaders lived. They didn't all worship Viteus, but as more dragons gathered in the Graveyard Trees, more temples popped up and the area became more of an open place to worship any god. Thistin even worshipped a different god than his aunt, a goddess of hunting called Vurla who, according to his aunt, had been brought into the pantheon less than a century ago.

When Asith knocked on his aunt's door, Thistin's deep voice called out to ask who it was. He smiled as best he could, trying to sound unshaken by the strange visions he'd seen in the square. "It's Asith."

Thistin threw it open, her unstrung bow in hand. A toothy grin spread across her face that was almost girlish if Asith didn't know she was quite a bit older than him. Her soft features matched her ebony skin, which shone almost blue when hit by the sun, a trait that made her cheeks look even rounder than they already were. He had told her that once, that she looked young, and she responded by saying the key to her youthfulness was her happiness. It was endearing, even if it did make him fear for his own youth.

"Have you eaten?" Thistin closed the door behind Asith once he'd stepped inside. Her tightly coiled hair pulled into a high ponytail bounced as she slipped past him into the small kitchen where Lestash had her sword laid out with a whetstone.

"Yes, thank you," Asith said. Thistin narrowed her eyes. They were a warm brown color yet discerning. She never seemed to trust him when it came to breakfast, though, in her defense, Asith tried to lie about having eaten to her rather often. He hadn't been hungry in the morning lately.

"I'll make some oats." Thistin nodded, setting her bow on the table and heading into the kitchen.

Lestash chuckled softly as Asith sat with her at the table. "You should know better than to lie to her by now." Lestash picked up her sword and tied it to her belt before she tucked the whetstone into her bag. "Are you here to work with your sword more?"

Asith nodded. "I was hoping so."

"I will gladly train you still." She looked at Thistin in the kitchen and smiled. "I had to admit, I've enjoyed getting to teach someone again. It's been a long time since I was on the guard."

"Thank you." Asith forced a smile. "I'm glad you're at least enjoying it."

Lestash hummed softly and looked at Asith with more concern. "Have you spoken with your parents yet?"

Asith swallowed, looking down at his hands. Every time he tried to lie about more than breakfast, he heard Dradevai's voice saying they didn't like it. He wasn't even sure they had ever told him that before. Asith shook his head. Going to his parents' home felt as if a rabbit crept into his ribs and settled there, shaking as a fox dug at the entrance to its burrow. So he avoided them as much as possible.

"I know it's not easy." Lestash rested her elbows on the table, arms folding over so that her bracers clacked together. "But talking to your father's twin doesn't count as talking to your father. Even if we look alike."

"I know." Asith sighed. He found Lestash easier to speak with than most people in the Graveyard Trees. It wasn't because she was his aunt; rather, she had spent years in the Drake Sentry fighting Blues and Greens, and because of that, she understood him easily. And he understood her too.

Thistin set a bowl of oatmeal in front of him, and Asith thanked her softly. She had sprinkled dark sugar on top, something Asith had never tried until he came to the Graveyard Trees. It was apparently honey that had been refined with magic, and Asith was starting to think it was a gift directly from the gods.

"I do go sometimes," Asith admitted to Lestash as he poked at the oatmeal. "I try. But I never make it all the way there."

"I know it's difficult, but please keep trying." Lestash smiled slightly.

Asith nodded and started to eat. If he at least started, she would probably be satisfied. She shared a look with Thistin, something that seemed to be a private form of communication, since Thistin nodded back. Asith had only ever experienced something similar when he was small, sitting between two adults as they communicated about him. The last time it happened was when the woman he knew as his grandmother exchanged looks with his mother. He wondered if he would get to share a similar look with Dradevai someday. Asith remembered the ghost they'd heard under the

Maeria Spire calling for Dradevai. Had they dreamed of sharing glances like that with their partner during Dradevai's childhood?

Asith needed to stop thinking about it. "What are we going to do today?"

"I was thinking today might be a good day to spar with real weapons." Lestash grinned, her narrow face looking wide for just a moment. "Can I trust you to not actually hit me?"

Asith's stomach turned, a vision of blood running down the blade of his sword toward his hands, rattling his spine. They were only using wooden swords until that point. He just nodded.

"Good." Lestash chuckled. "Then we'll go as soon as you finish eating."

He managed to eat the oatmeal despite not really wanting it and washed his bowl for Thistin. Lestash led him to the very edge of the grave trees, and as they walked along the massive roots, Lestash chatted about some things going on in town. She spoke of the city-state of Thecoria on the other side of the Barren Rise mountains and their fears as the Wacot empire continued to advance north. She was well known for striking an agreement with the Thecorians to protect their secret in exchange for some powerful magic that made the soil of the Graveyard Trees more fertile. But Wacot's advance could mean that secret becoming known outside of Thecoria. Asith offered validation of her concerns, but he couldn't really offer advice. Diplomacy and striking defense treaties seemed like work for someone who had much more schooling than him.

Lestash lamented about a few things, particularly some giants who had taken over a portion of the mine. She searched for the sun as she explained, speaking to Viteus as much as she was speaking to Asith. He listened carefully to her concerns, then added, "Could you make them think the mine is unsafe with acid? You're using it in the mining process already, and the dragons who produce it would be unbothered and could continue to mine."

"I hadn't thought of that." Lestash grew quiet and turned her face toward the sun, clearly communicating with Viteus in some small way. When they arrived in the clearing between several grave trees, she dropped her bag at Asith's feet and handed him a breastplate made of metal and leather. Asith slipped it on and tied it down; it wasn't quite his size, but it would work. Lestash pulled on something similar, only hers fit her properly.

"All right." Lestash moved to the center of the clearing, pressed her foot into the dirt gently, and settled into a fighting pose. She clearly had more training with a sword than Asith ever had. The dragon knights mainly fought with longer weapons like glaives, axes, and spears.

When Lestash held her sword, it seemed almost like an extension of herself, with a natural posture and an upturned chin. Asith, on the other hand, held his sword like a tool, or at least that's what Lestash told him. He did his best to mimic her, but unlearning the muscle memory proved difficult.

"Ready." Asith positioned himself across from Lestash, his sword pointed out and his eyes trained on her. Lestash could run quick. And after a nod, Lestash rushed forward and swung, which Asith parried easily.

Her next swing threw him off. Lestash didn't land the swing, of course, waiting for Asith to right himself. Then they began again, drilling that way so he could get used to the weight and hold of his sword. He preferred the sword over its wooden counterpart, for it seemed more like an extension of his arm. He returned his focus to blocking, and when he felt comfortable, he parried again. Then Lestash encouraged him to strike, handling each of his attacks with a precision that Asith's eyes struggled to follow. She just moved too quickly for him sometimes.

That's what got him into trouble; his eyes couldn't follow the way Lestash moved. Images of blood dripping down the blade flickered across his vision. It would last only a moment, his arms and shoulders tensing, but she was too quick for him. He overcorrected, swinging too hard just once, and the unmistakable sensation of his sword meeting flesh struck him. His body stopped as blood flowed from Lestash's arm and down his blade.

Time grew long as Lestash dropped her sword with a yelp, her hand shooting to the wound. Asith could hear Lestash talking but couldn't drag his eyes away from the blood snaking around her fingers.

Asith dropped his sword and took two steps back before running to the roots of the nearest tree. He stumbled into the solid wood and heaved until he emptied his stomach, and then he kept gagging when nothing was left. He shivered, wiping his mouth once he'd finally stopped.

Lestash's hand rested on his shoulder. "I'm sorry." Asith took the waterskin she offered. "It's okay, you just nicked me." Lestash helped him stand and brought him back over to her bag. "I think we might be done for the day."

Asith nodded and drank, sitting when she told him to. He wasn't really in a position to argue.

"Are you afraid of blood?" Lestash asked, securing a bandage on her arm.

Dizziness crashed over him again. "No, I—" He considered it. Maybe he was afraid of blood. "I didn't used to be, at least."

"What happened?"

"Dragon hunters attacked Dradevai and me in their hoard. I killed one of them." Asith took a deep breath; he remembered the blood covering the stone floor of the hoard. Scavenger birds must have picked the body clean by then, but the thought of it almost made him vomit once more.

"You'd never killed another person before, I would imagine?" Asith shook his head. She said, "It's hard, the first time. I've killed a few hunters, ones we didn't manage to just scare away."

"You've dealt with hunters here?" Lestash hummed. Asith said, "I can't imagine what they thought they'd gain. There are enough guards here to be an army."

"I know, and keeping out hunters is really all the guards here do. Usually, we scare them off just by presenting ourselves; six or seven of us does the trick. Sometimes the men took it as a challenge." Lestash sat against her bag and wrapped her arms around her knees. "I still remember the first time I was forced to taste human blood. After that, I always tried to fight them with my sword."

Asith grimaced, the hair on the back of his neck standing, so he slapped his hand over it.

"Even just defending yourself," Lestash said, "you can start to feel guilty. I wish I could offer advice on what would help, but I don't really know if there's anything that can."

"It's all right. I know that I was just defending the two of us. Just, with them gone, it's been worse."

"Did they usually comfort you about it?" Lestash's eyes held a cool look. They hadn't talked about Asith's relationship with Dradevai. She'd only said hearing the way Asith said their name explained enough.

"Yes." Asith allowed the stomach-curling sadness to creep into him. It always started low and worked its way to his chest, then his shoulders and neck. Eventually, it settled behind his eyes until he cried.

Lestash took a deep breath. "Viteus teaches us that sometimes when everything seems to no longer make sense, the best thing we can do is pick up the pieces of ourselves and refashion them into something new."

Asith hadn't heard Lestash talk about her faith before. Usually, she stuck to facts about the gods and their temples. Seeing Asith's blank expression, she laughed.

"Sorry." She looked up at the branches. "What that means is, sometimes the best we can do is look into ourselves, and even if we're a little broken, it's okay. At least to me it does."

"I think I see what you're saying." Asith drank from the waterskin.

"You know, Viteus also teaches that when we are hurting, we should seek the help of those who are already reaching out to us." Lestash smiled at Asith, cheeky and unwavering.

Asith's shoulders dropped. "I promise, I will try harder with my parents."

Lestash laughed. "Thank you."

Lestash spoke with his father regularly and had already hinted that his father wanted to know more about him. Despite that, Asith kept his distance, for the guilt about that had long since settled into Asith's already upset stomach. At that point, he couldn't feel worse.

"Does he ask you about me?" Asith fiddled with the seam on his pants.

"He does. He's worried, so he asks how you're doing." Lestash studied her wounded arm, checking the bandage. "I tell him that we've been training and try not to get too detailed. It's your choice whether you want to tell him anything you tell me."

"Thank you." He wondered how it might feel for her to hold back comforting details about Asith from her twin.

"Of course. You're a good kid, Asith. When I have children, I hope I get as lucky as my brother did."

Asith took a deep breath, his face warming. It faded quickly, though, as he looked down at his hands, remembering the harm he'd just caused with them.

"Come on." Lestash patted Asith's shoulder and then groaned as she stood. "Let's get back into town."

Asith removed the ill-fitting breastplate and carried the armor; it was the least he could do after cutting her. She took it back in front of the temple of Viteus, smiling at Asith.

"Go home, get some rest, I can take this from here." Lestash headed inside the temple, so Asith wandered through the temple district, finding the bustling market set up in front of the temple to Phela. People weaved around him as they carried goods to their stalls.

"*Asith.*"

Pystra's voice filled Asith's mind. She had communicated with him that way before, using a spell to speak to him at a distance.

"*Delri and I are heading into the Capitol. Would you like to meet us? We can see if Dradevai returned there looking for you.*"

Bile rose into Asith's throat. He walked into an alleyway and pressed his back against the cool stone of a temple.

"I am working with my father on a spell to find them," he lied. "You two don't need to look for them. I'll find them."

Asith heaved once he'd finished the message, nothing in his stomach to lose. The spell burned out, the connection between him and Pystra severing. Maybe he should have lied about Dradevai being missing when he'd first heard from her months ago. All those conversations did was remind him of his inaction toward finding Dradevai. The winter had settled in so harshly in the Graveyard Trees, prohibiting travel. His aunt had offered to fly him to their hoard, but Asith wouldn't have been able to direct her to it, nor was there any reason to believe they might be there. There was potentially some magic he could use, but Asith didn't know enough to cast a ritual like the one that found his father, and that had only worked because of Asith's blood. It's not like he had a sample of Dradevai's blood to use.

After an hour, he decided feeling better wasn't going to happen. He returned to the home he was staying in and stood in his small kitchen, staring at the cabinet as if he might eat something. When he couldn't stand the sight of his kitchen anymore, he walked to his parents' house. It was just down the boardwalk from his, randomly assigned by a friend of his aunt's who handled new refugees. The separation hadn't been purposeful, the friend had assumed Asith didn't want to live with his parents, but if Asith were honest, the split felt almost like mercy. After how his mother had looked when he returned with his father and without Dradevai, Asith couldn't unsee the wide-eyed worry that overtook her expression. With his parents safely in the Graveyard Trees, Asith had little to do beyond watch the snow pile around the grave trees outside his small window. It had taken Lestash showing up one day and offering to train him in sword fighting for him to leave the house. His mother had even brought some raw leather to fashion into useful items for trade, but it still sat unused in a corner on the floor, pressed against the wall so Asith wouldn't trip over it on the rare occasion he made dinner.

About a few hundred yards from his parents' house, he caught sight of his mother talking to her neighbor, with a smile on her face that didn't reach her eyes. Asith tucked himself against a neighboring house as his heart drummed in his throat. He tried to control his breathing, not really getting a handle on it. Once his mother had gone inside, he gave up and stumbled out of his hiding place. Asith had only been inside there once after they first arrived.

He crouched near the window of his mother and father's home, failing to get nearer to the door. He nearly screamed when the window flew open, the sound of his mother's voice almost admonishing as she said, "Really, I can't see why we haven't done it already."

Asith froze, his fingers tense against the plaster-covered wood.

"I asked Tash if Thistin can get me a few things for some potions when she's out next," his father said.

Tash was his father's nickname for his sister; apparently having such similar names as kids led them to take on Lis and Tash instead. After his father disappeared, though, his aunt slowly became known as Lestash, and only his father called her Tash.

But Asith hung on the bitter way his father said his sister's name. It wasn't directed at his sister, but not at him either.

"Which potion?" his mother asked. "I thought you were looking into rituals?"

His father's voice sounded tight. "No, I…I don't think I could do a ritual right now. I'm too weak."

"Oh." His mother's voice grew gentle. "It's okay, Listesh. You need to heal. Try not to push yourself."

"I know." His father sighed. "But at least I can maybe bring home some more food. Even bring some to Asith."

"I think he'd appreciate that." His mother sounded unlike herself. He realized it was simply the voice she used for soothing his father, her husband, rather than the one she used for Asith, her son. Asith's lips curved into a little smile; it was easier being happy for his mother than for himself. After all, it only took a few moments for the bright colors of the houses to dull, once he recognized he had a special voice reserved for Dradevai.

"It's the least I can do for him." His father's voice cracked. "Maybe with a little more time, I can do a ritual that will help him more than I can now."

It was as if someone had forced him to swallow a chunk of ice, the sensation closing his throat and sending a chill through his chest. He hadn't expected that rawness in his father's voice.

His legs moved before his brain could put together a plan, and he pushed up, only to slam his head into the window frame. His mother, rightfully, yelped as if a bird had hit the glass. Asith staggered and fell onto the planks below him.

"Asith!" his mother called frantically. She was already out the front door and at his side; perhaps he blacked out for a moment. "Are you all right? Here, let me help."

She helped him to his feet and looked at his father, who just reached the front door.

"I think I'm okay." Asith had a blooming headache, so he let his mother drag him inside and sit him in a chair.

"Are you okay?" his father asked gently. "What were you doing there?"

Asith's head still swam, but his father waited patiently as Asith tried to collect himself.

"Lestash kept telling me I should come talk to the two of you," Asith said.

His mother pressed a cool washcloth to Asith's head where he'd hit the window frame. Her pressure made it sting, and when he looked down, a little blood coated his hands. He might throw up again.

His father said, "Asith, I'm sorry. We didn't mean to pressure you…"

Asith shook his head. "No, it's okay." His mother was removing blood from his hair and face, then switched to wipe the blood from his hands. "You didn't pressure me, it's not that I didn't want to come here, it's just that…"

"It's okay. We understand," his father replied, with a confused yet soft expression. "At least, I think we both do."

Asith's mother sighed. "I don't think I do."

"I'm sorry, Mama." Asith looked her in the eye, and her frustration subsided slightly. He didn't expect to cry, but the tears just happened. After crying silently on his own so many times, he sobbed, loud gasps escaping his lips. "I should have stopped them. You told me to protect Dradevai, and I let them run right back into that prison."

His parents shared a look, and then his mother, her jaw hanging open, took a deep breath and swallowed. She picked up a pot of sticky sap with clean hands and applied some to the cut on Asith's forehead.

"And I…" Asith wiped at his face, struggling to breathe. "In the Capitol, another dragon was calling out to Dradevai. It was probably one of their parents and I made them leave, I told them it wasn't real and then—"

"Asith, honey." His mother squeezed his shoulder. "Take a breath, please. This isn't your fault. No one is blaming you for any of this."

"I'm sure Dradevai wouldn't blame you either," his father added.

Asith swallowed. He didn't particularly think they were right, but he didn't have an argument against it.

His mother smoothed his hair and kissed the top of his head. "Stay for dinner. We were about to eat."

He nodded, tears rolling down his cheeks. The tree sap was drying on his wound, pulling his skin tight as he shifted, and his stomach still felt like rocks were sitting at the bottom. There wasn't much in the world that could make him want to eat, even his mother's cooking, but he cared more about staying for her than his own rolling intestines.

"Are you going to be able to eat?" his father asked. "You look pale, even for a Silver." His father said it lightly, as if it were a joke.

Asith sniffed, his brows furrowing. "A Silver?"

"You're a Silver dragonborn."

No one had called him that before. He asked, "Would someone call me a Silver the same way that they'd refer to Lestash or you? Or Dradevai a Bronze?" The pain in Asith's head was sharper.

"Oh." His father's face twisted. "Yes, they would. They might follow it with dragonborn, but sometimes not."

It felt as if his father had just realized something, but Asith wasn't sure what he'd given away. His mother returned with three plates of food and set them in front of Asith and his father first before taking her own. It was a meat pie Asith had never seen her make, but she was probably learning new recipes.

"You know, it's impressive how you overthink just like your father, considering you've only just met him," his mother said. Asith didn't entirely understand until he looked at his father, who was scowling. His father let it go, turning to Asith instead.

"Have you done anything else to try to locate Dradevai? I know Tash couldn't bring you to their hoard, but they taught you some magic, didn't they? Maybe that could help?"

"I haven't," Asith said. "The way we found you required three casters and my blood. I don't know another way."

"You mentioned that maybe one of their parents was in the Capitol? They rarely moved us. Maybe if you get them out, they'll let you use their blood to find Dradevai."

Asith's eyes swam over the table, at his father's untouched food. "I don't even know if they're Dradevai's parent, and I'm not sure how I'd get them out in the first place."

"I know a few spells that could help." His father rubbed the back of his head. "I'm certain you could learn them if Dradevai was already teaching you magic."

"I'm not sure if I'm really on that level." Asith's shoulders sank, and he pressed a hand to his pulsing temple.

"Then let me teach you until you are." His father leaned forward, a radiant glow coming to his eyes. "I can teach you more formally than Dradevai did. It might be enough to get you where you need to be."

Asith's limbs tingled. "I really only know basic enchantment, though."

"That's okay. I know you learned a lot from Dradevai, but most of what they taught you was fire magic. Lightning will probably come to you much more easily due to our ancestry."

Asith's brow furrowed. His father breathed lightning in the prison they'd rescued him from, and every time his father had done magic in front of Asith since, the magic snaked like dry lightning across the sky before a windstorm hit. Even if he was only creating a small light or putting up a small tent for them to stay in on their travels, all his father's magic appeared like lightning.

"It's worth trying," Asith said. "If you think you'll be able to teach me."

His father nodded. "I know I will."

The flutter of Asith's lungs rocked him, making him feel dizzy. He hadn't realized how much he'd needed this help, and as his mother smiled and reached to smooth his hair down again, Asith cried.

CHAPTER 2

4th of Asdel
130 Days

Asith stared at Dradevai's spell book from his small armchair, trying to prepare for what he might find inside. Dradevai wrote all sorts of things, including portions of potion recipes, instructions for cooking eggs, a list of novels to read, and spell ideas. There might be some things they didn't want him to see.

He opened the book, his own sitting nearby in case he needed to copy some spells. That way, he would only have to look at Dradevai's spell book once and it would be less of a breach of their trust and privacy. He started at the back and moved through the pages backward. Asith copied the spell they'd used to find his father, but it was only portions of it since it had been a ritual and they'd had Pystra's book to reference.

Asith tried to skim the pages as he went, but one diary entry included his name. Dradevai's handwriting was neat, as always, but it usually veered toward the book's binding with each new line, slowly getting close until Dradevai corrected it, only to repeat it after a few lines.

That entry read:

> *I'm worried what finding Asith's father might mean for the both of us. The thought that we might discover his father among a bunch of other dragons is terrifying. I don't think they could ever accept me; it would be no different from when I went into towns to try to speak with humans. I am going to stick out. They are going to know.*
>
> *I won't stop Asith, though; he deserves to get something out of the trouble I've caused him. Even in the Capitol with the library, I might have gotten him marked as a criminal. When so many people looked up to him and treated him so well for being a dragon knight, I can't help but think I've ruined his reputation.*
>
> *That voice calling to me in the holds still comes to me in my dreams. I don't think it's ever going to let me go…*

Asith sighed and set his head in his hand. Dradevai's facade of grandeur was completely gone in favor of all the anxiety. But if Asith were being honest with himself, he wasn't much different. He was just less confident than Dradevai; well, maybe pompous was a better word.

He flipped to another entry, long before they had met. The handwriting was distinctly Dradevai's but not incredibly neat.

> *My feathers are so strange, sometimes they don't even look bronze. But I was born knowing myself as a Bronze, so I should be a Bronze. Maybe I'm just thinking about it too hard, I wish I could speak to someone about it.*

Asith flipped through more pages, his eyes scanning the dates on the entries until he found one close to when Dradevai had first taken him from his home. He shouldn't have read those entries, but his curiosity got the better of him.

> *Asith has taken to poking through the various items in my hoard. It seems as though he is unaware that I've noticed, but really it doesn't bother me that he's doing this. I find it kind of nice to watch the way his hands move as he picks things up. In fact, I find it difficult to look away from him often, but especially when he has a book in his hands. Something about the way he threads his fingers between the pages excites me. I understand that this isn't unlike the tingling feeling that is sometimes described by the women in the novels I read, the female characters burning with desire over the minuscule details of a man's hands or lips. I believe, if given the chance to see Asith, any of these authors would instantly want to make their next leading man look like him, his features are so striking. It makes me warm whenever he looks my way, even when he is frowning or frustrated with me, the little bit of attention sends a thrill down my spine and awakens...*

He closed the book. Asith shouldn't have been reading Dradevai's private writings, anyway. Heat ran like water up and down his entire body, so he settled on his bed, and to his surprise, his body became heavy. Asith looked at the wall next to him, thinking of how Dradevai would curl against him, and he stacked pillows on his arm and chest to mimic the sensation. He fell asleep faster than he had in weeks.

Asith woke to loud and persistent knocking on the door. He sat up, groaning as he looked at the window across the room. By the look of the light, the sun was barely over the horizon, let alone over the trees. He typically didn't see light for a few hours. Even as the first sun came over the horizon in the North, the full light didn't occur until the second sun rose in the east several hours later.

The knocking grew louder as Asith pawed around for his shirt from the day before and, more importantly, his pants.

"Coming!" He didn't bother with shoes. Asith swung the door open, still in the middle of tying his belt, to find his father standing there.

"Sorry," he said. "I probably should have asked before I showed up this early."

"It's all right." Asith straightened. "Is everything okay?"

"Nothing's wrong. But I thought I could start teaching you today." His father rubbed a scar over his wrist, something that probably happened to him in the dungeon.

"Of course, yes, please." Asith studied his bare feet. "Come in, I need to…I was still in bed."

"It's okay. Like I said, I should have thought this through more." He followed Asith inside, taking in the surroundings. Meanwhile, Asith ducked into his bedroom, picked up clothes, and changed.

With socks and a better tunic on, Asith reemerged. "I used to do that to my friends actually. When I was training to be a dragon knight. Wake them up early on accident." He sat at the table with his father and put his boots on the floor.

His father chuckled, a hint of admiration in his eyes Asith hadn't noticed before. "Sorry, I think you got that from me. Your mother used to complain that I would wake her up as I got out of bed in the morning."

Asith smiled. He hadn't wished for a father as a child, for his mother was more than enough. It wasn't until adulthood that Asith started the search. Knowing that his father had always wanted to come back to them, and that he still loved Asith's mother, he couldn't hold any resentment. So he had simply won a second parent.

"She used to complain when I would get her up early too." He started to lace his boots and pulled up the tongue carefully before it snapped against his shin. "During the harvest celebrations, I'd wake her hours before the games even started. She never yelled at me for it, but she certainly never seemed happy about it."

His father laughed, warming Asith's skin. Lately, he couldn't put his worries out of his mind long enough to achieve much of anything but training and eating. His bones felt lighter from making someone laugh, even if he wished it were from Dradevai.

"That doesn't surprise me," his father said. "Are you ready? I'm hoping we can start a little more advanced since you already have some training."

"What are we going to do?" Asith stood, picking up the journal Dradevai had given him. His aunt taught swords and healing magic, but his father had been a renowned mage before he'd disappeared. Asith had a feeling where his father's thoughts were headed.

"We're going to find you a familiar." His father led him outside. "And that will be much easier if you have a wand or a staff. Can you show me a spell Dradevai taught you? Something simple, perhaps?"

Asith ran a hand through his hair. There were many spells Dradevai had taught him, but a numerous number of them could light his home on fire. He stepped back and straightened his posture as Dradevai had shown him, before twisting his fingers in the air as if he were plucking strings, moving them in a clunky arch. The last time he performed the spell was when he first met Pystra, so he stumbled with his words and the movements but finished the spell with his arms crossing his chest. He then imagined a boy about his age with black hair and rounded ears, his complexion more like the color of fresh birch bark peeled from a tree. It must have worked because his father's eyes lit up like silver flames and he rubbed his hands together with a smile.

"That's great. That's a rather complicated illusion spell." His father eyed Asith's hands. "Though you were struggling with the movements a little bit, you still successfully cast it."

"Thank you." Asith looked at his feet, letting the magic slip from his concentration like a tablecloth sliding off a worn wooden table. He felt fully awake, the warmth of his praise spreading over him. "I think I am just out of practice."

His father rubbed his jaw and shook his head. "It could be, but you'd do better focusing your magic through a wand like I do."

Asith studied Dradevai's spell book on the table. He had never seen them use a wand, though magic came to them as if it were an extension of their body. In their hoard, they moved their fingers into all sorts of complicated symbols, drawing magic out of the air as if it were music being drawn from the strings of a lyre.

"Will that make the hand movements less complicated?" Asith stepped closer to his father, his hand sliding to his journal. He probably should have been taking notes, for his father had a lot to teach him. But the faster he learned, the closer he was to seeing Dradevai again.

"In a way. A wand allows you to do the movements required to cast a spell with your entire body, which always came more naturally to me."

Asith pressed his lips together, picturing the mages at the Stonegarde. Eroan, the mage in his group, never used a wand. But Dradevai and Eroan looked nothing alike when they cast. Perhaps, Asith was getting caught up about what a mage should look like. Even if he felt he'd never be a real mage, he still had to try for Dradevai's sake.

"Could you show me how I can get a wand?" Asith asked.

Lips curving into a smile, his father nodded, a bounce to his movements that reminded Asith of Dradevai's excitement.

"Yes. While we walk, can you tell me what other sorts of magic Dradevai taught you?"

"Mostly enchanting and things to make fire."

His father's face twisted in confusion, which surprised Asith.

"Dradevai could do fire magic?" he asked.

"That seemed to be all they knew. That and illusions."

"Did Dradevai breathe fire as well?"

"They did." Asith looked ahead. "Why do you ask?"

"Well, it's not unheard of, but it's unusual for a Bronze." His father considered the idea further. "In fact, a dragon that breathes fire has not been born in a rather long time."

"Really? I didn't know certain types of dragons are rare." Asith had seen so many dragons in the Graveyard Trees, many of which were smaller than Dradevai, but some seemed about the same size. Some breathed acid, giving them work in the mines, and others could produce toxic smog or lightning.

"It's not that a particular type is rare, necessarily, but combinations of feather color and certain traits are rare, much like specific traits in people can be rare. For example, having your mother's green eyes and silver hair is about as unusual as a Bronze breathing fire."

"I see what you're saying. The same way red hair is unusual when one of the parents has black hair."

They continued talking as they headed into the town. The Graveyard Trees had never been so quiet to Asith; few people were awake at that hour in the marketplace. Wayward merchants were setting up their stalls, the fabric awnings a vivid mix of yellow, red, and orange. Hanging over the wooden stalls, they blended into the glowing light of the morning, smoke rising out of some stalls from a small chimney stuck through the top, while others displayed vegetables lined up in large crates. The bumpy cobblestone streets barely registered under Asith's feet as he fought to keep up with his father. Asith considered buying some oats and brown sugar later that day if he had the time. It wasn't much, but it would be better than not eating at all.

They reached the far end of the market and turned left, heading north toward the mountainside and mines. After a while, his father took a sharp turn that led down a winding street lined with old buildings. They didn't match those of the city, with their leaning spires and thick shingles holding tightly to precarious cone shapes. It was the sort of design only achieved by using magic.

Eventually, they stood among towering trees that bordered the city and on soft earth that lay between them. There wasn't much grass, by Asith's guess, due to the lack of sunlight. His father walked along the roots as closely as he could, carefully stepping on the moss instead of the dirt. He counted softly under his breath, as if to reaffirm he was heading to the right place.

He turned down one of the narrow rows, which left little room for an army or anything to slip through on either side. But as they walked closer to the main wall, the trees lost their placement pattern. Some trees were pressed close together, while others had wider gaps.

Finally, his father stopped in front of one tree, looked up, and smiled.

"Who is it?" Asith asked.

His father raised his eyebrows as his cheeks became rosy, and he snorted. "This is my mother's grave tree." He grimaced. "I think. I can't remember if Lestash said my mother was on the left or right."

Asith peered down the row of trees. "Is there a way to tell?"

"Yes." His father's eyes flicked between the two trees, and in a burst of light and the sizzle of lightning, his father transformed into a lithe silvery dragon. Asith hadn't seen his father in that form since he and Dradevai had first found him. His feathers had grown back over the bald patches. Asith's chest swelled as he attempted to swallow a lump in his throat, but a broad smile came over his face. He was happy to see his father getting better and safely resting in his mother's care.

His father wiggled his tail before hopping on the tree and climbing the bark awkwardly. One of his wings hung at a strange angle, as if it were pinned against his back. Upon reaching a massive branch, he bit it off and let it plummet to the ground. The branch was as thick as Asith's waist. He realized almost too late that he needed to move, running out of the way just before the branch crashed against the ground.

"Sorry!" His father let go and fluttered like a chicken to the ground. He returned to his smaller form and met Asith on the other side of the branch. "Are you okay?"

"I'm fine." Asith reviewed the distance between him and the branch. He might have overreacted about how close it was.

"Good, your mother would have killed me." His father began poking at the smaller branches along the wood. "Can you help me find a long, fairly straight branch?"

"This isn't, like, desecrating a grave, is it?"

His father considered it, but answered, "It isn't in our culture. We did build the city into the sides of the trees."

As Asith studied the trees again, he saw etchings, some of the bark even stripped away on others. It probably wasn't much different from clipping the grass around a gravestone.

When Asith found a long, straight branch, he knelt and snapped it off. It was about the width of a broomstick, maybe a little thinner. "How is this?" Asith held it up.

His father's eyes brightened. "Perfect." He picked up the large bow and dragged it as far away from the path as he could. His father also held a branch for himself while pulling two knives from his belt. "Have you ever whittled before?"

Asith shook his head, following his father to the base of his grandmother's tree. His father sat with his back against a large root and gestured for Asith to sit among the gnarled tendrils that held the tree into the ground.

"I was close with my mother, the way you are with yours," he said, after Asith sat. "That's a good place to start for spellcasting focus. Something dependable, like a mother can be."

His father explained he would peel back the bark, then cut the soft inside to a desirable length. "Once you've done that, you're going to need to channel a little magic into it." His father displayed his branch, which shimmered and crackled softly, much like the lightning.

Asith looked at his branch, took a deep breath, and tried to focus his magic first in his hand and then push it into the wood. Dradevai and he had tried it that way whenever they enchanted things together. He did not, however, expect the branch to be far less willing to take his magic than a piece of fabric. His attention remained on his hands as he struggled to channel energy into the stick. Static would spark at some moments, but as soon as his father gave more instructions, he lost his focus. Asith took a deep breath and started over.

His hands squeezing the stick, Asith tried to visualize the movement of magic another way. Speaking words of power in Endethi didn't seem to have much effect, other than raise the temperature of his body. He remembered Dradevai again, listening to their words, trying to hear their voice directing him. The memory hurt his stomach. Finally, he imagined the magic as streaks of lightning drawn to a tree, and the energy transferred. His fatigued hands couldn't keep their grip on the wood, which was dry from the magic, and the branch shattered against the ground.

Asith frowned, his hands shaking, and he stomped on the branch. After Asith kicked the bits of wood away and huffed, his father silently placed another branch into Asith's hands.

It took four attempts to imbue the stick with magic. He hadn't even started to whittle the end. When he tried, he didn't know how to keep the branch in one hand while he whittled with his other. Which meant starting at the beginning.

"Here." His father set his hand on Asith's shoulder. "Think of it this way. This stick will help you find Dradevai. Focus your thoughts on finding them instead."

Asith wanted to yell at his father, as a child would yell at a teacher, but he bit his lip. He frowned, taking in the valleys in the back of the branch, the lines like lightning across the sky.

"I don't know if I can keep the magic in the branch while I try to whittle." Come to think of it, Asith had never been good at dual-wielding a pair of weapons either. Delri was phenomenal at that, which was why she frequently used a pair of short swords if she lost her glaive.

"Don't worry about the whittling; that will come on its own. Close your eyes and focus on Dradevai."

Asith, though sullen, nodded. He was certain it wouldn't work, wondering if he could make a spellcasting focus out of a needle and thread instead, but he would try once more.

He closed his eyes, refocusing his energy into his right hand as he held the knife with his left. As he centered himself, he remembered all the times Delri said he should improve his meditation, that his mind worked all the time and never rested. She was probably right.

Still, he couldn't just give up, so he took a few deep breaths and cleared his mind of everything but Dradevai. He remembered the vest he had made for Dradevai, the black velvet with red and yellow embroidery on either side. He rather liked the way he had cut it; the careful decorative stitches lined their waist, around to back with his design of the flowers and a sun. The design had come to his mind so easily, and the enchantment had worked with little effort.

His hand twitched, and when he opened his eyes, he saw his hand moving on its own. Static crackled as he carved a sun at one end, and the same flowers he had stitched for Dradevai on the other. It was a strange yet natural sensation.

Asith kept his magic running through the branch evenly, shaping the soft branch into a long, narrow rod. It couldn't be too short, though, for the design singed when he stopped working on it, as if he were running a heated knife over it. The wood changed color as well, a soft, shimmering gold, and appeared metallic, much like Dradevai's feathers.

When his hand finally stopped, an intricate vine of flowers ran toward the narrow end, with the sun at the wider base. The wood rested at two feet long, not quite long enough to be a cane but too long to be much else. It reminded him of the short broom his mother had sometimes used in her home in South Cairn. At the top was the simplified shape of a dragon with four horns wrapped around a ball, protecting it.

"I had a feeling that might work better." His father gently took the focus from Asith, turning it over in his hands, and then settled it back in Asith's. "Gold is an unusual color. Your aunt Tash would say it's a sign Phela smiled upon you."

"Really?" Asith looked at his father. "What does that mean?"

"I don't really know. I was never very religious."

Asith gaped and then laughed. "So, what do we do next?" The dragons of the Graveyard Trees had to be awake by then, for he could hear the distant din of the city, wings fluttering and flapping.

"I have a spell to teach you, but we need to go to the market to get a few things." His father stood up, and only then did Asith notice he was also holding a fresh wand. It was white with a bolt of lightning running down it. Seeing Asith looking at it, he showed it to Asith. "It always looks about the same when I do it. I've had to remake mine several times."

"Why have you had to remake it?" Asith stood and followed his father, who was making his way down the row of trees.

"Sometimes, it can explode if you make a mistake when doing powerful magic. That's why most dragons choose to use materials like softwood. It's less likely to hurt you than metal or gemstones if something goes wrong."

Asith paled. "How will I know if I've done something wrong?"

"Well, for one thing, your focus will explode." His father smirked. "That's usually a good sign. But if it gets too hot for you to hold, that is typically also a sign your spell might not be working."

"Oh, that's actually happened to me before." He had burned his hands trying to do a spell with Dradevai once or twice.

"Everyone does when they're still learning. And sometimes when they're well practiced and just not paying enough attention."

His father displayed his wand again and smiled, then turned it over to reveal two names written in a language not of Cairn. He had carved Listesh and Lestash, but farther down, he saw Maryan and his own name. Apparently, reading Endethi was innate to dragons and dragonborn.

In the city, Asith's father stopped at a run-down shop at the very edge of the market. His father offered a bundle he had been carrying on his belt to an elderly woman, and she gave him several pastries, all of which seemed to be filled with some form of sweet jam and topped with sticky honey. He handed one to Asith.

"I used to stop here a lot when I was on my way to my friend's home." His father didn't offer further explanation, and Asith was wondering what he had traded with the woman until he tasted the sweet, buttery pastry. They reminded him of something he'd had in the Capitol; sometimes, they were filled with chocolate. Though, he was often unwilling to give up the money to buy one. He needed to bring Dradevai to that shop once he found them.

His stomach churned. It was the first time he imagined Dradevai returning. To prevent himself from spiraling, he looked over the colorful awnings, people dipping in and out of stalls. One stall was brimming with dyed fabrics that were waxed, creating patterns along the edges that could be cut to create trim or wear near the hem of a sleeve. The myriad of yellows, oranges, and reds would look perfect against Dradevai's soft ochre skin. When they returned, he could craft something for them, but Asith had nothing to trade for it. He wouldn't even have enough if he spent a month fashioning the loose leather in his home into gloves or armor fittings.

"Are you all right?" His father nudged his arm gently.

It was enough to pull him from his thoughts. Asith shook his head. "Yes." He bit into his pastry so he wouldn't have to add more.

His father hummed. "You said yes but shook your head like you were meaning to say no."

Asith sighed. "I did, I'm sorry."

"It's okay. You don't have to tell me. But I'll listen if you want to."

"Thank you. But I'm fine, really." Asith took another bite, examining the flat stones under his feet. "I just had a thought that I might actually be able to find them for the first time since we've been separated."

His father smiled. "That's a good thing, if you have some confidence in what we're doing. But I have to admit, I had similar moments when I was in that prison."

"What was it like there?" Asith returned his gaze to his father. "Do you have any idea what they were doing?"

"Well, I spent a lot of time locked in that cage you found me in. Sometimes they'd come and harvest my feathers, my blood, my scales, and other times, they'd knock me out and take me to this place …" His face grew pale.

"It's okay. You don't have to tell me." Then Asith added, "But I'm willing to listen to you too. If you need to talk."

"Thank you." His father offered Asith another pastry. "I think they were running experiments. They kept me away from the other dragons on purpose. We were the most intelligent creatures they were keeping."

"What could they want to experiment on dragons for?" Asith frowned, and his stomach lurched. "Wait, they were taking your blood?"

"Yes. Probably for potions."

Asith handed the pastry back to his father and mumbled quick words about feeling sick. The mages who worked for the dragon knights said their healing potions contained dragon's blood, to make them more potent.

"Are you okay?" his father asked.

Asith entered an alley and swayed, his father right behind. He was going to lose his stomach.

"What's wrong?"

Just the thought of drinking a potion with dragon's blood in it made him want to puke. Anger burned in his stomach as well, from the thought they could be taking Dradevai's blood for potions. He hated it.

Asith collected himself and said, "The dragon knights made healing potions with dragon's blood. They were using you to supply us." Asith frowned, the words uncomfortable against his teeth.

His father's face tightened. A whole new wave of fear that Dradevai was right where his father had been crashed over Asith.

"Hopefully they're not in one of those facilities," his father said, "but we need to find Dradevai as soon as possible."

Asith straightened his posture. If Dradevai wasn't in a facility like the one his father was in, they would have found him already. He needed to move faster yet wasn't sure how.

They returned to the center of the city, his father bringing him to another small store. The young man standing behind the open booth took a bottle from his father. After examining the quality of its contents, he gruffly asked what his father wanted.

He listed the ingredients, some of which Asith didn't catch, most of them sounding foreign. He caught a request for chocolate too. When his father finished listing what he needed, the shop owner slowly turned his gaze to the bottle's contents again.

His father sighed and pulled out another bottle, seemingly from thin air, and extended it forward. The owner smiled, then told them he'd be right back.

"What did you give him?" Asith asked nervously.

"A potion. They're hard to make but the ingredients in them are common, so two was actually probably a fair price."

"Oh, what do they do?"

His father gave him an even look. "They're for enhancing the virility in a person who does not have enough on their own." He spoke casually, his expression like that of a doctor speaking about some fairly uncomfortable topic. Asith, however, was not immune to feeling flustered by the subject.

"They're difficult to make?" he asked.

His father nodded. "It's difficult to invoke passion in the passionless sometimes." He said it so simply that it left Asith thinking the phrase over as if it had some additional meaning.

"Do you make potions often?" Asith asked. The owner returned and was gathering ingredients into a basket.

"Potion making was always my specialty." His father accepted the full basket from the owner and thanked him. "I spent a lot of time making potions for the Drake Sentry."

"And in the town you lived in with my mother and her uncle?" Asith followed his father toward home.

His father nodded and smiled. "Actually, I made that particular virility potion much more in that town." He grimaced. "A lot of the people there married because they hadn't left their hometown and didn't seek out someone they really loved."

Asith thought of South Cairn. He probably would have done the same, before meeting Dradevai. The butcher's son had been trying to see more of Asith. He even made a promise with Delri at the Stonegarde that they would marry if they were both unmarried by thirty. Of course, they were drunk, and while Asith did love Delri, it was just a different kind of love than what his father spoke about.

"Does the same thing happen here a lot?" It wasn't like the dragons in the Graveyard Trees could easily travel. But they did sometimes travel to countries other than Cairn.

"It might. Some dragons have a history of arranged marriages. I actually had a fiancée my parents intended for me to marry."

Asith startled, and his father laughed.

"She didn't want to marry me either. The two of us initially left the Graveyard Trees together, along with her partner. I haven't seen either of them since we got separated."

"Oh." They ascended the stairs until they reached the level they lived on. "So when you met Mama, it was after you got separated from your friend?"

"Yes." His father shifted his gaze to his feet.

Asith frowned. "I'm sorry."

His father shook his head and reached out to smooth the hair on the back of Asith's head. "I was happy where I was."

In a rare moment of understanding, Asith stopped to hug his father tightly. He felt his father tremble as he wrapped his free arm around Asith.

"I'm glad you're here with us, Papa."

His father cried, which surprised Asith. Then again, he wasn't sure if he had called him papa before. Asith tried to apologize, but his father's cries turned into laughs and he wiped his face before stepping back and waving Asith off.

"It's okay, you didn't do anything wrong. I'm just glad to be home." He smiled. "Let's bring Dradevai home too."

Asith nodded, and they finished their walk home, discussing the spell Asith needed to find a familiar.

CHAPTER 3

5th of Asdel
131 Days

Asith and his father sat at the table in his parents' kitchen to copy the spell he needed to locate Dradevai into his book. It turned out his father had bought the chocolate because they needed a few things Dradevai liked to perform the spell. Asith regretted trading their books, but he still had one under his pillow. The pages were filled with little scratchy notes Asith hadn't noticed before, so at least he had something. Meanwhile, he needed to think of more things he might have of Dradevai's. It was Asith's homework, according to his father. He might have been joking, but Asith wasn't particularly sure.

At one point, his mother made them take a break to eat. Though, all she had on hand to feed them were purple sweet rolls. Asith enjoyed their earthy, almost chocolatey, flavor. He couldn't wait for Dradevai to try them. While his mother fried a few eggs to pad out their meal, Asith felt Dradevai's absence like an icy wind howling down an alleyway between tall buildings on a spring day; unexpected and disheartening.

After they had eaten, Asith could at least distract himself better. His father waved his hand, and a spell book appeared, then floated down to meet his fingers. He turned it to a page titled, 'For Attracting a New Familiar,' written neatly and straight. Asith's inability to write in a straight line must have come from his mother.

"I bought enough for you to try the spell twice." His father laid the book in front of Asith. "I have a feeling this might come more easily to you."

"What makes you say that?" Asith looked over the spell and grabbed the pen and ink Dradevai had purchased for him.

"You're loyal. Familiars are often creatures of the fae, but not always, and they like loyalty." His father sorted the components for the spell into the correct amounts. It seemed the leftovers were either for himself or for a different spell.

He had seen fae creatures and familiars with the mages at the Stonegarde; in particular, he remembered one getting crushed by a dragon. It resulted in the mage creating an explosion of fire in the dragon's face, which really had no effect, but several days later, the cat was trailing after him again. So, it must have simply gone somewhere else for a while. The realm of the fae made as much sense as any other.

"I guess that makes sense. What do we do if this doesn't work?"

His father shook his head quickly. "It will work." His father met Asith's eyes. "When you're still new to magic, it's better for you to not have a backup plan."

Asith scrunched up his nose, examining the spell he had partially copied. "That doesn't make any sense. It's likely that it won't work."

His father took a deep breath as he looked at the ceiling. He blinked a few times, his lips pursed as he brought a hand to his jaw. "When you fought Blues and Greens, what was the worst thing you could have done?"

Asith straightened, blinking as he looked down at the many lines of couplets he needed to copy and memorize to complete the spell. His heart quickened as he remembered all the times he'd moved at just the right moment or delivered the final blow as a Blue was about to catch Hamon, Eroan, or Delri in its fire breath.

"Hesitating," Asith answered.

His father smiled, his eyes shifting back to Asith. "That's what Tash would have said too. But with magic, thinking you may fail is like hesitating in a fight. It gives an opening for it to slip out of your grip."

Asith finished writing a couplet. He wasn't particularly following his father's logic. When they'd enter a town that was overrun, their first plan rarely ever worked. So, they would pivot their tactics to protect each other or gain the upper hand.

His father's shoulders dropped. "You don't look convinced."

Asith set his pen down. "It is hard for me to imagine fighting a Blue or Green without a backup plan." He wanted to understand, because understanding meant being closer to finding Dradevai.

"How much do you know about how magic works?" his father asked.

"Well, I know that spells have movements, incantations, and sometimes ingredients to work. And, admittedly, not much else…"

Asith rubbed the back of his head, and his shoulders dropped. He had never thought to ask Dradevai how magic worked, instead just letting them teach him whatever they felt would help him learn. Trying to learn more formal magic with his father, Asith knew he had holes in his fundamental knowledge. He felt dumb for never asking.

"That's okay." His father stood, then grabbed a pincushion and a scrap of fabric. His mother had been making several dresses, so the supplies were easy to find. After setting the pincushion on the table, his father draped the fabric over it and explained how the pincushion was the planet of Desta itself.

"The fabric is the magic that naturally exists on Desta," his father said. "It's there for all of us to use, and it permeates the very core of our world. This is the magic we tap into when we cast spells. It's very different from the magic of the gods, like what Tash does."

Asith had seen Lestash mend a small tear in her clothes or lift a stain. She could heal people, too, but he had always assumed it was similar to the healing magic that Dradevai did.

"What does this have to do with not having another plan?" Asith said with a frown.

"I promise, I'm getting to that." His father chuckled. "When we cast a spell, we're taking a bit of this fabric and forming it into a new shape. Like when you cut a bolt of fabric to make a dress."

Asith tilted his head as his father cut a small piece away and tried to fold it over, but it kept flopping open and sliding back into its preferred shape.

He took a pin and said, "Because the fabric wants to remain the shape it's always been, we put a pin in to make it stay where we want it before sewing it into place."

His father stuck the pin into the fabric at a strange angle. The fabric was rumpled and uneven, but the pin still held the fabric into place. Asith resisted the urge to pick it up and fix it. Chuckling at Asith's squirming, his father picked the fabric up and straightened the pin before laying the small triangle of fabric flat on the table.

"Likewise, a mage needs to force their will upon magic. However, magic is much more difficult to force into the shape you'd like than fabric." His father ran his fingers over the material. "You need to have the confidence you're doing it right."

"Ah, like how lace trim can smell your fear?" Asith joked.

Laughter barked from the room where his mother was working. She used to make that joke to Asith quite often when he would help her with dressmaking.

His father smiled at the doorway. "Yes, your mind must be clear of everything besides your will and what you'd like the magic to do."

Asith nodded and looked at the spell book again. "So, I have to believe this is going to work."

"And if it doesn't, then you find another plan. Not before."

"What if I'm concerned I might mispronounce some of these words?"

His father's eyes shined, perhaps with tears. He didn't acknowledge it, though, shifting his eyes to the couplets again, but felt his warm arm pressed against Asith's. A smile curled at the edges of Asith's mouth, his stomach settling as his father explained how they could adjust them to make Asith feel more confident about the incantation.

The lesson continued like that, his father gentle even when Asith smeared the ink of the line he'd just written. His thin fingers helped blot the paper, and he encouraged Asith to keep writing on the same page; it wouldn't make a difference if a smeared ink stain appeared in the middle of the spell.

As they worked, Asith felt lighter. It was a step toward Dradevai, but his father's presence also eased him and kept Asith busy. He drew a few versions of the spell circle in his book, each more accurate to the example than the last, his hand more confident as he drew the shapes. A giddiness came over him, the excitement of doing something correctly and earning his father's praise mixing with the satisfaction of progress. Finally, he could settle into the thought that he'd leave to find Dradevai soon, a thought he'd pushed off for a long time.

"Have you ever had a familiar?" Asith asked as he rearranged items to make space for the spell circle.

His father shook his head. "I have never really been interested in looking."

"Why do you think I need one, then?"

"They can play a supporting role in larger rituals. It will be easier for you to complete the ritual to find Dradevai if you have one."

Asith nodded. "That makes sense."

He carefully removed a few pages of his spell book, just enough to draw the circle at the proper size when he laid them out on the table. His father offered slight adjustments as they went, overlapping the paper more, using charcoal to draw the circle rather than the pen, and rearranging ingredients.

When the circle was completely set, Asith rubbed the charcoal onto his hands and picked up his wand and spell book. His father had shown him how to hold it and where to tap the paper, so he was fairly certain he could coordinate it.

During his first attempt, his wand grew so hot that he dropped it and the charcoal exploded. As a result, his mother angrily kicked them out of the kitchen, for black dust coated her fabrics.

"I am working on a wedding dress in the other room." She set her hands on her hips. "It's yellow and pink!"

Even after his father cast a spell to clean the fabric, she pushed them out the door.

"I promise, that probably won't happen again." His father stood awkwardly outside their home, his arms full of whatever spell components he could grab. Soot covered his silver hair, his fingerprints marking the sides of the containers and bottles. Asith held the rest of the collection, along with his spell book and warm-to-the-touch wand.

"Go do this at Asith's." His mother waved toward his house and then unceremoniously slammed the door in their faces.

"I don't have a table," Asith said.

His father sighed. "Guess we're working on the floor."

Asith pressed his lips together, studying the soot on his own hands and all over everything except his spell book. Luckily, what little magic Asith had imparted also kept the book clean. At least that's how Dradevai had explained it once.

They walked the short way to Asith's home, and his father cleaned them and the spell components with a magic spell before they changed clothes. Asith lent his father some clothing, for they both knew his mother was not about to let him back in her house to get his own. That time, after they reset the spell, his father walked Asith through the steps without attempting to cast anything in hopes of preventing another explosion. They worked until late into the night, carving the charcoal together as his father told him stories about his childhood arcana tutor.

"He would smack our wrists with a stick if I did the movements wrong. So, I put a spell on the stick to make it really light and bendable. He was so confused when he went to pick it up that he didn't even notice my friends and me leaving from the back of the room."

"Why would he hit you with a stick?" Asith frowned, using a needle to carve divots into the charcoal. The movement was similar to poking holes into a potato going into a fire so that steam could release. It was a horribly boring task, though, which meant Asith had plenty of time to hear about his father's old teachers. Even if they were jerks.

"Because that's what his teacher did to him, and he never thought deeply enough about it to realize it wasn't actually useful." His father shrugged and set his piece of charcoal on their pile of finished pieces.

"Dradevai was always worried when I accidentally hurt myself when they were teaching me," Asith said.

His father's head popped up, his eyes a little wide. "Well…" He looked at his hands. "Really, that's the way it should be."

Asith nodded. "Yes, probably."

His father told more stories until they were finished with the charcoal, then Asith drew the spell circle again, larger that time. It was a bit clearer that way and might prevent a repeat of the exploding charcoal.

"Don't be afraid to start." His father had pressed himself into a corner. "Remember, a lot of getting magic right is confidence."

Asith snorted. "That must have been why Dradevai was so good at it. They could convince themself to be confident in most situations. Even when they were incorrect."

His father's eyes lit up, his lips turning up and his shoulders shaking as he laughed. Telling a story about Dradevai and making someone laugh felt normal and easy.

"Funny enough, that's exactly how I would have described your mother when I first met her," he said. Asith laughed, his whole body shaking enough that he lost his grip on his spell book. He caught it, his father flinching as if he would have tried to catch it.

They laughed, taking a few minutes to recover before Asith straightened himself again. He took a few deep breaths to center himself, then raised his book and wand. Asith spoke the incantation, his wand over the circle, and it immediately glowed. He tapped the various smaller circles, and the charcoal rose and spun. The pieces seemed to condense and then looked as if they'd been turned into small crystals.

Those spun at a more rapid pace, and the glowing ink on his spell book grew brighter. But his wand stayed the same temperature. That had to be a good sign. He finished the passage and snapped the book shut to focus on his wand. He traced the complex circle with the tip in the air three times, and then, with a crackle of static, a small creature appeared, sitting in the fog of the paper that burned but gave off no heat.

When the paper had completely disintegrated, the crystals fell to the table, the flames dying much more slowly until only the rough gems and a black blinking rabbit remained. Asith had been expecting a cat, a dog maybe, but not a rabbit. It blinked its large black eyes, and its whiskers shivered, with black fur and a tinge of gray on the bottom of its feet.

His father chuckled. "Well, that is somehow both surprising and unsurprising."

"What?" Asith said.

The rabbit raised on its back legs, looking at Asith intently. Its fur shimmered silver, which was sort of pretty, but he still couldn't imagine why his familiar was a rabbit of all creatures.

"A rabbit just seems to suit you somehow." His father looked amused. "It will understand you and will follow your every command. See if you can find out its name."

"How does it suit me?" Asith frowned while the rabbit sniffed in his direction.

His father smiled but said firmly, "You are not easy to trust, but when you do, you're gentle. Also, you're pretty quick on your feet. Go on, though, ask their name."

Heat rose to Asith's face and ears. He hadn't expected his father to be so blunt. Though, his chest warmed to know his father thought of him that way, even after Asith had been so cold those past few months. Meanwhile, the little rabbit was sniffing its own feet, as if it were still getting used to the shape.

"Hello," Asith said awkwardly, but he pushed on. "I'm Asith. What is your name?"

The sensation of hearing the rabbit's name was odd. It was like his own voice was offering him the answer, rather than hearing the rabbit's voice.

"Yarrow." He looked at his father. "Her name is Yarrow."

Yarrow had approached him and was pressing her small face into his stomach. Sensing her happiness, Asith carefully scooped the rabbit up like he would a cat. She wriggled, so he adjusted his arms to the way she wanted to be held.

His father said, "Yarrow will show you how the two of you can work together. Just listen to her, and she'll tell you."

Asith smiled at Yarrow. Something about her being in his arms made his muscles unwind. He could understand why the mages at the Stonegarde would get horribly upset if their familiar was hurt, even if they could just bring them right back. He rubbed her ears and nose, already knowing she liked it, and she climbed onto his shoulder, where she fit well.

"Thank you." Asith felt more relaxed than he had in months.

"Of course." His father yawned, beginning to collect his things. "Let's continue in the morning."

Asith set Yarrow on the floor to help his father. Before leaving, he gave Asith a tight hug and said goodbye to Yarrow, who stood near Asith's feet.

Watching his father walk down the dark boardwalk, lit only by the few windows that still had candles burning in them, Asith felt his heart race in an eager way. A smile came to his face as he turned back into his home, looking over the scraps of paper leftover from the spell. He closed the door behind him, and the low candlelight barely illuminated

Yarrow as she darted to the center of the room, hopped, and twisted her body gracefully.

Asith laughed as she repeated those movements across the floor, as if she were showing off for him. Her elation bled into his limbs, and he squeezed his fists as he walked into his room to find Dradevai's spell book. He hugged it to his chest, then pressed his lips against the cover, with Yarrow standing between his feet. Asith's mind raced frivolously as he listed everything from the Graveyard Trees he wanted to show Dradevai when he returned.

CHAPTER 4

6th of Asdel
132 Days

When his father arrived in the morning, he carried a basket of food; soft bread and several steamed duck eggs he had bought from a vendor on his way there. Asith had eaten the eggs a few times since arriving in the Graveyard Trees, and he was excited for Dradevai to try them, as the eggs were partially incubated, which gave them a unique flavor. The other dragons ate the shells, much like Dradevai, so they might be excited to freely eat eggs as they liked.

He smiled as he pictured Dradevai buying the steamed eggs from one of the vendor carts and eating them as they walked. In the meantime, his father was looking for a spell in his book, an egg in hand. After he found it, Asith copied it while he set up in a corner to make a potion. Yarrow settled in Asith's lap and occasionally poked her head up to see if food was nearby. She didn't seem interested in Asith's bread and butter, no matter how many times he let her sniff it. Asith set a hand on her head and rubbed her nose with his thumb instead, which seemed to satisfy her.

Asith finished copying the spell for the ritual, realizing he had filled easily thirty pages of his spell book. The many notes, the long incantation, and the intricate spell circle seemed daunting compared to the spell he'd used to summon Yarrow.

"Have you finished?" his father asked lowly, breaking the quiet that had come over them.

Asith nodded. Yarrow shifted in his lap before hopping to the floor when his father set a few completed potions beside Asith.

"I was just thinking of how much bigger this ritual will be," Asith said. Yarrow was sniffing the potion bottles, her ears tilted forward.

"It will be, but you will be all right." His father smiled. "If you could summon Yarrow successfully, you can successfully do this ritual."

Asith sighed. "I hope you're right."

"I am." He leaned toward Asith and set a hand on his shoulder, giving it a squeeze. Asith smiled and thanked his father, who then picked up the potion bottles. "I'm going to try trading these for a table. I think you need one at this point, or maybe a desk."

Asith laughed. "I guess sitting on the floor isn't the best solution."

"No, my back feels terrible." His father stood and gathered his things. "I'm going to try getting a table, and I think you should maybe take a break."

Asith chuckled as he stood and followed his father to the door. "All right, I'll try to take a break."

His father tucked the potions into his basket and wrapped Asith in a tight hug, a warm hand on the back of his head. Asith melted into the touch. His father left, and Asith closed the door behind him.

When Asith turned around, Yarrow was sitting in the middle of the room, one of her large back feet in her mouth.

"Does your foot taste good?" Asith asked.

Yarrow set her foot down, not justifying Asith with any sort of response. She settled on the ground as if she might take a nap, tucking her feet up under her so that she looked like a freshly baked bun someone had left in the oven too long.

Asith cast his eyes toward his soft bed and the blankets there. He had stayed up quite late the day before, and though his father hadn't come as early as the previous day, he was still tired. Yarrow stood on her little front feet and stretched before she hopped toward Asith's bed and jumped in. She settled on his pillow, returning to her bun shape. In that strange way she communicated with him, she invited Asith to join her, to lay his heavy bones on the bed for a nap.

It was easier to fall asleep with her presence nearby, for her gentle movements as she adjusted for him lulled him into a calm he hadn't experienced in a long while. When he woke, she had flopped on her side like she was dead, her eyes closed and small front paws crossed underneath her chin. When Asith shifted, she lazily rolled onto her feet and stretched with her butt in the air. She then bathed herself again, her foot back in her mouth.

Asith got up to wash his face and put clean clothes on. It was late afternoon, and while he could review the spell sitting on the floor, he wanted to stretch his legs.

"Do I need to feed you?" Asith asked Yarrow, who was still on the bed. She looked far too small to be real, only about the size of the cantaloupe melons farmers would sometimes sell in the market back in South Cairn.

Yarrow tilted her head, her foot stretching forward as her toes splayed out, revealing the thick gray fur there. She then shook, her entire body shivering, and she stepped to the edge of the bed. Asith held out a small satchel, and Yarrow hopped in before they left for the market to buy her greens. She didn't actually need to eat, but according to her, she liked it, so Asith traded a leather belt to get some. He had intended to keep it for himself, but he could make another. He let Yarrow pick a good number of fresh carrots, and he chose some potatoes and eggs for himself.

When he returned, he put his groceries away, set a plate of herbs down, and sat on his bed. He reviewed the spell, keeping in mind what he'd done wrong when trying to summon Yarrow in the first place. That spell didn't call for charcoal, but Asith wasn't sure he wanted to know what would happen if the pieces of lightning glass he needed exploded. The spell to find Dradevai had to wait until night, so he made something to eat. Once he had food in front of him, and Yarrow had finished bathing herself post-breakfast, he asked her questions about the spell.

Despite her advice, Asith still didn't understand some matters, for the spell spoke of summoning a guide rather than giving him directions. He wasn't sure what sort of guide could lead him to Dradevai or if it could even lead him there directly. However, Yarrow assured him it was the correct spell. His father didn't stop by, and while Asith wanted to speak with him about it first, Yarrow urged him to cast the spell that night, when the moon would be nearly full. That way, if they needed the power of the full moon, they'd still have a chance to try again.

Asith agreed, lying down in the evening before their walk into the woods but unable to rest. By the way she spoke, Yarrow seemed completely confident about completing the spell as intended, and she made herself comfortable at the foot of Asith's bed while he prepared the items needed for the ritual.

CHAPTER 5

6th of Asdel
132 Days

Asith shivered in the chilled mountain air. On the cliff, he walked around the circle drawn for the spell, Yarrow standing on his back legs in the middle and sniffing up at the sky. Asith forced crystals into the ground at the points of the constellation that made up most of the design. It was Sula Major, a constellation his father had suggested, since it was named for the god Sula, who was Viteus's guide.

He placed the final crystal, then walked the edge of the circle twice before standing behind Yarrow. With his book in one hand and his wand in the other, Asith took a deep breath and picked up the chant at the beginning. He'd practiced it over and over, but that time, his eyes followed the lines of the circle and lifted to Sula's star.

From the corner of his eye, Asith saw Yarrow's eyes glow. The magic seemed to be working so far. Asith continued his chant, even as the light of Sula's star wavered. The constellation drew itself in the sky, and the crystals at the edge of his vision glimmered.

Asith's vision went black. His father had warned him that blindness was an essential part of the spell. It startled him slightly, for he hadn't expected it to come so suddenly, but he needed to continue chanting and keep his head turned up toward the star, despite no longer being able to see.

When he finished the chant, a weight landed on his shoulders and pushed him down until he was on his knees, as the spell requested.

"Please, I request your guidance," Asith said. He bent his head, and to his surprise, his vision returned.

"You are looking for your lover," said a voice, smooth and warm like snow settling on Asith's hair. A chill starting at his collar bones and working over his shoulders ran down his back.

"Sula asked me to guide you. Raise your head."

Asith's eyes followed the lines of a flowing velvet kirtle with a billowing blouse underneath. The neckline plunged between their breasts, yet was soft, and made their neck appear long and regal.

"Who are you?" Asith asked. He didn't know a person would be talking to him. But as her lips turned up into a soft, caring smile, he had a feeling she wasn't a person at all.

"I am Phela, goddess of love and wife of Sula." She approached Yarrow slowly. "And I am the first dragon."

Goosebumps rose on the back of Asith's neck as what little of the thin mountain air in his lungs left them. A lightheadedness came over him that eradicated the cold. Although the spell mentioned summoning a guide, Asith had not expected a goddess. He didn't know what to offer a goddess, nor did he particularly understand why a goddess would wish to speak with him.

Asith's eyes caught on the thick wavering horns that appeared like the tail of two moving snakes. Jewelry dangled at the very tips, and chains extended to a cuff around the base. Her black hair hung long, similar to Dradevai's, and was braided on either side of her head like heavy ropes draped over her shoulders.

Asith must have been gawking at her because she laughed softly, mimicking the chime of temple bells.

"Sula felt it was only fitting to send their lover to help you find your own. I do have one request of you."

Asith's brain clicked back, and he nodded. "I will answer your request if you will guide me."

"Then we have a deal. My only request is that you become my champion, and at my side, you will help me bring balance back to the people of Cairn. All of them, including the dragons."

The goddess smiled, her eyes sparkling in the moonlight as she leaned down to pick up Yarrow. She kissed Yarrow on the top of her head. "She will know the way."

"I do not know if I am the right choice for that task." Weight increased on his shoulders again as Phela set Yarrow down. She smiled, the light in her eyes new and brighter than the stars above.

"You are." Phela pressed a finger to her lips. "But don't tell Viteus I've asked you to be my champion. I'll be in trouble."

Asith's mouth fell open, so Phela added, "That means don't tell your aunt." The smile on Phela's face grew, and she giggled. "Viteus keeps a close eye on her."

"Oh." Asith had more questions than answers, but Phela kept speaking as she stepped toward him, a sword appearing at her side.

"Come here," she said.

Asith closed the distance between them, and she carefully removed the leather necklace with Dradevai's feather on it. She touched it to her lips and twisted the loop in her fingers, and as she raised it to Asith's head, he glimpsed something metal.

After tying the leather into Asith's hair, she said, "With this, our deal is struck. I will come to you again once you have found Dradevai."

Asith nodded. "Thank you. I will serve your name well."

"I trust that you will."

Phela's voice sounded distant, and Asith's vision turned black.

When it returned, she was gone. Meanwhile, Yarrow was cleaning off her face.

"Did you not like her kissing you?"

Yarrow shot him an indignant look. Asith picked up his book and wand and laughed. He scooped her up, then tried his best to scatter the remnants of the circle, but it had been burned into the ground.

Yarrow settled on Asith's shoulder, which he felt shouldn't work but she always seemed to stay tucked against his neck. He certainly didn't mind the extra heat as he walked back down the trail into the increasingly cool air.

The moon appeared quite lower from when he'd started the ritual, even though he hadn't felt time passing. Asith reached for the metal in his hair but couldn't distinguish the shape, so he removed it.

The small charm was a silver axe, with colors rippling through it as he tilted it in the moonlight. Something else was carved into it, but he'd have to examine it again in the daytime. Dradevai's feather was attached to the charm; the feather probably worked just as well to protect him in his hair as it did around his neck.

The more Asith learned about the gods, the more he realized how prominently Viteus stuck out in Cairn. People in South Cairn worshipped other gods, too, but in the Capitol and most other parts of Cairn, temples to other gods rarely existed. Though, one could find the occasional visage of Sula along the roads, watching over travelers and collecting offerings. It still seemed strange since, according to his aunt, the gods weren't at odds with each other. Phela's warning about keeping their deal secret felt much more like that time when Delri told his mother that he had lost his job while training at the Stonegarde so that she would send Asith money. It was for his own good, since Asith had been too proud to ask for help, but he realized eventually Delri did the right thing.

Even by the time the first sun rose, Asith's eyes struggled to focus on the charm's inscription. He yawned, looking at Yarrow on his shoulder.

"I don't think I can read when I'm this tired."

Yarrow's nose twitched, and as he entered the massive front gates of the city, exhaustion overwhelmed him. His stomach churned as he made his way through the quiet streets, and Asith shivered, his chest tightening at the thought of how vague Phela's offer had been. Asith had accepted it without thinking it through, but the promise of finding Dradevai had lured him in a way he couldn't resist.

At the edge of the temple square, he peered up at the statue of Phela holding the rabbit. Asith considered going to his aunt's to sleep, for the thought of going up all the stairs to his house seemed daunting, but Yarrow encouraged him to go home; he wasn't sure he'd be able to keep his secret from his aunt, anyway. When he opened the door to his home, a table and two chairs sat in the center of the kitchen. Asith touched the smooth wood and smiled, thinking of his father and Dradevai, before flattening himself onto his bed.

Asith woke sometime near midday, rubbing his eyes and finding the axe and feather tied back into his hair. He didn't remember doing that, but Yarrow might have put it there so he wouldn't lose it. After untying the axe, he examined the carving, which was a running rabbit. On one side, its legs were crossed, and on the other, it was stretched out mid-hop. When he spun the charm in his fingers, it appeared as if the rabbit were running.

Yarrow was resting on the pillow above his head, her ears laid flat and her eyes shut, reminding him of a sweet bun he'd had in the Capitol with Delri. The pastry was made with a root vegetable and dyed black with flowers, and Delri had giggled as she ate hers. He should bring Dradevai to get one sometime.

"Wake up." Asith ran his fingers over Yarrow's ears, and her eyes peeked open. "We need to get ready to leave."

Yarrow shook herself out and stretched, yawning with her large front teeth and tiny mouth protruding from her silky fur. She hopped off Asith's bed and followed him to his speckled mirror, where he got dressed. Running a comb through his hair, Asith felt like he was pulling hundreds of knots out. His hair had gotten long because he'd been ignoring it and tying it back. Maybe he should start braiding it. His father and aunt both did, though his aunt's were detailed and laid flat against her head. His father simply braided his hair off to the side.

Once he combed all the knots out, he retied the axe charm and feather into his hair and opened his bag for Yarrow to jump in. She peered up at him and blinked expectantly.

"What?" Asith thought she might have been frowning, but then it occurred to him. "Do you want something to eat?"

Yarrow ran in a little circle and stood on her back legs. Asith sighed, grabbing greens from the kitchen. She munched loudly as she inhaled the herbs, and in response to watching her eat, his stomach growled, so Asith made some eggs.

After they had eaten, Yarrow hopped into Asith's bag, and he carried her down to his parents' house. He needed some help with trading, and his father probably wanted to know how the spell went.

When he entered, a woman was trading a large bundle of fabric for his mother's cloaks. He should probably be making armor fittings and sewing. That might get what he needed.

"Ah, Asith," his mother said jovially as the woman passed Asith out of the house. "Good morning! Have you eaten?"

"I have, Mama." She pulled him in to kiss his cheek and then leaned down to kiss Yarrow's head. She seemed to think she was a real rabbit, but that wasn't a bad thing.

"Good." She touched the feather in Asith's hair. "What is this? Can I help you with something?"

"I need to make a few things for trade, and I came to talk to Papa about it. Also, it's what I got from the spell last night."

"Oh, the big spell!" His mother looked as if she'd forgotten. "How did it go? Listesh!"

Her stern yell surprised Asith. His father poked his head out of the back room with a confused expression, wearing a strange pair of goggles and a headpiece that covered his ears.

"Asith!" His father removed his various implements and dropped them unceremoniously on the table. "How did the spell go? Did it work?"

Asith nodded. "I was given this." He touched the axe in his hair.

His father stepped forward to get a better look. "You were given it? By whom?"

Asith remembered his promise that his aunt wouldn't find out. His father would absolutely tell his sister if he wasn't careful, but he trusted his father to keep a secret.

"You can't tell Lestash." Asith looked between his parents, and they nodded. "But it was the goddess Phela. She's worried about Viteus finding out."

His father went through several phases of emotion, ending with surprise.

"The entity that came to you called herself Phela?" His father expressed concern, studying the charm, and asked to see it.

"She did." Asith untied the axe from his hair. "She said she was the first dragon."

His father examined the charm in his hand, then retrieved his spell book from the back room. He spread it out on the table, Asith's mother sweeping up the fabric and a few other things blocking the space. After performing a few spells on the axe, probably to ascertain its purpose, he handed it back.

"I have no idea what this does. If she told you she was the first dragon, it's likely that it was really her. It's too bad you can't talk to Lestash about it. She would know a lot more."

It was such a strange little object, making Asith feel horribly afraid of what he'd agreed to so easily. Yet the sight of it made his limbs twitch, made him want to run, find Dradevai in Cairn, as if that were all he needed to find them safely.

"Maybe I need to spend some time with it. She gave Yarrow the directions to Dradevai," Asith said.

"I'm sure it will help you somehow." His father closed his book and set his head in his hand.

"I trust her," Asith said, tying the charm in his hair, "but I want to leave soon. I just need to get supplies."

"I can help." His mother was setting sewing supplies on the table. "Lestash was asking after armor fittings for the guard."

Asith perked up. "Can she provide the material?"

"Yes. Go talk to your aunt. If you need more, I could use some help making things."

"Thank you." Asith kissed his mother on the cheek. "I'm going to go talk to her."

"Say hi to her for me." His father laughed and waved as Asith ran off. Yarrow was still in his bag, bouncing and wiggling as he jogged to the stairs. She convinced him to walk once they reached the stairs, but slowing down was difficult; he finally had a path forward.

His aunt was speaking with Thistin and a group of other serious-looking Drake Sentry outside their home. Asith waited, not wanting to interrupt, until Lestash turned to him. She smiled, but the gesture was tight, her face not growing as wide and open as it usually did. Alongside Thistin, she ushered him into the house and closed the door.

"Is everything all right?" Asith asked.

His aunt shifted on her feet and glanced at Thistin, who sat in a chair in the kitchen.

"We have been seeing an increase in Blues and Greens." She rubbed the back of her head. "We always get a few here or there, but there have been so many, it's like they're being drawn to the city."

Asith frowned. "Has there been any unusual weather? Or something that could have displaced them?"

"No." She shook her head, crossing her arms. "And it's strange that they're coming from the East, not the South, as they usually do."

"What does that mean?" Asith asked.

His aunt shrugged. "I wish I knew, but they've requested I return to the Sentries for the time being to help organize." His aunt pressed a hand over her mouth, her eyes turned towards her wife. Thistin's jaw was set hard, and her brow lowered as she looked at the table.

"I take it they must be desperate, yes?" Asith asked.

His aunt's shoulders fell, and she sighed, her eyes turning to the ceiling. "Yes, they are. I haven't made a decision yet, though."

"I understand." Asith rubbed his left shoulder, thinking of the Green that picked him up and nearly killed him. "But if something unusual is going on and there are more of them…"

"There is little else I can do." His aunt shook her head. "Sorry, you were looking for me, yes?"

"My mother told me you may have some work I can handle. Armor fittings? I'm happy to make as many as you need if it means I can trade for supplies. I must return to Cairn."

"Return to Cairn?" His aunt's lips parted, her brow furrowing

"I have a lead on Dradevai."

Her reaction was slow, his aunt's eyes coming to light first, then she wrapped him in a tight hug and ruffled his hair, causing it to fall out of his braid, but he didn't care.

"Oh, Asith, I'm so happy for you!" Lestash pulled away, her hands on his shoulders still, her grin making her cheeks round and her face wide. It was infectious, Asith's lips curving into a smile as he thanked her. She called over Thistin, saying Asith had a lead on Dradevai.

"Tell us, how did you find a lead?" Lestash asked.

Asith paused, his lips parting, but no lie came to mind. "I did a ritual my father taught me."

"Was it the one for the spiritual guide?" Lestash crossed her arms and tilted her head. When he didn't answer immediately, her chin jutted toward him, her eyes narrowing. "What kind of guide did you find?"

Asith looked at his feet, his shoulders slumping. Of course she would want to know details about the ritual. "I can't say. Not to you."

Lestash tsked. When Asith looked up, her lips were pressed together, and she was looking at Thistin, whose eyes were wide, her full lips pressed into a small circle. He knew what Thistin was thinking, because Asith was also thinking it: Lestash would not like his answer.

"Why not?" Lestash's voice dropped, stern and goading. Her eyes bore holes into Asith, so he shrunk, similar to when Yarrow would sit like a loaf of bread. Asith would very much prefer to be a loaf of bread right then.

"I promised them that I wouldn't," Asith said.

"That you wouldn't tell anyone, or me specifically?" Lestash dropped her arms to her sides. "Asith, I was hoping I could go with you."

Asith blinked as Yarrow shifted in his bag. "You wanted to go with me?"

"Yes." Lestash looked at Thistin, who nodded. "I wasn't just going to let my nephew save their partner on his own from the people who took my brother and held him captive for a quarter of a century."

His arms felt light as he smiled at Lestash and Thistin. "Thank you, Auntie, really, but they need you here."

"And you need me more!" Lestash groaned, then pressed her hands to her face. "Thistin."

Thistin pressed her hand to his aunt's back and rubbed gently. She wiped tears from her face and said, "Asith, is this something you think you need to do on your own?"

Asith nodded. "I think it is. I think I need to find my own way of doing this."

"Then, Lestash, I think we have to let him."

Lestash frowned at Thistin and pulled away from her touch. She bared her teeth and grunted. "And you really can't tell me who is guiding you?"

Asith cast his eyes down. He wanted to, so badly. He wanted to tell her everything and invite Lestash, but the Graveyard Trees needed his aunt. His parents were also safer with Lestash working with the Drake Sentry in the city.

"I can't."

His aunt swallowed audibly and sniffled as tears streamed down her face. She leaned back into Thistin, who comforted her again. The room was mostly quiet, the only sound belonging to Lestash gathering herself.

Finally, she took a deep breath and nodded. "Okay. But I have something I want you to bring with you."

She walked to a trunk pressed into the corner of their small living space. Lestash rummaged through it before returning with a glass orb about the size of Asith's palm. Blue smoke swirled inside. She pressed it into Asith's hand and squeezed it.

"If you need me," she said, "break this, and I will come to you as quickly as I can."

"What does it do?"

"It will alert me." Lestash held up her hand, showing Asith a leather bracelet around her wrist. On one side was a large glass bead, filled with similar-looking smoke. "When it's broken, the smoke will come out of this bead, and I'll know you need me."

Asith frowned at the little ball. He didn't understand how she'd locate him if he broke the orb, but it was very clearly magic and he trusted she knew how it worked.

He tucked the ball into his bag alongside Yarrow. "I'll be sure to use it if I need your help."

His aunt's eyes froze on his face, then she opened her mouth, but closed it, instead running her hands through her hair.

"You said you wanted to make armor fittings for trade?"

CHAPTER 6

15th of Asdel
156 Days

It took Asith three days to make all the fittings, but he created enough to fit most of the guards and Drake Sentry with new armor, even if theirs hadn't broken yet. He also made them easier to adjust, a trick that he then taught the blacksmith which earned him some spare leather, as a thank-you. With the extra leather, he made a harness to hold his spell book close to his side, and for the armor fittings, he received a thick cloak, some heavy pants, and a good amount of rations.

Asith spent his free time over the following weeks at the library reading about magic, fixing his old armor to accommodate the book harness, and studying spells with Yarrow. Even with some extra distractions, the spring days seemed both horribly long and short. As the hours passed, he always felt like he didn't get enough done. Then, when he would sit down at night to eat, the seconds couldn't pass fast enough. The agony tightened his skin as though he were being stretched out against his will.

Yarrow hadn't told him where they were going yet, only that she knew the way. Asith would have to put a lot of faith into the hands of gods he didn't even fully understand, but there was no other option. Doubt would sometimes creep into the center of his bones and cause his limbs to shake.

Holding the axe charm in his fingers and focusing on it as his father had shown him, Asith wished he could know what it did before he left. He twirled it between his thumb and forefinger, watching the rabbit run and run, then closed his eyes to visualize how it might help him on his journey. A rabbit could certainly run fast, so perhaps the charm could make him faster. But Asith was already fast on his own.

As he sat on his bed, his eyes swam over his room, the weight of the charm heavy against his skin. His eyes landed on Dradevai's spell book, and he remembered the many useful spells he'd seen them use, including turning invisible to sneak into the cave. Yarrow's small feet pushed against him, urging him to follow the thought.

Asith squeezed the axe and visualized himself disappearing, his body as transparent as glass. That didn't get him anywhere. He closed his eyes, took a deep breath, and imagined a piece of fabric being draped over him, obscuring him from the world so that he perfectly blended into the surroundings. The axe warmed, and his eyes snapped open. The charm shimmered in the light coming through the window. It was communicating with him, a lot like when Yarrow first said her name; he didn't hear a voice in his head but knew he could hide him from people's view. He jumped out of his bed to find his father, Yarrow hopping after him.

Over the next few weeks, his mother helped Asith as much as she could, trading some intense embroidery work for a new backpack and heavy fabric to quilt. Asith helped in whatever way he could, especially seeing her customers, because they sometimes provided opportunities for Asith to get more supplies. Even an offer to clean an older Silver dragon's home would give him access to down feathers. By helping his mother, he also acquired a warm doublet for the mountains and a map.

Asith wanted to leave before spring truly started. The trees were shedding their needles to prepare for the new ones they would grow in the spring. People swept them up and used them to scent their homes or candles, some dried them to use in tea or spirits, and many burned theirs in fires. Though the air grew warmer each morning, Asith's mother reminded him he might need oils for his lips and face to keep them from drying and cracking when he was high in the mountains, and something to cover his head if the wind blew his hood off.

However, the heavy snow surrounding the Graveyard Trees hadn't fully melted. He would need snowshoes and a doublet twice as warm. One day, though, his mother presented him with a thick wool doublet stuffed with his father's down feathers. She grinned ear to ear as she held it up.

"It should fit with enough room to put more layers underneath it." She slipped it over his arms and checked the hems. "I felt as though I couldn't send you away without at least one thing that I made myself."

"Thank you, Mama." Asith fastened the doublet at the front and side and hugged her tightly. "I always prefer your clothes, anyway."

She chuckled and kissed his cheek before running her hand over his shoulder. "It helps that it's very easy to get down here, with so many dragons absolutely covered in feathers. Your father was shocked when I asked for it."

"Well," Asith said, "Dradevai never did need a coat the entire time we were up in the mountains together."

"It makes a lot of sense to me now." His mother stepped back to admire her work. She had embroidered the collar with two little running rabbits.

"I had this made for you too."

She picked up a small wrapped package and handed it to him. Asith untied the twine carefully and found a brooch about the size of his palm. His fingers brushed over the brooch; it was so small and perfect. The circular part was fairly plain and flat, but the rabbit that ran through it looked like the one on the axe charm.

"I thought you should wear her symbol with pride," his mother said. "She has given you a lot, after all."

He pinned it to his doublet. "You're right. This is a good way to honor her help."

Asith didn't know what he would do without his mother. His mother's trust soothed some of his worries, but he couldn't help but think of the promise he made to Phela about balance. His inability to understand her words made his heart turn over in his chest, rattling his ribs. But Asith pulled his mother in for a hug, and she wrapped her arms around him in return. Her love would always be a comfort, even when worry and stress blinded him.

"Thank you, Mama."

"You're welcome." His mother put tea leaves into a small teapot and faced Asith. "You have to come home safe, though. Do you promise?"

Asith chuckled. "I promise."

"Good." His mother turned back to brewing the tea and added a piece of wood to the stove. "You know, I was hoping that once you returned with Dradevai, you'd be able to settle down here. But seeing you wear Phela's symbol, her asking you to be her champion, I don't know…"

"We'll make it back, I promise." Asith furrowed his brow, trying to read his mother's tight expression.

"It's not that," his mother said. "I just have this feeling that there's going to be more involved. That you will go off and save the world after you've found Dradevai."

Asith laughed and wrapped an arm around his mother's shoulders. It had been so long since the two of them had talked in that manner. "I don't think I'm going to be saving the world, Mama." But when he looked at the teapot, chills ran down his spine. Phela certainly couldn't have meant saving the world when she asked him to bring balance back to the people of Cairn.

"I think you're underselling yourself." His mother set a hand on his cheek. "I always knew you'd grow to be a leader. You always had that spark in you."

Asith's shoulders drew in, his frame collapsing on itself with that thought. He hadn't even liked speaking in front of a crowd of people unless he was teaching them to wield an axe. Even if he was Phela's champion, he couldn't lead anyone.

"Thank you, Mama." Asith set his head against hers, his thoughts still scattering.

She smiled. "Let's get you the last of what you need to find Dradevai."

Asith started his travels on a morning unusually warm for that time of year. Both suns were rising high and melting the snow. He put on his goggles from when he'd flown with Dradevai, in case it snowed later, and his aunt had agreed to partially fly him down the mountain so he'd be on the softer hills and could avoid the steep trails.

His mother and father hugged him tightly, and each gave him a small package to take with him. Hers was specifically for Dradevai, so Asith tucked it in the middle of his pack. His father handed him a potion in a bottle about the size of his palm. It glittered like polished quartz in the sun but otherwise looked milky white. The potion would improve his strength temporarily, but it would also sell for quite a bit of money if Asith needed coin. Asith didn't know how to respond, thanking his parents for all they had done, but promising that was not a final goodbye. He held back his tears until he was in his aunt's paw, and he had to take off his goggles to wipe his face with his sleeve.

After an hour, his aunt dropped him off in the hills, and Asith could no longer see the tall trees that made up the walls of the Graveyard Trees. In a burst of static, she shrunk to her humanoid form and wrapped her arms tightly around Asith.

"Be safe. Trust in the guidance you have received. And if you need me, you know how to reach me."

"I do. I'll be safe. I'll be home soon."

She wiped away some tears, something he didn't expect to see from someone so strong, but she turned back into her silvery dragon form, which looked just like his father's. With a flutter of her wings, she kicked up snow and water, then she was high enough in the sky that Asith could barely make her out. He wished he could do that himself.

Asith looked down the rolling hills and toward the valley where Cairn was nestled in the browns and whites of patchy snow. The valley had always been fairly warm, giving it a long growing season and making it ideal for farming. South Cairn wasn't far, putting him near the south side of the Barren Rise. During that time of year, the walkways and roads would have already been built up with a layer of dirt and straw, then be topped with rocks so that they would float above the water as the raised houses did. South Cairn had always looked prettiest buried under fresh snow, and he was tempted to walk south just to see his old home and the people there. But given what his mother had told him, Asith knew better than to go there. Guards were looking for him, so he needed to stay out of sight as much as possible; otherwise, he'd find himself in jail, or worse, in a facility much like the one he'd found his father in.

Yarrow reminded Asith of the axe, but he shook his head. He should save it for emergencies. As Yarrow shifted on his shoulder, he studied the outline of the small round homes sitting above the vast farmland where he'd grown up. He would stay on the main road that went around South Cairn.

CHAPTER 7

19^(th) of Asdel
159 Days

It took him two days to walk the edges of South Cairn. He occasionally recognized the shape of a person, probably someone he knew, but they were too far away to tell. His fingers twitched to cup his mouth and yell for their attention, but he couldn't risk giving himself away to authorities or endangering anyone in town. Yarrow agreed that was the right choice, making him feel less alone, as she hopped along at his feet or sat on his shoulder.

Asith thought about Dradevai to pass the time, and when he was alone on the road, he'd sometimes tell Yarrow about them. He said he wanted to show Dradevai the library in the Graveyard Trees, where countless books about Sterling history had been gathered by a group of dedicated archivists.

A half-day beyond South Cairn, sleet drenched the fields. Asith picked Yarrow up and put her back in the bag to warm her feet. They stayed the night at a small inn in the next town. The following day, Asith rented a horse, which Yarrow approved of, though she didn't much like being atop the horse, even inside his bag.

Arriving in the Capitol took far less time than it had with a cart, but he had to figure out how to explain himself to the guards. He sat on his horse in the line of people entering, remembering how Dradevai's disguise spell had failed the first time they'd gone through. If wanted signs were posted for Asith, he might not be able to enter the normal way.

His hair was longer and he could maybe pass for a foreigner, but he couldn't speak any other languages. He got off his horse and watched the crowd move about as he patted the horse's shoulder. The only sign that he was a dragon knight was his sword, and it wasn't actually from the Stonegarde; it had come from his father. He might need to create a more convincing lie.

So, Asith combed his hair and braided it neatly, then used a spell his father had taught him to clean himself up. He would pretend to be a mage traveling for an education at the Macria Spire. Even though he wasn't young enough to be seeking magic lessons for the first time, his spell book and wand would make it more believable. It was as good a lie as any other he had come up with, and at that point, he had to go with it. However, Asith couldn't remember when the Maeria Spire typically interviewed interested students. Eroan had said once he'd thought he'd failed his interview but still had gotten in. Asith tried to remember the entire story, hoping he could strengthen his lie with details from Eroan's life.

As he fleshed out his lie, a group of gilliedhu men were rolling their sleeves up. They likely were trying to absorb as much sun as possible into their green skin. Their cart was full of leather goods, and as the men chatted amiably, Asith wished he hadn't trekked there alone. It wouldn't have been easy to get both him and Lestash into the Capitol, but at least he wouldn't have been trying to figure out passage by himself.

A halfling man walked up to the group and shook the hand of one of the gilliedhu men. Two other men hugged him and spoke to each other in Malenki, a language most common in Froiland, the country just to the south of Cairn. The man had a big smile, but what really caught Asith's attention was the velvet ribbon tied back in his hair. It was old, embroidered with fine thread by a delicate hand, but the most notable feature was the design. Asith had only ever seen that type of embroidery in the Graveyard Trees, in the ties that sewists made for blouses. Thistin sometimes wore one if she wasn't in her hunting clothes, the gauzy fabric held together at the front by a similar ribbon. It shared the same width, too, about as narrow as Asith's finger, because the needle they used was made from the tiniest of dragon feathers.

Yarrow shifted in Asith's bag. Then he caught an exchange between the gilliedhu man and the halfling. It was a quick and trained movement, with years of skill behind it. Trying to track the gesture was much like studying an arcane illusion; the sleight of hand could be obvious with a good eye, but with a slip of one's gaze, it could be lost. As soon as the halfling secured the item, he said goodbye to the men and wandered off to the tree line. No one paid him any mind; not even the gilliedhu men watched him go.

Yarrow's nose nudged his arm. Asith was unsure if he wanted to confront the man, his eyes still on the ribbon in the man's hair. But Yarrow's nudging persisted; she didn't want Asith to lose sight of him. He stepped away from his horse and started toward the halfling man. Asith didn't receive any odd looks, not even from the horse, so he followed the man into the trees.

The man was hard to follow in the dense forest wrapping around the Capitol's walls, but Asith kept up. The man took quick turns down what appeared to be a hunting trail. Asith looked down to step over a root, but when he peered up, the halfling had disappeared into the leaves.

Something felt off. Asith removed Yarrow from his bag and let her sniff the ground. She hopped down the trail slowly, stopping where Asith had last seen the halfling. Yarrow stuck her head through the bushes.

The man kicked, his foot emerging from the leaves. Luckily, she had ducked out of the way already, too fast for him.

"What the hell kind of rabbit…" The man swatted at Yarrow, so Asith picked her up.

"Stop," Asith said. "I just want to speak with you."

"I'm not going to speak with the weirdo who followed me into the woods." The man pushed his way out of the bush and stood. He wore thick clothes and reached the height of Asith's waist, maybe a bit taller.

Asith pressed his hands to his face, feeling Yarrow hop onto his shoulder. He hadn't considered how following someone into the woods would come across. Obviously, it would be strange, but Asith just listened to Yarrow, which, in hindsight, was maybe not the best idea, as she was a rabbit.

"I'm sorry." Asith held up his hands. "I just wanted to speak to you."

"Speak to me about what?" The man's brow wrinkled, his eyes darting up and down Asith's body.

Asith had just been thinking about how nice it would be to have someone to help him, but that wasn't really what he had in mind. The halfling was a criminal of some sort. But as someone who was wanted by the Capitol, Asith maybe needed a criminal's help. Asking him for help was likely his best option, so he needed to make it work.

"I need to get into the city discreetly." Asith dropped his hands to his sides. "I have coin."

"Oh." The man straightened. "*That's* why you were watching me since the moment I walked up to the line?"

Asith blinked. "You knew I was watching?"

"Yes. You were staring. It wasn't subtle." The man rubbed his temples and then looked at the trees. His eyes lingered on Yarrow, and he chewed his lower lip. Asith wasn't sure how to be persuasive, and he had little to prove he didn't have it out for that man. So, he offered the only thing he could think of.

"I can pay you with this." Asith pulled out the potion bottle his father had given him. "It's a potion of gem skin. It could easily sell for 250 gold."

The man's jaw dropped, his eyes so wide that Asith could see all the edges of his gray irises. "And you *just* want me to get you into the city?"

"Yes, just into the city, discreetly."

The man's eyes narrowed, and his shoulders tensed. He leaned forward to see the potion, but somewhere deep in his eyes, distrust was forming.

"What's the base of this potion?" The man asked. "It's clearer than any I've ever seen."

Asith had no idea how his father had made his potion. His mind raced before he spat out the first thing he could think of.

"Quartz, of course." Asith was pretty sure his father used quartz a lot, though that bottle could have none at all. He just hoped the man bought it.

"I'll get ya' in," he said. "But I need a fifty-gold retaining fee so I know you won't run off with the potion. You'll get it back when you give it to me."

Asith balked. "You could just run off with my potion and my gold."

The man stuck his hand out, his eyes hard and his lips pressed together. He was probably being taken advantage of, but he didn't really have other options.

Asith offered the man his hand. "Deal."

They shook hands, and Asith pulled gold from the various places he'd hidden it. He placed the potion in a small bag on his belt where the man could see it, to hopefully earn him some trust. Once he'd handed off the money, the man dropped it into his wallet and grinned.

"Name's Farin, by the way." He crossed his arms. "Nice to meet you."

"Asith, and this is Yarrow." Asith gestured at his shoulder, but Farin only gave the rabbit a quick glance.

"We should get moving." Farin nodded in the direction of the trail.

"Then lead the way."

As they walked, they stayed deep in the trees, avoiding a gap of about thirty feet where the trees were cut back, leaving only prairie grasses. They worked their way to an offshoot of the river that bisected the Capitol. Farin led them along the bank until they reached a hill that blocked their path. A large stone pipe was built into the side, with water drifting out.

"I hope you have good boots." Farin hopped into the fast-moving stream and moved ahead quickly, partially obscured by the darkness.

Asith scrunched his nose at the vile smell, and he tried to hold his breath as his stomach turned. It was good his father had enchanted his boots to be waterproof, but he still questioned his decision to follow Farin as he stepped into the shallow water. Asith remembered Dradevai might be enduring much worse conditions, and as he looked at the ribbon in Farin's hair, he knew he was on the right path.

"I'll be all right." Asith bent down to follow Farin into the pipe, and they quickly approached a portcullis. The metal had twisted, leaving a gap between the frame and the stone wall. Farin slipped through easily, but Asith had to curve awkwardly, forcing Yarrow to hop onto a stone.

After Asith forced his way through, Farin was staring at Yarrow. "So, you're a mage, huh? That's why you thought you couldn't get into the city?"

"Yes," Asith lied.

In the dim light, Farin set his jaw and held his arms tight to his body. "I understand. What're you in town for then?"

"You're asking quite a few questions for someone who is willing to sneak someone into the Capitol." Asith rubbed his nose with the back of his hand, trying to remove the smell from it.

Farin scoffed. "I think I'm allowed questions since you followed me into the woods like a weirdo."

Asith didn't know how to respond. After all, Farin was correct. The halfling moved down the tunnel, so Asith put Yarrow in his bag and followed close behind. When Farin wasn't checking marks on the wall with the light of a match, he was looking over his tense shoulders at Asith. After the second time he lit a match, Asith whispered a spell, which brought floating lights.

Farin turned on Asith and pressed his lips into a flat line. "Nifty trick."

"Thanks." Asith's eyes caught on the embroidered ribbon, and a compulsion hit him like a wave before sliding up his arms and into his throat. Even though Yarrow stamped her back foot against his side, Asith couldn't remove his stare, or stop his next words. "Where did you get that tie in your hair? The embroidery is unusual."

The splashing of the water stopped. Asith could barely register why Farin had halted when a strike came to his gut. He fell into the chilled water and gasped. Asith was pulled up by the collar, then a cold blade was pressed to his throat, all while Asith tried to adjust his vision.

"Are you another mage here to experiment on her?" Farin barked and shook Asith. "Are you?"

Asith put his hands up as he coughed. "N-No!"

"You're not here to experiment on a dragon in the holds?"

Hearing Yarrow splash in the water, Asith tried to retract from the blade without success. He considered reaching for his sword, but he couldn't risk it.

"I came from the Graveyard Trees," Asith answered, summoning a shock of fear that ran over his skin, down to the very tips of his fingers and toes. He might have just given away too much information.

"What the hell is that?" Farin pulled back, his brow furrowing.

Asith knocked Farin's hand away and scrambled to his feet. He moved backward from Farin, who lost his footing, grabbed Yarrow, and pressed his back to the wall.

"I'm not here to experiment on anyone, especially not dragons," Asith said. "I'm looking for my partner's mother."

Farin got up, his shoulders squared and his dagger poised at Asith. "You're not here for dragon parts to better your magic?"

"No!" Asith removed his belt bag with the potion and held it out to Farin. "Please, I promise you, I am dragonborn, I am not here for that. You can have the potion now if that helps you trust me."

"Dragonborn?" Farin scanned Asith, then slid the dagger into his boot. He paced, pressing his hands to his head. "Shit." Farin stomped. "Shit, I've been looking for a dragonborn, and when I finally find one, I assault them!"

"Uh, him," Asith said with a frown. "But it's all right."

Asith lowered his shoulders, no longer seeing Farin as a threat but trying to gather whatever the hell was going on in his head. Farin bowed his head as he mumbled in Malenki.

"It's not. I need help from a dragonborn. *You* are a dragonborn, but why would you help me now since I've gone and thrown you into sewer water?" Farin groaned as he paced.

Asith rubbed his temples. "Please, just take me into the city. I wasn't kidding, take the potion, let's go." Asith shivered, and Yarrow was cowering. He shook the belt bag at Farin. "We can speak about this at a tavern or something."

Farin stopped. "You still want to come with me?"

"I don't know the way out of here."

Farin reached out slowly and took the bag with the potion, his brow furrowed. "I guess that's true, I just thought you'd go back the way we came."

"If you want help from a dragonborn, maybe I'll actually help you, if you get me into the city like I paid you to do."

"Right." Farin moved forward again. "This way."

Asith sighed. He used the rest of their trip to dry Yarrow and his bag with magic, then put her inside. By the time Farin led them up a ladder to a hatch in the street, Asith was still wet and cold. Farin popped his head out before exiting the tunnel, then gestured for Asith to follow.

As Asith emerged, the sun made his eyes ache. Yarrow poked her head out of the bag, while Farin wrung his hands, peering at his feet.

"Listen, I know this situation is…precarious. But I know an inn, a safe place. I can take you there."

Although it could be dangerous, Asith needed Farin; it was the only lead on the dragon in the holds, a person who could very well be Dradevai's parent.

Asith nodded, and they walked again. The trip to the inn was thankfully short, even as Farin kept to the alleyways. They both stunk like sewer water, so it was probably for the best if they steered clear of everyone. Eventually, Farin stopped at the back door of a little inn. When they entered, the warmth hit Asith immediately, thanks to a large fire in the hearth near the center of a seating area. Only a few people were there, including a middle-aged woman with the same dark flowing curls as Farin. She looked up from her cleaning, sighing at the sight of them.

"What did you do this time, Farin?" She set a kettle among the coals of the fire, standing an inch shorter than Farin.

"I found us a customer," Farin said. Asith frowned at Farin's light tone. He hadn't forgiven the halfling yet.

"And you clearly dunked him in the river." The woman gestured at Asith. "I mean, look at him, he looks like a drowned rat. And you both smell awful." She locked eyes with Asith. "Sorry for my son. I'm Herleva, it's nice to meet you."

"Nice to meet you as well." Asith looked down at Farin. "You gave me your real name?"

"My mother uses it no matter what I do, so there's no use in lying to people. She doesn't understand the first bit about aliases." Farin huffed and crossed his arms.

Herleva handed Asith a warm towel from a small shelf nearby, then grabbed one for Farin. "Of course, Farin is your name." Herleva set her hands on her hips. "And I really wish you'd stop doing things where you need to use a fake name."

Farin rolled his eyes, taking the towel and wiping his face. "Mama, I got us a customer, that's all that matters."

It was a bit like listening to himself and his own mother somehow. "Listen…" Asith started.

Herleva interjected, "Oh, don't tell me him dunking you in the river has made you not want to stay here." Farin's face grew indignant as he crossed his arms and grumbled something Asith couldn't hear.

"No, I was going to ask for my room so I could change."

Herleva's eyes lit up. "Oh, of course, just a moment." She practically skipped away to get a key off the wall. Her cheery attitude was much like the one Farin had when he approached the gilliedhu in line to the Capitol.

"Thank you," Farin said, practically hiding his face in his towel.

"I need you to explain what the hell all of that was about," Asith whispered, hoping Herleva didn't hear.

"Yes, I'd say I owe you an explanation." He pulled the ribbon from his hair and squeezed it with the towel. "I promise you one, but I need to be in dry clothes."

"Well, at least we agree there."

When Herleva returned with the key, Asith smiled and thanked her, then dipped into the assigned room he'd been given. He removed all his clothes on him and from his bag, and thankfully, they didn't take too long to dry with magic. His boots were mostly dry, and after he redressed, he checked on Yarrow. She had settled under the blankets on the bed and did not want to move, but Asith couldn't blame her.

He reentered the open tavern area, and Herleva and Farin were sitting near the hearth. They were speaking quietly, rapidly, in Malenki. Their Matsic hadn't been as fluid, so Asith guessed Malenki might have been their first language. They stopped as Asith approached, and Herleva offered him tea. He pressed his hands around the teacup, the delicate porcelain heating his skin almost to the point of pain.

"I'll leave the two of you to it." She got up and headed out of the room and into what seemed to be a kitchen near the back.

Farin pressed his lips together. "So, I thought I should apologize. It's just that there have been mages coming through here a lot lately looking for dragon parts."

"And you know where they're coming from? The dragon parts?"

"Unfortunately. I met the ghost under the holds."

Asith's shoulders stiffened. "She's still there?"

"You know about her?"

"I heard her once. At the time, I didn't know she might be a dragon."

Farin chewed on his lip and peered down at his cup of tea. "I want to get her out. I'm just not, I'm not enough, and I lost my job in the holds."

"If you want to get her out, then you and I are on the same side, I assure you."

"You said you are a dragonborn." Farin met Asith's eyes. "So, you know what's being done to the Sterling dragons?"

"I am unfortunately more familiar with what they are doing to the Sterling dragons than anyone else."

Farin's face fell. "Then there are others being held like her?"

Asith nodded. Farin pressed his hands around his mug as his leg bounced just enough to shake the table. His shoulders drew in tight, and Asith mimicked his speechless state, the only sound being their lips slurping at the edges of their cups and the clinks as they set them against the table.

"Can you tell me more?" Asith asked. "About what's happening to her?"

Farin took a deep breath. "It's not good."

"I want to know anyway."

Farin nodded, then refilled their tea before he explained. After he finished, Asith excused himself to his room for the night.

Asith stared at his drying clothes scattered about the various flat surfaces with his back pressed to the door. His heartbeat thudded in his ears, his blood sinking to his feet. His stomach ached, even though he had already guessed the woman was being stored in similar conditions to his father. But Farin's confirmation had knocked him off balance.

Farin had worked at the holds primarily for the Maeria Spire. Down below the city, he'd met a woman who refused to give him her name, her arms and legs chained to the wall. She had told him of some things that had been done to her, and they sounded much like the stories Asith's father had told him.

His stomach reared its ugly head, the small dinner that Herleva had given him threatening to come up. He swallowed, took a deep breath, and spun the axe chain between his fingers. He couldn't do anything about his past decision to not pursue the ghost, someone who was probably Dradevai's parent, but that didn't stop his body from reacting against his will. Even as Yarrow left his spot and pressed herself against his chest, Asith couldn't calm down, his breath coming in faster and faster. He searched for a waste bin or chamber pot but ultimately vomited into a washbasin.

As he finished losing his stomach, a knock sounded on the door.

"Can I talk to you?" Farin asked from the other side. "I, um, brought some mint tea. My mother said you may need it."

Asith nodded, more to himself than anything else, and opened the door. Farin's hair was properly cared for and dry, with the narrow ribbon having been cleaned and replaced.

"Wow." Farin blinked. "You somehow look paler than a ghost in the snow."

"Thank you." Asith took the cup of tea and rinsed his mouth before spitting it into the washbasin. He wished his body's response to any bit of trouble was not throwing up, but he was, unfortunately, growing used to it. "What did you need to speak to me about?"

"Right, um, the woman in the holds, the dragon." Farin's shoulders sank, his eyes cast to the floor as he worried the ends of the ribbon tied in his hair. "She's the one who gave me this ribbon; she asked me to find a dragonborn. She said they might be able to help her but that I shouldn't try to help her on my own. Made me promise I wouldn't."

"Are you trying to ask if I intend to help her?" Asith asked.

Farin looked nervous, as if preparing to not like Asith's response. "Yes," he answered.

"I'm going to help her."

Farin's eyes lit up with genuine happiness, which Asith had only seen a few times in his life, one of those being when his father had seen his mother again after all those years apart.

"I'll help you however I can. She said I shouldn't try alone, I promised, but I never said anything about using that dragonborn to break her out."

Asith took a deep breath. "Are you sure that's what you want?"

Farin's eyes shifted to his feet, and then he stared at the corner. He pressed his lips together, looking at Asith. "I'm sure it will worry my mother."

Asith softened, his hands touching his tunic, remembering his mother's smile and the bounce of her red curls. Yarrow shifted at his feet.

"I know it's hard to worry your mother," Asith said. "I wouldn't blame you if you stayed behind for her sake."

"Thank you." Farin straightened himself. "But I think my mother would want me to help you, to help her."

"The people of the Maeria Spire might come after you. Your mother too." Asith crossed his arms, frowning at Farin.

"I can't keep thinking about her down there, and I'm sure my mother would understand." Farin set his jaw, his hands balling into fists.

Asith needed the help and Farin was throwing himself at his feet, but he couldn't help but think of the blade at his throat a few hours earlier. Yarrow hopped over to Farin to sniff at his feet. Her ears twitched, then she bounced around him in a little circle. She liked him, even if Asith was still hesitant to trust him.

"You tried to attack me earlier," Asith said. "How am I supposed to trust you?"

Farin stammered, his hands gesticulating as he tried to form an explanation. Eventually, he settled on pointing directly at Asith, almost wagging his finger at him. "Only because I thought you were another mage coming to take her hair or blood or eyelashes or whatever!" Farin threw his hands up into the air. "You were acting so strangely, and I couldn't let you hurt her."

Farin held no fear in his eyes, just unmoving loyalty. Not to Asith but to the dragon. That could be an asset. Though, he knew he shouldn't think of Farin as a pawn to find Dradevai again. Neither was the dragon in the holds, whether she was Dradevai's parent.

"I need you to understand," Asith said. "My mother had to run from her home twice because of her association with my father and then with me."

"Farin doesn't need to worry about that."

Herleva stood in the doorway, her arms crossed tightly.

"He has my blessing. If I have to run, I've run before, and I'll do it again."

Farin spun around. "M-Mama, are you sure?"

Herleva laughed, uncrossing her arms. She had heard everything, but he couldn't do anything about it.

"I'm sure." Herleva smoothed down Farin's hair and hugged him tightly. "You're doing the right thing, even if I'm not happy about you putting yourself in danger."

"If you can get me to her," Asith said. "I can try to get her out."

Farin nodded rapidly. "Okay, yes. I can do that."

CHAPTER 8

20ᵗʰ *of Asdel*
145 Days

The following morning, Farin joined Asith wearing his holds uniform. His confidence already increasing, Asith crossed his hand over his chest, casting the spell Dradevai had developed, and made his clothes look just like Farin's, while also giving himself dark hair and rounded ears and hiding his green eyes behind brown. The illusion also allowed him to disguise his wand and spell book as a part of his bulky frame. Yarrow nestled into his bag so that she could scout ahead if necessary. Although Asith didn't love that idea entirely, he remembered she could disappear from existence temporarily; it just felt better when he didn't have to ask that of her.

"If something goes wrong," Asith asked, "will you be able to get out or hold your own?"

"I can hold my own." Farin revealed the concealed dagger he'd attacked Asith with the day before. He then turned his arm over to reveal another in his sleeve.

"I'm glad you're on my side this time," Asith said.

"I'm hoping we can put that behind us," Farin said lightly.

"Sure, it's no big deal to trust people less than a day after they attack me." Asith crossed his arms, looking down his nose at Farin, but something about Farin's charisma was endearing, so Asith couldn't help but joke with him. An irrepressible little smile spread over Farin's face.

Farin twirled a knife in his fingers before hiding it. "I would like to think that we could, in time, put it behind us. I never said today."

Asith rolled his eyes. "All right, are you ready?"

Farin nodded, opened the back door of the inn, and led Asith into the alleyway. He didn't ask if Farin had told Herleva they were leaving already, but they'd decided the night before that early morning would be the best time to depart. They walked quickly toward the holds, as two workers would on their way to work; tired and maybe a bit hungover.

Asith kept close to Farin as they neared the entrance. A constant shiver was running up and down his spine. The entrance had enchantments on it; he just hoped they wouldn't remove magical disguises. Farin walked with the same confidence as Delri when she had snuck Asith and Dradevai inside. Stepping onto the stairs, Asith took a deep breath, happy he had eaten nothing because his stomach was already uncomfortable.

"I'm glad you turned up when you did," Farin whispered as they approached the door. "Otherwise, I'd be doing this on my own."

"I thought you promised her you wouldn't?"

"I was close to breaking that promise." Farin's voice was resolute, and he inhaled sharply. "We'll get her out."

Asith shook Farin's hand discreetly right before they slipped inside. No one seemed to pay them any mind, which meant his spell was still firmly in place, though he wondered what the enchantment on the door did.

Farin strode through the halls, so Asith tried to match his air, keeping a step behind him as they turned down old corridors that led deeper into the holds. They descended a set of stairs that took them to a long hallway made of a sand-colored stone, much like those under the library of the Maeria Spire that Asith had seen with Delri and Dradevai. To Asith's surprise, Farin's footsteps became as light as a feather, but Asith wasn't as good at keeping quiet, his feet thunking against the ground. He had never been so aware of his own footsteps; even with Blues and Greens, he could have been as loud as he wanted, and it wouldn't have made a difference. But there in the holds, he used an entirely different set of muscles, and his calves ached quickly.

When they paused outside a stone door with a small glass window, Farin gestured at some runes written along the right-hand side. The door didn't have a knob or handle, so one would need magic to open and close it.

His father had taught him a spell to open doors; he just hoped an alarm wasn't built within the runes, for he didn't know how to disarm one. Asith pulled his book out and touched the runes, chanting as quietly as he could. The runes sparked and then faded as if he'd broken them, and the door slid open slowly. Asith, in awe of himself, stared before Farin shoved him inside of the room. Apparently, Farin had been rushing him, but he hadn't noticed.

"Can you close the door?" Farin had grown frantic. Asith shook his head. When he'd broken the magic, the door had slid into the wall, hardly a seam showing. Asith didn't know how to get it back out. "There's someone coming. We have to hurry."

Farin was halfway to the woman who had been shackled to the wall. She was frail, her form lying atop a bedroll. Farin pointed to a door on the other side of the room. "Try opening that door; I'll get her out."

Asith ran to the door and repeated the process against the runes as quickly as he could. The door was opening just as footsteps clinked behind him. Guards.

He spun, only to see the woman lying limp on the mattress, with Farin nowhere in sight. Asith's stomach dropped. Had Farin ditched them? He imagined the rope of a hunter's trap wrapping around his ankle, threatening to suspend him from a tree. His stomach churned, hands shaking as he rushed to the woman. Even if he was on his own, Asith could find a way to break her from the shackles.

The woman was thin but not as emaciated as his father had been. Her long black hair hung on either side of her head in matted locks, and her dark brown eyes were severe and round, with a slight downturn at the corners. Asith's throat clenched at the curve of her lips, the shape of her jaw, the angle of her pointed ears; she looked very much like Dradevai.

She reared her head back and gestured at the collar around her neck. He studied the runes on it, and that was when Asith noticed all her other bindings had been removed. Asith started the spell to remove the runes, but his breathing and thoughts were strained. Doing so many spells close together tired him out in a way he hadn't expected. When he'd practiced, he'd taken a leisurely amount of time to reset the lock his father had given him to practice on.

Asith pulled out his wand and focused his magic through it, pushing through the burning pain in his lungs. He was only halfway through the spell when two guards appeared at the door and shouted. If he broke his focus, he'd have to start over. Maybe the woman could help in the way his father had at the other facility. Asith sped up his incantation, but the metal of the collar burned bright. She hissed and slapped his shoulder. He slowed down, his stomach lurching as he struggled to keep his focus.

Grunts and punches sounded in the background. Armor clanged against blades, the guards' voices sharp as they traded blows with someone. Then a weapon clattered to the ground, but Asith wouldn't dare look to see whom it belonged to.

With no one stopping him, Asith calmed his composure and evened his voice. When Asith said the last words of the spell, the runes darkened, and the collar opened. The woman ripped it off, exposing her bruised and burned skin. She tried to stand but wobbled, so Asith offered his hands to support her.

"I'm so sorry," Asith said.

She shook her head and gestured at the second door. Farin was standing there, waving them along. He had taken care of the guards, who were out cold on the floor. Asith tried to ignore their still figures, remembering their rescue mission, and bent to offer his back to the woman. She studied Asith's face closely before she squeezed her eyes shut and climbed onto his back. Asith wanted to ask her questions so badly, but they didn't have time. So Asith followed Farin through the door.

That door led to another long hallway without any turns, meaning any guards coming their way would spot them immediately. Asith adjusted how he was holding the woman, letting Yarrow down off his shoulder, and ran. She gripped his shoulders as she bounced from side to side. His panting was loud and out of control, and he wasn't sure how much farther he could run.

Yarrow darted between his legs, forcing him to stop, and dug at his foot. A rapid thought streamed from her to Asith. The charm, she was thinking of the charm.

Asith didn't know if it would work, but he caught up to Farin, grabbed his arm, and pulled him against the wall. He yanked out the axe, along with some strands of hair.

Farin struggled in his grip. "What are you doing?"

"Trust me." Asith focused on becoming unseen and said the activation chant. Phela hadn't explained how to use the charm, so he only had his instincts and Yarrow.

"Where'd you go?" Farin's voice whispered. He wasn't visible either. Asith didn't respond and clapped his hand over Farin's mouth. Farin squirmed but quieted as the guards approached.

The guards shouted orders at each other and ran in opposing directions. But as they reached the spot where the three of them pressed against the wall, the guards ran right past. Asith stood stock still, and even the woman on his back didn't shift despite the discomfort she was likely experiencing.

When all the guards had left, Farin said, "They can't see us."

"Yes," Asith replied. "Let's go before a mage who can actually see us gets down here."

Asith kept one hand on Farin's shoulder as he led them down the hallways, stopping whenever guards passed them. They finally arrived at a stairway that led out onto the streets of the Capitol.

As soon as they tucked themselves into an alley, Asith let go of Farin, and he became visible again. Asith looked where he felt the weight of the charm in his palm, and he and the woman returned to normal as well.

"That…" Farin said, "was the coolest thing I have ever done in my life."

Farin looked as though he had stars in his eyes before he practically hopped down the alley. Asith couldn't help but smile, for Farin's joy was a little contagious and he had pulled his weight in saving Asith from the guards.

"We need to get back," Asith said. "She's weak."

Nearing the entrance to the inn, they had to push through a crowd forming by Herleva's tavern. People eyed them strangely, so Asith tried to avoid eye contact and kept his head down. Once inside a room Farin and his mother used, they laid the woman on a small couch in the common area. Her eyes were shut, but she was breathing at a steady pace.

"I think she'll be okay if we give her time to recover," Asith said. "And then food, and a lot of water."

"Do you think she's your partner's mother?" Farin shifted pillows underneath the woman's head. "Were you right?"

Asith chewed the inside of his cheek, studying the face of the woman. It wasn't just her hair, and it didn't matter that her eyes were a different color; she looked like Dradevai.

But Asith said, "No. I think I was wrong."

Farin's eyes widened, and he blinked rapidly. He shook his head at Asith. "Why are you lying?"

Asith's shoulders tensed, and he held his breath until he couldn't anymore. He waved for Farin to follow him into a different room and shut the door behind them. Farin crossed his arms, and the knot in Asith's stomach grew.

"My partner might be in that same exact situation as her, or worse." Asith stared at his feet. "If that's the case, I can't tell her they might be out there, because what if they're not? Maybe it's better if she doesn't know."

Farin pressed his hands to his face, and his eyes darted to the door they'd just entered through. Then he shoved his hands into his pockets and nodded.

"I think you're right. I don't think we should tell her."

They grew silent, until Asith walked to the door. "We should be there when she wakes up."

Farin followed. "You're still in disguise, by the way."

Asith looked down at the disguise he'd created. "Right."

He dropped the spell, and they returned to the side of the woman, listening to the noises of the tavern. Herleva was cooking lunch for the few customers and chatting. They were discussing the break-in at the holds, and Herleva acted like she had no idea what they were talking about.

CHAPTER 9

20th *of Asdel*
145 Days

Farin left to change out of his uniform, and he returned with a notebook and a pencil and set them near the sleeping woman.

Examining Asith, he said, "You look like you maybe need something to eat. My mother will feed you. I'll keep an eye on her."

The woman seemed to be sleeping soundly. Farin settled in a chair across from her and picked up a book from the table. They'd be safe for a bit, so Asith went out to the front. It would probably help if people saw him, as if he were coming down from his room for the first time that day. Herleva happily served him a plate of eggs and bacon, which Asith consumed quickly. Then he retraced his path as if he were returning to his room but slipped into the innkeeper's suite instead.

She was sitting up, with a short, thick shawl draped over her shoulders; perhaps it belonged to Herleva. On the floor, Farin was holding a bowl of water for her as she combed out the matted locks of her hair.

"Asith," Farin said, "this is Pherrosh. She's finally awake."

"It's nice to meet you." Asith sat next to Farin. "I'm Asith, how are you feeling?"

Pherrosh switched her comb for the pencil and picked up the notebook. Asith realized she had not said a single word when they rescued her. But she could hear them fine enough.

Like death, she wrote.

Asith couldn't help but chuckle. His father had said something similar shortly after they'd saved him.

Relaxed a little, Asith said, "I'm sorry. Hopefully, you'll feel better after some food and water. And maybe a bath."

"I'll get you more water, and some food," Farin said. He set the bowl down and picked up the empty water cup from the table, then headed out. Asith folded his arms around his legs as Pherrosh wrote in the notebook.

Are you a dragonborn?

"I am."

Her shoulders lowered, and she took a deep breath. He probably should have revealed that sooner, but it had slipped his mind. After all, he wasn't exactly used to telling people his identity.

What color are you?

"You *are* a dragon, then?"

She stared at him in silence, as if she were assessing why he didn't know for sure what she was.

"Sorry, I only had Farin's word to go on. I'm a Silver."

She nodded. *I understand.*

Farin returned with water and a hot potato. She set aside the notebook in favor of both and quickly ate the food and drank the water. Her eyes darted back and forth over Asith and Farin, her lashes sometimes covering her dark irises. When she drank, she only tipped her head back ever so slightly. She looked like Dradevai when they were scared, which made him release his arms around his legs, trying to open himself up to her, at least in posture.

"Do you know of the Graveyard Trees?" Asith asked.

Pherrosh nodded and picked up her notebook again, finishing her water and balancing the plate on her knees. She tilted the notebook to write, a little more awkwardly that time.

I'm from the Graveyard Trees.

She might know his father, then, but he wrote that off. The Graveyard Trees was fairly large, anyway.

"That's where I came from," Asith said. "My father brought me there."

Were there others where they kept me?

Asith shook his head, and Farin did the same. "I worked down there for nearly a year and only ever saw you."

"Do you know if there are other places they may be keeping dragons?" Asith asked, fidgeting with the seam of his pants. It had puckered from getting wet and then drying it with magic the day before.

There are two more facilities.

"Is one in the mountains to the north?" That was where his father had been.

It was broken into. I heard one of the mages say so. They don't use it anymore.

Asith smiled. "Good. My partner and I are the ones who broke in."

Pherrosh looked surprised. *Is your plan to do it again?*

"Yes." Asith's heart raced faster than Yarrow's as he realized she might show him where Dradevai was being kept. "Can you tell me where the other facility is?"

I can take you to the other facility. Pherrosh's writing was slanted and hurried.

"Will you be well enough to help him break in?" Farin asked, his voice startling Asith. His world had tunneled down to just Pherrosh, and he couldn't believe Farin had been following the conversation.

Pherrosh straightened her back, raising her chin. *I'll be fine.*

Farin made brief eye contact with Asith. The curve of his brow signaled that he didn't think Pherrosh would be strong enough. Frankly, Asith agreed.

"I think that maybe you should fly home," Asith said to Pherrosh. "I'm sure you haven't hunted in a long time, and you need time to eat and heal."

Pherrosh's gaze flicked up toward the ceiling, a twitch in her cheek as she wrote.

I am not letting you go alone.

She pointed at Asith and then crossed her arms, looking down her nose at Farin.

"He won't be alone. I'll be with him," Farin said. "We can take you home before we storm the facility. You deserve to go home and rest."

"Well, it might be faster if she flew home. But you're right, we can handle this."

Hopefully, she was not as stubborn as Dradevai. Pherrosh pressed her lips together, brow furrowed as she squeezed the pencil. She took a breath, closed her eyes, and let her shoulders fall. When she opened them again, she wrote her next words with trembling fingers.

Get me to the mountains. Then I can draw you a map to the facility and fly home.

"That sounds good to me," Farin said to Asith, who nodded. He turned to Pherrosh, with squared shoulders and a set jaw "I promise you, we'll help anyone that was in a similar situation to you."

Pherrosh smiled, but it looked sad and tired.

"If you don't mind my asking," Asith asked Pherrosh, "how do you know where the other facility is?"

I overheard the guards. They thought I would never get out, so they rarely hid their conversations from me. Pherrosh was crossing her arms, with a smile crawling over her lips and her jaw jutted out.

"Can you tell me what they're doing with the dragons, then?"

I'll tell you everything I remember.

Before she could write, Herleva walked in with several bundles of clothing in her arms.

"How are you feeling?" she said gently. Pherrosh wrote and only showed the notebook to Herleva, who smiled. "That's good. I'm sorry none of our clothes would fit you, but these are things guests at the inn have left behind. Some only have a few small holes…"

"I can fix them," Asith said. "If there's something that will fit you but it needs to be repaired, I can fix it."

Pherrosh smiled and gestured in a way that Asith had learned meant thank you.

"That's perfect, then." Herleva set the clothes on the couch. "Let me bring you all a meal now."

"Let me help you, Mama," Farin said.

Pherrosh's face twitched, her chin trembling and water coming to her eyes. She collected herself quickly, though, pressing her eyes closed and biting the potato.

Asith played with the seam of his pant leg. The thread on it had been doubled the whole way down, with the seams finished on both sides, something his mother always did so his pants would not immediately fall apart. As he thought about his mother, Asith realized he was sitting with Dradevai's mother, unable to even tell her how wonderful her child was.

Someone tapped his shoulder, and Pherrosh was holding the notebook again. *Are you looking for someone at the facility?*

His eyes watered. He took a deep breath and nodded as Yarrow crawled into his lap. Asith scooped her into his arms and cradled her to his chest.

"My partner," he said, rubbing Yarrow's ears. "We broke my father out of another facility, and I lost them in the process."

Pherrosh's lips quivered as she squeezed the notebook.

It's likely they're alive. They wouldn't kill a dragon senselessly. She showed Asith the notebook and then added more. Make them pay for whatever they've done to your father and partner.

Asith turned his face to the ceiling, tears streaming down his face. It had been so long since he'd felt angry at anyone other than himself for what might have happened to Dradevai. He tasted bitterness on his tongue, and he ground his teeth. Asith gripped the seam of his pants, the static making his hair raise on end like when he'd cast magic.

"I'm going to. I'm going to get them back for what they've done to you as well."

Pherrosh set a hand on Asith's shoulder and squeezed. Then she finished her food and sorted through the clothes. By the time Farin and Herleva returned with food for the three of them, she had selected a few items. So they ate first, and then Asith started to mend the clothes. Meanwhile, Farin was on the floor helping Pherrosh rub oil into her hair and comb the knots out. After a while, she allowed Farin to take over completely, but his face flushed and he kept dropping the comb.

"So, dragons can really turn into people, huh?" Farin said, probably to distract himself from his blunders. "I mean, well, I knew that, but…"

For the first time, Pherrosh chuckled. It was soft and shallow, but it was a laugh. From there, she seemed to relax slightly. She nodded at Farin, which indicated that what he'd said was close enough.

"What kind of dragon are you? If that's okay to ask."

Pherrosh pointed at the small satchel of money Farin had tied to his belt. He opened it, and she removed a copper and a silver piece, then wagged her finger.

"Not Copper or Silver…" Asith mumbled. "Gold?"

Pherrosh smiled and nodded. It was unusual, but Asith didn't have a reason not to believe her. That color was as unusual as green eyes would be to a person, he guessed. Their mother being a gold would also explain their size, something Pystra and his father had both commented on when they first saw Dradevai. He wondered what their other parent must have looked like. If Dradevai was a Bronze, then their other parent might have been as well. He wished he'd asked his father more about it.

"The Graveyard Trees, what exactly is that?" Farin asked. He'd brushed over the significance of Pherrosh being a Gold; in fact, he didn't even take the money back from her, focusing instead on detangling her hair.

Pherrosh gestured to Asith, as if she wanted him to explain.

"It's a city the dragons who lived in Cairn moved into after the war. When dragons die, they turn into massive trees, so the dragons who lost their lives during the war made a wall around the city to protect it."

Farin's eyes enlarged to the size of dinner plates, and he asked questions while Asith continued to explain the territory. They continued like that, Asith mending clothes and Farin working the knots out of her hair, while Pherrosh ate her entire bowl of stew. Herleva left to get another bowl, and Pherrosh picked up her notebook again.

It sounds like it hasn't changed a bit.

She appeared happy hearing the details about her home. Asith warmed at the thought of her returning after being away for so long.

"I grew up in Cairn. But I liked the time I spent in the Graveyard Trees."

Eventually, with a bit of Herleva's help, Pherrosh's hair became sleek-straight. Her black hair spilled over her shoulders, still wet as she ran her fingers through it for the first time in what must have been a long while. Herleva took her into the washroom to get her cleaned up, and she put on the clothes Asith had finished mending. When she emerged, she looked much better, not because she was no longer wearing rags or she was less dirty, but because she was genuinely feeling better.

When she sat back on the couch, she cast magic on her old clothes to clean them. While the blouse was torn and partially destroyed, it was clear the ribbon Farin wore in his hair had come from the bodice of that shirt.

"Would you like me to fix these as well?" Asith asked.

Pherrosh stroked the front of the skirt and examined the pants she'd been wearing underneath, but ultimately, she shook her head.

It wasn't late, but they agreed they should go to bed. Herleva gave her an old nightgown someone had left at the inn, and it fit well. Asith went up to his room and found Yarrow asleep on his bed. Even as Asith ran his fingers over her soft head, she didn't rouse. He sat at the table pressed into the corner and ran his fingers through his hair, brushing against the axe. Asith didn't remember tying it back, but he must have done so. He thanked Phela, for, without her, without Yarrow, they'd have been caught in the holds.

Asith pulled his spell book from his bag and opened it to the lightning spell his father had tried to teach him. He hadn't taken to it well, finding it much easier to bend magic into a shield. His father had stressed the importance of harnessing spells for attacking, rather than just defending, especially when fighting mages. If they had confronted mages in the holds, they might not have made it out. They had been lucky only the guards had run past, but he couldn't rely on luck.

He traced his fingers over the few notes his father had added, tricks to make it easier to cast. In some places, his father had scratched out a rune because he'd written it backward, something Asith was prone to doing if his mind was elsewhere. He'd done that as a child learning Matsic in school, so he wasn't entirely surprised. With Dradevai in their hoard, Asith had taken all the time and attention he needed to write spells or draw circles. Asith didn't possess that leisurely amount of time anymore. Even if he could take his time slowly preparing spells and casting them, he would never cast like his father and Dradevai did. They seemed leagues ahead.

Asith copied the spell again to hopefully make it clearer, but his hand shook. His lines grew unsteady, imperfect, a collection of wobbly reminders he did not take to those inscriptions as naturally as he once thought he did. His fingers found the charm in his hair, tracing the shape of the rabbit, and he removed it from the tie. He spun the handle of the axe between his fingers, and the rabbit ran. But then it stopped entirely.

Asith furrowed his brow, and on the side where the rabbit's legs crossed, a scratch ran along the long ears and down to the rabbit's back. He rubbed it in case it was a smudge, but his fingers caught against the jagged edges of the scratch. He bowed his head, skin crawling as he tried again to rub the scratch away, but its imperfect form remained unchanged. Something from the day had marred the gift, but his mind came up empty on what could have happened to it.

Tears sprang to his eyes as he tried again to clean the small axe. Phela should not have trusted him with something so precious. He couldn't truly be her champion. She was the goddess of love. Yes, he loved Dradevai dearly, but she was also the ruler of magic. As his eyes drifted from the damaged axe to the shaky runes littering his spell book, Asith felt like a child again, trying to read his schoolbooks in his kitchen while his mother sewed. Phela might have chosen him, but it was up to him to succeed. And he had scratched the gift she had so graciously given him.

Yarrow hopped into his lap and nudged his hands out of her way. Then she set her front feet on his chest and sniffed at the broach his mother had given him, the metal still shiny from her polishing it. She was reminding him of Phela's presence, as her symbol was on the broach, so Asith wiped his tears from his face and eyes. She attempted to lure him to bed, but he picked up his pen and copied the spell again, his hands still shaking.

CHAPTER 10

20th of Asdel
145 Days

Asith woke at the table with Yarrow in his lap, her ears back and her legs underneath her like a loaf of burned bread. He sat up stiffly, his head on his folded arms where he'd fallen asleep, and stretched his legs out before petting Yarrow's silken fur. He examined his shakily written spell, which he would need to redo if he expected to properly memorize the couplets and the spell circle.

It was dark outside the window, so Asith wasn't sure what had woken him. He couldn't have been asleep for very long, as he wasn't stiff enough from a full night's sleep. The sounds of people moving on the street down below caught his ear, and Yarrow's ears wiggled, and then shook faster, before her head twitched and she rose.

"The window?" Asith set her on the table, and Yarrow stood tall on her back legs while he edged to the curtains. He barely moved the fabric and held his breath as he peered at the group of armed guards discussing something in front of the inn.

He'd already packed in case they had to flee, so he closed his book and set it into his bag. After tucking Yarrow into his coat, he double-checked he hadn't left anything and pulled on his boots. Downstairs, Farin was sneaking down the hall towards the stairs with a pack on his back, presumably to get Asith. They saw each other, and Farin gestured at the front door.

"You noticed too?" Asith whispered.

"Yes. I think we need to leave."

Asith nodded, and they moved to alert Pherrosh, who was stirring awake. Ignoring the chill running down his back, Asith pressed his finger to her lips, only to receive a disappointing look. In his defense, he had only forgotten she didn't speak because the icy chill had been distracting.

The guards pounded on the door, so Asith offered Pherrosh one hand and Farin took his other. Farin pulled them along the hallway. "What's the plan?" Farin asked as they neared the storage room.

Asith's eyes darted between Farin and Pherrosh, and he realized they were seeking help from him. He frowned at his feet. Asith wasn't sure the axe would work since it was scratched and they didn't know if there were soldiers at the back door too.

"I…I don't have one."

Farin balked. "Shit."

Herleva appeared in the hallway, and taking one look at them, she mouthed, Go. She gestured wildly at the back door, so Farin pulled Pherrosh and Asith into the corner of the storage room, just on the other side of the back door.

Farin tucked Pherrosh behind a barrel smelling strongly of vinegar, which she scrunched her nose at. She disappeared from view, but when Farin turned to Asith, he grimaced.

"You're too damn tall." Farin pushed Asith toward a cupboard across from Pherrosh, and Asith frowned at the thought of climbing inside. To his relief, Farin shoved him toward a low shelf on the wall. "Lie down under there." Asith followed his orders, and Farin stacked flour bags in front of him. Asith sped it up by pulling them close as Farin set them down.

The pounding of heavy metal boots filled the inn, Asith's heart skipping and his breath sticking in his throat. He pressed himself against the wall, Yarrow wiggling inside his coat.

"Make for the door on my signal," Farin said before tucking himself behind the barrel with Pherrosh. Asith could only see Pherrosh's golden eyes glowing in the dim light. When the guards' shouts filled the inn to the brim, Pherrosh shut her eyes, so Asith did the same.

The guards questioned Herleva, but she lied like it was her career. Her answers were quick, with just the right tone of confusion. She sounded like she was earnestly trying to help the guards, but each answer was incorrect or slightly off, a grain of truth concealing each one.

"We're looking for a man with silver hair, pointy ears, probably elven. And one of your folk. People said it sounded like your son."

"Well, my son left yesterday morning to head north to see a girl," Herleva said, her voice traveling closer. "We had a man here with hair like that, but his ears were rounded."

Asith really needed to ask Farin where he and his mother learned to deceive people. Her words were filled with such confidence that he almost checked his ears to see if they were actually pointed.

"Did he have a woman with him?"

"He was alone, had a cat with him, though. Can I ask what this is about?"

"No," the guard said gruffly. That was when Asith recognized the voice.

He opened his eyes, and light had filled the room from the open doorway. His eyes swam over the group of men at the front of the room, and his breath still caught in his throat when he saw Kosor towering over Herleva.

Asith swallowed, closing his eyes again as he pressed himself harder against the wall. His fingers shifted ever so slightly for his wand in his belt, but he couldn't risk trying to pull it out. So, he pressed his lips together as hard as he could to prevent any noises of fear from slipping out.

"The guest with the silver hair, was he pale and quiet?" Kosor asked.

"No. His skin was dark, and he talked to me quite a bit."

Footsteps settled near Farin and Pherrosh. He wondered if she might cast a spell, but Kosor didn't have magic, so he'd only find them if they somehow gave themselves away. Still, the man who had harassed Delri and started a street fight with Dradevai made Asith tremble. Delri had gotten him out of the situation last time, and he didn't know how to deal with Kosor on his own.

Asith sucked in the smallest bit of air but stopped cold when Kosor stomped over to his side of the room and yanked the doors of the cupboard open, the hinges cracking from the force.

"Now what was that for?" Herleva admonished. "You broke them!"

She stepped into the room, and he wondered if Herleva even knew where they hid, which could work to their advantage.

"They're not in here," Kosor called out, and he stormed out of the room. She stomped her own feet after him, demanding he pay for her broken cupboard.

Asith opened his eyes, and Farin poked his head around the barrel. He waved for Asith to follow, and Asith had barely pushed himself out from under the shelf by the time Farin had pulled Pherrosh to the back door. Farin grabbed Asith's hand and opened the door, revealing an alleyway. Poking his head out to check for guards, Farin hesitated for a moment before he gestured for Asith to move first. All the while, Herleva was yelling near the front of the inn, with Kosor's voice louder than hers.

After exiting, Asith pressed against the back wall of the inn, while Yarrow popped her head out of his coat. Pherrosh shook as she exited, her arms wrapped around her middle. Asith let her hang on him for support, then offered his back for her to climb onto as Farin shut the door. When Pherrosh climbed onto Asith's back, Yarrow hopped onto his shoulder and settled next to Pherrosh's hand. She then nudged the charm in his hair, but Asith hadn't forgotten its power. He wasn't about to test its strength at that moment.

Farin pulled his cloak off and draped it around Pherrosh's shoulders, and she pulled the hood up. They began down the alleyway, and Farin grabbed Asith's hand. "Stay close to me. Turn us invisible when I tell you to."

"About that…" Asith whispered. "I'm not sure that will work right now."

Farin's hand grew clammy, and he looked over his shoulder. "What do you mean? We'll need that to get through the gates."

"It got damaged when we were getting out of the holds." They ducked under a low archway, Asith barely getting low enough to protect Pherrosh's head.

"It didn't look damaged," Farin countered with tensed shoulders. Then he jogged, so Asith matched his pace. Pherrosh drew something on the back of Asith's shoulder. Works. But it was hard to tell if she meant that, being jostled by Asith's running.

"You think it works?" Asith asked. Yarrow concurred with Pherrosh, telling Asith it would be fine.

"Pherrosh says it will be fine," Asith said to Farin.

"Why does she know better than you?" Farin scoffed and stopped in his tracks.

"I'm still new to magic, okay?" Asith pushed on Farin's arm; they had to keep moving. "I was a dragon knight before all of this."

Farin said something in Melanki, perhaps a curse. He walked, though, tugging Asith behind him.

"Whatever, so long as we can use it to get through the gates. We should find a place to hide near the wall and leave once the gates are open."

"Can't we leave through the sewer?"

"They'll check the sewers first if they're looking for someone. Better to slip out the main gates where they're least expecting it."

Asith didn't love that idea, but he kept walking. They were entering darker alleys, which Farin said were less frequently used. They eventually stopped and sat near the East wall, near an exit to the countryside. Asith offered Pherrosh his waterskin and told her to drink as much as she wanted, because they'd be walking along the river once they escaped. If they really believed Farin went north the day prior, as Herleva had said, Kosor might head in that direction.

"Will your mom be okay?" Asith asked softly, with Yarrow in his lap.

"Oh, definitely. She lies like someone cheating on their spouse."

Pherrosh chirped, which Asith guessed was a laugh. She smiled, waving her hand as if she couldn't stop laughing, and Farin looked rather pleased with himself.

"Why is she such a good liar? And why are you so good at sneaking around?"

"My dad was horrid to the two of us." Farin's delighted expression withered. "We spent a few years running away from him, and we did what we could to survive."

Pherrosh stopped laughing, her lips turning down, and she patted Farin on the shoulder.

"I'm sorry. I probably shouldn't have pried."

"It's all right." Farin smiled. "I'm proud of how far we've come."

"You should be."

"I have a more important question, though." Farin squared his shoulders toward Asith. "You were a dragon knight? But you're a dragonborn."

"I was. I only found out I was a dragonborn a little over a year ago."

He could feel Pherrosh's eyes on him while Farin's jaw slackened and his eyes widened. "So, you didn't even know you were killing your own?"

"I wasn't. Blues and Greens aren't dragons. Sterlings, like Pherrosh, are the only real dragons. The others are…something else. Mimics."

"Oh." Farin's shoulders relaxed, his eyes darting across the alleyway as if a memory clouded him. Pherrosh tapped Asith's shoulder, and she quickly gestured toward her hair. She was asking where the charm was from.

"It was given to me by Phela." Asith pulled it out of his hair and frowned at the scratch, feeling the metal catch on his fingers.

Pherrosh's eyes widened too. She probably had more questions, but they hadn't grabbed her notebook in the rush of escaping. That was a serious failure on his and Farin's part.

"I can explain more when we've made it out safely," Asith said.

Farin's head thumped against the wall behind them. "The gates won't open for another hour or so."

"Do you think we'll need a better hiding spot until then?"

"No, there's only one street entrance to this alley, and it's not used often." Farin wrapped his arms around his knees. "We should be safe here so long as we stay quiet."

They sat in silence as the suns slowly rose. As the first one came up, Asith pulled his bag of jerky from a side pocket on his pack and offered them each a piece. Relief washed over Asith as the light of the first sun shined on their surroundings. Farin stood and stretched, and Pherrosh followed suit.

With the rise of the second sun, Farin and Pherrosh grabbed Asith's arm, and Asith touched his charm with shaky fingers as he said the chant.

Thankfully, they disappeared. Asith let go of the charm, and Farin took his free hand.

Farin took the lead, and they carefully approached the archway, where a few people were still trickling in and out. The number of guards had increased significantly, likely for the opening of the gate. Asith pressed his shoulders into the jagged stone of the wall to stay as close as possible; he'd probably find scratches later. At the exit, Farin stopped. The guards milled about the front, doing their best to avoid being touched, and Asith cringed each time the gaze of a guard seemed to settle on them. He chewed the inside of his cheek raw.

The guards called to welcome people into the city, and the gate rose. Just as the portcullis reached high enough, Farin tugged Asith underneath. The chains clanked, the metal rattled, and the spikes above his head seemed daunting, but they made it through. Relief struck Asith.

While they wove around the tents and crowds of people ready to enter, Asith bumped into a few, but they looked around confused or blamed someone nearby. Then they ducked behind a tent, after Asith announced the charm's magic would wear off soon. Visible again, Farin took the cloak from Pherrosh, and Asith gave her his doublet. Asith tucked his broach away, leaving him in his plain tunic, as Farin stripped himself of any easily identifiable clothing.

After that, they tried to stay out of sight. Asith's skin crawled when anyone so much as glanced in their direction, but no one's eyes lingered. Most were focused on getting their belongings into their carts to head into the Capitol. Asith didn't feel safe until they passed the very end of the line waiting to enter. They finally slowed their pace, for both Farin and Pherrosh looked weary.

"How much longer should we walk?" Farin asked, his face pale, with dark circles under his eyes. Pherrosh dragged her feet, and her shoulders were slumped. She straightened up when she realized Asith was looking.

"Just into the trees up there," Asith said and pointed to the nearest thicket.

Farin appeared relieved. Asith led them well into the trees until he found just enough space to lay his spell book. He cast a spell to produce a small tent, which his father had taught him. A dome of light encircled Asith, and the tent materialized around them, though its walls appeared translucent from the inside, they would appear solid to passersby. Asith unpacked his bag, finding paper and a pencil at the very bottom. He also found the glass ball his aunt had given him and rubbed his fingers over the smooth glass. Farin offered Pherrosh a bedroll, and she looked grateful for both the writing supplies and the bedding.

"It's warm in here," Farin said, settled on his bedroll, with his boots next to him.

"It's part of the magic," Asith explained, putting away everything he'd pulled from his bag and spreading out his bedroll. He returned the broach to his doublet, then took off his boots and relaxed. Pherrosh closed her eyes as she lay down too. She'd be able to sleep for a while, for they'd move at night until they were off the main road.

Farin untied a handkerchief and revealed cookies. He nudged Pherrosh. "You should eat something before you sleep."

Pherrosh sighed, sat up, and took a cookie. Farin tossed one to Asith too. He then pulled a cauldron from his pack, large and heavy enough that Asith scoffed. There was no way they needed that. Farin pursed his lips, tapped the edge twice, and said a few words. It promptly filled up with stew, similar to what his mother had made the night before. Asith stopped eating his cookie, his mouth hanging open.

"I wouldn't have brought it if I didn't have a good reason." Farin smirked, crossing his arms. Asith frowned, but the cauldron was incredibly useful.

Asith pulled some cups from his pack and handed one to Pherrosh. It quickly became clear they all needed food, because they finished out the very last dregs of stew from the bowl. Farin wiped the cauldron and tucked it away.

Asith only slept a few hours and woke in the early evening, after a dream where he found a thin and weak Dradevai in a cage similar to the one in which his father was locked up in. Their hands had grasped at the bars as they demanded why Asith let them stay. Asith rubbed his temples. He couldn't have convinced Dradevai to leave that night. Still, the thought of them in a cage facing terrible treatment made Asith's spine shake and his ribs rattle. He sat up and curled his arms around his legs, listening to Farin snore softly while Yarrow slept in his lap.

Farin woke second, stretching his hands beyond the invisible edge of the tent. He shivered and rubbed his hands. "What a rude way to wake up."

"You were the one who chose to sleep so close to the edge," Asith said.

Farin grumbled and glowered at him before setting his cauldron in the middle. He filled it with fresh berries and oatmeal. Asith fed Yarrow some fruit while Farin dished out oatmeal for himself. Asith nudged Pherrosh awake, and when she sat up and grabbed the paper to write, she looked more lively than earlier that day.

I'm going to hunt. I should be able to get a deer at least.

"It's probably not a good idea to hunt. You might be seen."

But Pherrosh was already standing, waving away Asith's worries. She walked past the protection of the tent and transformed into a flurry of smoke. Asith's jaw fell open. She was large, much larger than his father. Her neck was long and sleek, like any other dragon's, but her head was big, if not a little bigger than Dradevai's. Though slightly dulled, her feathers shimmered a beautiful gold that reminded Asith of the ornate decorations on the central buildings in the Capitol. Her horns were the most mesmerizing, though; they were tall and had waves from the base all the way to the tip, perfectly symmetrical like Phela's horns. She flapped her wings and took off into the trees.

Yarrow seemed to agree Pherrosh looked a lot like Phela. Perhaps that was why Phela had led him to her, rather than directly to Dradevai. It seemed unlikely they were related, since Phela was a goddess, but maybe she was under Phela's protection for some reason, as his aunt was with Viteus. His mind was racing, and he almost missed Farin's voice.

"She's beautiful."

Farin stared at where Pherrosh had been, with a slackened jaw and wide eyes. His reaction to seeing a dragon transform to their larger form for the first time was endearing.

"Your partner, do they look like that?"

Asith shook his head. "They're a Bronze dragon, so they're a different color and smaller, but not by much."

Now that he thought about it, Pherrosh's feathers carried a bronze tone when the barest hints of the second sun hit her. Asith furrowed his brow, picturing the golden tones of Dradevai's feathers. If he hadn't known better, Asith would have thought Pherrosh and Dradevai were the same color. He wondered what Pherrosh's partner looked like.

"Wow." Farin seemed lost in thought, so Asith focused on eating.

When Pherrosh returned, her eyes were brighter and her amber skin seemed to sparkle as if gold were underneath. Her hair shined, and her cheeks carried a plumpness that made her face look rounder, more like Dradevai's. She wrapped up her bedroll and carried it on her back. Farin asked if she'd be okay with the weight, and she nodded.

"I take it you got something real to eat?" Asith asked. They were making their way back onto the road.

Pherrosh grinned, carrying a bit more strength in her steps. As they walked, she asked and answered questions via the paper and book Asith had given her. Then Farin asked if she had any friends back in the Graveyard Trees, and she withered in a way that made even Yarrow sad. She read what she'd written, then scratched it out. After writing something new, she turned the paper around.

I don't know if I do.

"I'm sorry," Asith said. "Hopefully, some of them are still in the Graveyard Trees."

She nodded but didn't seem hopeful. Asith didn't know how to make her feel better, so he kept quiet.

"You've got friends in us," Farin said. "I don't know about the two of you, but performing a jailbreak and sneaking out of the city together forms a bit of a bond. That and my mom's always happy to bring in more people. That's why she runs a tavern."

Pherrosh chuckled. She turned to Farin and set a hand on his shoulder, squeezing it. Farin beamed. He walked with a spring in his step into the darkness of the evening, heading east into the vast forest covering the middle part of Cairn. Asith and Farin didn't know the woods well, but Pherrosh led them confidently.

"Have you been here before?" Asith asked once they reached a less central road. They hadn't passed anyone for miles, despite the cart tracks in the path, which meant a village could have been nearby.

I lived near here for a while.

"Do you know how long it's been since you were caught?" Farin asked.

I know I was in the Capitol for about two years. Before that, I'm not sure.

Asith frowned. Two years ago, he didn't even know Dradevai. It was hard to imagine that Pherrosh had been suffering in the Capitol long before he and Dradevai arrived. He rubbed along the seam of his pants, trying to direct his thoughts away or he'd grow angry with the world.

"You were in one of the other facilities before that, then?" Pherrosh nodded. "Was it the cavern I described? The one with many other magical creatures."

Your father and I must have been there at the same time. They separated the dragons so we couldn't work together.

"You had allies so close," Farin said and squeezed the straps of his pack, his frown forming deep lines in his pudgy cheeks.

"What were they doing with you all?" Asith asked. "It's not like the mages at the Maeria Spire need that many dragon feathers or griffon claws.

They can't use them all."

Pherrosh stopped in the road to write, pressing Asith's book against her stomach for stability. Dradevai had mimicked that exact gesture. The more time he spent with Pherrosh, the more he believed she was Dradevai's mother.

They sold them to Wacot, largely. From what I understand, they have an agreement with the Cerulean Visage, and they also sell to private mages in Froiland and the Zotia coast. Also, they make the dragon feathers into pens, so they take a lot of them.

Asith's shoulders fell. "My father had bald spots in his larger form where they'd been taking them."

Farin shook his head and scrunched his nose. "Wait, to Froiland too?" Farin hugged himself, shrinking to an even smaller size. "There were mages there who helped us…"

"Don't blame yourself," Asith said. "You couldn't have known. I was a dragon knight, so I don't know how many potions I drank with dragon's blood in them."

Farin pressed a hand over his mouth and dropped his pack before darting into the trees and retching.

Asith rubbed the back of his head. "I maybe should have worded that more carefully." Pherrosh shrugged and hugged her writing supplies to her chest.

"Do you know-"

Farin made a particularly horrid noise, like a defeated goose after a fox clamped on its neck. A quick check determined he was still throwing up, so Asith said to Pherrosh, "Do you know who at the Maeria Spire is involved? Why were you there alone?"

I was there to be the headmaster's personal power font. I don't know exactly what his intentions were, but he would force me to bring all the magic I could into my body and then channel it into various things, sometimes other dragon feathers, sometimes a gem. All I really know is that it hurt.

A pale Farin wobbled out of the woods, but he picked up his pack and pulled the straps over his shoulders. Meanwhile, Pherrosh had written one name and a note:

> *Vetrish*
> *Heskel*

"Elaqen Vetrish is the headmaster of the Maeria Spire," Asith said. "And Heskel, did he ever have an elven man with him? Called Eroan?"

Pherrosh's brow wrinkled, and she sighed, shaking her head. *No. But he had a big man, blue eyes, dark hair, rather handsome but cruel. Called Kosor.*

Asith had considered visiting Eroan the night he'd lost Dradevai. He'd clearly seen Asith and his father but allowed them to escape. It felt as if he were trying to untie a knotted ball of thread, and his brain almost seemed to rattle against his skull.

"Can we keep moving now?" Farin asked. "If I keep standing here, thinking about it, I'm going to puke again."

"Yes, sorry." Asith started ahead, losing himself to his thoughts. Delri had reported Kosor for harassing her, which meant he likely could no longer work as a dragon knight. So, Elaqen Vetrish must have picked him up; that was the only part that made sense. He wished he could ask Delri, but she probably knew as little about the Maeria Spire as he did. Though, she might know about Eroan.

The trees rustled in the breeze as they navigated an empty road for the rest of the evening. Before sunrise, they made camp just off the dirt road to hide amongst the bushes. Farin still seemed a bit jumpy, but he calmed down once he asked his cauldron for shepherd's pie.

Pherrosh left them to hunt, and she returned with more gold under her skin, which shined like a fresh acorn in the rising sun. She settled on a bedroll and stretched her shoulders out. In the Graveyard Trees, Asith had seen plenty of dragons do the same gesture, only they would take their time stretching their wings too.

Farin had eaten most of the shepherd's pie, since it had never been Asith's favorite. As they sat in their warm, magical tent, Asith worried a little. Pherrosh would leave once they made it to the mountains, so that left him with Farin, who he'd only met a few days prior. Farin had been eager to help Asith break into the holds, which gave him a certain amount of credibility, but he was more concerned about putting Farin and Herleva in unnecessary danger.

"You're thinkin' pretty loud over there."

Farin's voice brought Asith out of his thoughts. He sighed softly. "Sorry." Asith finished off his bowl and added, "There's just a lot on my mind."

Pherrosh picked up her writing supplies. *I think we all do. Except for maybe Farin. So far, only the thing about the potions has bothered him.*

Asith chuckled. "Well, it did bother him when he thought I was a mage looking to take your feathers."

Farin rolled his eyes, grumbling as he rinsed his cauldron out. "I thought we agreed to let that go?"

"You agreed," Asith said.

Pherrosh raised an eyebrow and turned to Farin. Asith smiled. "He was being protective of you, that's all."

Farin's face bloomed, despite his skin matching the color of crisp autumn leaves. The reddish blaze moved all the way up to his wide pointed ears. He shifted, mumbling for a moment, and then looked at Pherrosh.

"No, Pherrosh is right," he said, completely ignoring Asith's comment. "Nothing really bothers me. Besides that thing about the potions."

Asith scoffed. "And I'm worried about everything."

"We can tell; it's written all over your face." When Asith frowned, he added, "I mean no offense. You're just better off telling us about it so that we can help you."

"You're right." Asith washed out his bowl. "The last facility I broke into was heavily guarded, and the magic we used couldn't release the shackles from my father. On top of that, a mage I knew saw me. I also don't know what these people are after."

"Well, you broke the shackles somehow, yes? And Pherrosh's collar? All that other stuff, I don't have an answer for it."

"My father removed his own shackles; he taught me the spell. But I barely made it work to remove Pherrosh's collar."

"Oh." Farin's shoulders dropped, and he stashed the cauldron away.

A spell like the one you used wouldn't work on a large number of cages either.

"That's what I was afraid of." Asith chewed on his lip and looked at Yarrow at his feet. Even if he disguised himself with magic, mages as powerful as Heskel and Vetrish could remove a simple illusion. Asith hadn't figured out the lightning spell, either, so he could only shield them if they got into trouble. "My father used a lightning spell to destroy the locks on the cages, but I am still unable to cast that spell."

I'll think on it. I might be able to help you somehow. Make the spell easier.

"Really?"

Pherrosh performed a few hand motions, and a thick book appeared from thin air and landed in her hands. Pherrosh's careful handwriting filled the pages, in a neatness that resembled the beginnings of Dradevai's spell book. Asith's stomach sank, and he tried to avoid blurting every last thing he knew about Dradevai. But he remembered why he hadn't told her yet.

When she found what she was looking for, she set the book down between them. The spell seemed incomprehensible with its runes and various layouts, but the very edges of it looked familiar. Like a much more complex version of the lightning spell his father had been teaching him.

Is this the spell you're trying to learn?

"Yes, but…" Asith whispered, thinking about the shaky runes he'd recorded just the night before. "This version is far beyond me."

That's okay. Let's try anyway. May I see your wand?

Asith didn't want to argue, so he drew his wand from his belt and smoothed his hands over it. "I'm not sure I want to risk my wand breaking." Asith extended it to Pherrosh, resisting an instinct to retract it. He felt as if a single touch of his wand would reveal the flaws in his casting abilities, even though he was fairly certain it didn't work that way. He just hoped she didn't ask to see his spell book.

Pherrosh took the wand, and her body froze. Asith's stomach flipped, but her pinched expression gave no hint as to what was going through her head.

"Pherrosh?" Asith's voice trembled. Maybe she realized he was too inadequate a mage to cast the spell after all.

Her head whipped to Asith, her eyes filling with tears, not daring to fall just yet. She gestured for him to place his hand on the wand as well. Asith furrowed his brow, but Pherrosh's gesturing only became more frantic, so he reached out and touched the end of his wand.

A voice filled his head that sounded just like the ghost he had heard a year ago under the Maeria Spire. It was loud and desperate, crackling like a wet log set on a roaring fire.

Your father, is your father Listesh? Is he safe?

Her lips didn't move, which made Asith rear back, his hair standing on end and his skin crawling.

I'm sorry, this is uncomfortable for me, too, but please, your father, please tell me Listesh is safe.

Asith nodded, blinking as he forced words out of his mouth. "Yes, Listesh is safe."

Pherrosh's tears poured down her face as she devolved into sobs. The connection between them broke. He glanced at Farin, whose head was tilted harshly, his brow low. Farin seemed confused, but Asith understood; she knew his father.

"Are you okay?" Asith asked.

He tried to catch her eyes, but Pherrosh was squeezing them shut as a few sobs shook her frame.

"What just happened?" Farin asked. "You two were staring at each other and not speaking."

Asith couldn't remember if he'd spoken out loud. He rubbed Pherrosh's shoulder, and she took a deep breath, releasing the tension from her body like rain sliding down a roof tile, taking the dirt with it.

"She knew my father," Asith explained. "She wanted to know if he was safe."

Pherrosh grabbed the paper again. *I have friends in the Graveyard Trees.*

"I'm sorry. I should have said something sooner, I just…" Honestly, it had crossed Asith's mind a few times, but it seemed like a coincidence they would know each other. The Graveyard Trees was bigger than South Cairn, and Asith didn't know everyone who lived there.

Pherrosh shook her head and hugged him tightly. Asith held her, and her warmth spread over him, like when Lestash had hugged him after she'd carried him from the Graveyard Trees. Farin smiled, and Pherrosh pulled him into the hug too. He laughed as they huddled in the warmth of the little tent.

They traveled for a few more days, Pherrosh growing stronger with each hunt. She stepped with renewed vigor, asking Asith questions about his father and mother. Asith liked answering them, though he avoided certain details about his father's containment, not that she asked about that subject to begin with; she seemed to understand it might hurt them both to discuss it.

Pherrosh spent the following days teaching Asith the lightning spell. She used a stick in place of a wand, as she rarely used one, which didn't surprise Asith because Dradevai didn't use one either. Her version of the spell didn't rely on the circle as much, so it was easier to practice. He just had to get the movements right. Without sigils and runes to draw, he had to be confident enough to bend the magic in just the right way to cast a lightning bolt. It felt a bit like trying to sew without a needle.

Seeing he struggled with runes in all his spells, Pherrosh drew lines in Asith's spell book using another sheet of paper as a straightedge, hoping it might be easier. His lines still wobbled, but he succeeded in keeping his runes the same size. That could also affect the success of a spell, much like the uniformity of the stitches in a seam would alter the fit of a garment. It might be easier for him to do magic if he related everything to sewing, so he recorded that example. Soon enough, he realized he had started writing in his spell book as if it were a journal, remembering some of the pages of Dradevai's that he'd read. He felt closer to them, so he continued doing it even if it wasted precious page space, even if they could not get additional paper.

To practice, Asith used Pherrosh's method of creating guidelines with spells he already knew, which reminded him of following the chalk markings his mother would draw on fabric for him to add smocking. He loosened, the peace of being in his home with his mother as a child finding him, of helping her make another dress or suit for someone in South Cairn.

"What language is that?" Farin asked, pointing to some parts of his father's lightning spell.

"Endethi, the language of the dragons. Dragons and dragonborn know it innately."

"Really? You didn't have to learn to read it?" Asith and Pherrosh shook their heads, and he scoffed. "That'd be useful. It took me years to learn to read Matsic, and I'm still not very good at it."

Pherrosh smiled and wrote, *You're good at other things.*

She pulled a few of her shimmering golden feathers from her bag and tied them to Asith's wand before offering one to Farin and explaining it meant good luck if given willingly. She also advised him never to steal a dragon's feather, and Asith instinctively touched the leather strap that held Dradevai's around his neck. He sewed one of her feathers onto a piece of leather for Farin so that he could put it on a chain or a necklace.

Asith didn't fully understand the connection between Farin and Pherrosh, as it seemed like Farin was just an average person next to Pherrosh. He wasn't good or bad, just normal. But people could very well say the same about him with Dradevai or even Delri. If he really thought about it, Farin had a gentle side that Pherrosh brought out, so maybe it was that.

The following evening, they reached the mountains, where Pherrosh stopped and wrote, *I'm going to leave from here. Be safe, you two.*

She had already drawn them a map to the facility, so they gave her some food and money just in case. Pherrosh hugged Asith first, her eyes watering as she stepped back. When she turned to Farin, her smile grew soft, and she hugged him tightly and kissed him on the cheek. Farin's cheeks turned red, and he trembled.

With a beaming smile, Pherrosh burst into smoke, and her sleek golden wings spread out as her long, elegant neck turned up to the sky. Her feet lifted off the ground, and her twisting horns pointed toward the ground.

"Be safe!" Farin yelled. "Don't let anyone see you!"

She fluttered, acknowledging Farin's words, before flying straight up into the clouds hanging low on the mountain.

"We'll get back to her," Asith said, breaking their stretched silence. "I promise."

Farin nodded. "We will. Let's find your partner now."

Asith squeezed Farin's shoulder before they turned back to the trail and headed farther into the clouded mountains.

CHAPTER 11

27th *of Asdel*
151 Days

Asith clasped hands with Farin and hauled him up a ridge he was too short to hop onto.

"Why couldn't we take the main road again?" Farin fell forward onto his belly when Asith let go, wallowing on the rocks while he caught his breath. With his pack on his back, he looked like a snail.

"Because we don't want to risk being seen." Asith sat next to Farin and pulled out his waterskin. Yarrow hopped out of his bag while he took a long drink, and then he dripped some onto his hand for Yarrow to sip on.

"Would they even know who we are if you used that spell to disguise yourself?" Farin rolled over and looked up at the sky. "It's not like they know me."

"I can't cast that spell every time we might pass someone on the road."

"And why not? Mr. Big Shot Dragonborn Mage can't even make himself look like a regular-degular human for five minutes?" Farin huffed, sat up, and drank from his waterskin.

Asith sighed dramatically and tilted his face to the sun. It only warmed his skin a little. Spring hadn't set in, and as they got higher into the mountains, snow still clung to the trees and rocks.

"Bending the fabric of magic to your will is tiring, and I am not very good at it." Asith became aware of Yarrow's teeth against his palm. "I would rather have the energy to do other things rather than wear myself out. It isn't necessary if we just walk a bit off the road."

Farin paused his drinking. His expression was subdued, his brows knitting together.

"Sorry, I was only teasin' you." Farin nudged Asith's arm. Yarrow hopped away, and she brushed off the remaining water on her fur with her front feet. She bathed the rest of her body, grabbing at her ears to lick them.

"It's okay." Asith capped his waterskin and tucked it into his bag. He brushed his fingers over Dradevai's leather spell book, imagining Pherrosh's careful handwriting in the front. He hadn't had the heart to look at it since he'd realized it was hers. She had left the carefully drawn spell circles and notes for Dradevai, and Dradevai had added notes and spells to them; a love letter to their own mother they hadn't even known they were writing.

"Is that book your partner's?" Farin asked. He was leaning over, eying the book in Asith's bag, though not really invading Asith's personal space.

Asith touched the worn parchment and globs of dried glue at the spine where it had been repaired. He thought of the state his father and Pherrosh had first been in, their bodies weak and broken, in need of fixing, much like a well-used spell book. Dradevai could be in a similar state, their body needing to be put back together. They were not a book, though, a body was much harder to fix, and they could be getting treated more cruelly for breaking out the dragons.

"It was." Asith closed his bag, scooped Yarrow up, and stood. She moved to his shoulder and pressed against his neck. She was trying to reassure him, but the more he thought of Dradevai's state, the more his stomach turned. Grinding his teeth, he tried to hold something in his throat, but he wasn't sure what exactly it was.

"Hey," Farin said sharply, hopping up onto his feet as he frowned. "Don't talk like that. It *is* theirs. It is still theirs, not was. We'll find them, okay?"

Asith's mouth fell open, his eyes welling with tears. He raised a hand to his face, sniffling as he tried to speak.

Farin leaned forward, trying to catch Asith's eyes. "What's their name? What's your partner's name? Can you tell me about them?"

"Dradevai, their name is Dradevai." Asith took a shaky breath, closing his eyes. Tears were running down his cheeks, and he allowed the blackness closing his eyes afforded him. But it didn't last long as he imagined the sight of Dradevai in a cage, weak and pinned down like his father. The vision came so quick and so heavy that he opened his eyes to escape.

"What were they like?" Farin asked.

Asith swayed on his feet, and Yarrow hopped off his shoulder. "Like the dawn." Asith covered his eyes, darkening the world around him.

"What do you mean by that exactly?"

Asith listened to the sound of Farin's boots shuffling on the stone, hoping it might ground him. "They were…" Asith swallowed, shaking his head. In his mind's eye, he viewed Dradevai grinning with confidence, their cheeks so high that their eyes looked like the crests of hills and their nose wrinkled. They looked like that when Asith complimented their magic, when they had done something difficult, when they succeeded in their goals; the Dradevai that Asith had fallen in love with in their hoard and continued to love even when he didn't understand that's what he was doing. Dradevai had opened themselves to him, and Asith hadn't even said he loved them because he was too afraid.

"Bright and hopeful," Asith answered.

Farin didn't respond, looking at Asith with his brow worried. But Asith couldn't continue. His mouth opened and closed, and he hiccupped as he realized how long it had taken him to understand his own feelings. He might never get to tell them of anything he'd felt, nor hold them in his arms again.

Farin touched Asith's arm, but Asith shut his mouth tightly. He didn't look at Yarrow or Farin but sensed them drawing closer.

"Maybe…" Farin said. "Maybe it would be easier for you to tell me their favorite food?"

Asith pressed his lips into a hard line, and fresh tears streamed down his face even as he imagined Dradevai crunching a raw egg between his teeth.

"They really liked eggs," Asith said, a sob rocking his body.

"O-Okay. How did they like them cooked?"

"They ate them raw, with the shell still on." Asith looked at Farin through blurry tears, and Farin's eyes had enlarged, with a small gap between his lips.

"They did what now?" Farin's voice had gone up about three octaves.

Asith's chest heaved, but a smile encroached on his lips. "I swear, they'd eat them raw, shell and all." A laugh tore through him. "I had to keep telling them not to do it in the Capitol so people wouldn't catch on to their true identity."

"Yeah, I'd say that would fuckin' give them away if they ate a raw egg in front of someone!" Farin's face pinched, his brow low over his eyes. "Wouldn't that hurt them?"

"It didn't for whatever reason." Asith picked Yarrow up and cradled her against his chest.

Farin tugged his pack onto his shoulders. "Well, when we find them, I'll have to ask them about it."

"Yeah." Asith rubbed his face, taking some deep breaths. "I'm sorry."

"It's okay." Farin wrapped his hands around the straps of his pack, suddenly looking much, much older than Asith. His eyes softened, and he added, "I don't know what it's like, but I'm sure it's hard."

Asith swallowed and ran his fingers over Yarrow's head. Dradevai was bright and hopeful, but they were also smart and confident. It would take a lot for them to be captured, and even if they had been, Dradevai's spirit wouldn't easily break. Asith closed his eyes and repeated that train of thought. Taking in the warmth of Yarrow's soft fur and letting it spread up his arm and through his chest, Asith opened his eyes and looked at the path before them. Well, it was really more of an old hunting trail they had found, but it made him feel closer to Dradevai than any other road or mountain pass so far.

The trail was confusing to follow, but Farin ultimately noticed deer hoofprints in the mud. Perhaps the animals made the path themselves, rather than hunters, but regardless, it would be a smart path to follow.

As they walked, the trees created a dark canopy overhead, broken only in areas where large boulders had fallen from the rocky hills above. Asith helped Farin get up and over several boulders, and they took turns discussing topics other than their current task. He was glad they had convinced Pherrosh to fly home as they approached the timberline and the climb became steeper. Her health had improved, but she was weaker than she let on. Even walking up a foothill winded her, and if she had flown to the top, she might have been seen.

He hoped she was taking plenty of breaks and pacing herself. Flying was probably just as tiring as climbing, especially if she was staying low in the trees and couldn't glide. A part of Asith wished he had broken the orb Lestash had given him so that Pherrosh could have flown with her, but it was too valuable to use before finding Dradevai. He might also need his aunt's help to break into the facility.

Farin talked for a long time about some toy duck he'd had as a kid stolen by another kid at school. Asith couldn't even remember how they'd gotten on the topic, but listening kept his mind off everything else. Upon hearing all the details, he also agreed Farin was in the right and the other kid was a jerk.

"And then the asshole brought it to school a week later for show and tell!" Farin threw his arms up into the air. "The nerve of that asshole. Takin' my wooden duck and pretending it was his right in front of my— hey, what is that?"

Asith stopped as Farin stepped into the bushes, going until Asith couldn't see him. He tried to follow Farin's movement, for he barely parted them at the top, but he eventually popped out between two tall evergreen trees.

"I can't see what you're looking at." Asith stood on his toes, leaning to the side. He didn't want to go into the bushes either, for he wasn't as small as the halfling and wouldn't be able to navigate as easily.

"Sorry, thought it was something," Farin said. "I think it's just a deer leg? Like with fur still on it?"

"Wait." Asith entered the bushes. "Does it have teeth marks?"

"Um…I'm really more of a city boy."

"If it has teeth marks, then a wolf pulled it off the deer."

Farin pressed his lips together. "I'm starting to wish I hadn't pointed this out to you."

When his father hunted, while Asith was trying to learn the lightning spell, he often didn't eat the limbs of animals he caught, for they carried too little meat for them to be worth digesting the bone and hoof.

"If there are no teeth marks on it, then it's possible a dragon bit away the leg from the body." Asith studied the brown fur of the appendage, but there were no obvious teeth marks or signs that something tore away the flesh. It appeared just like the deer legs his father would leave behind. That meant a Sterling dragon was in the area.

"Okay, your reasoning has made this less weird, but why does it matter if it was eaten by a wolf or a dragon?" Farin slipped on a glove and turned the leg over gently, frowning so deeply that it distorted his sharp jawline.

"It means there are free dragons around here." Asith stomped back to the trail. "The facility wouldn't let the dragons in cages out to hunt deer."

"Oh, well, that actually sounds like useful information." Farin shrugged. "You think a dragon ate it then?"

"I do think a dragon ate it. Did you think I was staring at a severed deer leg for no reason?"

"Honestly, you're kind of weird. I wouldn't have put it past you." A grin spread across Farin's face.

Asith rubbed his temples. "You were the one who pointed it out to me. What did you even think it was?" Yarrow shifted and popped her head out of his bag.

"A nice walking stick." Farin gave a crisp nod. "Anyway, let's keep walking."

Asith's shoulders dropped, and he ran a hand over Yarrow's head. "I'm not that weird, am I?"

Yarrow blinked slowly at him.

"You're talking to a rabbit," Farin said.

Asith covered Yarrow's ears. "She's not just a rabbit; she's my familiar."

Farin chuckled. "What exactly is the difference?"

"There are lots of differences!" Asith's brows knitted together. "She helps me cast spells, and she can communicate with me in her own way."

"All right, I'm sorry. I know she's not a normal rabbit; I was only teasing you."

"I knew that…"

Farin snorted at Asith's shaky tone and followed him to the trail. "We should probably try to find a spot to camp soon. There's a cave up ahead, maybe there?"

Asith looked at the treetops, gauging when the suns might fully rise. Farin was right about stopping soon, especially if they wanted to find somewhere flat to sleep. He scrunched his nose at the thought of sleeping in a rocky cave with not even so much as dirt under them to soften the granite.

"You're right. But maybe with all these pine trees, we might find somewhere softer to sleep than a cave."

From the corner of Asith's eye, something flittered with movement. It could've just been the leaves rustling in the wind, but his hair was standing on end. A hiss sounded, which he'd heard plenty of times and was only ever followed by a spray of acid that could melt a shield in seconds. His stomach fluttered, and bile rose into his throat as the figure encroached upon the sky. It dove, and on instinct alone, Asith grabbed Farin by the collar and dragged him under a rocky overhang. It was hard to see in the dark, but he swore he caught a flash of green. He pushed Farin against the wall, covering him as much as he could, fearing the worst when a squelch rose over the harsh wind.

"Holy shit." Farin trembled. "Turn us invisible, what are you doing? Make us unable to be seen."

Asith looked back toward the trail, unable to see where the acid had landed.

"Asith, wake up, make us invisible." Farin tugged at Asith's tunic. "*Please.*"

He pulled the charm from his hair and tried to remember the chant, but the words wouldn't leave his mouth. Instead, he stammered as leathery wings rose over the tree line. It hadn't descended toward them, and in its claws was the shape of a person, their limbs flailing and their scarf falling off. Even though it was flying away, Asith's left shoulder ached, a phantom pain from the old wound where a Green had pierced him with its claw and then dropped him. Eroan had narrowly saved him, and Asith had retired shortly after.

It was a Green. And it let go of the person. Doing exactly what one had done to Asith.

Asith stuffed his hand into a pouch on his belt and grasped a feather.

"What are you doing? Asith?" Farin's voice cracked, and he pulled away from Asith and took two steps from the overhang.

Asith raised his arms and hands, casting one of the first spells Dradevai had taught him. He had only considered using it to save himself in case he fell from Dradevai's hoard, but there was no restriction on whom he could cast it on. Dradevai had likely learned it for the sake of Asith's safety, and that was just like them.

Asith snapped his hand forward and shouted the words for the spell. The falling person halted in the air, their arms thrashing around, before the magic lowered them below the trees. The Green turned on Asith, its tongue lashing out.

The mages at the Maeria Spire always changed locations after using a spell, for dragons could follow the scent of magic directly back to the caster. But Farin was the one pulling Asith away from the Green.

"Good job, we need to move. That invisibility would still be good anytime."

Asith made sure he was still holding the charm and let Farin guide him, his eyes on the sky. The Green hovered, likely tracking the scent of magic, but its attention was also caught on where the person had fallen. By the way it swung its head, Asith knew it hadn't found them yet.

"Greens mostly hunt by smell, so invisibility wouldn't help." Asith jogged to maintain his pace with Farin's sprint. "We need to get into water or mud or under leaves."

"How's a cave?" Farin asked.

Asith studied the Green, which didn't have any front legs. That meant it couldn't dig them out of the rocks. "Cave will work."

"Good." Farin sped up as he made for a nearby gap in the rocks. Asith reluctantly turned his back on the Green to sprint as well, listening carefully for a hissing sound or gargling or any sign of an acid bath coming their way.

When they were a good fifty feet from a cave entrance, the wind kicked up, and the beating of the Green's wings drew closer. Asith looked back, trying to remember everything Dradevai and his father had taught him. It had been a long while since he'd wished for his axe, though he wouldn't want to get close to a Green without his armor.

Yarrow hopped from his bag and zipped after Farin as she sent Asith a single mental image—lightning striking across the sky.

Asith stopped, whipped around, and pulled his wand from his belt. He held it out straight in his left hand, his hair rising, and spoke the chant his father had taught him. A bright light burned at the end of his staff, the flowers along the shaft flaring as if they were burning hot. When Asith moved to grab the ball of light at the end of his staff, the Green hissed, and his focus turned to the impending spray of acid. His fingers slid through the ball of lightning, and the spell shattered, the flowers on his wand going dark.

He tried to shake the wand as if that would help, but he abandoned the spell entirely when the hissing grew louder and its neck bent back like a snake preparing to strike. Knowing he was better with shields, Asith visualized a shield as he extended his left arm above his head. He drew his wand down like he was towing a heavy piece of freshly washed canvas over a drying line and pictured the image directly in front of the Green's nose. The acid sprang from its mouth, but it hit the barrier and splattered all over the Green's face and neck.

The Green screeched, and its black eyes widened as it writhed and plummeted through the tree line. It smashed against the ground with a concussive boom, shattering branches and knocking some smaller trees over.

The dust settled, and every sound of nature fell quiet, until the quick patter of Farin's feet broke the silence. Asith spun on his heel to follow Farin into the cave, his skin tingling as a strange giddiness swept over him. He couldn't believe that had worked. Gripping his wand, he sprinted to the cave, hearing the rustling of bushes and growls of pain as the Green gathered itself. It reminded Asith of a downed pheasant that had taken an arrow but not yet dead.

Farin dove into the cave, and Asith crouched and crawled inside. As the Green made louder noises and broke more tree branches, he stared at Farin, and they both panted, trying to recover their breath.

"That was clever," Farin whispered, his voice thin and breathless. "Using its acid against it."

"Thanks." Asith moved farther into the cave, feeling Yarrow brush past him in the dark. Thanks to her black fur, she was impossible to see. "Sleep in here today?"

"Absolutely," Farin said. "Please set up that magic tent."

Asith sat up and rubbed his face, taking a deep breath. Hoping the person the Green had attacked was okay, Asith cast a spell for the tent, the edges of it forming along the rocky walls of the cave and Farin moved closer to him in the warmth. Together, they listened to the sounds of the Green until they faded away.

CHAPTER 12

28ᵗʰ *of Asdel*
152 Days

The cave was both quiet and loud, with the dripping of water echoing off the hard rocks and no noise coming through the opening at the front. Light had partially entered with the rising suns, and Asith's eyes followed the shapes in the stone ceiling to avoid thoughts of the Green that had nearly killed them. Farin had fallen asleep at some point, his breathing more even than it had been at first; more jagged than the rocks.

They stayed like that until nightfall, Asith unable to fall asleep. Closing his eyes, Asith breathed in slowly and focused his attention on the sounds, eventually hearing a rustling of leaves from outside the cave. He clung to the noise, the howling of the wind just loud enough to tell it didn't belong to the beating of leathery wings. The Green was probably long gone, but Asith's skin still crawled and his fingers moved toward his sword.

"Asith, it's Pystra."

The voice came in loud, as if she were right next to him. He sat up quickly, scraping his head against the ceiling of the cave despite the tent. The magic was not enough to protect him from the rocks apparently.

"Any word on Dradevai?"

Asith rubbed the top of his head, groaning loudly enough that Farin stirred. "No, I'm still trying to find them, but I helped free a dragon from under the Maeria Spire."

The words had spilled out of his mouth before he thought them through. He hadn't tried to contact Pystra and Delri before he left because he feared putting them in danger, and since his departure, he'd been too distracted to communicate with them. A pause stretched out before Pystra answered.

"Okay. Delri wanted me to tell you the Stonegarde is mobilizing large units. Going northeast toward what she called Old High Cairn."

Farin sat up, rubbing his eyes and mumbling. "Strange," Asith said. They were in the Northeast, not the Northwest. "I'm in the Eastern mountains."

"Who are you talking to?" Farin shook Asith's shoulder. "You're not sleep talking, are you?"

Asith tapped on his head. "No, magic." Farin nodded.

"Delri and I are in the Capitol. Things are…strange? We'll try to figure out what they're doing."

"Tell me if you find anything out. Especially if it's about me," Asith said.

"We'll keep our eyes and ears open and let you know. Be safe." Pystra's voice held an air of finality Asith didn't particularly like, but he let it be.

"I will. You too."

When nothing additional came from Pystra, Asith relayed the information to Farin.

"Is that Graveyard Trees of yours to the northeast?" Farin asked. Asith's skin felt terribly cold, his blood rushing to his feet.

"It is, but…" A strange shiver ran down Asith's spine. The Graveyard Trees had a great deal of magic around it that kept it hidden, but he couldn't shake the possibility that its location had somehow been compromised. After all, more Blues and Greens had been causing problems there lately. It seemed unlikely that the dragon knights were headed there, like Pystra was hinting at, and perhaps the Blues and Greens were just tracing the magic around the Graveyard Trees. A lot of it was certainly being used in and around the city, and that Green had pinpointed him fairly quickly after one spell that day.

"But?" Farin asked, his voice wavering.

"It's well hidden," Asith said. "They use a lot of magic to conceal it."

Farin shifted. "But it was a bunch of mages keeping Pherrosh captive. Couldn't they see through something like that?"

Asith bit his lip until he tasted iron. He released his jaw, running his tongue along the wound. Farin didn't seem convinced the Graveyard Trees was completely safe, and Asith couldn't ignore it anymore.

"Powerful mages like Heskel and Vetrish might see through it, and Pherrosh said they're selling the dragon parts. Now that they've lost a couple dragons, they might be looking for more." Asith pulled from his pack a glowing crystal Dradevai had given him so he could read at night in their hoard. That was so long ago, and he wanted nothing more than to rest among the heated pillows, shaking off the chill of winter. He wished he could sleep on Dradevai's warm paws again, their head nestled at his side and their wings protecting him as they had in Pystra's hoard. Asith shivered, tears gathering in his eyes, but he wiped them away.

He placed the glowing crystal in a crevice above them, providing light to the cave. Farin's body was curling inward like a rabbit making itself smaller to hide. Yarrow walked off Asith's lap and set her front feet on Farin's thigh. Smiling, Farin sighed and let Yarrow onto his lap.

"I hope we're wrong," Farin said in a low voice, the light dancing across his long eyelashes and reflecting off his wet eyes.

"Me too."

Yarrow snuggled against Farin's stomach, while he kept his eyes on the ground. "You know," Farin said, "shortly after I met Pherrosh, she gave me one of her feathers to sell." Farin rubbed the back of his neck. "When I met her, Mama and I were in some money trouble, so I had snuck under the Maeria Spire for something I could steal. Earn some quick gold."

Asith wrapped his arms around his knees. "The two of you knew each other for longer than I realized."

"We did."

Asith placed a hand on Farin's shoulder, which was trembling, so Asith slipped an extra blanket to Farin. It was thin, but he wrapped it around his form, encasing Yarrow within.

"Anyway, Pherrosh was scared of me at first. I told her I'd help her get out right then and there, but she didn't trust me." Farin looked at Asith, his eyes watering. "I spoke to her as often as I could, snuck her food. Eventually, she started to trust me, and when I told her what I was doing, she gave me one of her feathers and told me to sell it."

A small smile tugged at Asith's lips. Somehow, it did not shock him to learn that Pherrosh was just as caring as Dradevai could be.

"Thank you," Asith said. "That makes things a lot clearer."

Farin sniffled and coughed. "What I don't get is the difference between Sterlings and Blues and Greens. Why not just catch the Blues and Greens? They're hurting people anyway."

"Blues and Greens aren't dragons. They're mimicking dragons. Why, I'm not entirely sure. Maybe just evolution."

"Evolution doesn't make sense, does it?"

Asith's brow furrowed. "No, not really. The friend who contacted me just now was trying to research where they came from and why before I met her."

Farin pressed his lips together, opening the blanket so Yarrow could pop her head out. Her ears perked up and swiveled to the mouth of the cave. Asith listened, but he could barely hear anything beyond the cave. Then he caught the distinct sound of bushes rustling, but that time, it was louder than the Green had been.

"Is that the dragon again?" Farin asked. "I mean the Green."

Asith crawled toward the edge of the tent and peeked out. Perhaps he had imagined it, but Farin and Yarrow had clearly heard it too. He extended himself farther to scan the tree line.

Farin shoved himself under Asith's arm, fitting in what was left of the cave opening. "The sound is gone."

"I know." Asith's eyes moved lower. It helped that the trees were mostly bare at that time of year, a few evergreens hanging onto their needles, but that was all in his sight.

"Wait, what's that?" Farin pointed at two reflective eyes partially obscured by some bushes. The eyes were close together and forward facing, so they didn't belong to a deer or an elk. Asith wished he had some sort of spell to see in the dark. He searched for signs of fur or the wet nose of a bear, but something about the vague shape of its head didn't read bear either and no ears seemed to sit on top of its head. Whatever it was, Asith wouldn't figure it out without getting closer.

He put his hand on the stone below and pulled himself out of the cave. As he emerged, moonlight caught on the creature's eyes and reflected in a way Asith had only seen happen with Dradevai's eyes.

"Hello?" he called, hoping he hadn't just drawn a bear's attention. A startled noise was followed by a cacophony of breaking branches and crunching snow. The eyes disappeared, and a flurry of mist rose from the bushes, wings flapping desperately as they tried to climb above the tree line.

"Wait, please don't run!"

The dragon was small, about the size of an ox, with dark gray feathers that shimmered in the moonlight. They flew towards him, and Asith fell back, their long tail feathers grazing the top of his head. Asith rolled over in the wet snow, the dragon fluttering desperately like a chicken trying to outrun a fox. They climbed only a little higher than the trees.

"Wait!" Farin yelled, crawling to Asith's side, and threw his hands in the air. "We're friends!"

The dragon paid them no mind, continuing to glide away.

"Let's follow them," Asith said and helped Farin get up. "Quick, come on."

CHAPTER 13

They swept up their belongings into their packs as quickly as they could and ran along a small break in the trees between the rocky cliffs and the forest. The dragon didn't get too far, their wings carrying them toward an edge that tumbled down into a steep gorge, the sound of the rushing water loud.

"Stop! Please!" Asith yelled.

The dragon's wings beat the air rapidly, but they didn't catch much air in their feathers. They wouldn't make it over the gorge if they tried crossing. "I'm dragonborn, please!"

Farin was close on his heels, occasionally yelling about a rock or tree so Asith didn't crash into it. Asith let Farin take the lead through the darkened landscape and slowed his pace to match Farin's, which wore him out less anyway.

"Yarrow, please." Asith pulled her out of his bag and tossed her into the snow. She darted off, much faster than Asith or Farin could travel, her strong back legs closing the distance between herself and the dragon. Asith pulled out his wand and decided to cast a net spell, hoping he could shoot it from Yarrow. When she glowed, he knew he'd done something right, and a dark green light emitted from her.

The dragon called out as they neared the cliff side, lowered to the ground, and then hopped forward with all their might.

"No!" Asith didn't finish the spell before the dragon was fluttering toward the center at a poor angle. He wasn't good at math, but he knew falling at a speed that fast wouldn't be safe.

He whipped out a feather and sprinted to the cliff side, his heart pounding in his ears. The magic released from his hand instead of from Yarrow, rippling like a sheet caught in the wind. But the dragon plummeted to the rocks below.

A burst of feathers appeared from the face of the opposite cliff. A second dragon, their wings spreading wide as it descended toward the small dragon. In a flash, they had captured the falling dragon in their paws. The wind escaped Asith's lungs as the second dragon dropped the other safely about ten feet above the opposite cliff.

Asith stopped at the edge, Farin still far behind him. His knees ached from running up such rough terrain. As he tilted his head up at the dragon's form, Asith tried to distinguish its features in the dark. They were much larger and probably older. They crossed the gap and Asith grew breathless, his eyes studying the feathers for any signs of bronze, but the moon wasn't revealing much, other than silhouetting them. Trembling, Asith examined every shimmer of light bouncing off the dragon's wings. Their long neck extended, and they dove faster than Asith had ever seen something move.

Asith's legs shook, his stomach unsettling as the dragon rotated ever so slightly. The moonlight caught on the double set of horns on either side of their head. Asith's fingers clenched into a fist, trying to ready himself for the chance his instinct was completely wrong, but Pystra had said four horns were a rare feature in dragons.

It had to be Dradevai, he had to have found them. He sucked in a heavy breath, and they opened their mouth slowly, smoke gathering at the edges as they flashed their teeth.

Asith's body froze, his head filling with a cloud of unspun wool, caught somewhere between terror and elation when he raised his empty hands. He possessed nothing to protect himself if the dragon chose to attack. Their honey amber eyes removed all the air from his lungs.

Dradevai. It was Dradevai.

"Dradevai!" Asith screamed. He was unaware his voice could be that loud. "Dradevai!"

"Asith!" Farin's voice was still far off. "Move."

Asith bounced up and down and yelled their name again and again. The dragon's mouth clapped shut, the smoke dissipating. They blinked quickly, their eyes turning back into the soft round shape Asith remembered. They flung their wings forward to slow their descent as Asith continued to move erratically, his arms reaching out as if he could close the distance with them alone.

"Asith!" Dradevai's voice cut clear through the cold air. When they were close enough, they transformed into their smaller form and dove headfirst with their arms extended.

As they collided, Asith barely even felt their weight as he fell onto his back, Dradevai thudding on top. Dradevai must have done something because it should have hurt more, but he simply drew them in to the tightest hug he could give. Their arms looped around his neck in return. He buried his face in their shoulder, a sob shaking his entire body as he clung to them with all his might. Asith had finally found them, he had saved their mother and sent her home, and they had hopefully never been captive like she and his father had been.

"I'm so glad you're safe," Dradevai said, his voice cracking. They pulled away from Asith and cupped his face with warm hands, tears pouring down their cheeks. Brushing some of his hair back, Dradevai said, "You're so cold, oh, Asith."

"I love you." The words spilled out of Asith's mouth as he sat them both up. "I'm so sorry I didn't say it sooner, I love you, I was so worried I would never get to tell you."

Dradevai snorted, which then devolved into a fit of laughter. They wiped at their face and pressed themself into Asith's shoulder. "I love you too."

Asith grasped their jaw, trying to be gentle, but his hand shook and nothing felt real. He kissed Dradevai's warm lips, then pressed their foreheads together, not wanting to go far. A smile spread across Dradevai's face, all the way to their cheeks, which were flushed in the moonlight. They appeared mostly the same, though their hair had been cropped to barely graze their shoulders and their bangs had grown out. Their hair fluttered in the breeze, haloing their head as they wiped at their eyes with the back of their hand. Dradevai wore a plain brown tunic with the leggings Asith had made for them, except they were torn in awkward places and fraying at the seams. His eyes caught on a fresh scar on the right side of their neck that trailed down to their collarbone. Asith brushed his fingers over the irritated skin, the texture jagged.

"What happened?" Asith asked.

Dradevai turned their head as if they could look at the scar, their eyes unfocused while they thought. "A guard shot me with a crossbow bolt as I was leaving the facility we broke into."

Asith's chest tightened. "I'm sorry I wasn't there to help." Even with Dradevai in his arms, he couldn't help but regret leaving them that night.

They shook their head. "It's okay. It didn't even really hurt when it happened. I was too focused on other things."

Dradevai smiled, but it wasn't the same unshakeable smile Asith remembered. It didn't hit their eyes, and their lips remained closed over their teeth.

"Then you weren't ever caught by them or kept there?" Asith's brow wrinkled, his hand smoothing down their shoulders.

"No, they never caught me." Dradevai's smile grew. "They even came after us at one point, but I got us away and found us a much better place."

"Us?" Asith hadn't even considered they might have more dragons with them. Something in his chest swelled, the thought of Dradevai successfully saving other dragons bringing a lightness to his limbs he hadn't felt in a long time. Asith should have known better, for Dradevai was far too determined to get captured or leave that facility alone.

"There are a few, yes." Dradevai's head tilted, their nose wrinkling ever so slightly, and their eyes landed on the charm tied next to their feather around Asith's neck. They touched the axe gently before finding the brooch pinned to his doublet. "What are these?"

"It's a long story and I want to tell you the whole thing when we have more time, but the charm is a gift from Phela. I used a spell to call to her, and she helped me find you."

"What spell did you—" Dradevai froze, their eyes moving toward something behind Asith's head. Asith looked over his shoulder to see Farin, his hands covering his ears.

"Sorry, I was trying to give you some privacy." Farin lowered his hands and picked up Yarrow at his feet. She didn't look particularly pleased, but being on a lower rock, she had no choice in how to get up.

Asith sighed. "Sorry, Vai, this is Farin. Farin, this is my partner, Dradevai."

Dradevai's eyes lit up at Asith's last words, when he called them "partner." They stood and helped Asith off the ground.

"It's nice to meet you," Dradevai said to Farin. A sad call cried from the distance, and Dradevai spun toward the dragon on the far cliff. "Oh, I need to go get him."

"Nice to meet you too." Farin handed Yarrow to Asith. "Go get the kid. We can talk more once they're safe."

Dradevai gave Farin a soft smile and nodded at Asith. "I'll come right back for the two of you."

Asith said, "I know you will."

Dradevai changed into their larger form. The moonlight caught their soft feathers, their horns a tiny bit longer than the last time Asith had seen them. They hopped off the cliff in a single motion and glided to the other side. Upon reaching the ledge, they nudged the smaller dragon toward the edge, and the dragon ultimately fluttered onto a small ridge on the opposite cliff face, Dradevai right behind. Then they slipped past the rocks, and an illusion rippled, obscuring them from view.

"Wow, they just disappeared." Farin was leaning forward on his toes, still several feet from the edge.

When Dradevai returned, they explained that the dragon had safely made it inside their temporary home, and they would head there too. They scooped Farin into their paw while Asith perched himself on their back. He adjusted the goggles Dradevai had made over his eyes, warming his cold skin. Asith had not bothered to put his coat on when they'd chased the dragon, but he hadn't felt the cold until then.

It was only a short flight from one cliff face to another, but Farin yelled in fear most of the way. When they approached the hoard, Farin made it quite clear he didn't like heights, and Dradevai set Farin down before they landed. Farin wobbled around on the stone as if he might be sick. It all reminded Asith of how he'd first felt in Dradevai's paw.

An illusion was carved into the rocks around the smooth cave entrance, making it look much like the tunnel in Dradevai's old hoard. The light was dim inside the cave, but it was spacious, curving back into the cliff side.

"Is this your new hoard?" Asith asked.

"No, hiding here was meant to be a temporary solution to a rather complicated problem, but we've been here for a while." Dradevai hit the rocks, emitting a clapping sound.

"What's the complicated problem?" Farin asked.

As the clap echoed, rows of magical flames lit up on either side of the walls, following the curve of the cavern back into the rest of the cave. It was narrower than he'd realized, for Dradevai had floated in so easily. A small set of hands wrapped around the bend of the cave, followed by a tiny face peering around the corner. She had dark brown hair just barely covering her pointed ears. Two little horns curved up from her messy bangs, not yet long enough to know what direction they'd twist in. With her eyes being a warm dark brown, she reminded Asith of a fawn that should still be with her mother. She wore the reddish tunic Asith had made for Dradevai, but it was too large and poorly stitched in places. The fabric belt Asith had also made was secured around her waist. She didn't even have shoes.

"How many are there?" Asith asked Dradevai. "How many other dragons?"

Dradevai sighed, waving at the girl, and she squeaked like she had been caught. But she stopped when Dradevai asked her to bring everyone over.

"Oh no, she's so little." Farin's voice cracked, and his eyes appeared hollow. His mouth hung open, making his face look older and gaunt, and a green undertone shone beneath his ochre skin.

"I think you see why I said this is a complicated problem." Dradevai guided them to the back of the cavern, where the girl had gathered two older boys. They lowered their voice as they added, "There are just three of them, but none of them can really fly."

One boy looked about thirteen, if he was even that old, based on his height and the awkward length of his limbs. It appeared as if he hadn't grown into them quite yet. His skin was a pale peach tone, and copper hair curled around his head in a way that made his face look round, betraying his otherwise sharp features, like the horns sticking straight up like tree trunks. A smatter of nearly metallic freckles dotted his cheeks, nose, and shoulders. He was frail, but his jaw was set and he held himself high, his blue eyes locked on Asith and Farin like he was ready to fight if need be. On his body was a simple wrap of what looked to be a torn bedsheet, haphazardly held together with a piece of rope. He wore a pair of thin sandals, with the same rope as the fabric belt wrapping around his ankles.

Clinging nervously to his companion, the other boy had dark, nearly onyx skin, with big brown eyes turning downward at the edges. His hair was a gray halo around his head. At the oldest, he looked about eight, his fingers and hands still tiny with dirt underneath his nails. His eyes darted between Asith, Farin, and Dradevai as if he had done something wrong. He was also wearing makeshift clothes, including a nightshirt torn off at the bottom, with the vest Asith had made Dradevai over it.

"I'm sorry, I didn't mean to lead anybody here," said the younger boy, who Dradevai had saved. Tears gathered on in his long lower lashes, and his voice wobbled as he said, "I just thought if I could get more food...I just wanted to help."

"It's okay, Idhe. Remember how I told you I had a partner who was probably looking for me?"

All three kids nodded.

"This is him, this is my partner, Asith, and his friend Farin. They won't hurt us."

The boys looked at Dradevai like they didn't entirely trust their words, but the girl smiled and waved. Farin and Asith waved back. He'd never felt more like an only child in his life.

Dradevai introduced the older boy as Mysse and the girl as Cemi. Mysse barely acknowledged them, while Cemi looked up at Dradevai.

"Then this means you're going to get the dragons out of that other place, right?" Cemi asked. Her eyes widened, looking between Dradevai and Asith. "You said you'd try once your partner came."

"R-Right." Dradevai shifted their weight and kneeled to reach Cemi's level. Before they could say anything, Asith bent down and spoke.

"Yes. I just broke another dragon out of a facility like that. My friend here helped me. We'll do our best to get the other dragons out, but we might need to wait a little before we do, okay?"

Cemi flashed a smile of yellowed teeth, with two missing. Asith smiled back while Yarrow hopped around her feet and then sniffed Mysse's ankle.

"I understand." Cemi turned to Idhe and Mysse. "See, I told you two them being here had to be a good thing!"

Idhe smiled, though he still looked around nervously. Mysse, on the other hand, huffed, pulled away from Idhe, and stomped to the back of the cavern, startling Yarrow at his feet.

Dradevai sighed, and, grimacing at Asith, stood up. Idhe was bickering with Cemi, as children sometimes did, and Dradevai's frown deepened. They schooled their expression back to a smile that didn't reach their eyes. He would have to speak to them later, for something was off, and though it might just be the pressure of keeping those little dragons safe, he didn't want to leave them alone in their worries anymore. It was a small burden to take on that load.

"Hey," Farin said, tugging Asith's sleeve. "How about we eat?"

"We don't have much..." Dradevai began, rubbing the back of their head.

"Don't worry, I have it." Farin puffed out his chest and pulled out his cauldron. Dradevai gathered the few bowls they owned, Asith following to see if he could help. Something in the way they moved and rubbed their temples made Asith desire to reach out for them, but that was not the right time.

Farin filled his cauldron with mashed potatoes and dished them out into some bowls and one cup. Then he wiped the cauldron out and filled it with stew. The smell grabbed the kids' attention, even Mysse walking over to peer at Farin. Cemi helped serve the stew over the potatoes, and then she picked a bowl up and brought it to Dradevai.

"Here. You didn't eat last time we had food."

Dradevai's shoulders dropped, their mouth falling open. They started to explain the three of them should eat first, being the smallest, but Cemi insisted.

"Go ahead, you saved Idhe and did all that flying," Farin said with a wave. He filled the cauldron a second time with stew. "Plus, there's plenty. I can do this twice more today."

"All right." Dradevai sat next to Asith as Cemi handed the bowls to the boys and then to Asith and Farin. Yarrow sniffed along the floor until she settled between Mysse and Idhe, resuming her typical position of appearing as a bread roll. Asith took the smaller serving in the cup since he wasn't very hungry after everything. Farin took a smaller portion as well.

The cave grew quiet except for the sounds of the three kids gobbling up their food and a distant rumble of water. Asith found himself comfortably warm in the humid air, which made him think a hot spring was somewhere inside. There also seemed to be more rooms beyond his sight.

Eventually, his eyes found Dradevai, wandering over the back of their neck to their cropped hair. They didn't notice him looking, their eyes straight ahead as they chewed on their food. Asith's chest clenched as he thought about how much he had to tell them. Even though he wanted to blurt out everything about Pherrosh right then and there, he had to wait.

"Oh," Asith said, setting down his cup and spoon to rifle through his bag. Dradevai perked up and turned toward him. After pulling out his coat and the bedroll, he produced Dradevai's spell book. "I wanted to make sure to return this. I have a pen for you too."

Dradevai's eyes filled with tears faster than Asith had ever seen them. They reached out for the book, hiccupping before they started to sob. Asith wrapped his arms around them and pulled them into a tight hug as he glanced at the kids and Farin. Mysse's chin raised, looking down his nose at Asith as if Dradevai's reaction was his fault somehow.

"Hey, Vai, it's okay." Asith rubbed their back and set his cheek against their head, twitching when his temple hit one of their horns. "Here, come on."

Asith made to move, but Dradevai leaned back, their eyes darting to Farin. They whispered, "Are you sure he's…" Dradevai gripped Asith's shoulder, their fingers tangling in his tunic. "Is it safe to leave him with them?"

"Yes." Asith had seen how Farin treated Pherrosh with such care that he didn't doubt the kids' safety. Dradevai's concerns were valid, though, so he nudged them to earn their attention again. "I promise you. I wouldn't bring anyone unsafe here."

Dradevai's lips quivered, their eyes still wet with tears, but they took Asith's outstretched hand. After picking up their food, he helped Dradevai to their feet while they cradled the spell book to their chest, their knees nearly giving out. Mysse rose as if he might follow them, but Dradevai put their hand out.

"Mysse, keep an eye, please?" They glanced at Farin, who gave them a thumbs up. Mysse grimaced but nodded slowly as he sat again. Yarrow got to her feet and looked at Mysse briefly before following Asith.

Dradevai held onto Asith, instructing him to head to a wooden door. It seemed to predate their arrival, puffy from absorbing water and the carvings near the handle worn down. When they entered, a small room greeted them, with a bedroll on the floor and, beside it, a collection of pillows, blankets, partial mattresses, and feathers that were formed into a sort of dilapidated nest. The sound of water was louder, and steam rose from an alcove near the back. The room smelled strongly of minerals typically released from the rocks into the water, and Asith wondered if they'd been drinking from there. Though he hadn't looked too closely, river water might have been in the main chamber.

"I'm sorry." Dradevai wiped at their face and turned the spell book over in their hands. "I just, I wasn't sure how I was going to keep doing this, and then you just turned up with everything I needed."

"It's okay." Asith wrapped them in a side hug. "I'm sorry it took me so long."

Dradevai hiccupped, tears streaming down their face. Their voice came out strained and cracked. "It's okay."

Asith kissed their forehead and wiped their tears away. He offered them some of his water, and while they collected themselves, Yarrow stationed herself against Dradevai's foot. They looked at Yarrow with their eyebrows squished together in confusion but didn't probe about her presence. The questions would come eventually. They took a deep breath and swallowed audibly.

"You could have turned up with nothing but the clothes on your back and I would have been just as happy to see you." Dradevai set their hands on his chest. "And instead, you showed up with food and, just, look at you…"

Asith studied his appearance and said, "I haven't bathed in over a week, so I'm not sure I entirely see what you mean."

Dradevai closed their eyes, which turned into happy little arches as they hiccupped through a laugh. They pressed their face into his chest, devolving into a fit of giggles.

"You do smell," they said.

"Sorry." Asith cupped their cheek and smiled when they looked up at him.

"I don't mind." Dradevai got up on their toes and kissed him gently as Asith looped an arm around their waist. He was still holding their food, so when he pulled away, he offered that to them. They accepted it, and Asith smoothed their hair down.

"Your hair looks nice like this." Asith twisted his fingers through the ends of their soft hair, admiring how the strands shined in the light.

"Oh, thank you," Dradevai said, touching their hair. "When I first got them out, Cemi's hair was so matted that I had to cut it all off, so I cut mine, too, to help her feel better about it."

Asith kissed the bridge of Dradevai's nose. "That sounds like you."

Dradevai's lips curved up, their bottom lip jutting out in just a bit of a pout. They didn't respond, just leaning on Asith again.

"Why don't you eat?" Asith asked. "It seems like you need it."

"I should, you're right." Dradevai looked at the door. "Stay in here with me for a little while?"

"Of course."

Asith sat with Dradevai on the bedroll, Yarrow pressing herself against their thigh. Dradevai studied her appearance before hesitantly smoothing two fingers over her head. When Yarrow's whiskers danced, they smiled.

"Is this rabbit yours?" Dradevai switched their attention to their bowl and swallowed some food, humming softly.

"She's my familiar." Asith reached over Dradevai to wiggle her ears, which made Dradevai chuckle.

"Her presence feels…similar to yours?" Dradevai said. "I'm not sure that makes sense."

"It makes about as much sense as anything else," Asith said as Dradevai savored every bite. In the light of the magic torches, their cheekbones jutted out, and their eyes appeared sunken.

"What?" Dradevai met his gaze. "Why are you looking at me like that?"

Asith sighed. "I was worrying about you. Are you really okay?"

Dradevai pressed their lips together, their shoulders tightening, and they looked at Yarrow again. They ran their fingers over her fur and relaxed ever so slightly.

"I'm not." Tears ran down their face again, reaching all the way to their chin. "I want to free more dragons, but I have been afraid to do more than scout."

Asith kissed their head and cupped their cheek before wiping away some tears. Asith had felt like Dradevai did when he hadn't progressed toward finding them while in the Graveyard Trees.

"You're doing your best, Vai. And I'm here now. I promise I will help get the other dragons out."

Dradevai leaned into his chest, their tense shoulders relaxing into Asith's rounded shape. He held them there, and Yarrow shifted closer.

"Can you tell me about the Graveyard Trees?" Dradevai asked. "Have you been learning from your father? He was a mage too, right?"

Asith nodded and encouraged them to eat again as he spoke about the Graveyard Trees. He showed them his wand, and Dradevai held it, admiring the carved flowers.

"Then my father started teaching me magic so I could come find you,"

Asith finished. He wrapped an arm around his knees, the other still holding Dradevai. They were finally finished with their bowl of stew.

"I'm happy for you." Dradevai smiled at the wand, their fingers following the carving. "I'm glad that you've gotten to spend time with him."

"Me too." Asith looked at his feet and then at Dradevai again. "I have something to tell you. A lot to tell you, actually."

"Oh?" Dradevai set their bowl on the ground, and a feather drifted into it.

"I'm not sure if now is a good time. I know tonight has been a lot and it's late. But it's important…"

Dradevai tilted their head just a bit, their face stony. Then they stood and said, "Let's get you cleaned up first. It will give me some time to prepare myself."

Offering Asith their hands, Dradevai pulled Asith up, and they led him into the alcove. There was a short tunnel filled with steam, and it led to a small cavern that had thick air and was warmer than the rest of the cave. A large spring bath had been carved into the floor.

"Just one moment. I need my bag." He pulled their hand to his lips and kissed their knuckles. "I will meet you at the spring."

"Okay." Dradevai probed at the collar of their shirt and pulled it off in an easy motion.

Asith struggled to pull his eyes away, but he turned and headed back to where they'd left the kids with Farin. He treaded quietly, though it wasn't particularly difficult to conceal his steps because Cemi and Idhe were cheering as Farin performed magic tricks for them. Farin's eyes briefly met Asith's, but he continued to keep the kids distracted. Asith would need to thank him for that later.

Once Asith had his pack, he searched for the wrapped package he'd stowed toward the bottom while in the Graveyard Trees. He dug as he walked and haphazardly dropped a dirty tunic on Yarrow. She grunted, her little feet scrambling while she tried to escape from under it. Asith plucked it off her, and she hopped ahead, kicking her back feet out at him.

"Sorry," Asith said when he reached the bedroll, where she was bathing herself. She ignored him entirely, and he shook his head, finally pulling the beaten-up package out. Then he headed to the alcove to join Dradevai.

CHAPTER 14

When Asith entered the cavern, Dradevai was sitting on the edge of the spring, their outstretched arm nudging a few stones on the other side of the small pool. Each movement caused steam to rise as cool water hit the spring. The water in the air clung to their brown-amber skin, and their bare chest and neck had gathered beads of sweat. Their wrist and ankle bones jutted out harshly, something that Asith didn't particularly like, not because Dradevai looked bad but because they were likely feeding the kids over themself. It didn't surprise Asith, but he wanted them to be healthy.

Their face was still as round as ever, and their cheeks glowed when they noticed Asith lingering near the entrance. They waved for Asith to join.

"I cooled the water down a bit, but you should still check it before you get in. I've found my tolerance for this sort of thing is higher than other people's."

"Well, you do breathe fire. You probably are a bit more fireproof than I would be." Asith set the gift for Dradevai near their clothes on the ground.

Dradevai chuckled. "I do, I hadn't thought of it that way."

Asith pulled his clothes off, the heat of the spring already sticking to him. Asith hadn't experienced that kind of heat before, especially with his hair so long. Strands of hair clung to his neck and shoulders uncomfortably, and he tried separating them from his skin.

"Your hair looks nice this long," Dradevai said. "What's in the package?"

Asith gave up on his hair and slipped his pants off, and when he realized Dradevai was watching him closely, a flush rushed to his skin. Their eyes glossed over, and a surge of energy ran down his spine, his skin tingling as he joined Dradevai on the stones. He dipped his legs slowly, the relief climbing up his tired feet and calves. The warm water was drawing out the soreness in his muscles so nicely that he was tempted to plunge in fully. He hadn't yet acknowledged the pain from scaling the mountain on the hunter's path, and his muscles twitched as if they were excited to get rest.

"Clothes for you," Asith answered. He ran his fingers down Dradevai's arm and kissed their shoulder. "From my mother. I think sewing helped take her mind off her worries about you."

"I can understand that. Mysse, Idhe, and Cemi at least have taken my mind off things somewhat. Here, let me help you with your hair."

Dradevai set their hand on Asith's shoulder and guided him into the water. His feet hit the bottom, and he sat on a small bench carved into the stone in which Dradevai could still reach him while the water soothed his aching elbows and knees.

"Is it that much of a mess?" Asith asked. Dradevai carefully undid Asith's lazy braid. It had been much easier to braid Dradevai's hair rather than his own.

"There are leaves in it." Dradevai chuckled. "But otherwise, it's not too bad." Dradevai sniffed the top of his head and gagged. "Okay, never mind, it's bad."

"I've been in the woods for about two weeks, so I'm not surprised." Asith chuckled, then shivered as Dradevai poured water onto his head with a ladle.

"We'll have to let Farin take a bath after this." Dradevai rubbed a bar of soap between their palms and lathered it into Asith's hair. "He probably smells just as bad as you do. Where did you find him anyway?"

"I paid him to sneak me into the Capitol." Asith leaned into Dradevai's touch, their long nails dragging along his scalp and making him shiver pleasantly. "And then he attacked me in the sewers when he thought I was a mage there to hurt the dragon under the Maeria Spire."

He wouldn't mention yet that Pherrosh might be their mother, but the thought made his tongue swell and his shoulders curl inward. He felt like he was doing something wrong by keeping it to himself even though Dradevai hadn't asked him to reveal it yet. They hummed, gently pulling the knots out from the ends of his hair and occasionally removing a leaf, letting it fall into the water and float out where the water escaped the cave.

"Was it the ghost?" Dradevai asked. "The dragon you rescued from under the Maeria Spire?"

Asith's eyes unfocused as he pressed his lips together. He hesitated, unsure where to begin. Dradevai was far too smart; if he said yes, Dradevai would know she was their mother, but they asked him not to tell them. And Dradevai didn't like when he lied.

"Asith." Dradevai's voice was so, so quiet. "Was it one of my parents?"

Asith looked up at Dradevai. Their blank expression was schooled and intentional, as if they had prepared themself before asking. Asith took a deep breath and turned toward them fully. Then he pulled Dradevai into the water with him, set them at eye level, and placed his arms around their middle.

"Your mother," Asith said. "Her name is Pherrosh. She was weak, so I suggested she go back to the Graveyard Trees."

Dradevai swallowed, the scar on their neck moving slightly. Asith ran his thumb over it, memorizing the shape as if he needed to etch them into his mind as much as he could.

"Did you tell her about me?" Dradevai asked.

He stopped moving his thumb, considering his words, but too many thoughts filled his head. "I didn't know where you were or if you were safe. I'm sorry. I just, thought I should spare her if you weren't—"

Dradevai's lips turned up, and they shook their head before they submerged themself. Asith kept a hand on them as their hair floated to the surface, but they got low enough that it dragged under.

When they resurfaced, their hair stuck to their skin in awkward clumps, parted so far to one side that all the strands wouldn't stay put.

"Thank you," they said. "You did exactly what I would have wanted you to do."

Asith's hands trembled against Dradevai's soft skin as he drew them back in. "Really?"

Dradevai nodded and returned to washing Asith's hair, resuming their position behind Asith.

"Cemi has a sister in another facility near here. And I'm sure others are in there too. If we're going to get them, I'd rather our parents not know what we're doing."

"That's a good point actually. Though, I think my father knows."

Dradevai hummed. Asith didn't add anything else, letting the sound of the water overtake him. With the water running over his scalp, Asith could finally relax. Dradevai ran their fingers through his hair one last time, and then they offered him the bar of soap and a washcloth before sitting back on the bench and sinking into the water up to their neck.

"I never knew how nice taking a bath felt," Dradevai said, their eyes upward, studying the etchings from chisels and pickaxes, which were likely used to make the room bigger.

"A bath like this is certainly relaxing," Asith said, rubbing soap onto his chest. "The only bathhouse in South Cairn charged a lot of money to have a heated bath."

Dradevai snapped their head straight at Asith, their eyes wide as they stammered, "They aren't always warm?"

Asith snorted. "No, a hot bath is a luxury unless you live near a spring like this."

"How much effort is it to heat a bit of water?" Dradevai's brows knitted together.

"Well, without magic, you have to transport the water, chop wood, start a fire under the tub, keep the fire going until the water is warm, then feed the fire until the person is done in the bath. Sometimes you even heat extra buckets in case the person needs extra—"

"Why do you know so much about this?" Dradevai's eyes were lidded, their chin in the palm of their hand. He lifted his necklace and tossed it behind his back to continue washing himself, trying to ignore Dradevai's wandering eyes. A tingle ran down his abs.

"I worked in a bathhouse while I was training at the Stonegarde for pocket money." Asith met Dradevai's eyes, and they straightened, trying to act demure. But Asith caught the flush creeping across their cheeks.

Asith's feet moved on their own, and he kissed them. Dradevai twitched and pulled away for just a moment, but they met Asith's lips again, their hand finding his chest, the soft pads of their fingers gliding over his wet skin.

"How often were you thinking of this when you were staring at me in your hoard?" Asith asked. He backed away just enough to see Dradevai's face. Their skin was darkening all the way to the very tips of their pointed ears, and their eyes grew wide, the golden edges reflecting the low torchlight. Their nose crinkled as their brow pinched.

"Get the soap off and wash your face." Dradevai huffed, splashing Asith.

"I'm sorry." Asith wiped the droplets off his nose and cheeks, shaking his head to get the rest off. Dradevai's eyes were bright and glossy, and they laughed.

"It's okay." They pressed a kiss on Asith's lips. "I missed you."

"I missed you too."

When Asith finished cleaning himself, Dradevai straddled his lap and looped their arms around his neck. They kissed him again, and Asith placed his hands on their waist, happy he couldn't feel their ribs under their skin. He sank against the warm stone and slid his hands down Dradevai's sides, reveling in the way they shivered.

He kissed their jaw, and Dradevai threaded their fingers into Asith's hair. He trailed down their neck, lingering on their pulse, savoring how it quickened under his tongue. When he squeezed their thigh, their muscles flexed, and their hips jerked forward, fingers tightening around Asith's hair.

Asith slid his hand between their legs but saw Dradevai's face had pinched, their eyes squeezed shut. Their shoulders had drawn in tight, and their tense muscles carved hollows above their clavicle.

"Vai?" Asith lowered his voice. "Are you okay?"

Dradevai twitched, their eyes popping open. They nodded, but they trembled. "I'm fine, I'm sorry." Dradevai shook their head, forcing their shoulders down. Asith cupped their cheek and scanned their face in hopes of parsing out whatever was going on.

"We don't have to do anything if you don't want to." Asith rubbed their arm, but Dradevai slapped their hands onto his shoulders.

"No, no, I would like—" A pretty flush crept across their cheeks. Asith's skin warmed, starting where their hands touched his shoulders and spreading to his chest, where Dradevai moved their hands.

"I'm sorry." They sighed. "I thought about going to another facility to save more dragons and I don't—my mind started to scatter. I lost focus and I just…It's not you. I'm happy to see you." They pressed their forehead against Asith's and nuzzled at his cheek.

"Are you stressed about getting the other dragons?"

"I am. I don't want to leave any dragons in facilities like that, but…" Dradevai swallowed, their eyes wandering to the stones behind Asith. "But if something goes wrong, if we get caught? What happens to Cemi, Idhe, and Mysse?"

"That's understandable." Asith rubbed his thumb over their cheek, and they pressed their palm onto the back of his hand. "It's not something we can find a solution for tonight, but we will make sure they're going to be safe. Even if something happens to us."

Dradevai's brow wrinkled, their hand moving to their temple. "You're right."

"Do you want me to help you take your mind off it?" Asith slid his hand down their neck. He wanted to offer them more, but all he had was a distraction from their thoughts. "It might help."

Dradevai's eyes narrowed. "What do you mean?"

Asith slipped his hands under Dradevai's thighs, taking advantage of their buoyancy in the water, and lifted them onto the edge of the stones. He kissed their knee and pinned their thigh to keep their legs spread. Though, if he was honest, they could overpower him. The thought made him shiver.

"Sometimes this can help," Asith said. "More than anything else when you're stressed."

"Sex?" Dradevai tilted their head and propped their hands on the stone behind them.

"Yes." Asith planted kisses on their soft inner thigh, causing the black hair on their legs to stand. "Pleasure can be a good distraction. From a lot of things."

Dradevai's nails skidded on Asith's scalp and caught on his hair, their knees bumping Asith's shoulders. They hummed in the back of their throat, but their body hadn't loosened yet. The muscles in their neck and collarbones were visibly stiff, even as they inclined their head back, a shaky breath running down the plains of their chest.

"Is this okay?" Asith kissed Dradevai's navel, sliding his hands across the silky skin on the back of their thighs.

"Yes," they mumbled. "Please? I want to forget about all of this for a while."

Asith elevated their legs onto his shoulders in a swift motion, making Dradevai squeak.

"Sorry." He chuckled and spread them open with his thumbs. Asith started slow, his tongue lingering to fully taste Dradevai. He'd only thought about sex a handful of times since they'd been separated, since his focus had been on their safety, but since they were secure, he realized how desperate he was to hear their voice laced with bliss.

Their voice cracked, raw and heady as their grip on Asith's hair loosened, their hands moving to support his neck. Dradevai struggled to keep their legs open as their toes curled against his back.

"I forgot…" Dradevai moaned, a flicker of magic sparking at their fingertips. Asith wondered if they were casting a spell to muffle the sound. "I forgot how good you are at this."

Asith snickered, his nose still planted in the soft hair between their legs. He rested his forehead against their belly as Dradevai laughed too.

"Don't get a big head." There was no bite to it, no actual lecture, just Dradevai giggling.

"How could I not?" Asith's chest lightened, and he squeezed Dradevai's butt, just light enough to make them jump. "I love you."

Dradevai bopped him on the head and pushed Asith backward. Asith only had a moment to register he was floating before Dradevai hopped into his arms and wrapped their legs around his middle. They kissed him, their tongue tracing his teeth, coaxing a muffled moan out of Asith and swallowing it.

Asith wasn't sure exactly how it happened, but Dradevai's tongue had him on edge, enough for him to be hard enough to meet Dradevai exactly where they were at. They took advantage of it, shifting their legs just enough to slide Asith inside of them with a sigh. His breathing hitched, and Dradevai ate it up, their tongue moving to his jaw, their lips sealing on his neck. He lost track of the noises he was making, folding under Dradevai's touch entirely.

"I love you too." Dradevai's words were lost in a sea of desperate sighs, but Asith still managed to grab their jaw and pull them into a kiss. The warm water wrapped around them like a thick blanket, Dradevai's magic licking up the walls and keeping their sounds between them.

CHAPTER 15

The world swayed around Asith slowly. He might have been in the hot spring a bit too long. His back against the cool stones on the far side of the cavern, Asith knew he should get back to Farin and the kids. Dradevai probably wanted that as well.

"I wish I could clean these better." Dradevai was squatted near their pile of clothes, sorting out theirs from Asith's.

"Don't forget the gift." Asith pushed off the wall and wrapped a towel around his middle. "From my mother for you."

He picked up the package and offered it to Dradevai before grabbing his cleanest leggings and tunic, though they smelled like the smoked sausage he'd stored inside his pack.

Dradevai untied the finely embroidered ribbon around it, much like the one that Farin wore, and took off the wax wrapping. "Clean clothes!" Dradevai cried in relief, his voice tinged with excitement as they looked them over. They set them down to squeeze the last of the water from their hair and tie it back into a short ponytail. They slipped on the wide-legged pants first, then secured the ties at their ankles, and buttoned the high waist just over their navel. The soft wool tunic fit well tucked into their pants, the collar hanging in a V that stretched to the bottom of their sternum. Their amber necklace framed the black fabric, and for a moment, they looked like a pillar of black, the pants and the tunic melding together to fill out their form, even though the pants weren't quite tight enough.

Next, Dradevai pulled on a long jacket, a series of orange, yellow, and red diamonds creating a gradient from bottom to top, the sleeves a rich goldenrod. Gold lace trimmed each diamond, every other holding a golden sun embroidered with enchanted thread that glinted in the light. On the back, a single diamond in the center held a glittering red sun, much like the first sun that rose each day. The jacket folded over, covering Dradevai from the middle of their thigh up to their shoulder, and a belt at the middle could secure it if they wanted to.

It looked wonderful on them.

"The pockets are so deep." Dradevai's hands were deep inside the fur-lined pockets on the jacket, which his mother had inserted because she feared they'd be cold in the Graveyard Trees. Dradevai was rarely cold, but he had seen even fire-breathing dragons shiver in the winter among the tall trees.

"I'm glad you like it." Asith cupped Dradevai's cheek and tucked a strand of hair behind their ear. They grinned, toothy and showing off their snaggled canines. Asith's skin warmed.

"I will have to thank her in person." Dradevai leaned into Asith's hand, before a voice screeched from the other room. They jerked their head toward the door. It had sounded like Idhe.

Asith pulled on his leggings and tunic and ran after Dradevai. When they reentered the cave, a rambunctious scene was playing out in front of them, the room filled with Cemi's raucous laughter and Idhe's elated screams.

Farin, who looked a bit worse for wear, was laid out on the floor with Idhe on his back. A copper dragon about the size of a wolf giggled in a girlish voice, meaning it was Cemi. She stood just out of reach of Farin's hands, which were grasping for her tail. A scrap of fabric was tied around it in a cute bow, her feathers a bit askew.

"Oh, thank god!" Farin exclaimed dramatically. "Asith, Dradevai, get the fabric off her tail so I can stop giving Idhe a piggyback ride!"

Cemi and Idhe erupted with laughter. Idhe kicked his feet in the air and sat upright on Farin's back. Even Mysse, who sat a few feet away with a small book, smiled.

"I have a better idea." Dradevai approached them. "How about the two of you go to bed, and we let Farin go and take a bath?"

"There's a bath here?" Farin's eyes grew to the size of dinner plates. He looked like he desperately needed sleep, and Asith did as well, but the call of a warm bath was hard to ignore, considering how dirty they were.

"Awe, can't we play with Uncle Farin a little longer?" Cemi's shoulders slumped, her round, bird-like head tilting to the side. "Please?"

"It's the middle of the night," Dradevai said. "Come on, we all could use some sleep."

They scooped Cemi up and bobbed her in their arms until she turned back into her smaller form. Idhe stood and offered to help Farin stand. They weren't much different in height, though Farin was taller.

"I'll show Farin to the bath." Asith approached Dradevai, smiling at Cemi as she waved at him. "And then I can help you with them?"

Dradevai nodded, their eyes appearing tired but a smile crawling over their face. So Asith led Farin to the hot spring and cleared away his and Dradevai's dirty clothes. Farin stripped and stepped into the water, sinking all the way down so that his head dipped under the surface.

When he rose, his hair was stuck to his face, then he floated while emitting a deep sigh.

"There is something to that story of Viteus being healed in a hot spring after he'd tirelessly searched for Sula when they'd gone missing," Farin said wearily. "This could heal a god if one needed it."

"I'll come check on you in ten minutes to make sure you haven't fallen asleep," Asith said.

Farin righted himself, with a frown so deep that it distorted his jaw. "Ten minutes!?" Farin flailed his arms, splashing water. "You two were in here for the better part of an hour while two kids used me for pony rides."

Asith laughed. "I only said I'd make sure you weren't asleep, not that you had to get out."

"Oh." Farin crossed his arms. "Well, fine then, thank you."

He tossed a bar of soap to Farin, who scooped it up and scrubbed his arms and chest. "By the way, the older dragon…" Farin sank deeper into the water. "Mysse wouldn't even come near me, and it wasn't just that he didn't trust me. It seemed like he was afraid."

"Afraid?" Asith asked, drawing closer.

"Terrified, actually. Reminded me a lot of myself at that age."

Asith's fingers tingled. Farin had mentioned his father wasn't a good person. As Farin's shoulders hunched and a familiar distant look fell over his eyes, Asith knew he was implying something similar might have happened to Mysse.

"I think it's going to take a lot before he really trusts either of us," Farin added.

"Yeah," Asith said. He turned to go help Dradevai, but he couldn't move forward. He might start crying. But he didn't have time for a breakdown; Dradevai needed their help, as they'd been alone for far too long. He took a steady breath and walked again.

When he returned, the lights were low, and Mysse lay on a bedroll, his eyes on Asith, his expression pinched. He broke eye contact and rolled onto his other side. Cemi was sitting in Dradevai's lap, and Idhe lay outstretched next to them in his larger form. Despite being older and taller than Cemi, he was only the size of a hefty tomcat, his horns resembling the antlers of a deer.

Asith sat next to Dradevai on their narrow bedroll, causing Cemi to shift into her larger form, and she curled up between Idhe and Mysse on a pile of thick blankets. Once she settled, the feathers on the back of her head perked, creating a crown of pointed spikes, and her horns were not long enough to be seen through her downy coat.

"I was just finishing telling them about your mother," Dradevai said. "They were asking about the clothes."

Dradevai's coat was hanging on a protruding rock, their new pants folded neatly underneath it. The loose black tunic reached the middle of their thigh.

"That makes sense," Asith said. "The coat is rather flashy."

"It suits them," Cemi said firmly. "They deserve it."

Dradevai chuckled. "This also means I can give Mysse my other tunic so he's not in the sheet anymore."

"I'm fine in the sheet." Mysse rolled over, his shoulders tight as he wrapped himself in a blanket.

"But you're always so cold." Idhe lifted his head. "And you never sleep in your larger form, so you shiver most of the night."

"Shut up, Idhe." Mysse snarled, his teeth bared. Idhe cried.

"Whoa, hey." Dradevai shifted onto their knees and rubbed Idhe as tears streamed down his face. Idhe's cries quickly subdued into hiccups. Dradevai turned to Mysse, but he was already out of his bed, stomping out with loud slaps against the stone.

"Mysse!" Dradevai called.

Asith set a hand on their shoulder. "Make sure Farin doesn't fall asleep in the bath." He stood. "Let me try to speak with Mysse."

Dradevai's brows knitted, but Idhe was still crying so they let Asith go with a nod. Asith pulled his warm doublet from his bag. It wouldn't do him any use while sleeping next to Dradevai in the humid bedroom, so perhaps he could get Mysse to take it.

Asith walked out, rubbing his jaw as he thought about what to say. He didn't really know if anything he said would make him feel better, but he had to try. After all, Dradevai had their hands full with Idhe and Farin.

Eventually, Asith found Mysse in the darkened chamber shivering in a corner and sniffling. When he saw Asith, he pressed his nose into his elbow and secured his arms around his knees.

"Hey," Asith said, knowing that asking if he was all right wouldn't accomplish anything.

"I don't want to talk," Mysse said, pressing his face into his arm. "Leave me alone."

Asith sat near the small boy, remembering all the times his mother had spoken to him when he was sad or angry. But he didn't know how to transfer anything he'd experienced as a kid to that situation.

"I don't think Dradevai will want you to spend the whole night out here." Asith smoothed the hem of his tunic down against his leg.

Mysse hiccuped and began to cry. "You're going to hurt them. You're going to bring us back, aren't you?"

Asith's brow furrowed, a defense on the tip of his tongue as a fire rose from his stomach all the way to his ears. He ground his teeth painfully to stop himself from reacting. His experience with kids was basically zero, and in the negatives with children who had been kept and harvested as his father had.

"What would make you say that?" Asith said, unable to hide his angry tone well. Mysse flinched, his grip on his knees tightening.

"I don't trust you."

It wasn't really an answer to Asith's question, but it was the best he was going to get. He was tempted to get up and leave, but Yarrow reminded him that Mysse was still shivering from the cold.

"Okay." Asith took a deep breath and picked Yarrow up. "Can you hold her for me for a bit?"

Mysse lifted his head, his face scrunched. Asith didn't wait for a response and simply settled Yarrow in Mysse's lap. If he wouldn't accept the doublet, at least Yarrow could help keep him warm.

"Why did you come here?" Mysse studied Yarrow, his face distorted in anger and confusion.

"Honestly?" Asith set his head back against the wall. "It was entirely selfish. I love Dradevai, and I missed them. I just wanted to be with them again."

"I had never seen Dradevai cry before today." Mysse tentatively set a hand on Yarrow's back and stroked her. Yarrow relaxed her ears against her head, affirming Asith had made the right choice. Though, he had always made the right choice when it resulted in her being pet.

Asith sighed. "I overwhelmed Dradevai by accident. I had only seen them cry once or twice before that."

"What did you do to make them cry before?"

Asith glowered at the ceiling, his chest tightening in guilt. Mysse's tone was accusatory, but he couldn't blame him for being angry with the world. "I didn't do anything either time. The first time, it was my mother telling them that my father grew up with his parents and sister in a town full of dragons."

Mysse's eyes were narrowed, but Asith continued. "The second time, they had a nightmare."

"Then why were they alone when they rescued us?"

"We were together, but they made me leave with my father, who had been in your facility too." Asith wrapped his arms around his knees. He had replayed that night in his head so many times, wishing he had done something different, even though it wouldn't have made any difference at all.

"And where is your father now?"

"In the Graveyard Trees with my mother." Asith looked at the wall. "I promised Dradevai I would get him to safety, so I did."

Mysse returned his head to his arms, squishing Yarrow between his stomach and legs. There was something Mysse wasn't revealing. Maybe Mysse was just acting childish, but that didn't seem to be the case. He seemed to have firm beliefs about something, which could be why he didn't like Asith but trusted Dradevai.

Asith wanted to probe but remembered Farin's comment from before. He was afraid of them. When Asith was Mysse's age, the last thing he ever wanted was for someone to call out his fear of something. After what just happened with Idhe, he didn't want Mysse yelling at him either.

Yarrow stepped off Mysse's lap to climb into Asith's. He cradled her against his chest, running his fingers along the edge of her ear. After adjusting Yarrow to his shoulder, he wrapped the doublet he'd brought around Mysse's shoulders. He bristled slightly but didn't argue, eventually pulling the doublet tighter against his body.

"Why won't you leave me alone?" Mysse tucked his legs inside the doublet, the brooch his mother had given him still pinned to the front. The rabbit on it was taunting him. He wished his mother were there, for she would know how to handle Mysse. She was always good at dealing with children. Asith wished she had imparted more of that to him.

"Because…" Asith said with an edge of frustration, stroking Yarrow's head as a chill brushed over his skin. "Because I know that it is the right thing to do."

His mouth twitched slightly, as if he might snarl at Asith, but he set his head on his knees and pulled himself into a tighter ball. Asith considered coaxing Mysse to snap at him because that could tire him out and he could carry him to bed. But Yarrow hopped off his shoulder and slipped under Mysse's bent knees. He shifted to open his legs before looking at Asith.

"Why does she keep doing this?"

Asith shrugged. "She doesn't like it when I cry or I'm upset. She probably wants to make you feel better."

"Do you really cry that often?" Mysse straightened his legs and let Yarrow climb back into his lap, shivering as the cool air hit the exposed areas of his body. His feet were dirty, no thanks to the dilapidated sandals.

"I have always cried easily and often. Since I was Cemi's age." Asith ran a hand through his hair, pushing his bangs out of his face.

"You're an adult. You shouldn't cry easily."

Asith's shoulders fell, his eyes on the ceiling as he reminded himself that Mysse didn't know any better. At that age, he'd said plenty of things to his mother that made her feel just as frustrated.

"I don't think adults crying is a bad thing." Asith returned his gaze to Mysse. "Crying tells other people that you need their help."

Mysse didn't respond. One moment, he had a furrow to his brow, eyes on the ground, but in the next, his head was dipping, nodding off despite his efforts to stay awake. Asith waited, his fingers trembling from the cold, before he scooped Mysse, who didn't offer much resistance. Asith stood and adjusted the doublet to make sure he didn't get cold.

"Your father," Mysse whispered. "He was Listesh, wasn't he?"

Asith smiled. Dradevai had probably told the kids about him and his father, and the thought made warmth spread over his chest. "He still is. He's safe in the Graveyard Trees, I promise."

Mysse wrapped his arms around Asith's neck, sleep starting to take him. "He protected us when he could."

Tears filled Asith's eyes. Mysse was likely speaking of his father's actions in the facility, and even though it reminded him of his father's weak state, Asith grew proud that he'd tried his best to protect Mysse, Idhe, and Cemi. Not wanting Mysse to comment on his crying again, Asith silently carried him back into the warm room, where Farin was speaking softly with Dradevai. They looked up at Asith, but neither moved, likely because Cemi and Idhe were asleep in a small pile of wings and tails.

He laid Mysse on the bedroll next to the kids, and he slipped his arms into Asith's doublet, settling on his stomach. Asith draped a thin blanket over him, to which Dradevai and Farin gave weak smiles in sync. Farin then crawled to his bedroll, which he'd laid at the foot of Dradevai's against the wall, making room for Asith to join.

Asith stepped over the sleeping kids and sat beside Dradevai, his hand cupping their cheek. He kissed their temple, and they leaned on him. A few minutes later, Farin was snoring, and Dradevai pulled Asith down so that they were reclining and draped an arm over his middle.

"Mysse doesn't trust me," Asith whispered against Dradevai's hair.

Dradevai breathed deeply. "I had a feeling." Their fingers followed the quilt lines on his tunic where his mother had stitched the two layers together. "He's not a trusting kid. I don't think I did enough to teach him better because his suspicion helped me keep the three of them safe."

"It's okay, you didn't foster his distrust any more than the people in that facility did." Since Asith didn't know if Mysse had told Dradevai about what happened to him, Asith refrained from discussing the topic further.

Dradevai sighed. "You think I can do no wrong."

"In this situation? No." Asith chuckled. "In others, you can definitely do things wrong. You kidnapped me, remember?"

Dradevai turned into his neck, their smile pressed against his skin. "Don't start that again. I apologized."

"I think I have every right to keep bringing up that you kidnapped me as many times as I like." Asith brushed their hair away to kiss their round cheek.

"All right, all right." Dradevai set their chin on Asith's chest and brushed his hair back while he ran his fingers down their back. Asith basked in the comfort of holding on to Dradevai for the first time in nearly a year, sleep still far off despite how tired he was.

CHAPTER 16

The morning in the cave came and went, no one moving until the early afternoon. Asith was clutching pins in his mouth, a discontented Mysse refusing to put his arms into the sleeves of Dradevai's old tunic. The scowl on his face looked like a crack between mountains.

"I know you don't like this, but would you at least do it for Dradevai's peace of mind?" Asith pulled the pins from his mouth and rubbed the back of his head. He was hungry and wanted to be with Dradevai, but they had taken Farin down to the river to collect water and set up a trap for some fish.

"I don't see why Dradevai couldn't be doing this." Mysse crossed his arms underneath the tunic. "Or why you have to pin the tunic while it's on me."

"Dradevai doesn't know how to sew." Asith rubbed his eyes, his thumb pressing deep enough that colors flurried behind his eyelids.

"Mysse, why do you want to make everything so difficult?" Cemi barked from nearby, spinning in circles as she tried to bite down on her tail.

"Mind your own business, Cemi." Mysse ground his teeth, closing his eyes as he finally stuck his arms through the sleeves. Asith simply lifted Mysse's arms and placed some pins.

"Cemi," Asith said, "could you go to my bag and bring me the doublet that's on the bottom?"

Cemi stopped chasing her tail, her head turning toward the other room. When she fluttered away, she moved like a chicken, as Idhe had, and bumped into a wall. She got up fine, though. She was resilient; they all were.

"Listen, I know you don't trust me, and that's okay." Asith marked where the tunic needed to be taken in on each side, using fewer pins than normal to get it over with. He also left some extra room because Mysse would grow quickly. "If you really don't want these clothes, I won't make you take them, but I think it's important for you to have clothes that fit."

"Just finish fixing them." Mysse grumbled at his feet. "Please."

In the light of day, Mysse looked short and so horribly young, despite the million years behind his green eyes. The worry and terror had set into his skin, and Asith realized Mysse looked much like his mother had the day Asith had trudged into the field to confront Dradevai for the first time.

Their red hair and freckles, which had been obscured in the dark, made the comparison even more obvious.

"Why are you looking at me like that?" Mysse asked.

Asith slipped the tunic off Mysse. The sooner he started sewing, the more likely he'd correctly judge if the excess fabric was enough to make leggings for Cemi or Idhe. He wondered if Phela, when he agreed to be her champion, envisioned Asith getting heckled by a preteen while trying to alter an old tunic so he didn't freeze to death. Asith should get back to studying his magic; that would probably please Phela. He was better at sewing, though.

"I was thinking that you look like my mother." Asith crossed his legs on the floor and threaded a needle.

"Your mother is a human, isn't she?" Mysse tilted his head as genuine confusion washed over him. Somehow, Asith had managed to disarm him, which he hadn't expected was possible.

"She is." Asith turned the tunic inside out and started with a new side seam. "But she has red hair and freckles and green eyes like yours."

Mysse's teeth clicked as he shut his mouth. Cemi returned with Asith's spare doublet, and he handed it to Mysse, who slipped it over his head without comment. The slight shake in his shoulders stopped. He must have been cold quite often, which made Asith desperate to ask what sort of dragon he was. It would upset him, though, as he refused to switch into his larger form every time Cemi and Idhe pestered him about it.

"Can you teach me how to sew?" Cemi turned into her smaller form and studied Asith's hands at his side. With Asith's attention on Cemi, Mysse sat on the rock he'd been standing on.

"If you'd like to learn." Asith smiled. Cemi was grinning, her black eyes wide and full of excitement.

"I want to learn to make dresses." Cemi toyed with the hem of her tunic. "Can you teach me that?"

"Well," Asith said, "I'm not a very good dressmaker. But I could teach you the basics and make you a promise."

Cemi blinked. "What's the promise?"

"I promise to have my mother teach you to make dresses when we get to the Graveyard Trees." Asith dipped his needle back and forth through Mysse's tunic.

She contemplated his promise, then nodded. "Yes, please." Cemi moved closer to examine Asith's needlework.

Mysse scoffed and crossed his arms, glaring at the entrance to the cave. Cemi spun on him, a frown on her face as she slapped her hands on the ground. The noise startled Mysse.

"Stop being such a grouch!" she yelled. "Just because *you're* not happy about Asith being here, despite him being nothing but nice to us, doesn't mean you get to ruin it for the rest of us."

"Cemi, it's okay." Asith put a hand on her shoulder, but she whipped toward him.

"It's not okay!" Cemi shook her head. "Dradevai was so happy to see you. He shouldn't be so mean to you."

"I'm older than you, Cemi, you wouldn't understand." Mysse huffed.

Asith tried to grab Cemi's shoulder again, but she was on her feet and in Mysse's face, forcing him backward until he fell off the rock.

"Just because you're older doesn't mean you're smarter. And just because I'm nicer doesn't mean I'm being stupid."

"You're such a little kid!"

"And you're a moody brat!"

"Okay, okay!" Asith stood and scooped up Cemi by the armpits. He set her a few feet away, and she stuck her tongue out at Mysse. "Enough," Asith said.

Cemi crossed her arms and pressed her lips into a hard line, her eyes locked on Mysse as he righted himself. If it were any colder, steam would be rising off her head. Asith wished he had stopped the fighting before it started, especially since their yelling had drawn Idhe out of the bedroom, where he'd been reading a book Farin had loaned him.

"Cemi, I know you're angry with him, but I think you owe Mysse an apology," Asith said.

Cemi and Mysse gaped at him like fish he'd just reeled in.

"Why do I owe him an apology!?" Cemi balled her hands into fists. "I was defending you! Why aren't you on *my* side?"

"Because Mysse has every right to distrust me if he wants to. I'm not angry with him for it, and you shouldn't be either."

"You're so strange," Mysse said and wrinkled his nose. "Just defend yourself. It would be less strange."

Asith pinched the bridge of his nose. "It doesn't matter if it's strange. I'm trying to do what's right."

"Well, what's right is that he shouldn't be causing problems on purpose." Cemi set her hands on her hips.

"All right, that's fair." Asith patted her on the head. "But that doesn't give you the right to yell at him if he's just huffing and not hurting anyone, okay? It doesn't help anything."

"Fine." Cemi crossed her arms, looking at Mysse. "I'm sorry for yelling at you."

"It's…" Mysse shifted, his eyes darting around the room. "It's okay."

They stood awkwardly before Cemi set her hands on her hips again, standing taller. "You should apologize to Asith too," she said.

Mysse flinched, then rubbed his arm, saying, "I'm sorry, Asith."

"It's okay," Asith said, studying the fit of the doublet on Mysse. "Also, why don't I resize the doublet for you as well?"

Mysse's lips pulled at the edges, and he nodded. After that, he remained quiet as Asith showed Cemi basic stitches. Idhe fully emerged from the bedroom to sit with them, listening to Asith's lesson but not engaging as Cemi was.

When Dradevai and Farin returned, Asith was pinning the doublet to resize it for Mysse. He wouldn't bother with the side seams or sleeves, just add belt loops; that way, Mysse could close it with a belt.

Farin had a trap under his arm brimming with fish, and he gladly showed Idhe how to clean them. Meanwhile, Dradevai lined the buckets of river water they'd collected along one wall. After receiving his new tunic, Mysse helped them carry the water and fish. There wasn't enough fabric for leggings, so Asith would make leg warmers for Idhe.

"How were things here?" Dradevai asked in a low voice as they settled next to Asith. Cemi had wandered off to sit with Farin and Idhe.

"All right." Asith returned his eyes to the belt loop he'd created, stitching them across the top. He should at least double them, or they might break.

"Did something happen?" Dradevai asked.

Asith picked his head up, looking at Dradevai and then following their eyes to Mysse.

"Not really, why?" Asith slipped his needle through the fabric and lifted his hand above his head as he pulled the thread tight.

Yarrow hopped at Mysse's heels as he continued moving buckets of water. She seemed to like him a lot. There wasn't a huge difference in how he was acting, but maybe she would help him feel more comfortable with Asith and Farin's presence. When Mysse finished, he scooped some water into a cup to drink.

"He doesn't usually smile this easily," Dradevai said. Mysse filled another cup with water and gave it to Yarrow. Asith studied Mysse's lips and saw he did have a little smile. It was unusual, considering how Cemi had fought with him not long before Dradevai and Farin had returned.

"Cemi yelled at him and made him apologize to me for causing problems on purpose," Asith said. "That's all that really happened."

Dradevai blinked at Asith, then shifted their gaze to Mysse. "Well, I'm certain that couldn't have been what caused this."

Asith chuckled. "Perhaps just see it as a gift then."

Dradevai smiled and leaned on his shoulder, closing their eyes. "You're right."

Farin cooked the fish over an open fire that Dradevai made in the center of the cavern, the smoke slowly airing out through the small entrance on the cliff. Farin kept serving as much fish as the kids could eat, then made a second fish trap out of some reeds he'd collected by the river. Cemi and Idhe followed Farin as he moved about, while Mysse snapped sticks for the fire. Asith was sewing while Cemi's giggles filled the air. The scene was oddly happy, despite the impending need to infiltrate another facility and save more dragons.

His mother must have felt that way when he was a child, sewing while Asith played with little wooden toys on the floor. Asith's fingers slowed as Dradevai grinned at Mysse and ruffled his hair when he dropped sticks into the fire. Farin was teaching Idhe how to spear a fish with a stick he'd sharpened to a point. In all, Asith felt like he was where he was supposed to be. Much like his mother had always said, she felt most happy at home with him while she sewed, and he felt best while watching Dradevai and Farin take care of the young dragons.

Asith gazed at Dradevai's face, admiring the soft line of their jaw that led to the gentle curve of their earlobe. Their wide nose wrinkled at the edges each time their soft brown lips turned up. Their eyes found Asith's, honey-gold and softening as their smile brightened. Asith realized, it would be nice to marry them. It seemed brash, almost, in the face of everything they still had to do, but they could, one day, spend their time together as they did then in the Graveyard Trees, finding happiness in simple work.

Yarrow hopped in small circles around Dradevai and Mysse, her small ears flopping at her sides before standing again. Asith remembered Phela kissing her the night he'd promised to be her champion. Since Phela had helped him find Dradevai, he needed to uphold his end of their agreement.

Dradevai left to hunt, and they returned with a shine in their feathers and a stag in their teeth for the kids to split. They took Cemi and Idhe onto the cliff to eat in private, as Dradevai mentioned they struggled to eat in their dragon forms. Mysse politely refused the food, saying he had filled up on fish. Dradevai didn't press him, but they didn't seem to like that answer.

Farin was doing his best to help Asith mend clothes near the fire. His sewing wasn't where Asith's was, but if he stitched a patch down, Asith could embroider the edges so that it lay flat much faster. They had a good system.

It didn't take long for a few days to pass, Farin and Asith helping with the kids, allowing Dradevai more time to hunt and eat. Their bones already held more meat, and a roundness was returning to their hips, belly, and shoulders. Asith enjoyed running his fingers over their skin while they slept in his arms, the relief of Dradevai nourishing themself making it easier for Asith to think about the promise he'd made to Phela or the dragons in the facility they needed to rescue.

Farin, Asith, and Dradevai had quietly taken to slipping away during parts of the day to scout for the entrance to the facility. Farin proved to be invaluable, his skill with a pencil and a bit of paper earning them a detailed map of the front. He had even slowly pieced several small sheets together with a sticky sap to create a larger, clearer picture of the area. That way, they could brainstorm how they could escape. Of course, hunched over the map, they knew something unexpected would inevitably happen, but Asith found solace in how much more prepared they were compared to how he and Dradevai had been previously. They would rescue the dragons in the facility, they would return to The Graveyard Trees, and Dradevai could finally meet Pherrosh.

Despite only a few days passing, Asith, Dradevai, and Farin had settled into a routine, which brought the kids some comfort; even Mysse, though he still didn't seem to enjoy Asith's or Farin's presence. Farin was out scouting, so Asith practiced the chant for the lightning spell with Yarrow in his lap. However, his thoughts were tangled, and his focus drifted to Dradevai writing in their spell book and Cemi and Idhe chasing each other. The lightning spell was his only hope to deal with a mage like Heskel, but he kept mixing up the couplets and sometimes the sigils singed the spell circle in his book, forcing him to redraw it.

"Asith."

Pystra's voice filled Asith's ears, pulling him out of his thoughts.

"Sorry it took so long to get back to you. The Stonegarde, they're moving like an army. Getting ready to attack. Have you found Dradevai?"

"Yes," Asith said, perking up and looking at Dradevai. "Dradevai and I are safe. We are going to release more dragons."

Dradevai's brows furrowed, and they looked up at Asith, their pen going lax in their hand.

"It's Pystra, she's using a—"

"*In the East still?*" Pystra cut in. "*Delri says the dragon knights are being removed from their posts everywhere to centralize.*"

"We're in the East still, yes." Asith considered her implication. "You said they are mobilizing Northeast? Toward Old High Cairn?"

Dradevai closed their book and shifted closer to Asith. They set a hand on his knee, and Asith took it. Yarrow was shaking in his lap with her ears perked straight up, so he set a hand on her back as he visualized the map in his head. Only one location was near Old High Cairn. It was a city high in the Barren Rise mountains that Pystra had once pointed out to Asith and Dradevai. The Graveyard Trees.

"*Yes,*" Pystra confirmed, and something cold ran down his spine. "*They're gathering in Old High Cairn. Delri says she was told they'd move out from there, but they don't know where to.*"

Asith swallowed. "Can you and Delri get to the Graveyard Trees? Tell Lestash that the dragon knights are near."

Dradevai's skin paled, and they squeezed his hand.

"*We'll try. You both should try to return soon too. We'll meet you there.*" Pystra's voice shook slightly. He couldn't imagine Pystra crying, and to do so made him tremble.

"We'll do the same."

As the connection broke, Asith met Dradevai's eyes, his hand tightening around theirs. He laced their fingers together and said to them, "They're mobilizing dragon knights toward the Graveyard Trees."

"We need to go tonight, then," Dradevai said. "We'll go tonight, take the rest of the dragons, and flee to the Graveyard Trees."

Asith nodded. "Yes. We'll go tonight."

Farin returned with a sketch of a vent shaft they had found a day prior, only to be ambushed by the new information from Pystra. Startled, Farin looked at his sketch and pulled out his cobbled-together map.

"I could only see so much of this vent." Farin tapped his fist against his lip a few times, eyes narrowed. "If we have to go tonight, though, then I think we have to enter this way. The front is too risky."

"Should we really change the plan now?" Dradevai rubbed their jaw, gripping their elbow.

"I don't think we have a choice," Asith said. "I haven't made the smoke potions we were planning to use to distract the guards." He had been gathering materials and was planning to use his father's recipe, but the potions might not even work. They couldn't go in with untested potions.

Dradevai worried their lip between their teeth, their eyes darting to the kids. Mysse was staring at them, with Yarrow at his feet. She looked at Asith, then up at Mysse again before circling around his sandals and hopping to Asith's side. She must have wanted him to speak with Mysse about something.

"Okay," Dradevai said. "But we have to take the kids to the plateau before we go."

"We'll get them to safety first," Asith said. After all, none of them, including Asith and Farin, could safely get out of the cave without Dradevai transporting them.

Farin nudged Dradevai with his elbow. "I promise ye, Dradevai." Farin grinned. "I've been stealing things from rich bastards for years. I know this is the right choice."

Confidence settled into Dradevai's skin like an old friend, a haughty grin spreading across their face as they straightened. They extended their hand to Farin and squeezed it tightly.

"And I promise I'm a big enough dragon to carry any number of dragons out of there," Dradevai said.

Asith chuckled as Dradevai bumped Farin back with their elbow with a little too much strength. Farin wobbled, but he didn't seem to mind.

Dradevai went to retrieve the bags they'd been packing for the kids. Each contained some food and water, enough for Mysse to get them to town, if need be. Yarrow's nose pressed against Asith's leg, and he picked her up, his eyes trailing to Mysse.

Mysse was holding back tears, his arms stiff as he stood firmly where Cemi and Idhe had left him. He was wearing Asith's old doublet, the sleeves rolled up and the hem far too long, but was still shivering. Asith frowned and approached him slowly.

"Mysse?" Asith kneeled, setting Yarrow on the floor to put a hand on his shoulder. Yarrow leaned against one of Mysse's ankles.

"I don't want to talk." Tears dripped down Mysse's face, his arms moving slightly to wipe them away, and he pulled away from Asith's touch.

His frustration with Mysse had ebbed away over the past few days, and worry replaced it. He wouldn't let anybody help him, not even Dradevai.

"Are you sure you don't want to talk?" Asith asked, letting his hand fall to his side.

Mysse scrunched his nose and grumbled something Asith didn't understand.

"I know it's not easy," Asith said. "My father has a hard time speaking about his pain as well, but it might help."

Mysse's lips pulled into a wobbly frown, but he sat on the floor and picked Yarrow up. He cradled her against his chest and hiccupped. "You're going to leave them there, aren't you?" Mysse whispered, just barely audible.

Asith took a moment to fully process what Mysse had said. Then he bit on his tongue to avoid saying the first bit of vitriol that came to his mind. The thought of leaving Dradevai in that facility made his tongue taste acrid, and his throat burned as he swallowed.

"Why would you think that?" Asith couldn't hide the hurt in the edges of his words. It might be good for Mysse, anyway, to hear how his words affected Asith.

"Because, four years ago, someone brought me there." Mysse looked at the ground, his knuckles turning white as he gripped his arms. "She acted just like you. She told me she'd keep me safe, and she still took me to that place. I may have been stupid then, but I won't be stupid now."

"Someone brought you there?" Asith's voice cracked. "How? How old were you?"

Mysse picked his head up. He didn't speak right away, but eventually, he put his head on his arms, his face pinched and his lips pressed small like he had been given a lemon to lick.

"I was eight."

Asith grabbed the hem of his tunic. His hurt and anger were no longer directed at Mysse but at a person he didn't know. Someone who had found a child so young but gave him over to the Maeria Spire for a profit. A tinge of iron flared in his mouth, the taste making him open his lips.

"She was a dragonborn just like you." Mysse's words had lost all their fight, a lull in his voice indicating his exhaustion.

"I'm so sorry." Asith's anger had nowhere to go, boiling up in his chest and throat until he started to cry. "I'm so sorry she did that to you. I understand now why you never trusted me."

Mysse's eyes lidded as quiet washed over them. Asith wasn't sure how long the silence lasted; it might have actually been rather short.

"Crying isn't going to make me trust you," Mysse said flatly.

"I'm only crying because I'm so angry that I want to hit something." Asith rubbed his eyes, trying to suck in a breath caught in his throat. He coughed and shook his hands to push away some of his thoughts. Crossing his legs, Asith shifted directly in front of Mysse's eyes, which were large and so similar to his mother's. He didn't know what to say, as someone had already failed Mysse with words. There had to be something, though, because saying nothing felt like failing him as well.

"All I can do is promise that I would never do that to you." Asith wiped at the tears on his face. "And I'm angry she did that to you."

"I won't believe you until I see it." Mysse placed a hand on Yarrow's head, and she set her front feet on his chest.

"Then I'll prove it," Asith said. "I promise."

Mysse frowned but nodded. Asith wanted to reach out and squeeze his shoulder, or maybe even offer him a hug, but he would simply get rejected. He forced himself together as Farin returned with a light bag of items he'd need to get into the facility.

Looking between Asith and Mysse, Farin asked, "Everything okay?"

Asith nodded, and Yarrow hopped off Mysse's lap to sniff Farin's bag on the ground. Asith picked her up. "I should get my things."

As Asith walked away, Farin was saying something he couldn't hear, his attention tunneling to thoughts of Mysse being betrayed by a dragonborn. He would've done anything for his father to avoid that fate in the facility. And someone—no, not just someone—a person Mysse had implicitly trusted on some level, someone he might have even seen as family, sold him to that facility.

In the entrance to the bedroom, Asith swayed on his feet. Idhe, Cemi, and Dradevai were putting the final items into the kids' packs, all while Dradevai softly assured them they would be safe in response to the kids' questions. Cemi's eyes were bright, her hands gripping the straps of her pack and grinning like a kid going on their first trip to the Capitol. She looked like Asith must have once, his small bag on his back, ready to travel with his mother. Dradevai kneeled, smoothed down her coiled strands of hair, and smiled, as Asith's mother had once done to him.

"Asith?" Dradevai said. "Is everything okay?"

"Yes." Asith walked over and kissed their head, brushing their horn. "Would you like me to pack your things for you?"

Dradevai leaned into his touch and took Asith's hand in theirs. "Yes, thank you."

Asith gathered the minimum number of items they would need to cast spells, while Yarrow either sat on his foot or stood on his shoulder depending on his position. When it was time to leave, they tucked the kids into a warm hiding spot on the plateau above the cavern. Through welling eyes and a trembling voice, Mysse promised to protect Idhe and Cemi. Asith considered abandoning their plan in favor of taking the kids to the Graveyard Trees, but with the dragon knights mobilizing and his promise to Phela, Asith couldn't do that. Dradevai soothed the three children before Farin led them away. To Dradevai's credit, they did not change their mind to turn back, but they did glance over their shoulder at the hiding spot. They continued to do so even when they were too far to see it anymore.

CHAPTER 17

2ⁿᵈ of Katib

Asith, Dradevai, and Farin had been walking for a few hours, keeping close to each other as they neared Farin's planned entry point, a vent shaft of some sort they'd discovered two days ago. They had wanted more time to explore it, but they didn't have the luxury. Asith pulled out the orb from his aunt and considered breaking it, but he didn't know how much attention it might draw if she arrived to help. They needed the element of surprise, so he returned it to his bag, keeping it in mind in case they needed someone to fly them away.

"We lose tree cover here," Farin whispered, barely audible above the breeze. "Try to keep low to stay out of sight."

With his wand out, Asith crouched in the snow with Yarrow on his shoulder. Dradevai held three down feathers, which Asith had extracted from the makeshift beds somewhere along the way, and Farin removed the embroidered ribbon from his hair before tying it back with a piece of leather.

The vent shaft was just up ahead; a little farther and they would be delving into unexplored territory. Asith's thoughts scattered. What if Phela had never intended for him to break into a facility? If she had other plans for Asith, what would happen if he strayed? Yet he couldn't live with leaving dragons behind, and that, at least, settled his thoughts somewhat. It might not have been what Phela had in mind, but it was the right thing to do. That was what really mattered.

As the second sun dipped one-third below the horizon, Yarrow leaned forward to press her front feet into his hand. She looked at him with unblinking black eyes, and a thread of purplish-red light emanated from the flowers on his wand. The light curled and extended down his arm and around him like patterns of clouds floating across a late evening sky. His hair stood on end, and he sat up on his elbows as a mark like a glowing yellow sun settled under his sternum. It flashed bright, then settled into the same dimness as the sky above.

His haggard doublet and dirty leggings were replaced with leather armor holding tight to Asith's form. The greaves had metal but were easy to move in like the armor he had worn as a dragon knight, and the doublet was secured tightly around his middle under the breastplate. Gloves wrapped around the palm of his hand and ended at his fingers to provide dexterity for casting. The armor shared the same color as the purple clouds that had slid along his arms, with dark brownish grays in the creases.

Asith straightened from his crouch, feeling horribly light. The sun mark by his sternum had become a running rabbit, making Asith realize Yarrow was no longer sitting among them.

"Did your rabbit just turn into armor?" Farin asked.

Dradevai shushed him, so Farin pressed his hands over his mouth, his volume surprising even him.

As Asith sat on his knees, Dradevai's lips hung in a soft O, their eyes darting from Asith's chest to his shoulders to his hands, as if they weren't sure where to look.

"I know about as much as you two do," Asith said, touching his chest. He felt the same warmth that came whenever Yarrow set her front feet on him and leaned up to sniff his face. "But yes, I think my rabbit became armor."

"Can familiars just…do that?" Farin's eyes had grown to a size matching the top of his cauldron.

"Not that I know of?" Dradevai answered, their eyes still locked on Asith.

"Well, you don't have one. How much do you know about them?" Farin argued.

Dradevai tore their eyes away and nudged Farin with their elbow. "I've read plenty about familiars." Dradevai crossed their arms and lifted their chin.

"I hate to tell you this, but readin' about something isn't experiencing it."

Dradevai pursed their lips. "That isn't the point at the moment. Asith, what just happened?"

Asith ran his fingers over the sun on the breastplate. Yarrow was moving about his armor as if she were walking on him. She said Phela had given it to Yarrow when she kissed her on the head, as a gift for finding the right path.

Relief washed over him. Phela wasn't unhappy, and he was pursuing the correct path. Even if he wasn't the perfect mage or struggled with casting the lightning spell, Phela hadn't abandoned him. However, he desired clarity on what the larger picture looked like. His aunt would likely say he would just need faith, but he wasn't sure he was cut out for that sort of trust, even if it were in the hands of a goddess.

Asith explained the gift from Phela. Dradevai smoothed down their hair.

"Well, hopefully, that's a good sign for what we're about to do," they said.

Asith smiled, grateful for the small amount of optimism. Perhaps things would go well, and maybe he would be better off letting himself believe it. It was much like entering a town overrun by Blues and Greens. The knights were trained, but that didn't make it any less dangerous.

"Okay, lovebirds," Farin said. "Dradevai stop staring. We have to go."

Dradevai straightened, their mouth opening and closing before they said, "I wasn't staring."

Farin smiled. "You two are cute and I'm happy for you, I promise."

Heat spread all over Asith's body, which was unusual given the temperature's rapid descent as the second sun was dipping below the mountains.

"Farin, we're doing something serious," Asith whispered.

Farin snickered and crouched behind some rocks. "What fun is having five new siblings if I can't tease you whenever I want?" Farin pulled some rope off his belt and wrapped it around his palm.

A tingling sensation traveled up Asith's arms and down his chest. Dradevai was blinking with an open mouth. "Siblings?" they said.

"There's no way we won't be family after what's about to happen," Farin said, his voice lowering. "So I'm being preemptive, but I know I'm right."

A laugh rocked through Asith. Farin's optimism was hard to shake, and Asith almost envied it. Blind optimism wasn't always helpful, and he hoped it wouldn't get Farin into trouble inside the facility. But perhaps if he were more confident in his own memory and magic abilities, he could cast lightning.

Dradevai's face softened toward Farin, their shoulders relaxing. "I'm glad you were the one who helped Asith."

Farin winked before crawling along the ground toward the vent shaft.

Asith moved to follow, but Dradevai grabbed his shoulder and pulled him in for a kiss. His breath escaped him. When they pulled away, they pressed their forehead against Asith's.

"I love you."

"I love you too," Asith said.

They kissed him again and let him go. Asith cupped their cheek, savoring their warm skin before he crouched and followed Farin, with Dradevai close behind.

The vent shaft made the entire world loud, the metal vibrating all the way up from the fan at the bottom. Secured with rope, Asith and Farin descended into the cavity. However, each time they kicked against the wall for support, the sound echoed with an intensity that never seemed to end. So Dradevai cast a spell that helped them stick against the wall. When it was their turn to descend, they stuck to the wall as well, looking like a spider making its way across plaster, their hands splayed out as they crawled.

Farin reached the end of the rope and held himself in place. Asith stopped as well, shifting his feet to position himself better as he released one hand on the rope. He pulled one of Dradevai's down feathers from his pocket and grabbed the rope again, waiting for Dradevai to reach them.

Dradevai stopped just above the fan, turning over their shoulder to examine it. They stretched one hand toward the slowly spinning blades, their hair fluttering around their head as they carefully placed one foot in a safe spot, and then his other, so they could stop the chant they were using to stick to the wall. Their delicate fingers twisted, the vent shaft darkening as the second sun set completely, the glow of orange magic illuminating their face. A single fiery-red thread appeared between their fingers and snaked between the fan blades. It looped around one blade, and the fan groaned, Dradevai grasping the thread to stop the fan entirely. The mechanism clanked desperately, trying to move forward.

"Now!" Dradevai whispered, but their voice sounded so loud in the vent shaft that Farin shushed them. Asith chanted, and they both let go of the rope. They only fell for a moment before gently floating down to where Dradevai worked.

Farin grabbed a blade and wiggled between the crevice to get to the ground below. When Farin dropped, Asith met Dradevai's eyes, his mouth dry. Their arms shook as they struggled to maintain their grip. Blue sparks flew from the center mechanism, and Asith grabbed the edge of a blade and lowered himself as far as he could, licking his teeth to return moisture to his mouth. He couldn't help but picture what might happen if the blades spun again while passing between them. But Dradevai was a good mage so he tried to put the image out of his mind.

Asith let go, but the drop was much farther than he realized. He hit the ground hard, his knees buckling. He crumpled on the ground and groaned, Farin's hand slapping down on Asith's mouth to muffle him. More sparks jittered across the ceiling and rained on him and Farin as Dradevai's red thread held fast.

Pulling Farin's hand away from his mouth, Asith called up to Dradevai, "You're going to break it!"

Dradevai didn't have time to react as a sharp noise creaked and a series of blue runes inflamed the metal, revealing an enchantment. The fan blades jerked, and the thread snapped, causing Dradevai to fall backward against the wall of the vent. They hissed, and the fan crashed toward Asith.

Farin jumped to meet the fan, and Asith spoke the chant he'd used to lower himself and Farin. But the magic slid off. Farin caught the fan, but it pushed him to the ground, causing a bang that might have been worse if he didn't intervene at all.

"Fuck." Farin gently lowered the fan to the ground, his face pinched in pain.

Dradevai stuck their head through the gap before disappearing. They returned with rope in their hands and dropped one end to them. "Tie up the blade, hurry," Dradevai whispered.

Asith began wrapping it around the fan as Farin recovered, and then the halfling picked it up to help Dradevai pull it back into the vent.

"Good job," Farin said, rubbing his arms as Dradevai landed next to him. "We have to hide."

Asith studied the space around them, noting the closed doors in the hallway. Most had transom windows above them, and Asith led them to the first door without light shining through the glass. Asith tried the handle, but it didn't open. Farin whipped out a few tools and started picking the lock.

Voices sounded at the end of the hall, so Asith grabbed the axe charm on his necklace.

"Got it!" Farin said, pulling his tools from the lock.

Dradevai opened the door and pushed Farin and Asith inside, following without much regard for space before closing the door behind them. Dradevai tripped and knotted their limbs with Farin, so Asith grabbed them both to keep them from knocking over everything in the closet. He finally stilled them as the voices drew closer to the door.

A voice trembled. "What the hell was that?"

"It was probably just somebody dropping something in the barracks, calm down." The second voice sounded tired, with a yawn following.

"But it was so loud! Like something fell from the ceiling," the first voice claimed, sounding farther away.

"It wasn't that loud, was it?" the second voice said in front of the door. "Weird, that fan should be moving."

"Maybe it broke? We should tell someone." The sounds of the guards were falling off.

Asith didn't catch the second voice's response, but eventually, a door opened and slammed closed. Farin relaxed against Asith's hand on his shoulder, but Dradevai was trembling, their breathing quick.

"You didn't have to shove me," Farin said.

Dradevai's shoulders shrunk, their chest collapsing inward. "I know, sorry."

Farin's narrowed eyes relaxed, and he straightened his clothes. "It's okay, we should focus."

"Should I turn us invisible?" Asith suggested. "It sounded like they noticed the fan wasn't working."

Dradevai bit their lip, brow furrowing, but Farin answered, "No, no, no. We need to save that for a worst-case scenario."

"Is this not a worst-case scenario?" Dradevai posed. "We just made so much noise, and they said they were telling someone."

"I promise, it's not likely that anyone is suspicious yet." Farin touched the door handle. "But you're right, we have to go before they figure out the fan didn't break on its own."

"Okay." Dradevai pressed their lips together, looking around nervously. Farin nodded back at them and turned the handle.

Asith and Dradevai followed Farin's quiet footsteps out of the closet. They were alone in the hallway, passing doors in every direction, save for at the far end where a railing rose from the stone floor. It dipped down into a spiral staircase composed of perfectly triangular steps. They couldn't have predicted the stairwell would be so tight, but it was their best option as Farin tiptoed his way down. Before following, Dradevai pulled a small bag on their belt open and retrieved their spell book. They pulled two folded sheets of parchment from the pages before returning the book to their pouch.

The stairs tunneled into the rock of the mountainside, plunging several flights before they saw any sign of another level. When they reached a landing, a short hallway led to an open archway, greenish light illuminating a large room filled with cages. It wasn't as big as the facility where Asith's father had been stored, but at least ten large metal cages lined the walls. The glow belonged to the sigils in the center, and it seemed nothing else could offer them light to see better.

"Gods, this is worse than I expected," Farin said.

Asith scanned the cavern, the small forms in the cages unmoving and quiet. The damp air felt heavy, and the odor of sweat and unwashed skin tickled his nose.

"We need to turn the lights on," Dradevai said. "Otherwise, it'll be harder for you two to help."

"We can do it in the dark," Asith said. He couldn't see well, but they needed to go undetected for as long as possible.

"If you think it will be okay." Dradevai looked at Farin for confirmation. Farin nodded. "Look out for guards."

Yarrow stirred inside his armor, a warning coming to Asith's mind as he stepped over the threshold. He was too focused on his rage to pay attention, knowing that dragons like Mysse, Idhe, and Cemi were trapped in those cages. His stomach churned, but he set his jaw as he put a hand on his sword, Farin and Dradevai a step behind him.

A stone depressed under his weight, and yellow lights flashed as bright as the second sun. Asith flung his hand up, expecting to be hit, and Farin yowled like an upset cat, his forearm pressing over his eyes. Even Dradevai made a small noise as they squinted in the light. Asith was shifting his foot off the stone when a siren blared.

"Oh, no," Farin said, barely audible between the shrieks of the alarm.

At the last facility, Asith's father had electrified an arcane panel of some sort to open all the cages at once. That facility might not work exactly the same, but it was their best shot.

"Vai, protect Farin." Asith shot into the room as fast as he could, the dragons peering up at him with open mouths. He scanned the walls for a panel like the one in the previous facility. Arcane sigils ran across the stone but didn't connect anywhere.

"Asith!" Dradevai called over the noise. Asith looked back, and their arm was extended toward the stone panel near the center. He charged for it, and Dradevai, who was clutching a wobbling Farin to their side, met him there.

Asith stepped onto the platform and studied the markings he'd only seen a few times, their magic far more advanced than his, even with his father's tutoring. The Endethi symbols didn't make sense, with seemingly random words like "up" and "three" and "turn." He slapped one button, and the platform turned to the right. A cage shook before moving along a track toward the control panel.

The young dragon inside appeared around Mysse's size. As the cage stopped in front of Asith, their gray eyes widened, and they pressed against the back bars, their dull black hair hanging in dirty mats.

"Don't take me down there again today!" they shrieked. "Don't take me down!"

A chill ran down Asith's spine, and a blinking button on the panel caught his attention. He looked back at the young dragon, who had tears streaming down their face.

"Can I open the cages using this?" Asith asked.

Guards appeared on the stairs, weapons in hand. They lingered at the front of the room, likely forming a plan of attack.

"What?" the young dragon said, shrinking more against the bars. Other dragons yelled at Asith to leave the dragon alone. Their yells grew louder and louder, until Asith could barely hear anything at all. His mind filled with the call of a Green, and his hands shook.

"Can I open the cages with this panel?" Asith shouted. But the sounds of plated shoes melded with the shouting. The young dragon moved their lips, but he couldn't make out any of their words.

Remembering what his father had done, Asith slipped his wand from his belt, flipped open his spell book, and chanted. He moved his wand over the panel, losing hope that his energy would be preserved for Heskel. The magic rippled around him like a piece of slick silk, the waves making it difficult for Asith to hold it still. Visualizing a pin slipping into it, Asith spat out couplets as static rose in the air. But one pin wasn't enough, the magic slipping through his fingers and the silk floating to the ground. The magic returned to its original shape, and a spark popped at the end of his wand, the static fizzling.

Asith's limbs chilled as his head filled with the yells again, the words of the spell lost to him. They had done everything wrong. They were going to fail.

"Asith!" Farin smacked his arm. Asith hadn't noticed his presence. "Asith, this isn't the time, buddy, come on."

A Green roared in his mind, its teeth sharp as it snapped at him from the end of an alley. He swallowed, his mouth dry and muscles tight as he flexed his hands around the handle of his axe. He peered around the stone building protecting him and swung wildly at the Green, but his axe didn't connect with its flesh.

No, not his axe. His wand.

"Asith!"

The voice reminded him of Dradevai, but it belonged to a shrieking Blue overhead. It shoved its snout at him and kicked shingles off rooftops. His wand was his only weapon; not even his armor could protect him. He tried to cast a shield spell, but nothing happened.

Asith turned around slowly, a collection of guards moving in on a familiar-looking dragon who had been keeping them at bay, snapping with their teeth and swinging their tail to scare them off. One guard with cool gray skin looked up at the dragon with black eyes. Their jaw dropping, they abandoned their weapon and ran off to a door just beyond the cage, but nobody seemed to notice or follow them. Was that the only guard who was scared?

A Green hissed at Asith's back, so an acid shot would be soon to follow. He wouldn't be able to form a sturdy shield in time.

A halfling flung around his dagger at a guard who outmatched him with a sword.

Asith realized the shot of acid never came.

A familiar pressure touched Asith's chest, and air filled his lungs like he'd just emerged from deep water. Yarrow was there.

"Help!" The young dragon's voice broke Asith's thoughts. The surroundings of the cave returned in a clear blast, and Asith remembered why he was there. Dradevai and Farin were the ones fighting to protect him.

"Help, please! Are you the ones they sent to let us out?"

Asith didn't understand. No one had sent them, so whom were they talking about?

Dradevai threw a few guards around, some of them crashing into the walls and others fleeing. They flew to Asith and Farin and burst into their smaller form in a cloud of smoke. They breathed fire, sending several of the guards pursuing Farin stumbling backward.

"You were the ones they sent, right?" The young dragon's eyes had grown so large that their irises were perfectly round, surrounded by bloodshot white. They stepped toward Asith.

"Who?"

"Some of the guards were trying to get us out."

Asith swiveled to study the bodies on the ground. Some were just knocked out, but others had bent in a way that meant they were not as lucky.

"The guards were—" But Asith stopped as movement near the spiral staircase caught his attention.

"You will not be stealing any more of our inventory," Chancellor Heskel Ashe called, his bulky robes swaying as he shaped the air around him. He tucked it into a tight ball and angled it toward Dradevai and Farin, seemingly unconcerned about hitting his own guards in his path.

A mage of the Maeria Spire was not someone Asith could defeat on his own, but he charged at him anyway, hoping to at least defend his companions, and chanted as fast as he could.

Asith lifted his hand in the air as the ball of whirling air flicked off Heskel's fingertips. He imagined grabbing a bolt of fabric in his mother's home off the wall rack and yanking it over him. But Heskel's missile of air tore through it like thin cotton.

Asith flew backward and landed on the ground, the impact making Yarrow squirm. The armor flickered as he rolled a few times and stopped just out of reach of Farin. At least the shield had misdirected the hit. Farin looked down at Asith and cringed.

In that moment of distraction, a guard knocked Farin's dagger out of the way, and another raised their sword high and swung it down.

It met Farin's arm.

His hand thudded to the ground, followed by the clatter of the dagger as the fingers loosened, but Farin's scream never came. His brown skin grew ashen, and he fell backward and then crumbled onto the stone.

Asith jumped to his feet and plunged his sword into the belly of a guard who wore nothing but a breastplate. The blood pooled quickly, the guard falling to their knees as they tried to press their hands over the wound. They slowly lifted their head to Asith. They had lilac skin and dark black eyebrows, their eyes resembling a pool of black that had lost their shine as ink does when it dries. With their blood dripping down Asith's sword, they fell face-first onto the ground at Farin's feet.

Asith's hands trembled as static snapped against his skin. His stomach turned, but he swallowed back the bile and turned toward Dradevai instead, their spell book in hand. The last of the guards were bouncing off a shield they had formed, and they moved to Farin's other side.

"Asith, deal with the mage," Dradevai said calmly. They didn't have any visible injuries, but they were down to two, with at least fifteen young dragons to free. But Dradevai was right; Heskel was still a threat.

"Are you going to heal him?" Asith asked, unsure he could face the mage again. He was talented in physical combat, but Heskel wouldn't let him get close enough to use it.

"I'm going to try to heal him as much as I can, but this is not my area of expertise."

"It's okay," Farin said with a strained voice. "Better than nothing."

Dradevai placed their hands on what remained of Farin's forearm and chanted. Asith located Heskel as he finished a chant, his movements clean and swift in a way that even Dradevai's weren't. With heavy limbs, he attempted another shield with sedated movements, but it was all he could muster. Their plan had been too bold, too cocky, and if they hadn't been there, the dragons could have escaped with the guards.

Heskel growled. "You won't leave here alive!" He pressed his fingertips together, his robes billowing in the wind and his eyes glowing white. The shadows from his magic extended the creases on his face, but that didn't make Asith want to cower; it was the bright apricot of his pale skin, the silvery flicker to his hair, and the pink of his tongue. Heskel looked important, serious, pampered with heavy rings on his fingers and robes made of the finest fabrics, as a chancellor should; but with that came an eerie sense of power. Even if they escaped, even if Farin lived, even if they got the kids to the Graveyard Trees, that man would find them.

The shot from Heskel's hands was fast, spinning like a tornado on the plains of Southern Cairn that tore trees from the ground by their roots. Asith fumbled with his words and there was no fabric to grab that time, but he stretched his arms out anyway to at least attempt to protect Dradevai and Farin. He didn't look, didn't move, fearing the spell had been redirected around him.

His hair whipping around his face, Asith squinted through the cloud of stirred-up dirt. A purple shield was glimmering in front of him. It only took him a moment to recognize it, the shield that had saved his life many times over as a Blue or Green tried to sink its teeth into Asith. That shield was not the work of his own magic.

Eroan stood behind the cage of the cowering young dragon Asith had spoken to. His eyes glowed lilac, masking their dark brown color and making his tawny skin shine with a dewy life that Asith had only seen on Dradevai and Pystra while they cast magic. A grave shadow fell over his expression, giving a severity to his boyish features. The lines of his high cheekbones curved up to meet the edges of his long, pointed ears, which stuck out against his short silver hair.

He was surveying the situation, calculating as Asith had seen him do many times before. Only now, Eroan didn't look confident as he often did in a town swarmed by dragons. Asith, Dradevai, and Farin had unwittingly created a trap for him, and he had stepped into it willingly to protect them.

CHAPTER 18

The whirlwind stopped, and Eroan dropped the shield that had protected Asith, the purple glow only partially receding. Asith strengthened his stance and switched his staff for his sword. Heskel was a talented mage, but he couldn't match Asith in physical combat. If he got close enough, he could overwhelm Heskel.

"Eroan, what are you doing?" Heskel called. "*Catch them.*"

Eroan opened his mouth, but Dradevai shot in front of him, rapidly chanting and moving both loosely and chaotically. They expanded their chest and reached their hands to the ceiling as if they were pulling down a sheet from a clothesline.

Fire sprung from the top of the cave and spread to the floor, forming a wall. The heat ascended to an unbearable temperature, but they'd separated Heskel from the cages and his voice was muffled from the other side.

"That will slow him down, thank you," Eroan said. He turned to the console, pressed three buttons, and opened the doors to the cages. The dragons fled to the other end of the room.

Dradevai held their position with splayed fingers, the wall still burning as they gritted their teeth. The flames dispersed slightly, likely from Heskel trying to get through.

"Get Farin," Dradevai called. "Now!"

Asith sheathed his sword and lifted Farin into his arms. His arm was no longer bleeding, but his skin was damaged where Dradevai had melded the wound and his face was ghostly pale, matching the color of dried dirt. But his eyes had brightened. It appeared as if he received a few days of good medical care, along with some herbs from an apothecary. Asith's chest relaxed, until he remembered the dead guard on the ground he'd impaled, making his stomach turn. At least Farin might make it through.

"This way." Eroan waved for them to follow. Asith started to run with Farin and the small dragons, but he turned to see if Dradevai was coming. They shifted into their larger form, their long neck rising over their shoulders as the wall fell. They flapped their wings, showering the room with their feathers, and unleashed a torrent of fire on the stairs. Everything that was flammable burned, the flames quickly rising to lick the walls. If Heskel was still there, Asith couldn't find it in himself to care. Instead, the world fell away, Dradevai's glimmering feathers filling his mind's eye as they scorched the rock at the other end of the room.

Farin slapped Asith's forehead, nearly knocking him over.

"Stop gawking at your boyfriend and follow the dragons!" Farin gestured wildly at Eroan, who was waiting for them to follow.

Asith shook his head and stepped into the narrow hallway as Dradevai flew toward them. When they both arrived, Eroan rushed them up a set of straight stairs.

"Should I close this?" Dradevai asked, pointing at the hallway. "I can close it with stone."

"No," Eroan said sharply. "You three have done enough."

"What does that mean?" Dradevai balled their hands into fists.

"This is the second time the two of you have ruined our plans to free the dragons in these facilities. Get upstairs now. My people need this as an escape route."

Dradevai twitched, their eyes darting to Asith. He stopped on the stairs.

"Oh, shut your hole." Farin jabbed a finger in Eroan's face. "These two have gotten more dragons out than you have at this point, so quit makin' it seem like they're the problem here."

Asith's neck heated, the blood pumping past his ears and loudly in his head, but he had to be the reasonable one. "This isn't the time to fight. We'll leave it open if there are people who need a way out."

Dradevai's mouth dropped open, and they slowly shook their head.

"Vai, come on. Think of Cemi, Mysse, and Idhe. We have to get out of here."

Their body shook. But ultimately, they relaxed their shoulders. "Let's go." Dradevai passed Eroan and followed the group of young dragons up the stairs.

The gaggle of children was clustered next to some beds in what looked like barracks. Two guards stood at the door, and a third was prying a vent in the ceiling open from the top of a bunk bed.

"Eroan!" A guard with hair white as snow jogged over from the door, their skin a familiar cool gray color. They were the one who had fled upon seeing Dradevai. Their round face softened as they approached, the blackness in their eyes, with a light-yellow sclera, surprising Asith. He had only seen a few Irden elves in Cairn before.

"I'm okay, Uri. I promise." Eroan took the elf's hands and held their eye contact. Dradevai pressed closer to Asith's side, an eyebrow raised at the scene.

The realization crashed over Asith all at once. They had killed guards, perhaps some who were trying to break out the dragons. He hoped they hadn't targeted those.

"We have the doors to the barracks secured. Did you get everyone?" Uri asked. Their eyes moved away from Eroan's face, studying the group of children, some of whom were clinging to each other.

"There is one more in the lab area at the moment, but we have all of the guards," Eroan said.

The knot in his throat untied, the relief making his posture unstable. Farin shifted in his grip, so Asith set him down and he leaned on Asith instead.

"How are we going to get so many out?" Asith asked.

"You didn't have a plan for getting them out?" Eroan's voice rose.

"We were going to bring them through the vent shaft," Dradevai said. "We didn't know there would be so many here, though."

"Eroan, don't get angry." Uri set a hand on his shoulder. "They were only trying to help."

"If they wanted to help, Asith should have come to me sooner," Eroan spat.

Asith recoiled, his head shaking and his brow furrowed. "What are you talking about? I had no idea if you were on Heskel's side or not."

Eroan rubbed his temples. "You thought another dragon was just on Heskel Ashe's side?"

"What?" Asith's mind went blank. He'd known Eroan for years; they'd been friends. "I didn't know you were a dragon."

Eroan's jaw slackened, his eyes narrowing. "You never noticed?"

"I didn't even know I was a dragonborn until a little over a year ago."

Through the armor, Yarrow pressed her paws on his chest. Eroan's skin grew ashy, his eyebrows high and eyes wide.

"You never even knew you were a dragonborn?"

Uri looked between them rapidly, as the guard on the bunk bed popped off the vent cover.

"No! Did you know?"

"You are very obviously a dragonborn! Look at your hair, and your ears!"

Farin laughed deeply, his entire body shaking.

"I just thought I was an elf!" Asith tugged on one of his ears. "My mother was a human, and my father was in that other facility most of my life. How was I supposed to know?"

A bang shook the room, followed by a crack of thunder. Everyone froze before the guard on the bed climbed down to lift the kids onto the top bunk.

Dradevai asked Eroan, "What is your plan?"

"I'm going to teleport all of you to the Graveyard Trees." Eroan gestured at the kids and the guards. "And then I am going to try to get the last dragon who is currently in the lab."

"We can't go," Dradevai said. "We'll go with you and help."

Eroan shook his head. "No, I told you, you two have already done enough. Besides, he needs to go to the Graveyard Trees."

Farin was swaying, so Asith set a hand on his shoulder to steady him.

"There are three other dragons under thirteen we have to go back to." Asith shifted in front of Eroan to force eye contact. "I understand that we messed up your plan, but being belligerent won't help. It didn't help with the Blues and Greens either."

"Eroan, I don't want you going alone," Uri added and pointed at Asith and Dradevai. "Take these two, and I'll take their friend. Stop arguing, we don't have the time."

Eroan spun on his heels, but his words for Uri died on his tongue. Their face was pinched, their eyes darker than they already were, and their shoulders trembled, betraying their firm stance. Asith felt as though he shouldn't involve himself in whatever was going on between them, so he nudged Dradevai to huddle with Farin.

"Are you both okay with splitting up?" Asith asked.

Dradevai wrung their hands but said nothing.

"I'll be okay," Farin slurred. "I can do this. I'll be fine."

Dradevai met Asith's eyes, their head shaking slightly. So Asith shook his head too and said, "Farin, that's admirable..."

"I won't be helpful like this," Farin said, nudging the scorched skin where his forearm used to connect to his wrist. He winced.

Asith's shoulders sunk, his eyes finding Dradevai's face. Their jaw muscles flexed as tears gathered in their eyes.

"No, I think you would be helpful still," Asith said, "but I don't want you to die here. Think of your mother, how could I tell her?"

Farin looked up at Asith, his cheeks puffing like he didn't entirely believe him, but he said, "Okay, I'll go. For my mom."

"Thank you."

Dradevai's hands were fisted at their sides, and tears streaked down their face. They opened their lips, just barely, and took a shuddering breath.

"I know you're both right, but I don't like it. How can we trust Eroan? Or any of this?"

Farin sighed. "We can't, but it's our best option at the moment."

"I don't think Eroan is tricking us. He let my father and I escape at the last facility," Asith said. He leaned forward and lowered his voice. "And I have a way to call my aunt if we need help."

Dradevai swallowed and wiped their tears away. Farin squeezed their forearm and then tugged Asith's tunic.

"What?" Asith dropped to a knee. That close, he could see the hatred in Farin's eyes.

"Get. Evidence. If you do nothing else, get proof."

"Proof of…" Asith furrowed his brow, his knees throbbing uncomfortably.

"This facility! What they're doing!" Farin's lips quivered, and he shook violently.

"Farin, please." Dradevai kneeled. "Try not to move too much, if you get worked up—"

"I might die, I know." Tears streaked through the blood on Farin's face. "I want you both to promise you will get proof of what's been going on here."

"You're not going to die," Asith said.

Farin licked his lips, shaking his head. "That's not the point, Asith." Farin gestured at the room. "The people of Cairn, they wouldn't want this. You *know* they wouldn't."

Asith visualized the faces of people he'd grown up with in South Cairn, the ones who cared for him when he played in the streets, the ones who threw yarrow at his feet as he first left for the Capitol, and then again when he walked to face Dradevai alone. Delri smiled in his mind's eye, gushing about how much she wanted children one day, laughing as Asith told her she wouldn't be able to sleep in so late if she had them. Even the faces of the knights he trained with, the ones who lost friends and lovers to the Blues and Greens, were clearly in his head, and he imagined the way they'd turn to disgust if they knew even the smallest bit of what was happening in those facilities.

"You're right." Asith nodded. "You're right, we'll get proof. We promise."

"We promise," Dradevai echoed.

Farin's eyes grew unfocused as he clung to Asith. "You know, my father was a mage from Wacot," Farin said lowly, looking straight ahead. "Do you know who the Cerulean Visage is?"

"I know they are mages who work as part of the government in Wacot?"

"They are. My father is one of them, Lord Leonard Phylund. A pathetic weakling of a man, but good with magic. He was constantly receiving shipments of things: dragon's blood, feathers, dusted teeth, chunks of horn."

Asith's eyes widened. The facility he'd broken his father out of, along with that one, was supplying the mages of Wacot. But Cairn and Wacot were not allies. Cairn wouldn't fuel the mages of Wacot when they had their own to provide for at the Maeria Spire. Unless Heskel and the other mages were acting separately from the government of Cairn. But all of that work simply to become rich? Asith couldn't fathom it. However, someone else might do it for the power that came with wealth.

"I can see on your face that you don't understand," Farin said. "I don't either, but I think you can find a way to understand the connection there."

"I'll try. For now, I want you to take this."

Asith pulled a piece of paper from his pocket for spells and took Dradevai's pen from their belt. He wrote a note to his father, signed his name, and folded it up. The ink would smear slightly because he didn't let it dry, but Asith pressed it into Farin's hand and squeezed his shoulder.

"When you get to the Graveyard Trees, ask for Listesh and give him this. My parents will take care of you. Both of them have trained to be doctors."

"And what's your mother's name?"

"Maryan. Maryan and Listesh Evourin."

"Maryan and Listesh." Farin squeezed his eyes shut as if he were trying to force that into his memory.

Most of the children had moved into whatever the room was above the vent, and Eroan and Uri were whispering heated words.

"We're going with you," Asith announced, his voice loud enough to get Eroan and Uri's attention. "But Farin is going with them."

Uri folded their arms at Eroan, who took one look at Farin swaying and sighed. "Fine," Eroan said. Farin and Uri joined the last of the children going into the vent.

Another bang reverberated through the stone and reached Asith's ears with a thunderous crack. A fissure formed in the floor, just large enough for Heskel and two men to peer up at them. As the dust cleared, Asith studied the other men more closely, and one was eyeing him with a wicked grin.

Kosor was gripping a glaive, the edge a series of jagged spikes along one side and the pole obsidian.

The other man wore long decorated robes, the same rich reds belonging to the Maeria Spire. His face was cool, and his eyes were a piercing orange, like the leaves of a maple tree in autumn. His pale skin was immaculate, save for a few wrinkles around his eyes. A well-trimmed beard framed his squared jaw, black as coal, with speckles of ash gray in it, leading up to long hair pulled back in a complex plait.

"Elaqen Vetrish," Eroan said.

Asith's jaw fell. He had never seen the headmaster of the Maeria Spire. As Elaqen prepared to cast a spell with a cold stare, Dradevai tugged Asith away. He followed them to the vent and had just entered with Eroan when a spell split the floor of the room below them.

Asith felt horribly claustrophobic as he pressed up against Uri, whose arm supported Farin. A spell circle was carefully carved into the ground, the etching filled with glimmering silver metal, and sigils drawn in chalk lined the walls, with a paste made of herbs painted over each. It seemed like an advanced form of magic that took months to prepare, and perhaps that was why Eroan was confident he could transport a big group of people to an entirely different place in the blink of an eye.

The stone around them shook. Eroan chanted rapidly, each word rolling off with an ease that came with years of training. He didn't waver as stone crumbled to the floor. Each sigil glowed as he poetically finished a stanza, reminding Asith of air moving through the leaves of trees and the night sky.

Sparks fluttered along the chalk markings and burned away the herbs. The rest of the spell circle flared, and a purple light filled the room, static bouncing off the stone and making everyone's hair stand on end. Then a gateway appeared at the center of the circle.

"Go, now!" Uri shouted. They ran for the gate, Farin clinging to their side and clutching the hand of the smallest dragon. As they touched the gate, they disappeared. Air rushed through and popped as each guard and child ran through.

Eroan's eyes glowed purple, and he grimaced, his teeth bared like a growling dog. His chest sunk in, and he withered the moment the final dragon disappeared beyond the portal. His knees buckled, and the circle was gone, with some of the chalk markings lingering in places.

A glaive shot through the vent and hit the ceiling. Dradevai fell backward and scrambled to Asith's side. Asith pulled them toward Eroan, and once he had secured them both, he pressed them against the wall.

Eroan asked, "What are you—"

Asith slapped a hand over his mouth and grabbed the axe from around his neck. It might not work against Elaqen or Heskel, but it would on Kosor. He chanted quickly, and they disappeared as he shifted their position to make them one with the wall. Eroan pulled Asith's hand off his mouth but didn't say anything.

Kosor hopped into the room and picked up his glaive, which had clattered to the floor. Searching the room, he pulled a thick ledger from his belt, and then he scanned the pages.

"Specimens 336 through 341 and 343 through 351 are missing," Kosor called down.

Asith's ears perked and twitched at his words. He couldn't see the pages of the book, but he needed it. For Farin.

Elaqen rose through the vent, his eyes keen and his hands folded behind his back, with Heskel just a moment behind him. Elaqen's eyes flared, and a chant slipped through his lips at an almost imperceptible volume. Once he stopped, he studied the room slowly.

Sweat dripped down Asith's back, and he tightened his grip around Dradevai's shoulder. When Elaqen's gaze lingered on where they stood, Asith's stomach lurched, and he nearly gagged. He floated to the wall, but he stared at something above them.

"An enhancement for a teleportation spell," Elaqen said, his voice oozing with intrigue. "I'm going to have to tell the Visage about this."

"I promise, I will get them all back," Heskel said in a wavering voice and pointed below with trembling fingers. "And we still have one. We can meet our goals for this month."

"Kosor." Elaqen turned toward Kosor looming in the corner "Please secure our remaining asset. I will be down there to join you soon."

"Yes, sir." Kosor approached the gap they'd entered through and paused. In a flash, he hurled his glaive toward Asith, and it collided with the wall.

Eroan and Dradevai tensed in his arms while Asith held his breath. Then Kosor walked over to retrieve his glaive. "Just had to be sure," he said.

"Of course," Elaqen said.

Kosor dropped through the vent, and Heskel said, "Do you really need to bring that brute with you everywhere?"

Elaqen clicked his tongue, turning away from Asith, Dradevai, and Eroan. "I would be cautious who you call a brute."

"I'm not afraid of your lapdog, Vetrish." Heskel puffed out his chest.

But it deflated as Elaqen floated past him. "You should be," Elaqen replied and dipped below, leaving Heskel by himself.

Heskel balled his hands into fists and a growl escaped his lips. Then he left the room, leaving Asith, Dradevai, and Eroan unharmed.

CHAPTER 19

Asith stayed still as he listened to the sounds of Kosor, Elaqen, and Heskel fall away. When he was sure they were gone and not coming back, Asith let go of Eroan and released the spell. Eroan gasped, panting as he fell onto his hands and knees.

Dradevai clung to Asith, their nails digging into his biceps and their breathing rapid. They gave a knowing look to Eroan, seeming to silently understand something Asith did not.

"That shouldn't have worked," Eroan said.

"How did you cast that spell?" Dradevai asked.

"It was from the charm Phela gave to me." Based on everything Asith's father had taught him, the spell shouldn't have worked on Elaqen and Heskel.

Asith examined the rubble from the room below them. The bunk bed had been knocked over to its side, so he wasn't sure how they would get down, other than by climbing or jumping. He also wasn't sure how Kosor had gotten in and out of the vent so easily.

"Phela chose to be your patron?" Eroan's eyes had grown dull, a thousand-yard stare passing Asith entirely.

"That explains it." Dradevai hummed. "Divine magic."

"What?" Asith asked.

"Divine magic works differently." Dradevai nudged the charm. "It probably concealed us in a way that Vetrish's magic couldn't reveal."

"Oh." Asith picked up the charm and studied the scratch on the rabbit's leg. He tucked it back into his armor. Yarrow seemed to shake herself out from the inside.

"It's also unusual for Phela's paladin to fall on someone who does not study the arcane," Eroan added.

"She said that Sula asked her to help me because I was looking for Dradevai," Asith said.

"Who is Sula again?" Dradevai asked.

"We don't have time for this." Eroan's head twitched, and he rubbed sweat from his forehead.

"You're right, sorry." Dradevai paced around the hole in the floor. "We have one more dragon to rescue, and we have to get that book."

"We do." Asith nodded at Dradevai, glad they had the same thought. "We should be able to handle Kosor."

"Yes." Dradevai hopped to the lower level and held out their arms. "Asith, I'll catch you."

Asith jumped into Dradevai's arms, and their collision hurt slightly. But their bob with the motion stopped Asith without his feet hitting the ground. They straightened, with Asith in their arms like a new bride, before setting him on his feet. Asith kissed their temple.

"They've destroyed the hidden passageways we'd planned on using," Eroan said, floating to the floor.

"Should we use the back stairs, then?" Dradevai asked. "We should try to surprise Kosor, maybe cut him off from the mages."

Eroan agreed, and they walked toward the back stairwell, but Asith set a hand on Dradevai's forearm. Something deep in him rattled like a snake's tail. Its face belonged to Elaqen, who was poised at the base of the stairs, preparing to ambush young rabbits from a burrow.

"What's on your mind?" Eroan said. His sharp eyes narrowed at the staircase.

"I think we should take the main staircase. Then use the elevator shaft."

Eroan grimaced at the doors the guards had barricaded with furniture. But with the commotion, they were no longer blocked. "Why?"

"Yes, why?" Dradevai asked.

"Eroan knows the facility best, but I have a gut feeling." He turned to Eroan. "When we fought Blues, they'd lie in wait, hidden by houses, to take bites at us as we came around blind corners."

Eroan crossed his arms, his head tilting to one side. "Are you likening Elaqen to the imprudence of a Blue?"

"No, the cunning of a snake." Asith looked at Dradevai, hoping for some semblance of trust.

They rubbed their forehead, then nodded. "You're right." Dradevai shifted their glance to Eroan. "Asith's right."

"All right," Eroan said. "We'll take Asith's path, but our priority should be the dragon. I want the notebook, too, but her safety is most important."

"You're not going to fight with us on this plan?" Dradevai's voice cracked, and they touched their throat.

Eroan's eyes grew wet, his hands balling into fists. Not meeting their gaze, he said, "I don't like this. My plan is ruined." A frustrated growl passed his teeth.

Dradevai's shoulders drew in, their arms wrapping around their middle.

"But the last time I didn't listen to one of Asith's gut feelings…" Eroan took a deep breath. "We lost a man named Hamon who was very dear to me."

"Oh," Dradevai said.

Asith remembered Hamon's tightly coiled beard and infectious smile. His hair had been dark, shortly faded on the sides, the top a mix of tight coils arranged into various twists. He smelled of sunflower and lavender oil, and his umber skin would glimmer like glass in the sunlight. But Asith cherished his broad chest and soft arms the most, especially when he'd wrap them around anyone in need of comfort. Everyone in the troupe turned to Hamon for a funny story, which would bring them to a fit of glee only to be outshined by Hamon's full-bellied, bone-deep laughter that healed the soul. Eroan craved his presence the most, often pressing his lithe body against Hamon's soft belly, relaxing against Hamon's hand in his silver hair. Asith had been in that position many times, but he'd never realized how much Eroan must have yearned for that feeling after Hamon was gone.

"Eroan, that wasn't your fault. It was nobody's fault." Asith cradled his elbows as if he could relive the touch of Hamon.

Eroan shook his head. "We don't have time for this either. Let's take the front staircase. I trust you, Asith. Even if I am very angry with you."

Asith nodded. "I promise, I will make up for it somehow." Asith closed his eyes and listened to the sounds of falling rock and debris. Then Yarrow brushed his cheek with her whiskers, the collar of his armor touching his jaw.

Eroan led Asith and Dradevai to the door and inspected a short hallway before entering it. The place had grown eerily quiet. Once they reached the stairs, Dradevai led, since they made the least noise with their movements. They returned to the room that stored the dragons, the doors of empty cages creaking as they swung back and forth. For a moment, Asith soaked in the win. So many children were safe in the Graveyard Trees. It was a start.

"Listen," Eroan said to Asith and Dradevai. "Thank you for doing this, for being committed. Our goals are ultimately the same."

Frowning, Dradevai stepped over the tile that had set off the alarm earlier. "Don't say that now, like you think we won't survive."

"Vai," Asith chastised.

But Eroan let out a low chuckle. "It's okay, thank you. Let's hope you're right about surviving."

"I am," Dradevai said, shaking slightly. "I'm not leaving without that notebook Kosor had."

Asith squeezed their shoulder, and they approached the now empty gap where the top of the lift had been previously. The platform had been lowered to the level below, and Kosor's voice rose through the now empty shaft. Though he couldn't hear Elaqen or Heskel, he assumed they were there too.

"This is large enough I could fly down," Dradevai whispered a few feet from the edge.

"And small enough for you to be cornered by an explosive spell," Eroan said. "We should sneak down there."

While Dradevai and Eroan bickered about the plan in low voices, Asith caught Kosor's jagged shape on the floor below them. He walked to the edge of the lift, his glaive holstered on his back and the same book as before in his hands. Kosor shouted orders, then said, "Specimen 342, Silver, is to be brought to the Maeria Spire. Prepare her for transport." He scribbled something down and resumed ordering others around.

Asith jammed his hand into the pouch on his belt and pulled out a single downy feather that glittered in the torchlight. Approaching the edge of the hole, he looked back at Eroan and Dradevai. He wouldn't let Farin down or give Kosor the chance to destroy it.

"I'll get the book, you two get the dragon," Asith said.

Dradevai reached for him, their eyes wide and glowing in the firelight, but Asith hopped into the elevator shaft.

He fell fast, the air whipping his hair back. A warm breeze filled his nose, smelling of rot and bitter acid. Asith said his chant, and the feather in his hand heated until he finished. He slowed down and floated, his eyes trained on Kosor, who still had not noticed him.

When he was close enough, Asith drew his sword and brought it down on the glaive handle on Kosor's back. He yelped as Asith's sword sheered the blade clean off. It hit his armor with a heavy clunk, and Kosor thudded to the ground, along with the book face-down.

Asith released the chant and crashed into Kosor. The harsh movement threw the air from his lungs, and he rolled off while Kosor retrieved what was left of his glaive. He swung the handle at Asith and connected it with his shoulder, but the blow was dull and ineffective without the blade. Kosor's eyes grew wide, and he tossed the handle away.

"You always were a coward." Kosor sneered. "Looking to hide and deceive your targets rather than fighting them head-on."

He drew a sword from his belt, sending Asith a few steps back. Sometimes, dragon knights had shown looks of surprise upon learning

Asith was hidden in a city, watching him cut off a tail or claw of a Blue or Green. Asith swallowed, shaking his head. He didn't want to rise to Kosor's insults, for it wouldn't do him any good, even though his stomach roiled at the idea that Kosor, of all people, called him a coward.

"I see it's still easy to get a rise out of you." Kosor snorted and lunged. His sword connected with Asith's, his opponent's strength overbearing enough that Asith had to step back again, both his hands secured on the handle. "A coward defending the ones killing his people. I pity you for falling under a dragon's spell."

Asith's body pounded like a drum, trailing up his spine and to his ears, reminding him of a leather punch into a wooden block. His lips curled over his teeth, the dry skin stretching almost painfully as he redirected Kosor's sword. The blade flashed past him, and Kosor stepped on the book. Asith wanted to slide his sword through Kosor's throat.

"I'm a coward for defending children? At least I'm not trying to justify something so horrid."

"Shut your mouth," Kosor spat, but he lost his balance.

Asith shot forward and kicked the book to the side before swinging again. Kosor's guard was high, so Asith sidestepped him and ducked low, driving his sword underneath Kosor's guard.

Asith's blade connected with Kosor's jaw, leaving an ugly jagged mark and splattering blood across the ground. Yarrow's feet pattered down Asith's arm. It felt as if lightning were flowing through him, numbing his hand but filling his muscles with energy. He moved his arms at a blinding speed as he drew his sword back and moved to drive it between Kosor's ribs. But it skidded along the mail with an unpleasant screech.

"Still can't deal with armor, can you?" Kosor hissed, wiping blood from his jaw. He blocked Asith's following attack and redirected his sword to kick Asith square in the stomach.

Asith stumbled back, the rush of electricity moving to his diaphragm in an effort to soothe the ache from Kosor's foot. His vision blurred at the edges, the sight of a Blue's throat or their delicate ankle finding their way onto Kosor's body. Asith stepped past his opponent, expecting another blow, but it didn't come.

"At least I would never be so arrogant that I underestimate an opponent," Asith said.

He brought his sword down on the back of Kosor's ankle, where there was nothing but a leather fitting holding his grieve to his calf. His scream made Asith's blood warm. His body felt lighter as he backed away from Kosor and grabbed for the book, his trembling fingers slipping on the pages.

"Asith!"

Dradevai stood across the room with a young dragon clinging to their side. Her face was small, but she had big gray eyes that welled with tears. The short horns on her head curved backward in a familiar shape.

Then a scream came out of her that Asith couldn't parse, and static filled the air.

"*Coward.*" Kosor's voice shook. But his hand remained steady as he drove the severed blade of his glaive into Asith's thigh.

Asith coughed, searing pain gripping him and the lightning moving through his body dissipated into the floor. He lost his grip on the book and fell forward, quickly rolling to see Kosor hunched over him, his sword high.

"Coward!" Kosor screamed.

A spell whizzed through the air, smelling of sulfur. It landed so close to his head that he thought it had been meant to end him. But it collided with Kosor's chest and exploded in a fountain of sparks that sent him falling backward, his sword clattering to the floor. Using his elbows, Asith crawled toward Dradevai. Another rain of sparks exploded against Kosor's chest as Dradevai reached him halfway and kneeled. The young dragon had crumpled to the floor, a halo of dull silver hair blanketing over her head.

His vision blurring, Asith grasped for Dradevai's hand, their grip on his shoulder tight.

"The…" Asith coughed. His throat was too dry to speak, but he couldn't break his promise to Farin. They needed the book no matter what.

Yarrow walked on his back and brushed his jaw with her whiskers before digging her nails into the skin of his exposed collarbone.

"Vai…" Asith's eyes swam to the book, the smell of iron overtaking him. "I love you."

Dradevai set a warm hand on his skin and shook their head as his vision vignetted around them. The black drew in, slowly taking over everything, even Dradevai's honey-golden glowing eyes.

CHAPTER 20

"Are you okay?"

The voice washed over Asith like a warm breeze, the tingle of pollen in his nose as a world warmed by spring wrapped around him. His eyes opened slowly, and he closed them at the brightness of the second sun.

Someone brushed his hair from his forehead, sticky with sweat. The strands tried staying put, but the person was diligent and pushed them off. Asith's head was nestled against the person's thigh, and when he chanced peering through his eyelashes, he saw their form bending over him. Their blurry figure shifted to block the light, and Asith opened his eyes fully.

He didn't recognize them. But with their soft smile, they might be Dradevai, but that could not be. That person's frame was taller and broader, their hair a brown so dark that it was nearly black. They weren't round like Dradevai either. Their jawline was sharply squared, and their pointed nose sat high on their face, with a defined bump at the top of the bridge.

They looked very little like Dradevai but also so much like them. The tilt of their masculine lips and eyes reminded him of fresh honey dripping directly from the hive. It was as though the features were taken directly from Dradevai's face and placed onto that different one; or rather, those features had been taken from that face and placed on Dradevai.

"Who are you?" he asked, even though he knew the answer.

"A friend." They ran a warm hand over Asith's jaw and swept his hair behind his ear. "You can call me Meris."

"You are Dradevai's other parent?" Asith tried to move but found his limbs pinned to the ground.

Meris bobbed their head. "I am. You've been taking good care of them." They smiled. "I am sorry I will never get to truly know you both."

"That's okay." Asith looked to his left and saw a grassy outcropping. He recognized the strange shapes of the orange rocks and the deep reds of the valleys. They were atop a mountain in the Barren Rise range.

"Is this where you rooted?"

Meris nodded.

"I am never going to be able to bring Dradevai and Pherrosh here, am I?" Asith asked. Hot tears streamed down his face, stinging the corners of his eyes. His breathing stumbled as panic set in. He wasn't supposed to be there. He tried to sit up, but he couldn't so much as shift his shoulders.

Meris wiped his tears from his cheeks and temples, then shrugged. "I don't know if you can, but if that's true, I will be here to guide you."

Asith hiccupped. "You have to send me back."

"I don't have the power to do that." Meris's calm face withered, their shoulders slumping as they ran another gentle hand over a trail of Asith's tears.

"Phela can." Asith's voice cracked, and he searched the terrain for Yarrow. "Where's Yarrow? Where's my rabbit?"

Yarrow leaped onto his stomach and brushed her whiskers against the skin of Asith's collarbones.

"Ah, she belongs with you, then." Meris smiled. "That is a good sign."

Yarrow licked Asith's jaw, and as the second sun crested, a ring formed around Meris's head.

"I can't move," Asith said.

"That is a bad sign."

Asith groaned, trying to wiggle his fingers or toes or any body part beyond his neck. "Can't you help me?"

Meris shook their head. "I can't, I'm sorry."

Asith's tears flowed more freely, obscuring his vision. He strained his core as he commanded his waist to bend, his knee to shift, his foot to lift. Meris moved their hand so that Yarrow could lick another area of Asith's skin.

"I can't leave them," Asith cried. His ankle twitched, and when he tried to move it more, it felt like sliding out a poorly maintained drawer.

Meris's eyes darted to his foot, and a smile spread across their face. "You can't leave them."

Asith's tears stopped as he lifted his right knee, shattering hundreds of little roots that had pinned him to the ground.

"I can't leave them," Asith repeated, and he freed his right hand. If he could enforce his will on the very fabric of magic, maybe he could do the same there. There was no way he could leave Dradevai on their own again.

"You can't leave them."

"I can't leave them." Asith pushed himself into a sitting position. A massive wound on his thigh gushed blood, and it pooled in the grass and onto the wildflowers crushed under his weight. The sight startled him, but he did not feel that stomach-turning sensation he had become so used to when seeing blood.

"Meris, it's working." Asith turned to look at them, but they were nowhere to be found.

He was no longer on a grassy outcropping in the mountains. He was in a facility made of cold metal. Lab equipment whirled around him as someone clung to his form. He was weightless.

Meris's voice filled his ears, disembodied and gentle. "You're not away from the roots just yet. You can't leave them."

"I can't leave them."

6th of Katib

Asith's eyes slit open, the dark rock surrounding him unfamiliar. As soon as the humidity in the air reached his lungs, he could guess his location. Distant voices droned in and out like the buzz of hundreds of bees let loose from their hive after getting knocked off an old awning. He couldn't move, his head throbbed from a fever, and sweat caked every inch of his skin. His mouth was too dry to speak. And he desired to, because the thin form of Mysse sat next to him.

Mysse glanced over his shoulder before focusing on Asith again. If he knew Asith's eyes had opened, he didn't care. He dipped his hands into a pail of water, and Yarrow appeared from behind him.

"Shh, be very quiet," Mysse said to Yarrow. "And don't tell anyone I was here."

He removed his hands from the bucket, but bubbles of roiling water covered them. The liquid was as clear as a mountain stream, save for its slight mineral tinge. Asith lost sight of Yarrow but heard her frantic movements. Mysse checked over his shoulder again before carefully setting his hands against the wound on Asith's leg.

The water was warm, and a pale green light flashed. Asith's vision dwindled, washing out Mysse's face. He couldn't see what was happening, but a searing pain rushed up and down his leg. Asith had experienced that sensation before, when a dragon knight healer had closed a large wound from a Green with magic. The process had been slow to ease the patient's pain, but it wasn't always like that if there wasn't time. Either Mysse was working quickly or he simply didn't know about the spell to numb the pain.

His vision sharpened again, and Asith's leg screamed at him to move away, especially as Mysse dipped his hands back into the water and repeated the process. Mysse's teeth sunk into his bottom lip. Perhaps it was sympathy or focus or maybe a mix of both that made the dragon cringe. But Asith appreciated it.

When Mysse stopped, a cool shiver ran up his spine, and the pressure in Asith's head lightened, the sweat on his skin drying rapidly too. If his fever wasn't gone, it was at least drastically lower.

"Mysse." Asith's voice came out husky.

Mysse jumped, his hand moving to cover his face as if he might be struck from above. Asith didn't want him to be afraid, so he set a gentle hand on Mysse's.

"I won't tell." Asith coughed, his voice dry and hoarse. "Thank you."

"Oh." Mysse looked at Asith's hand over his.

Asith continued to hack and cough. "Water," he squeaked out, and then added, "Then go before they come to check."

Mysse slid the bucket close to Asith and put a full cup into Asith's hand before scampering off. Asith drank quickly and then drained another cup, his vision strengthening at the edges and his mind catching up to his situation. By the time he had filled a third cup, Dradevai entered.

They pressed an arm around his shoulders and tilted Asith upward. He continued to drink as if he had just escaped a desert. He didn't understand how his throat could ever be so dry when the humidity from the hot spring was leaking in.

Dradevai pressed their hand against Asith's temple. "Your fever broke." They brushed some hair back from his forehead, and tears streamed down their cheeks. Eroan entered with another pail of water and kneeled at Asith's side.

"I can't believe your fever broke." Dradevai clung to Asith and then refilled the cup, their movements stiff. Asith welcomed the touch, taking a few deep breaths.

"What, did you think a fever could kill me when a Blue or Green never could?" Asith joked.

Dradevai's eyes widened, and the frown that came over their face was deep. Eroan's features sharpened, as if he were ready to slap Asith across the face, and then he blinked away tears, turning his back on them.

"Don't joke at a time like this!" Dradevai sobbed, collapsing onto Asith's shoulder. But a moment later, they were laughing. "You're the worst! You never worry about yourself."

"I'm sorry. I knew you would laugh and it would help." Asith wrapped a heavy arm around their waist and Dradevai leaned into him, but he quickly discovered he couldn't hold their weight. "Oh, oh no, I'm falling."

Dradevai caught themself, but Asith fell into the bedroll hard, his head colliding with a makeshift pillow. Water spilled all over him, and he stared at the ceiling, unmoving.

"Are you okay?" Dradevai took his face between their warm palms.

"Yes." Asith slowly picked himself up with Dradevai's help.

"You're the same as ever." Eroan sighed, facing Asith again and wrapping his arms around his knees. "Glad you didn't die."

"Me too." Asith drank more water. "How long was I out?"

Dradevai's shoulders slumped, their eyes sliding over to Eroan. Yarrow shifted onto his lap, her ears perking and her nose twitching. Her nerves mirrored Asith's own, and his shoulders tensed.

"Four days," Dradevai said.

Asith choked on his water. When he gathered his bearings, Eroan lowered his eyes. His fine robes had torn in a few places, and the jacquard he had been wearing was gone, perhaps because of the humidity in the chamber. Dradevai wrapped their arms around their middle, their eyes puffy and their hair falling out of a short ponytail they'd obviously done several days ago. They no longer wore the coat Asith's mother had made them, and the sash she had sent for them was gone too. Then Asith realized the materials had been wrapped around his thigh.

"I'm sorry," Asith mumbled, moving his head to catch Dradevai's eyes. "I'm so sorry."

Dradevai shook their head. "If you hadn't done what you did, we wouldn't have been able to surprise Heskel, who had been activating a sigil to bring the entire facility down."

"Kosor was angry with you, but he never called for Heskel," Eroan added.

"I'm still sorry for scaring you." Asith set a hand on Dradevai's and turned to Eroan. "Both of you."

Eroan smiled slightly. Asith asked, "What about the little girl we were trying to save?"

Eroan's smile dissipated, and he slid his eyes to Dradevai. They threaded their fingers together with Asith's.

"The dragon, the little girl we were trying to save…" Dradevai's voice wavered, cracking in a way Asith had never heard before, not even when they discovered Asith's father had parents. "She didn't make it."

Asith's breathing slowed to a stop, his eyes moving to Dradevai's lips, which had pressed into a hard line. Eroan furrowed his brow, tears filling his eyes. "We got so many out," he said, his fingers balling into fists. "Just remember that."

"We did," Dradevai said. "We got so many out."

Asith took another long drink before running a hand through his hair. His fingers tugged painfully on his tangled braid, and Dradevai helped Asith remove his hand. His stomach tightened in the same way it had when Mysse had cowered from him moments earlier.

"But she was only a child." Asith pressed one hand to his face, not letting go of Dradevai's. Hot tears poured down his cheeks.

"We know." Dradevai shrunk. "We know."

"Did you manage to get the book?"

"It reacted much like the books from the Maeria Spire. The moment we took the ledger out of the facility, it turned to ash."

Asith's ribs tightened around his heart as numbness overtook him. He wrapped his arms around his knees and stared at the floor. A strange fatigue settled into his bones as a sorrow he couldn't quite explain filled him. He hadn't known the little girl, but that somehow made it worse. She had grown roots before she had even understood she was free. Asith wanted nothing more than to have gotten the chance to show her.

"What about the others who went to the Graveyard Trees? And Farin?" Asith's voice came out weak. He needed to hear at least one good thing.

Eroan's expression tightened, his tears threatening to spill over. Eventually, he said, "I'm going to get Asith something to eat."

Dradevai thanked him softly and met Asith's eyes after Eroan had left. "We haven't heard from the group that went to the Graveyard Trees. But we also have no reason to believe they didn't make it. Eroan cast that spell perfectly, you saw it."

"I see." Asith sipped his water. That was not the happy news he'd been hoping for, but Dradevai was right. Eroan had performed that spell as if he were a skilled bard reciting a poem they'd performed hundreds of times. Asith clung to that confidence.

"I'm glad you're okay," Dradevai said.

Asith thought of Mysse. His fever probably wouldn't have broken if it weren't for Mysse's intervention. He couldn't recall anything prior to waking up. Perhaps it had not been the first time Mysse had visited him.

"I could never leave you alone like that," Asith said and leaned on Dradevai's shoulder, pressing his nose against the nape of their neck.

Dradevai smiled. "Are you saying you're only back because you're stubborn?"

"Maybe." Asith peered at their face fully. "I think this is the only time I've ever seen you a mess."

"You've been dirtier in front of me before." Dradevai's lips curled into a feline smirk.

Asith chuckled. "I love you."

"I love you too."

CHAPTER 21

Eroan returned to the bedroom with food and a bottle filled with shimmering blue liquid. He offered Asith the bottle first, explaining it would prevent his stomach from losing the food if it was too rich, as they hadn't given him much besides broth while he was unconscious. Asith downed the potion and tried eating as slowly as he could, but it was difficult when he was so hungry. Meanwhile, Dradevai detangled his hair and tied it into a braid.

Idhe and Cemi realized he was sitting up and eating, and they hugged him with excitement. Cemi accidentally stepped on his wound, and Asith held his breath, hiding the deep cringe that ran through his body. Dradevai picked her up, suggesting she not treat Asith like a tree to play on, and she settled next to him after that, her small hands tucked in her lap per Dradevai's instruction so she didn't accidentally hit him while she spoke. Idhe sat patiently next to Eroan and questioned Asith's condition.

Eventually, Mysse walked in, holding the small pot that Farin had left behind, with Yarrow at his feet. He eyed Eroan and stepped around both him and Idhe to sit at Asith's side. Yarrow hopped after Mysse, her ears perked like a guard dog's.

"I thought you might need more than just jerky and bread." Mysse tapped the pot just as Farin always had, and a plain rice porridge appeared. That dish was rarely eaten in Cairn, since it came from the Zotia coast across the Western mountains, and Asith only recognized it because Delri's mother had made it for them once in Martivin while they were sick. She wound up taking care of them like children almost the entire time.

"Thank you," Asith said and patted him on the head.

Mysse grimaced, but he didn't pull away. Dradevai's eyes were glued to them, their head tilted and their eyes narrowed. But they pulled their eyes away when the kids distracted them.

Eroan and Dradevai didn't eat in favor of Asith and the kids having larger portions. When they all finished, they helped the kids clean up, and Asith took the chance to bathe. Walking to the chamber with the hot spring and getting in was not as easy as it once was. He hadn't looked too closely at his wound, but he had a feeling a large part of his muscle was damaged. Dried blood caked his skin and turned the water a pinkish color as he rinsed with soap. Something in his stomach welled until he felt like a hollow tree trunk rotting in the woods after the bugs and spiders had taken it, nearly reclaimed by the dirt of Desta itself. His breathing quickened as he ran his fingers over his leg, realizing how stiff it felt. It was as if the loss of muscle had turned his leg into a firm branch good only for supporting oneself briefly between steps.

He settled further into the water, his body clean, but his mind whirring. His condition might have been far worse without Mysse's magic, but even magic could only do so much. Even fully healed, he might not be able to walk or run like he used to. He swore quietly. Getting back to the Graveyard Trees would not be easy in his state, and he could not slow the group down. He hoped Delri and Pystra had gotten word to his aunt about the dragon knights moving toward their city, for they likely wouldn't make it in time to warn her.

The water started to feel like a prison, the lack of cloth on his skin making him feel too bare. He rinsed his hair one last time to ensure the blood was gone and carefully lifted himself out. After drying his body, he began dressing, but Mysse appeared at the doorway, rubbing his knuckles together, with his eyes cast down, as if to afford Asith privacy. Yarrow stood right in front of him.

"I will need to do what I did a few more times." Mysse shifted. "Just to be sure you're okay."

"Of course, we can find a way to keep it private." Asith kneeled to meet Mysse's eyes. "Thank you for what you did for me. I know you did not trust me."

Mysse lifted his eyes to meet Asith's gaze. "You really won't tell the others?"

Asith shook his head. "It's a secret that's not mine to tell, so I won't."

"Thank you. It doesn't…" Mysse's shoulders tightened, his eyes welling with tears. "It doesn't always work, and I don't want Dradevai or Cemi or Idhe to place their hopes in me only for me to fail."

Asith scanned his face, his reddish hair, and his freckled skin that so often reminded him of his mother. He laid a hand on Mysse's shoulder and smiled. "I can see why you hide it. I promise your secret is safe with me."

Mysse wrapped his arms around himself and cradled his elbows as tears ran down his cheeks. He hiccupped and rubbed his face as he looked down at his feet. "Okay. Thank you."

Asith frowned. "Do you want a hug?"

Mysse swallowed, still staring at the ground as he nodded. Asith wrapped his arms around Mysse tightly, his body small and his skin cool against his own, and then pressed his hand to the back of the boy's head. Mysse wiped at his face and pulled away from Asith, his eyes red at the edges. Asith stood, dipped his hand into the warm spring water, and cleaned the boy's face. He helped him dry off, and then the dragon, of his own accord, disappeared from the cavern.

Asith looked at Yarrow. "Thank you for looking after him."

Yarrow's whiskers quivered, her front feet extending forward as she stretched herself out. Asith smiled and picked her up to rub her cheeks and ears.

Asith walked back to the bedroom, and Eroan and Dradevai were exchanging tense words. With crossed arms, Dradevai studied Asith's gait and turned back to Eroan.

"We can't leave just yet," Dradevai said. "Idhe and Cemi's feathers have still not grown back properly and I've never even seen Mysse turn into a dragon, so I'm sure his wings were clipped as well."

"I know, but we will all be much safer in the Graveyard Trees." Eroan rubbed his temples, sounding exhausted by the debate. It might not have been the first time they had discussed that topic. "Asith, please. We need to go, we're still so close to the facility."

"But we are completely hidden!" Dradevai's arms fell with a slap to their thighs. "Asith just woke."

"I'm not saying we leave tonight…"

"But you're saying we leave tomorrow night." Dradevai set their shoulders back.

Asith set Yarrow down to avoid their gazes. He didn't know at all what the best solution was. Idhe and Mysse were too big to carry that far, and Asith probably couldn't ride on Dradevai's back in his state. But leaving immediately would mean getting back to his parents, his aunt, and even Farin faster. His concern for their safety quickly overshadowed his own need to heal, though he knew it shouldn't.

"I'm not sure what the answer is either." Asith took a few stunted steps toward them, his hand finding Dradevai's. "But I don't want to lose Mysse, Cemi, or Idhe. We've already lost one."

"I know!" Dradevai snapped, their eyes welling with tears. They looked at their feet, their brow furrowed. "I know."

Eroan and Asith exchanged a look, and to Asith's surprise, Eroan softened. He leaned toward Dradevai, gaining their attention.

"I understand Dradevai," Eroan said. "If Uri were in Asith's position,

I would not want to move yet either. But staying could leave us in a far more dangerous position."

"We can't fly, though," Dradevai said. "There is no way with where Asith's injury is, and I have no idea if Mysse can fly at all."

"Then we walk." Asith squeezed Dradevai's hand. "I've done it once before."

"When you weren't injured." Dradevai sighed. "I know you both are right. I really do."

"I have a way to shroud us on the ground." Eroan tapped a pouch on his belt three times, and it turned into a thick tome. That book differed from the simplistic one Eroan had carried with the dragon knights; it was made of purple suede, the design on the cover a mix of Endethi symbols with an opal inlaid in it.

"If we can stay hidden until we're deep enough in the mountains, we'll be much safer," Asith said.

Eroan opened the spell book to the proper page, and Dradevai took it. They read over the spell carefully, the lines of their face hard, but their expression ultimately softened.

"This spell is rather foolproof." Dradevai returned the book to Eroan. "But do you think you could beat someone like Heskel or…that other one."

"Elaqen," Asith provided.

"Yes, Elaqen."

Eroan sighed and shifted on his feet as he studied the spell book. "Elaqen is much more experienced than me. He has hundreds of years of study as an elf, and his magic is often difficult to predict."

"So… no?" Dradevai let go of Asith's hand and crossed their arms.

"That is not what I said." Eroan groaned. "We do not know if Elaqen will even be looking for us, and Heskel, I can handle."

"What if I handle Elaqen if we see him?" Asith asked.

They both stared at him, their mouths agape. While Dradevai and Eroan differed in unique ways, they both knew how to make one feel horribly small and illogical upon saying a single sentence.

"I am being serious. I may not be able to go toe to toe with him when it comes to magic, but if I snuck up on him and used a sword…"

Dradevai and Eroan didn't respond right away. Then Eroan said, "I know he can't see through your charm, but you're still rather hurt."

"And I hate to ask this," Dradevai said, "but do you think you can move fast enough?"

Asith's stomach tightened, constricting all the way to his throat, as if a root had wrapped itself around his innards and traveled up like a vine to hold him in a vice. But he nodded anyway. "I will move fast enough if it means protecting you all."

Eroan and Dradevai exchanged a look that meant they still didn't believe him. Asith looked at his leg, wondering if anything else might convince them. They might be right, though, and as much as Asith didn't like the feeling, he might need to acknowledge that.

"How about this?" Eroan said. "We wait three days, and if Asith is walking better, we move. For now, we'll discuss how we'll handle Heskel or Elaqen if we see them."

"That gives us time to gather food too." Dradevai straightened. "And time for us to think about Asith's idea."

Asith perked up, for he had expected to make a stronger case for himself. He nudged Dradevai's arm. "Thank you, Vai."

Dradevai looked up at him, their face still wrinkled with worry but their smile seeming genuine. They weren't just trying to placate Asith for the moment.

"Okay," Eroan said. "I think that's a good plan."

They divided up their duties for the following few days. Eroan and Dradevai took on more talks than Asith, which he couldn't really argue with. He could sew, but moving around too much wouldn't be good for his healing process. With Mysse's magic, though, Asith hoped he could walk well enough for them to leave in three days. That was the most important thing even if he still thought they should reconsider his idea about Elaqen.

The following evening, Asith couldn't find Dradevai in any of the caverns. They had been frantically preparing the kids for departure and helping Eroan gather the components for several spells. He approached the small ledge that hung over the canyon, the sound of the rushing water loud even from that far up. There, he found Dradevai, their arms draped around one leg and their other hanging over the ledge.

"Vai." Asith walked to their side. He had just finished another session with Mysse, and his leg felt better, though not all his movement was quite back yet. However, it didn't feel so much like he was turning into a yew tree, as some of his ancestors apparently had.

"Sorry," Dradevai said, with their cheek pressed to their raised knee. They offered their hand and slid farther back from the edge. It would have been fine to sit on the edge, for if he fell, Dradevai would simply catch him, as they always did. But he appreciated the gesture, and he found it easier to straighten his injured leg out that way.

"It's all right." Asith kissed their cheek, earning a little smile as they leaned on his shoulder. "Are you okay?"

"Just anxious." Dradevai gazed at the rocky cliffs, jagged from years of the river water wearing them down.

"Is that something one can feel outside of a romantic context?" Asith asked. He still hadn't forgotten that question Dradevai had posed once; something about it tickled him in the present and when he'd been alone in the Graveyard Trees.

"Shush, you." Dradevai rolled their eyes and straightened. Their shoulders had grown rounder, and the slight hollows in the cheeks had grown into soft chubby ones, the ones Asith remembered so well. They even filled out the pants his mother had made them, their stomach squished by the waistband a bit.

"You know…" Dradevai said, setting their jaw on their knee. "Mysse asked me something strange this morning."

"What did he ask you?" Asith tilted his head, trying his best to play dumb.

"He asked if you had told me anything about him." Dradevai narrowed his eyes, but they remained straight ahead on the horizon. "He wouldn't say what, but he seemed to be testing you, as if you were keeping a secret."

"That is strange." Asith hummed, looking forward as well. "I don't know what he could have been on about."

Dradevai turned to face Asith. From the corner of his eye, Asith saw them huff, their bangs fluttering. "It is still unnerving how well you lie."

Asith looked at Dradevai, his mouth opening to explain, but they shook their head. "It's okay." Dradevai opened their eyes fully. "You don't need to justify lying to keep Mysse's secret if he asked you to. I trust you."

"Thank you," Asith said.

A quiet came over them, and Dradevai leaned on Asith again. They sat like that until the first sun dipped under the horizon and the dim light of the second sun lingered.

"When this is all over," Dradevai said, "do you think everything will go back to how it was? With the dragons hiding in the Graveyard Trees and the dragons in Cairn hiding themselves?"

Asith's breath caught, his eyes leaving the horizon to focus on Dradevai. "I don't. I don't know."

Dradevai stared at Asith, then broke the silence again. "I don't want it to go back to that. I think you are the only one who can stop it from happening."

"Me?" Asith was almost certain his jaw had hit the rock below because it certainly felt like his mouth had opened wide enough. He shook his head, certain that Phela didn't want that from Asith specifically. It was such an important job. But considering Dradevai's suggestion more deeply, Asith realized that might have been Phela's intention, which scared him. "Why?"

Dradevai chuckled. "Don't think so little of yourself, Asith. A dragonborn who trained as a dragon knight, protected people from Blues and Greens, but didn't get hardened into an unfeeling person, so much so that you felt sympathy for me even after I kidnapped you."

"That was very different."

"Was it, though? Once you found sympathy for me, never once did you hate a dragon simply for being one."

Asith studied his hands in his lap. "I guess that is true. But I am just a person."

"Exactly," Dradevai said firmly, with a bright smile. "Who better to appeal to the people than just a person?"

"I'm not sure I understand. What are you suggesting, exactly? That, after this, I become a diplomat?"

Dradevai chuckled. "I'm not exactly sure what I'm suggesting. I just know that I am right about it."

Asith's shoulders sagged as he remembered the few times he'd spoken in front of new recruits at the Stonegarde. One time, he had explained the drills out of order, causing confusion and chaos when the recruits started practice.

"I would make a terrible diplomat. I am afraid of speaking in front of crowds," Asith said.

Dradevai laughed and kissed Asith on the cheek. They tucked his bangs behind his ear and adjusted his braid on his shoulder. When they pressed a warm hand to Asith's jaw, he couldn't help but smile.

"Okay, then maybe not a diplomat," Dradevai said. "But I do think you will be important. You were chosen by Phela; do you even know what that means?"

"Honestly, not really." Yarrow nosed her way under Asith's arm, and he allowed her to climb into his lap. She fell asleep fast.

Dradevai laughed. "I think you should find out on your own, then." Dradevai's honey eyes simmered with something Asith couldn't place. It was as though they were seeing all of him at once, making him feel bare. Yet it soothed him.

"Wait." Asith frowned. "No, tell me."

Dradevai giggled, shaking their head.

"You're so childish sometimes," Asith said. He could already tell he would not win the argument, and part of him wondered whether Dradevai had gotten better at hiding information or they just had no idea.

"What can you expect from someone who raised themself?" Dradevai shrugged, a smug smile lingering on their lips. Asith liked the thought that they had somewhat come to terms with their childhood. "I mean, it seems like it's so much easier when someone is simply telling you things, like we do with Mysse, Idhe, and Cemi."

Asith snorted. "You know, I would believe that."

Dradevai leaned on Asith lightly, as if they were a large dog that had figured out they couldn't lean fully on a small child. Asith nestled his nose in their hair as the wind moved his braid against his back.

CHAPTER 22

8th of Katib

Eroan pressed his palm over his mouth as Dradevai replicated the movements needed for Asith's lightning spell. "Something about it isn't right," he said, shaking his head.

"But I felt the lightning, briefly, when I was fighting Kosor." Asith looked over his wand and the spell circle in his book. "I could feel my own lightning inside me. Shouldn't that help me cast this spell?"

Dradevai crossed their arms, their mouth pinched into a tight circle. After not having much insight to help Asith, they had sought Eroan's assistance.

"I know, but it's hard to say what's wrong without seeing your father cast the spell." Eroan sighed. "The spell is rather anachronistic, and I generally don't cast with a wand. If I were to cast a spell like this, it would work differently."

"It's all right." Asith's shoulders slumped. With his injury and inability to cast a lightning spell, he wasn't really acting as the champion of Phela. "I was hoping I would have it before we potentially ran into Heskel or Elaqen again."

"Don't get too bogged down worrying about them," Dradevai said. "It's not like Eroan and I together couldn't overpower one of them."

"What if we get separated for some reason? We need a plan for that too."

Yarrow hopped between Asith's feet and wiggled her tail. She looked at Asith on her back legs and sniffed near his knee, though she couldn't quite reach it. The dim light in the cave made her look more like a shadow than a small animal. Her soft fur shimmered in the torchlight.

"I know…" Dradevai said.

With his eyes fixated on Yarrow, Asith assumed Dradevai was exchanging a look with Eroan. If he couldn't attack, Yarrow suggested, maybe he could defend. He agreed. A shield could be just as helpful.

"Vai, Pystra told me once you were better at shield magic than anyone she'd ever seen."

"Really?" Dradevai smiled. "I used it when I was moving rocks around on the mountainside. Sometimes they fell."

Asith frowned. "How old were you?"

"Probably no older than Idhe is now." Dradevai pursed their lips. "Why?"

"Well, I was thinking, maybe how long you've been doing it has something to do with how good you've gotten." Asith shifted his weight off his injured leg. "But more importantly, I was thinking maybe I'd be better off learning to make a shield than learning to shoot lightning."

Magic was still magic. He could probably live up to Phela's expectations if he could hone a skill he already knew. Like his mother used to say, it was easier for a sewist to learn a new stitch than it was to knit.

"Eroan would probably be much better if you want to learn about using shields in battles," Dradevai said, shifting his glance to Eroan. He had returned to whatever spell preparation he'd been doing before Dradevai had interrupted him. "I have to admit, we cast spells very differently, but he is very good at what he does."

The admiration that tinged Dradevai's words reminded Asith of how he spoke about Delri. Dradevai had made a friend on their own, without kidnapping anyone.

"I want to learn from you first." Asith stepped toward Dradevai. "I'll learn from Eroan, too, but you taught me magic in the first place. Your method may work better than Eroan's or the way my father taught me."

"I'll teach you, then." Dradevai's ears twitched, just the slightest hint of pink touching the tips.

Dradevai started with teaching the movements, since they might come more naturally to Asith. Once Asith got those down, they already wanted Asith to rest and eat food, even though he wanted to keep going. Eroan was preparing food for the kids with Farin's cauldron. Mysse had planted himself between Eroan and the others, his posture closed off to the mage. It seemed as if his distrust for Asith had simply transferred to Eroan. Though, he could tell the distrust bothered Eroan more, with his crinkled brow and pursed lips. Asith would have to advise him not to take it personally when he caught him alone.

Meanwhile, Idhe and Cemi had taken a shine to the mage, though, following him around like ducklings, involving themselves in whatever he was doing. Eroan included them, only saying no when something could be dangerous. Therefore, they treated him more like a parent and less like a friend or a sibling, as Farin had been to them.

After the kids had eaten, Mysse led Asith into a vacant cavern to do another healing session. The water didn't sting as much as the first time he remembered; he didn't want to know how it might have felt the first few times while Asith had been unconscious.

"Thank you again for not telling anyone about this." Water dripped from Mysse's fingertips into a small bucket of water.

"Of course." Asith snuck a glance at his bare leg, and it seemed to be missing a chunk of muscle. He looked away. Regardless, that method with Mysse probably felt better than the ways of a dragon knight healer. He wished the others knew how much Mysse had helped him. "You know, I do hope that, one day, you'll feel safe enough to tell everyone you meet about this."

"Maybe." Mysse's shoulders drew inward. "I may have to tell them once we're traveling anyway. Since there won't be places for us to hide while I do this."

"Well, I will keep your secret until you're ready. But I do think Dradevai will want to thank you for this someday."

Mysse nodded, the slightest curve coming to his lips. Mysse's boyish features were just starting to sharpen. He already had narrow eyes, which were deep set and tired despite being out of the facility for almost a year.

"Mysse." Asith shifted to stand. It was always harder to move right after Mysse's magic, but he'd feel better in a few hours. "Can I ask you something?"

Mysse offered Asith a hand and pulled him to his feet before picking up the pail of water. Then he looked directly at Asith and said, "Of course."

"After you're in the Graveyard Trees, and you're truly safe from dragon hunters and everything else, what do you want to do?"

Mysse's eyes grew wide as he scanned the rocks, and he bit his lip. But his shoulders relaxed, his grip on the bucket loosening.

"I don't know." Mysse turned back to Asith. "Honestly, I spent so much time locked away in that prison that I think I would like to see more of the world. But that's not really something I can do."

Asith inhaled sharply, his eyes darting away. He didn't want to cry in front of Mysse and make him worry. But his chest became cavernous and hollow, and his ribs began to crack inward, threatening to squeeze his chest so hard that he might cry.

But Dradevai's words about his potential returned to him, and his promise to Phela as well. The thought of being a diplomat still felt big, but a diplomat could work on making it safe for Mysse to travel.

He set a hand on Mysse's shoulder and kneeled on his good leg. He locked his gaze on Mysse's and squeezed his shoulders with both hands.

Mysse wouldn't like to be touched much more than that, even though he needed to be held more than any of the three children there.

"I'm going to make it so you can travel all of Desta safely, if that's what you want to do," Asith said. "I promise."

Mysse glanced away, a perplexed knot in his brows as he nodded. "Okay?"

"Sorry." Asith let go and hoisted himself up. "I think I was too in my own thoughts for a moment there."

"It's okay." Mysse looked at the bucket in his hands. "I would like it. If it was possible for you to make it safe for me to travel."

Asith started for the tunnel to the main cavern, but he stopped, turned back to Mysse, and smiled. "Then I'll keep that promise."

Mysse's eyes rose slowly, his lips pursed. "You're strange." He shook his head and followed Asith.

"What did I say to deserve that?" Asith said, his shoulders falling and his hands loose at his sides.

Mysse passed him. "You and Dradevai are. You're both so hopeful even though we're all so small and probably can't make a big difference anyway."

"I guess we are both strange by that standard."

Mysse turned around, his lips pressed into a hard line. Asith caught up to the boy and mussed his soft red hair as his mother had always done to him.

"You'll understand in time," Asith added. "I promise."

Mysse batted his hand away and grumbled. As they entered the main area, Asith chuckled, and Dradevai gave him a quizzical look. He settled where Dradevai was organizing their meager food supply.

"We had a good talk," Asith said.

Mysse shot him a look but said nothing, pouring out the bucket of water and then leaving.

"Interesting," Dradevai said. "Honestly, you would know better than me if that's the kind of face a kid would make after a good talk."

Asith snorted and stretched out his injured leg. "If I know anything from my own experiences, it's that sometimes a kid walks away looking like that, and, in several years, they realize it was a good talk."

"Several years?" Dradevai shook their head. "Why so long?"

Asith shrugged. "Just how kids his age work, I think."

Dradevai stared at him, perfectly still. "I'm starting to question your expertise with kids." They returned to counting bits of jerky and hardtack they'd salvaged from Asith and Farin's packs.

Asith laughed. "I never claimed to be an expert. I'm only speaking from experience."

"I'm starting to wonder if your experiences were maybe not average, then." Dradevai smiled. "I mean, from what Eroan has told me, you had an unusually close relationship with your mother."

Asith tilted his head. "What has Eroan told you?"

"Just that you would write to Maryan weekly when you lived in the Capitol." Dradevai shrugged. "I think he was trying to distract me however he could while you were still unconscious."

Dradevai slipped the jerky into a piece of wax paper, wrapped it with twine, and recorded the number of pieces on scrap paper, which Asith realized belonged to the wrapping around the cheese Farin and Asith had finished before they even entered the mountains.

"I don't think writing home often is that strange," Asith said and pouted. "But I'm glad that Eroan could be a friend to you while I was out."

"I wouldn't necessarily call Eroan…" Dradevai's eyes shifted to something behind Asith, and he turned to see what was going on.

Idhe was grinning from ear to ear as he entered the cave with a large rusted bucket. Something shiny had dried on his chin and around his lips like he had been eating.

"Dradevai! I found something very good." Idhe waddled over, his small arms trembling with the weight of the bucket, so Asith reached out to help him lower it. It was full of eggs the size of his palm. Asith had never seen eggs quite that large before, so he was lost to how Idhe had come across them.

"Idhe, where were you?" Dradevai asked.

"Just on top of the cliff." Idhe pulled his hands up to his chest, picking at a hangnail. "I flew up there really quietly, though."

"Was Cemi with you?" Dradevai straightened and glanced at the small bedroom behind them.

Idhe shook his head. "No, I went alone because I thought it would be quieter."

Dradevai's eyes widened, and their mouth dropped open. Their fingers trembled as they tilted one egg slightly enough to get a look, careful not to disturb the others.

"Did I… do something wrong?" Idhe asked. "I thought we needed more food."

Asith understood the boy's intentions. Farin's pot only went so far, and Eroan and Dradevai needed more protein and fat as adult dragons. During their travels, it wouldn't be easy to hunt for game, and eggs were a much better substitute than soup or stew; that was why Dradevai had always been eating them in their hoard.

Dradevai opened and closed their mouth, so Asith squeezed their shoulder. "Getting the eggs was a really good thing; we did need more food," Asith said. "But I think going out on your own was maybe not the best idea since we don't know who saw you, especially in your dragon form."

Idhe shook his head. "I only flew between the cliff and the entrance as a dragon, I promise. The geese nest was on the ground, so I just walked around and gathered eggs while they were away from their nests."

Dradevai's shoulders fell, their face dropping into their hands. They inhaled deeply a few times. Finally, they looked up. "You're so smart. Thank you, Idhe, but please don't do that again."

Idhe cradled his elbows. "I'm sorry. I did something I shouldn't have."

"It's okay." Dradevai smiled, but it was small and forced. Idhe accepted the approval and then ran off to tell Mysse and Cemi they should both take baths to prepare for departure the following day.

"That boy is going to kill me." Dradevai sighed, leaning all the way back onto the rocks, their hair splayed out like a halo, cut only by their horns.

"Where in hell did you get all of these eggs?"

Asith jumped at the sound of Eroan's voice. He hadn't seen the mage approaching. Dradevai snorted, rolling over onto their side as their laughs echoed.

Eroan stood over the bucket with an armful of herbs wrapped in cloth. "There's like two dozen eggs in here. Why didn't you tell me about them? I just spent an hour trying to find a deer and then gave up."

Eroan set a hand on his hip, blowing his bangs out of his face. He no longer maintained his manicured hair, typically pushed up into a beautiful coif, which seemed strange to Asith. He remembered him constantly going out of his way to fix it and trim it even when they'd been fighting Blues and Greens for days.

"I forgot you were out hunting," Asith said.

Dradevai was still laughing, their arms wrapped around their middle. Eroan was glowering and nudged their leg with his foot.

"Would you quit it?" Eroan crossed his arms. "It's not that funny."

"It's a little funny," Asith said.

Eroan moved to nudge Asith's leg too but thought better of it.

"Sorry." Dradevai sat up, still giggling. "You were just so annoyed over some goose eggs."

Eroan sat and piled the herbs with the rest of the food. "It's fine. Honestly, it's good that you both seem to be feeling better."

Dradevai plucked the herbs off the cloth and recorded the numbers on the paper. "Do you still feel good about leaving tomorrow?"

Eroan took some eggs out and set them on the cloth. "I feel much better now that we have all these goose eggs." Eroan turned one over in his hands. "Just one of these is probably enough for a meal for the littlest ones. Mysse might need two."

"How much more do you think Mysse needs than Cemi and Idhe in general?"

Asith couldn't contribute too much to their conversation, as he had never learned to fish or hunt and couldn't move around well enough to set traps, which he knew how to do on a basic level. He listened to their conversation in case there was a way he could help. They observed that Mysse hadn't eaten game, but he would eat fish.

When the conversation waned, Asith felt antsy, his fingers running along the seam of his leggings. Then he asked Dradevai, "Do you have time for another shield lesson?"

"I do," Dradevai said. They quickly explained their ledger system to Eroan and let him log the food before helping Asith to his feet.

Asith stood awkwardly with his wand in hand about twenty feet from them. He'd been using it as a cane, even though it was a bit too short, but without it, he had little support for his injury. While Dradevai prepared a heatless fire spell, Asith pushed his shoulders back and breathed deeply. When they cast the magic, Asith spun his wand clockwise in his fingers. It was like trying to play a lute for the first time; the movement didn't come naturally.

He gave up on that gesture and instead pulled down the roll of fabric as his father had taught him. But Dradevai's spell went right through it. Asith groaned.

"Your form is terrible," Eroan said, his pencil loose in his fingers.

Dradevai dismissed Eroan with a wave. "Don't be mean, he's still new to this."

"Yes, how about we let you use a sword for everyone to watch?" Asith said. He remembered how terrible Eroan was with just about any weapon, even a short sword.

"Oh." Eroan floated into a standing position. "A sword? That's a much better idea."

"What do you mean?"

Eroan lined up his shoulders with Asith's, though Eroan was a bit shorter. "I've seen you spin your sword in all sorts of weird ways. You should try what Dradevai taught you, but instead of spinning your wand with your fingers, spin it like you would your sword."

Dradevai's ears twitched and perked up, much like Yarrow's would. "That's a really good idea, actually."

Asith shrugged and adjusted his grip around the wand, near the end. The ball with the dragon at the tip felt heavy enough that he believed he might be successful in trying Eroan's suggestion. He flicked his wrist as he'd always done with his sword, and the wand slid over the back of his hand before it wrapped around and fell back into his palm.

Yarrow nestled herself between his feet, her little nose moving quickly as she looked up at him. "I'm glad you have confidence in me, Yarrow," Asith said.

Dradevai chuckled. "Let's try the spell again."

"And hold on to the confidence that Yarrow has in you," Eroan added and took a few steps backward. "You must remember that the trick to magic is imposing your will. You need the confidence that you can stop Dradevai's spell like you would with a physical shield."

Asith sighed and shifted his feet. "Okay, okay, I'll try."

He extended his wand with his hand on the end. When Dradevai pitched the spell at him, Asith set his jaw, spun the wand over his hand, and chanted. Yarrow nudged his leg with her nose. A silver shield materialized in front of him, round like the one he'd carried as a dragon knight. If that shield could stop acid, then it could stop Dradevai's spell. He finished his chant, and Dradevai's spell dispersed across the glimmering surface, while blue lightning bounced within the edges of the spell.

"Good job," Eroan said with a small smile. Dradevai hopped as the shield dissipated. Then they fell into a low stance, a mischievous look on their face before shooting a much faster spell at Asith.

Come visit me before you leave. I want to help you.

Asith flinched, unsure where the voice had come from. He spun his wand and chanted, then blocked the spell with another shield. Eroan scurried into the corner by the food, his eyes wide as Dradevai shifted their position and shot a third spell. He blocked that as well, and Dradevai was behind him, out of sight.

"Vai, I'm not—" Asith couldn't turn easily because of his leg, so he twisted around at the waist and chanted, pointing his wand toward

Dradevai's voice. The shield caught the edge of the spell, and flames licked at his clothes, though they didn't catch on the fabric.

"Good job!" Dradevai said at his side.

"Please don't do that again." Asith scanned the room for the source of the voice that had beckoned him. Cemi and Idhe were playing at the far end of the cavern, but it must have been them. It was the only option that made sense, even though the voice had echoed.

Dradevai laughed and kissed his shoulder. "Sorry, but I knew you could do it." Dradevai picked up Yarrow, who had been cowering against Asith's boot. "Sorry to you too."

They kissed Yarrow on the top of her head and rubbed her cheek until her whiskers pointed in all different directions on one side. Yarrow's eyes slowly closed, her ears falling back as she leaned into Dradevai's touch.

"It's okay," Asith said. "It did work, after all."

Dradevai grinned. "It did."

Asith's chest swelled with pride, even though he had only blocked a practice spell. It might not have been the lightning spell, but successfully casting the shield with Dradevai's pressure to go faster eased his mind about failing. He couldn't move as quickly as he used to, but he could at least shield himself and the others.

"You two should keep practicing," Eroan called from the floor by the food. "Asith needs it."

Asith pouted. "I'm going to tell Delri how much you're making fun of me when I see her next."

Eroan flinched like a younger sibling who knew their older sister was going to be angry with them. But he laughed and counted eggs. "I guess I deserve that."

They practiced well into the night, with real spells from a farther distance, only stopping once for Eroan to herd the kids into their beds. Then Eroan made Asith practice his forms without casting, and though his leg ached, he kept doing as Eroan said. He craved rest, but practice was the only way to protect himself.

CHAPTER 23

9th of Katib

Asith stood on the cliff side just above the entrance to the cave. It was strange to think they weren't coming back there. With his wand poised as a cane, Asith watched Yarrow lick her front feet and then bathe the rest of her body with a tilt to her head that was cuter than any animal he'd ever seen. She wiggled her tail and hopped toward some mostly dead grass to eat.

He'd dismissed the strange voice from the night before, but as the leaves rustled in the wind, he remembered that voice again. It hadn't sounded like a cavernous echo, but more like the fading edges of a dying wind.

Dradevai flew over the edge of the cliff, their feathers splayed out to propel them upward. They cradled Mysse in one of their large paws, their talons retracted, and carefully set him near Asith. Their wings blotted out the light of the second sun for only a moment before turning into their smaller form, smoke billowing around them. When they landed on their feet, Cemi and Idhe fluttered over the cliff with odd movements, thanks to their clipped wings. Eroan's sleek silver form followed them in case one of the children fell.

Idhe and Cemi both transitioned into their smaller forms mid-air, and Idhe landed on his feet with a wobble while Cemi promptly fell over. She popped up quickly, though, her eyes alight with excitement as Eroan landed behind her in his smaller form.

"I was finally able to make it all the way on my own!" Cemi cheered and ran toward Dradevai, preening at Dradevai's praise. Farin's pot clanked against her pack, hooked to the outside via a fabric braid. Each of the kids had been given one item to keep track of and carry, which took the weight off Dradevai and Eroan. Cemi had requested Farin's pot so that she could personally return it to him, which had made Asith's chest ache. If only Farin was there to carry it himself. Asith would carry the lightest items, though he didn't particularly like leaving the five of them with the majority of the load; he and Farin had brought most of those items in the first place.

While Asith put his pack over his shoulder, his wand vibrated.

Come see me before you leave here. I have something for you.

Asith scanned the trees. That time, the voice had been closer, as if it were directly next to his ears. No one else reacted, busy with making sure their packs were secured properly.

He turned, feeling Yarrow step between his legs and set her front feet on his boot. She looked toward the tree line, ears tilted forward.

I'm right here.

That time, the voice had traveled with the rustle of leaves, leading Asith's eyes to a lone tree that still had many leaves on its branches despite the passing of winter. He approached the tree, realizing those were not leaves, but needles like those of a balsam or pine, with little red berries tucked among them. It was a healthy yew, the sole yew amongst the oaks and elms and birches.

The branches curled toward him, as if they were leaning to meet him as he drew closer. With his eyes, he traced the massive bows and the trunk, which twisted upwards into the sky. He remembered his father's words, explaining yew was in their ancestry. It wasn't as large as those in the Graveyard Trees but taller than the others nearby, its roots having already dug deep into the rocky ground, and neither animals nor weather had worn the bark.

Asith's wand trembled underneath his hand as Yarrow circled the base of the tree and sniffed it. When she returned to Asith's side, twigs and branches stretched over his head and engulfed him in a flutter of needles, dropping berries at his feet. His heart pounded in his ears as the branches secured themselves around his wand and drew it upwards. He clung to it, his hands sliding along the shaft, until the branches lifted him off the ground. The vibrations from the wand numbed his hand, but he managed to hold fast. However, the branches relaxed slightly, lowering him so his feet were flat on the ground.

It's okay, I will give it back.

The voice flooded from all around him as Asith realized the needles and branches had caged him at the base of the tree. Asith released his wand, and the twigs wrapped around it. New designs appearing like embroidery sprung along the flower carvings, and yew berries were inscribed on the shaft, the lines of the design dotted like a stitching pattern. The wood of the branches merged with that of his grandmother's grave tree. Asith reached forward, and the yew needles wrapped around his fingers as if they were holding his hand. He grasped them, finding their hand no bigger than Idhe's but the grip weaker.

His breath leaving him, Asith remembered the little girl in the facility, the dragon who hadn't made it. Her presence surrounded him, the branches pressing against his body like a hug. He embraced the familial sensation, and tears filled his eyes. The needles wiped his fallen tears away, and Asith hiccupped. That same strange sorrow he'd felt when he'd heard about her death returned to Asith: a tree hollowed out by bugs years after its death.

He turned toward his wand, which had become a longer staff, taller than Asith, but thick and sturdy to lean on. The twigs and needles placed the wand into Asith's hand and withdrew themselves.

"Don't go yet," Asith said. The charm from Phela trembled against his chest, and the wind kicked up, carrying a childish giggle.

He studied every feature of the tree. Wiping tears from his eyes, Asith turned to see Dradevai standing nearby, their eyes wide and their brow furrowed beneath their bangs. Even though it felt like he'd only taken a few steps, Asith realized he had traveled down a path through the trees and was standing in a clearing at the edge of the cliff, amongst the tall grass where the birds would nest.

"Asith," Dradevai said, extending their hands. "Are you okay?"

"I'm fine." Asith looked at his wand. "I think she wanted to give me a gift."

Dradevai pressed their lips into a hard line. "That is the grave tree of the girl we couldn't save. How were you able to pick it out so easily?"

"She called to me."

Tears threatened to fill his eyes again, his chest hollowing, but he straightened. She hadn't wanted him to be sad over her death, so he could at least try to accomplish that, even though a deep grief lingered in his chest and flickered in pain. The placement and reasoning of it eluded him, and tears pushed past his eyelids again.

"Why are you crying?" Dradevai's hands settled on his biceps, their face contorted.

"I don't know." Asith wiped away his tears. He wasn't sobbing, and his breathing was even but heavy. He longed for the ease of understanding his emotions, despite pushing them away in the past. He said, "Maybe even losing one was too much for me."

"Oh." Dradevai's face relaxed, and they rubbed Asith's arms. "Oh, Asith, I'm sorry."

"You don't have to apologize." Asith flattened his palm against one of his eyes. "You did your best to save her too."

"No, it's not that." Dradevai met Asith's eyes before turning their own to their feet. Asith felt uneasy as he tried to find the source of Dradevai's guilt. He already felt like he didn't understand himself, so he at least wanted to understand Dradevai.

Dradevai pulled their hands away to wrap their arms around their middle. They were wearing the coat from Asith's mother, the flecks of gold glinting in the light of the second sun's dawn. "There is something I need to tell you." Dradevai's voice cracked. "Though, I'll admit, I was hoping I would not have to."

Asith tilted his head, wishing Dradevai would simply say what they had to. But he wouldn't use Dradevai as an outlet for his frustration. Dradevai's face was tight as they closed the distance between them and Asith. But the words didn't come out, their fingers sinking into the fabric of their coat, their mouth hanging open.

"What is it?" Asith cupped their cheek. "I promise I will not be angry with you, whatever it is."

Dradevai shook their head. "I don't think you will be angry. I think you will be sad."

Asith pursed his lips. His ribs were aching at the hollowness in his chest, yet he had a feeling that Dradevai's confession would not make him feel worse. Yarrow reminded him that Dradevai's words might help him understand why he was crying. Asith kissed Dradevai's forehead and smoothed some of their hair down.

"The little girl, she looked a lot like you…No, that's not right; she looked a lot like Listesh."

Bile rose in Asith's throat, and he tried to swallow it, his hand shaking against Dradevai's warm skin. His mind raced with theories as to why she might be connected to his father. His father and aunt had never mentioned any other siblings, Lestash hadn't had children, and his grandparents had been gone for a while too. Perhaps his aunt and Thistin were suffering in ways he didn't even know.

"Her name, did she tell you it?" Asith asked.

Dradevai set their hands on Asith's trembling biceps. "She said her name was Raystash. She was a Silver, with gray eyes like Listesh's."

Asith's stomach churned.

"I think Raystash may have been Listesh's daughter," Dradevai whispered, but the statement had come rushing out, as if it had been on their mind since meeting with Eroan.

"What?" Asith breathed. Raystash could not possibly be his father's daughter, for he had been locked in that facility for almost Asith's entire life. If she was born knowing her name, she had to be Lestash's daughter.

"Eroan said that facility was working on creating dragons without having to capture new ones. Using magic to create artificial dragon eggs. I think Raystash may have been your younger sister. Maybe a half-sister."

His grip on the wand tightened. That facility had been exclusively young dragons, many being younger than Mysse. His questions ceased, as if he innately knew better than to continue asking them. Tears streamed down his face, a deluge after a broken dam. A sister. Of course Asith had felt that much sorrow. He had lost a younger sister.

Asith turned away and stumbled toward the tree again, Dradevai steadying him with one hand. It wasn't his leg causing him pain; it was the way his eyes burned and his ribs collapsed around his lungs and heart. He leaned onto the base of the tree for support and placed his forehead against the trunk. With a shaky breath, Asith pressed his palm against the bark, then ran his fingers over the crags and crevices, the fabric of his doublet catching on the wood. He had seen his father do that to his grandparents' grave trees, so, if anything, he hoped the gesture would give Raystash some form of comfort.

As he lingered in that position, a small hand met his own, and a forehead pressed against his.

"I'm so sorry I did not come sooner, Raystash. Thank you for saving me. My mother would have loved to have a daughter."

The wind picked up, and the needles shifted above him. Dradevai approached Asith's side and mimicked his gesture. "I will take care of your brother, Raystash."

The wind rustled their hair. Dradevai closed their eyes, remaining perfectly still as if they weren't breathing. When they opened them, their horns became invisible with Dradevai's touch.

"Thank you," they said.

"What happened?" Asith asked.

"She taught me to hide my horns like Eroan does." Dradevai ran their hand through their hair, and while it would normally catch on a horn, it didn't that time.

"I didn't realize that needed to be taught," Asith said.

Dradevai smiled. "I didn't realize it could be."

Dradevai turned toward Eroan and the kids, who had walked to the head of the path and were peering at them from a slight slope. The kids' faces were small, their eyes seemingly too big for them, as Raystash's had been. Mysse was standing in front of Cemi and Idhe, as he often did. They needed Asith to be their shield so that Mysse wouldn't have to anymore.

Asith straightened. The hollowness had left. If he could find a balance between the people of Cairn and the dragons, Asith could create a safe world for every young dragon. All that time, he had thought achieving balance would require some great magic. But as Yarrow stepped onto his boot, she reminded him a different sort of magic could bring knowledge to people. It was not complicated or spectacular like a lightning spell, but significant, like perfectly matching damask along a seam in a wedding dress. When they returned to the Graveyard Trees, he and Dradevai would form a plan with Farin, his aunt, and Pherrosh, and they would find their way toward his goal.

"We should go," Asith said. He ran his fingers through Dradevai's hair to feel for their horns but didn't find them.

Dradevai grinned, took his hand from their hair, and kissed his knuckles. "Yes, we should."

Leaning on his wand, he followed Dradevai back up the narrow path. He would call his staff Raystash, and both the staff and Yarrow seemed to like it. Between Mysse's healing and having something better to lean on, Asith found it easier to move. They crossed the clearing together, and Yarrow darted ahead, leading them down a twisting dirt path headed north.

CHAPTER 24

11th of Katib

Thick mud stuck to Asith's boots as they followed the river toward the Graveyard Trees. His new staff had been spared, but Yarrow was not so lucky; she had attracted all of it. They'd realized early on that Cemi and Idhe would struggle to walk through the snow caking the mountainsides and it was far too cold for Mysse. He'd taken Asith's doublet on the first day after it had started snowing within hours of them leaving. On their fourth day, near the river, it was finally warmer, and spring had truly found its foothold on the landscape.

Mysse walked with light footsteps despite the weight in his pack, and his posture was straighter. It could have been because he was no longer frostbitten, but they were also walking along the same river that their makeshift home had overlooked, so that might have brought them comfort too. Mysse would stand on the rocks and watch the fish swim by despite Dradevai and Eroan's concern for the rapid clip of water that rushed south in roiling rapids. But it drew Mysse in like an old friend. Sometimes, he'd draw diagrams of the way the river bent. The notes confused Asith whenever he caught a glimpse of them, but he wasn't about to intervene, especially if his method of recording data brought him comfort.

"I'm hungry," Idhe said, his eyes glued to the river. They didn't have any fishing line and none of them knew how to make fishing traps like Farin had, so it was as though they were staring at food they were simply not allowed to eat.

Dradevai's shoulders dropped, and they scanned the scarce tree line. "I could maybe find a boar or a deer."

"Boar don't live in this area. They're only farther south," Asith said.

"It's because they come from Froiland, south of here," Mysse said. "They haven't made it this far north because there are fewer farms for them to dig up."

Eroan looked at Mysse with bulging eyes. "How did you know that?"

Idhe and Cemi fixed their gazes on Mysse, who shrunk in on himself. "I am from the northern part of Froiland originally," he said. "Before I came to Cairn with the woman who adopted me after my parents…"

His teeth sunk into his lower lip.

That woman was likely the one who brought him to the facility. As Mysse rubbed his forearm and his eyes grew unfocused, Asith opened his mouth, but Cemi beat him to it.

"It's okay, Mysse. We're all safe here, remember?" She had echoed Dradevai's words, which they had said whenever they began on a path that upset them. For a few days, she'd been talking and diffusing situations like Dradevai, which made Asith smile.

"Thank you." Mysse's shoulders relaxed. "But I went to school in Froiland for a little while. That's where I learned it."

Dradevai hummed. "Well, if there are no boar, perhaps I could get a deer."

"Actually…" Mysse hopped off a rock and tugged on Dradevai's sleeve. "I could maybe catch us some fish? And we could stop for lunch if you can make us a fire? I think Idhe can clean them."

"I can!" Idhe chirped.

Blinking, Dradevai nodded at Mysse. "I can get some wood and start a fire, certainly."

Mysse removed Asith's doublet and placed it atop his little pack before stepping toward the river. Then Asith realized Mysse's woven sandals and feet were free of mud, as if he'd been walking above the muck. The fabric wasn't waxed or made to repel dirt, so that didn't make sense.

He stepped into the water, and his transformation began at his hair and flowed down his body as if the river water had jumped up and engulfed him. Asith's mouth fell open, lips quickly drawing up into a wide smile. Dradevai was also grinning from ear to ear, their eyebrows nearly in their hair.

Mysse's body was long like an eel's, something Asith had only heard about and seen drawings of in books. His toes were webbed and his tail was thick at the base, tapering to a point with a flexible fin that stood vertically. On each side of his wide face, next to his blunt horns, three little fins wiggled in the wind, reminding Asith of fronds.

His body glinted bright orange, like the petal of a poppy flower, before he dove into the water. They had all gone completely still as his legs folded in and his tail propelled him forward. As he disappeared, Idhe's and Cemi's mouths hung open. Asith's fingers fidgeted along the length of his staff, remembering when he would cheer on Delri when she performed well in a sparring match, but Mysse probably wouldn't like that. Instead, he looked at Dradevai, taking in the elated gleam in their eyes. They gripped the edges of their coat and bounced slightly on their toes. When their eyes met Asith's, their cheeks rounded and their eyes arched.

"He swims," Dradevai said, their voice holding an air of pride, like a parent talking about their child.

Asith chuckled and squeezed Dradevai's hand. "He does," he said. Dradevai giggled and gave Asith a tight hug.

A fish popped out of the water and landed in the mud with a *splat*, and Eroan grabbed it before it could flop back in.

"I'm going to go get firewood," Dradevai said. They set down their pack and flew toward the trees, and Asith stayed to gather fish with Cemi, Idhe, and Eroan. They used the nearly empty bucket from the eggs, though it wasn't quite big enough for the many fish Mysse was tossing onto the shore. But it held enough that they could start taking out a few to clean while they tried to start a fire.

Thanks to a lesson from Farin, Idhe removed the scales as best as he could. Eroan also had some experience cleaning fish, but not as much as Idhe. It seemed as if Idhe was instructing Eroan, who scrunched his face each time he had to put his fingers inside a sliced fish. Idhe found that endlessly funny. While Cemi continued collecting fish from the shore, Asith tried to start the fire with Dradevai, but it wasn't going as well as he'd hoped due to the wet wood and sticks.

"Here, do that thing where you just heat them without the flames first," Asith suggested. He crouched next to them, leaning on his staff for support. Dradevai frowned at Asith's posture, then breathed heat onto the wood. Steam rose, so Asith positioned his doublet around the woodpile to both keep the heat and leave space for it to escape.

After a few minutes, condensation dripped down Dradevai's face. Asith moved the doublet, and Dradevai breathed fire again, that time successfully lighting the wood. They grinned, wiped their face with their sleeve, and started to organize the bigger logs nearby so that they could dry.

Eroan and Idhe walked over with a few fish speared on thick branches. Pressing one end into the mud, Eroan angled the fish just above the flames that licked the sky. He then taught Idhe how to do the same as Cemi wobbled over with the bucket of fish. When Mysse stepped out of the water, the orange fin on the top of his head wiggled, then disappeared as he turned back into his smaller form, though "small" was not the best choice of description, as he appeared the same size as his dragon form.

"You did such a good job, Mysse," Dradevai said, grinning. When he approached the fire, they wrapped their arm around his shoulders and hugged him tightly. "You're not too cold now, are you?"

Mysse shook his head. "No, I'm okay, thank you."

Asith wrapped the doublet around his shoulders anyway, then ruffled his hair as the boy sat next to him. A smile spread across Mysse's face, which he tried to conceal. Eroan distributed the cooked fish to the kids first, but Mysse denied his portion.

"I ate several while I was in the water. It seemed like the easiest way to do things."

"Well, have another," Eroan said. "You caught more than enough, and this one is warm."

Mysse considered it, then took the fish and sunk his teeth into the flesh. Everyone else received one whole fish for themselves, but Asith waited to make sure Mysse would eat. When he began clearing the bones of the meat, Asith ate his own. It only had a little salt, but it would go a long way since they had only eaten eggs and jerky for several days.

Cemi and Idhe thanked Mysse for fishing for them, and Mysse hid his eyes beneath his messy bangs. Dradevai beamed with pride. Despite the cold and the mud, Asith felt as if he'd returned to his mother's home in South Cairn, shortly after they'd arrived from Dradevai's hoard, eating warm stew with them.

Asith smiled at the kids' chattering, recognizing the way Mysse smiled to himself when Cemi and Idhe were laughing. Mysse wasn't the most talkative, but he stayed present, much like Asith at that age.

They traveled along the banks for a few days, eating Mysse's catch of fish around midday before camping on the moss-covered forest floor. Asith heard from Pystra a few times, and she contacted Dradevai as well, but after that conversation, they seemed pale and quiet as they sat beside Asith. They then insisted he review shield magic again. He obliged, noticing their demeanor relaxing.

After practice, Dradevai's nerves seemed less frayed, though they still bobbed their leg. Asith asked, "What did Pystra say?"

Dradevai looked at Asith from the corner of their eye and pursed their lips. "She and Delri are moving northeast to follow the army, but they've seen a mage in the area searching the woods."

Asith's heart raced. "Well, if it's Heskel or Elaqen, they're in the wrong spot."

Dradevai nodded, then pressed their face into the crook of Asith's neck. They might be looking for the Graveyard Trees, but it was well hidden. He wrapped his arms around Dradevai, trying to put the thought out of his mind. Once they returned home, he could ask Dradevai if Pystra had implied the mage was looking for the Graveyard Trees.

Upon leaving the banks, they traveled on a narrow hunting path that turned frequently. It was easier to walk through than the mud but still wet as the snow came down more frequently, even though it wasn't sticking just yet.

On the evening of the seventh day, Eroan stopped at a rocky lookout at the start of a trail that led from the foothills to the mountains proper. His jaw fell open, his eyes blank and wide. Asith followed his gaze and saw that North Cairn, the ruined former capital city, was brimming with life.

Large groups of dragon knights moved about, readying glaives and large axes, their armor made from the scales of the Blues and Greens. Based on their gray uniforms, the infantry consisted of men and women who had likely spent their time patrolling the roads of Cairn but were preparing for a battle. But what made Asith's stomach drop was what looked like an unorganized group of civilians wearing no uniforms at all awkwardly gathering supplies, probably posing as a temporary militia.

"What's going on?" Dradevai pressed into Asith's side, his eyes on the city ahead.

"They've mobilized the army too," Eroan said. "I had heard they were moving the dragon knights but not the whole army. Nor did I know they were enlisting civilians."

"They're going to attack the Graveyard Trees," Asith said. His heart pounded in his ears, his skin prickling all over. The faces of the children they'd sent alongside Farin and Uri flashed through his head.

"We…" Dradevai's mouth fell open. "We can't do anything about it right now."

"But we can warn the Graveyard Trees when we get there," Asith said, then bit down on his lip hard.

Cemi and Idhe looked up at them with mild confusion on their faces, but Mysse's brow was scrunched, much like Eroan's. Asith hated seeing them like that.

Asith asked Dradevai, "Do you know the spell that Pystra uses to contact us? Can we get ahold of her or Delri?"

Dradevai pulled their spell book from their belt and flipped through the pages rapidly. They paused on an old spell near the front of the book, and their eyes lifted and landed on Eroan. "Do you have a piece of clear quartz?"

Eroan tore his gaze away from the city to dig through his bag. He opened every pouch on his belt but only produced a small amethyst carved into an obelisk.

"I can try to make that work," Dradevai said, taking the stone from him.

"We shouldn't stop here, though," Eroan said, tracing the trail that wound up and away from the old capital.

Asith's hair stood on end as the shape of wings appeared from around the mountain.

"Get down!" Asith shouted and grabbed the kids. He pulled them into the bushes and against the rock wall. Eroan turned to follow, but his feet slid out from under him and he fell flat onto his stomach. Dradevai grabbed him and pressed themselves and Eroan against Asith and the kids. Cemi and Idhe shook against his chest while Mysse faced outward, poised to move.

Asith's leg ached from moving too quickly and crouching without keeping his leg straight. Eroan pulled spell components from his belt and readied something Asith couldn't see. As the pod of Blues and Greens flew overhead, he tightened his grip on the kids so they wouldn't scatter in fear and get lost.

A Green locked eyes with Asith through a break in the bushes, its tongue lashing back and forth along its lips. But it didn't stop. It followed the rest of the pod passing over them and sailed toward the people milling around.

"They didn't see us," Eroan said and relaxed against the rocks.

"No, they definitely saw us," Asith said. "One made eye contact with me."

Asith stood as another pod sailed overhead. In total, there were two massive Greens and four Blues of varying sizes.

Dradevai grabbed at Asith's belt. "What are you doing?"

Asith met the eyes of another predator that was passing on a seemingly easy meal. His hands shook, his stomach between his feet as he tried to wet his horribly dry throat.

"They saw us. They saw us and continued anyway."

"Why would they?" Eroan looked over his shoulder and then out at the Blues and Greens descending on the people below.

"They're mimics." Asith gripped his staff hard, because if he didn't, he might fall over. "And they've been given an order to obey."

"That doesn't make sense. Who would be giving them an order?" Dradevai said, standing alongside Asith. Upon seeing the Blues and Greens breathe fire, they promptly told the kids to cover their eyes. The dragon knights broke into their units and began to fight as Asith had once been trained to.

Eroan said, "You don't think they're—"

The Blues and Greens didn't attack the dragon knights but focused their fire on the army and civilians. The ones who weren't trained to handle them.

"They're sacrifices." Asith swallowed. "Someone is justifying a war."

A silence crept over them as a Blue spit acid over a scattering crowd of troops and civilian militia. Then the screams echoed through the valley.

CHAPTER 25

Eroan led the way to the Graveyard Trees while the kids followed instructions to keep their hands over their ears and look only at the trail ahead. As the first sun dipped below the mountain tops, Dradevai was studying the spell to contact someone from a distance, the piece of amethyst locked in one hand. Eroan had increased his pace, so Asith glanced at them frequently, making sure they didn't fall behind at the rear. With their hair fluttering around their head and their face lit up by the glow of magic in the obelisk, they looked older somehow.

"How's it going back there?" Eroan called, facing forward. Asith wasn't sure whom he was asking, but Asith grunted in response. Things were going about as well as nearly jogging on a bad leg injury could. The sharp pain in his thigh did not wane, even spreading to his knee and ultimately his ankle. And they still had a few days of walking.

"I think I might have this." Dradevai held the amethyst up and chanted.

"Just be careful, I need that for some of my more powerful spells," Eroan said.

Dradevai brought the crystal to their lips and spoke. "Delri, Blues and Greens attacking North Cairn. We think troops are—"

The crystal hissed, and a crack formed at the base. In a flash, it shattered, sending bits of crystal all around them.

Dradevai squeezed their eyes closed and turned away. "Shit," Dradevai said, their eyes finding Eroan's.

Eroan gaped. "Fuck."

They looked like two children who'd ripped a doll in half by fighting over it, dumbfounded and ready to cry. Eroan's eyes grew distant, his arms going limp at his sides.

"Uri saved for half a year to buy that for me," Eroan said in a monotonal voice, conveying that his significant other would be annoyed when they found out.

"I'm sure Uri will understand," Asith said, even though he didn't know Uri.

"What happened?" Idhe called out with his hands off his ears.

Dradevai balled their fingers into fists, their arms shaking slightly. Asith touched Dradevai's arm as their posture turned inward.

"The crystal broke," Mysse said.

"I have another crystal?" Cemi said and pulled out a shiny river stone from her pocket.

"That's not the kind of crystal I need!" Dradevai snapped, and tears spilled down their cheeks.

Cemi took a sharp step back from Dradevai while her eyes welled with tears.

"*Dradevai*," Eroan said calmly, and Dradevai twitched. Eroan kneeled in front of Cemi and rubbed her back, the kind yet awkward gesture making her cry.

"Vai, hey." Asith stepped in front of them, with Yarrow stirring on his shoulder. "It wasn't your fault, it's okay. You were doing your best."

"My best isn't good enough!" Dradevai's voice cracked. "I can't even get three kids to safety, let alone stop an army. We can't stop an army."

Asith set their hands on their shoulders, and they hugged their spell book to their chest. They hiccupped and shook their head hard. Searching for something to say, Asith cupped their cheek, trying to still their shaking.

Dradevai stopped all at once, but tears streamed down their face. "We don't have time for this. Let's keep moving."

Asith pressed his lips into a hard line but squeezed their hand before turning back to Eroan and the kids. Cemi had calmed down and was leaning on Eroan.

"Let's keep moving," Dradevai repeated.

Eroan scooped up Cemi and faced Dradevai, who shifted awkwardly and rubbed the back of their neck. But they looked her in the eyes and said, "I'm sorry for yelling at you."

"It's okay," Cemi said and sniffled, rubbing the tears from her cheeks.

They started walking again, and even when the second sun had dipped below the horizon, Dradevai urged them to continue. Idhe stumbled a few times, so Dradevai picked him up. Mysse kept up on his own, but Asith felt aches from his toes on his injured leg all the way up to his abdomen. He wouldn't let himself slow the group down, even though his wound bled for the first time in days. He'd likely get a poor night's sleep with that pain. To help himself ignore it, he thought of all the people in the Graveyard Trees: his parents, his aunt, Farin and Uri, and all the children. They needed to warn them as soon as possible.

Yarrow reminded Asith of the little glass orb his aunt had given him. Asith assured her he hadn't forgotten about it. But with the army bearing down on the city, the people of the Graveyard Trees needed his aunt more than he did. He wouldn't call her yet.

"Dradevai…" Eroan said, his glowing eyes flickering toward Asith like a cat. "We need to stop."

"We should keep going." Dradevai kept walking, but Eroan stood in their way, with a dozing Cemi in his arms.

"I'm not asking your opinion. Look at Asith, we need to stop."

Dradevai opened their mouth and turned around to look at Asith. Asith forced himself to straighten, about to say he was fine, but his breath caught in his throat. There wasn't quite enough air in Asith's lungs to speak, and he leaned on his staff.

Dradevai saw through the act and stopped. They looked at their feet and mumbled, "You're right, I'm sorry." Dradevai walked over and wrapped an arm around Asith's waist to hold him up. He wanted to protest, but since they had stopped, the pain was all he could think about. He needed to lie down, whether he liked it or not.

"It's okay," Eroan said. "Asith, can you make the tent?"

Asith nodded and squeezed Dradevai's shoulder before heading into the trees. Per Asith's request, Mysse stamped down on the grass and bushes to give them a flat space to sleep, then offered his shoulder to support Asith. But Asith chose to sit in the clearing, his injured leg extended in front of him and his spell book to the side of it. Yarrow sat in the crook of his bent leg, the soft tips of her ears brushing his arm as he tapped the three sigils on the page. As he chanted in the way his father had taught him, the tent shimmered around him before solidifying into a dome.

"It's ready," Asith said. He closed his book and patted Yarrow's head before shifting himself out of the middle for the others to have space.

Mysse entered first with a waterskin in his hand and kneeled next to Asith. He soaked his hands with water and began the process for healing. Asith was surprised he was doing so with everyone around but didn't say anything. The magic made his leg sting more than it had in days, but Asith's leg was already sore. The edge of the pain was already coming off, so much so that he'd probably sleep through the night.

Dradevai, who had taken Cemi into their arms, was setting her down and giving her a hug. The moment Dradevai pulled away, Cemi watched the glow of Mysse's healing magic. They were all watching actually, but Eroan and Idhe were sitting on the edge of the tent as if to give Mysse space. Understanding dawned on each of their faces, starting with Dradevai and Eroan, then Idhe and Cemi. Mysse finished, letting the water drip from his hands just outside the tent so he didn't wet the ground they'd be sleeping on.

Dradevai approached Asith and sat hip to hip with him, cupping his cheek. "I'm sorry."

"It's okay. I want to keep going. I just can't."

Dradevai nodded and draped their hands around their knees. When Mysse returned inside the tent, Dradevai reached out and pulled him into a tight hug. They secured a hand in his hair, and Mysse wrapped nervous arms around Dradevai, making Asith relax.

"Thank you." Dradevai pulled back, tears in their eyes. "You're a big part of the reason he's still here. Thank you."

Mysse looked at his hands. "Of course. You two are taking good care of us."

Dradevai's cheeks rounded with a smile. They let Mysse go and apologized to Eroan after Cemi and Idhe had settled in a pile of feathers near him. Eroan ruffled their hair and told them not to worry. Dradevai swatted his hand away and returned to his spot next to Asith. Their mannerisms had transitioned to normalcy so easily, considering what had just happened, reminding him of his bickering and making up with Delri.

The kids settled in for sleep, but Asith stayed up with Dradevai and Eroan. They likely found it harder to relax after the events of that day, like Asith did. They had only stopped hearing the screams from North Cairn after walking half a mile away.

Asith dozed off but was startled awake by what sounded like soldiers marching. It had to be his imagination. Dradevai set their hand on his chest and spoke softly until Asith's thoughts could no longer dwell on the horrors of that day. Eroan drew closer to them, and Yarrow moved to lie against his stomach to help settle him. He eventually started snoring softly, but Dradevai continued to whisper.

"I was born Freer of Wings. My whole life, I have known that my distinction could help free other dragons. I didn't think it would be so literal…"

Dradevai's voice grew softer as they neared sleep. Asith felt calmer but wasn't sure he'd be able to fall asleep, but at least Dradevai could get some much-needed rest.

Asith didn't remember falling asleep, but he remembered waking to the sound of breaking tree branches. His eyes snapped open.

"There you are, with three of our missing products." Heskel's voice filled the dome, wrapping around them like the wind. "How lucky am I."

Something strained on the tent, then drilled into the delicate fabric of magic Asith used to make it. He extended his hands straight up, trying to grasp onto the threads to keep them from fraying, but they shredded.

And Kosor was upon him.

CHAPTER 26

12th of Katib

Asith clawed at Kosor's hands and arms to remove his sweaty grip from around his neck, while Heskel's chant kicked up the wind and flung broken tree branches. Yarrow bit down on Kosor's wrist, but he didn't waver, his wide eyes piercing Asith like a glaive.

Dradevai cast a shield that knocked Kosor off Asith, and he hacked, rubbing his throat where Kosor's hands had assuredly left bruises. He grabbed for his staff but couldn't find it among the bedrolls and their other scattered belongings.

Asith locked eyes with Mysse and commanded, "Take Idhe and Cemi and run." He coughed as static rose around him. Mysse grabbed Cemi and took Idhe's hand before disappearing into the woods. Asith thanked the gods he could rely on the boy to take care of the little ones.

Kosor moved to chase Mysse, so Asith reached for his ankle. But his fingers slipped against the leather strap on his grieve, and Kosor shook him loose before running away. Asith's breathing hitched. He couldn't let him near the kids.

Yarrow shot out and snaked underneath Kosor's foot. Within moments, Kosor stumbled as if a root had hooked on his boot.

"Yarrow, on me." Asith reached out and Yarrow returned, her forehead colliding with his palm. The light of the setting sun burst into the clearing, which made Kosor hiss and cover his eyes with his arm. That gave Asith enough time to spring off his good leg and secure his arms around his opponent's waist.

Kosor spun and punched Asith's shoulder with a wild swing. Asith stumbled but held his grip, surprised Kosor could move that fast despite his injury. A jagged scar marked his throat where Asith had cut him, but his wound should have been raw and tender like Asith's. Even the potions at the Stonegarde and the best dragon knight healers couldn't restore someone so quickly.

"You're lucky I was told to bring you in alive," Kosor seethed, yanking on Asith's hair. But Asith tightened his grip around Kosor's waist, hoping to buy time for Mysse, Idhe, and Cemi. Getting captured was much better than losing the kids. Dradevai and Eroan were likely dealing with Heskel, so he had to stop Kosor on his own.

The heel of Kosor's fist collided with the top of Asith's head, and he ground his teeth to offset the painful ringing in his ears. But his grip loosened, and Kosor tossed Asith off, turning to chase after Mysse again.

"*Halt!*" Asith called in Endethi, recalling the word his father had taught him and instilling the strength that Dradevai had instructed him to hone. A bluish, semi-transparent shield sprang in front of Kosor, much like the one Eroan had cast in the facility. Kosor bounced off it and grunted before smacking it with an open palm. Asith wouldn't lose his will on the magic he had just bent. He had created a shield strong enough to block a dragon's acid before, and even though he was exhausted, he would not anyone near the kids.

It worked, long enough for Kosor to spin on his heels, draw a short sword, and pursue Asith.

"Learn a little magic and suddenly think you can take me?" Kosor lowered his stance. "You never could win in a training match against me, so you're resorting to dirty tricks? Or is it because you still can't move your leg?"

Asith stepped back and drew his sword from his belt, matching Kosor's stance as best as he could. He couldn't bend his leg the way he needed to, but he extended his right arm, flexing his fingers and chanting. A shield appeared on his arm. It was better than a sword, and he could stand firm despite his injury.

"What? Don't want to talk?" Kosor asked. "Or do you only speak the dragon's tongue now?"

Asith smirked. "I don't need to convince myself that this is an easy fight like you do."

Kosor's eyes widened, and a vein in his forehead popped out against his sweaty skin. He had always been easy to goad. He charged at Asith with his sword low, then raised it to jab at Asith's face. Asith had anticipated that, and the sword glanced off his shield like water on waxed fabric. He swung at Kosor from below, but Kosor dodged the blow toward his middle.

Kosor's blows grew heavy, forcing Asith backward, and he took his chance to knock Asith off his feet. Asith hissed in pain as he tore through the shrubs and moss and his tail bone connected with a stone or a root. The pain radiated up his spine.

Laughing sharply and loudly, Kosor raised his sword. His focus broken by the pain, Asith had lost his shield and blocked Kosor's blow with his sword instead. His arms throbbed as he tried to turn his sword, but he wasn't strong enough.

There is magic keeping him going.

That was Phela. She was helping him.

But Asith still couldn't turn his sword with Kosor's weight bearing on him. Asith growled.

"I'm going to enjoy beating you to death," Kosor said with a grin, his dark eyes ravenous and sunken into his face. That close, Asith saw the magic coursing through his veins, wrapping itself like a blanket around his entire being. It clothed him, kept him moving, made him stronger. Phela was right. And Asith had to break it.

"Don't touch him!"

Asith had expected to hear Dradevai at some point, but the voice didn't belong to them. It was Mysse's.

With his arms outstretched, Mysse looked tiny compared to Kosor. But before his opponent could react, the boy slapped his water-covered hands over Kosor's face. The water flowed into his nose and mouth, and he released his weight on the sword, then dropped it entirely. Mysse clung to his back like a cat and bit Kosor's neck whenever he tried to strike him.

Asith sat up and searched the clearing for his staff. Upon finding it, he crawled across the grass and grabbed the end as Kosor fell backward onto Mysse. The boy wheezed and tears streamed down his face, but he didn't let go. Kosor's struggles grew weaker as he drowned in the water Mysse was forcing into his lungs. The boy squeezed his eyes shut.

Asith wasn't about to let Mysse live with the weight of killing someone, even if it would be self-defense. "Mysse!" Asith called. "Mysse, let him go, now!"

His eyes flew open and connected with Asith's. Then he let go of Kosor's face, and the water splashed onto Kosor's clothes. While he rolled over and vomited water onto the ground, Asith pulled Mysse up to his feet.

"Thank you," Asith said. "Get out of here, now."

Asith pushed him toward the trees, but he turned around to look at Kosor again. Mysse's expression was unreadable, containing a mix of fear and shock that Asith couldn't place.

"Get out, now!" Asith yelled.

Mysse turned and stumbled before running back into the trees. Kosor's vomiting stopped, so Asith faced him.

Asith. Use the charm.

Asith nodded at Phela's command and positioned himself in a defensive stance, making his leg ache. Kosor grinned at the twist of pain on Asith's face and stood.

"Too bad you're such a whelp. You should have let the kid kill me; you won't stand a chance."

"Says the one who was almost killed by a preteen." Asith dropped his sword with shaking hands and gripped his staff for balance.

Kosor scoffed, threw his head back, and bared his teeth. "What? No fight left in you?" Kosor stepped back into his fighting stance, sword extended.

Asith reached for the axe charm and spoke the command word. Kosor's eyes widened as Asith disappeared entirely. He dragged himself to the side, even though his leg hurt. At least the moss dampened the sound.

"Cheap tricks again, but what are you going to do without your precious sword?" Kosor picked it up, and Asith bit his lip.

"I made you cry once. Remember? By taking it. You had to get the commanding officer to force me to give it back to you. She only took pity on you because you sobbed about your mother giving it to you."

Asith ground his teeth together. He had forgotten that incident entirely, and tears formed at the edges of his eyes. But that sword wasn't his only connection to his father anymore; he was well and alive in the Graveyard Trees, waiting for him. Asith's muscles relaxed. He thought of his mother, his aunt, Pherrosh, and Farin. Kosor did not have any of that; he only had an employer.

"Asith!" Dradevai's voice sailed over the trees.

Kosor chuckled, making Asith's skin crawl. He couldn't reveal his location just yet. If he trusted Phela's advice, he could destroy the sigil anchoring the magic.

"Sounds like Heskel is overpowering them." Kosor positioned both swords at the ready.

Asith walked closer to see the back of Kosor's neck. The sigil had to be somewhere near his injury but also somewhere that couldn't be easily accessible by someone else. That's what Asith would do if he were imbuing magic into clothes.

"Did you run away?" Kosor asked. "Leave your precious dragon to die with a useless mage at their side?"

When he turned his neck to search the clearing, Asith's eyes landed on a sigil on his tunic that peeked out from the back of Kosor's leather breastplate. A smile grew across Asith's face, and relief settled over him as he lunged off his good leg. The move felt awkward since it wasn't from his dominant side, but Asith was able to set his staff on the top of the small magic circle on Kosor's tunic. He spoke the command word, and a flame licked at Kosor's leather armor.

"What are you?" Kosor yelped and spun, grabbing at his back.

Asith dropped his invisibility and smirked. Kosor took a sluggish lunge as Asith began a chant, and surprise washed over his face, likely because of his dropped speed.

"I don't think I'm going to feel remorse for this," Asith said. It rattled his bones to say it, but it was true. Deep inside his chest, sympathy for Kosor did not exist. He had bullied Asith for years, harassed Delri, and aided in the torture and death of his sister. His skin prickled at the thought of Kosor's blood spilling, but it didn't scare him to know that he would cause it.

He finished his chant and extended his staff straight out, causing the end to glow. Kosor tried to dodge him, but without the magic woven into his tunic, he had slowed down; even the injury on his neck looked appropriately fresh.

Asith commanded a translucent bronze-tined shield to burst from his staff, and lightning trickled from the sides, causing static to rise. It collided with Kosor's face and sent him flying backward into a tree. An awful *snap* filled the air, and the wound on his throat gushed fluid and blood. He crumpled to the ground and coughed before reaching for his sword.

After taking a few slow steps toward the tree, Asith picked up his sword and kicked Kosor's out of reach. "Funny how you mocked me for using magic, yet it was the only thing keeping you going."

Kosor grabbed Asith's pants, trying to form words, but Asith merely looked down at him, the sheen of sweat on his brow, and his rapidly blinking eyes. He ignored his instinct to help someone suffering and stepped away, turning to find Dradevai and Eroan.

Asith walked away, breathing as quietly as he could in hopes of hearing Dradevai's voice. Then he hesitated, wondering if he should find the kids first, but Mysse would take care of them. If Dradevai and Eroan were fighting Heskel, they might need him more. His heart raced in his ears because it was too quiet for a fight between three mages. He wouldn't consider that Heskel had somehow overpowered both Dradevai and Eroan. If he called for them, he might bring Heskel upon himself, which he didn't have the strength for. It would be better to hunt for everyone silently.

His fingers trembled against his staff as he took labored steps. His mind quickly turned into a chaotic tangle of yarn, even as Yarrow moved within his armor, trying to provide some grounding. Then the shape of a woman with a sleek, long ponytail appeared in the distance. She lifted her head in his direction, stumbled, and then charged full speed at Asith. He recognized her, but Asith panicked as he realized she wasn't stopping and he was too weak to stop her.

"Wait, Delri!" Asith called. But she knocked him to the ground, and they tumbled around, with Delri landing on top. He groaned.

"Why didn't you bring us with you to find Dradevai?" Delri cried. Her voice was thick, and tears filled her eyes. "You should have told us you two got separated sooner! You should have asked for help, you idiot!"

Asith's heavy body ached. He cried from both guilt and physical pain. "I'm sorry." Asith pressed his hands to his face, his palms stinging from holding his sword against Kosor. "Please, this hurts, get off me."

Delri didn't have the chance to move because Mysse and Idhe burst from the bushes. In his larger form, Idhe snapped his teeth, but Pystra appeared at his side and simply picked him up like a misbehaving puppy. Idhe squirmed in her arms, his wings and tail flailing.

"Get off him!" Mysse hit Delri with a tree branch, which was so dry that it shattered over her back.

Delri grumbled. "Hey now, this is *my* best friend. I will jump on him and yell at him for being a fool all I want!"

Mysse held the end of the broken branch, his eyes blinking. Asith mirrored Mysse's confused expression. Where had Delri and Pystra even come from?

"They're not a threat, Mysse." Asith shoved Delri in the ribs to get her off. "I promise, Idhe. Stop trying to bite Pystra."

Idhe kept wiggling, while Cemi peeked out of the bushes. Relief washed over Asith's body, his muscles relaxing. They were safe, and his chest swelled as he looked at Delri. She and Pystra could help him find Dradevai and Eroan. He didn't understand what the hell they were doing there, but he was elated to see them regardless.

"Have the two of you seen Eroan or Dradevai?"

"Eroan?" Delri asked. "Like, from our dragon knight unit?"

"Yeah." Asith laughed. "Fuck, do I have a lot to explain to you."

"You shouldn't use that sort of language in front of children," Pystra admonished. She set Idhe down and scurried behind Mysse.

"Pystra, I don't think this is the time," Delri said.

A shadow slipped over the trees, and Dradevai's feathers shimmered in the moonlight. They landed next to Asith, and Eroan's smaller shape followed over the trees. They both turned into their smaller forms and ran toward Asith and the kids. He felt the safe and familiar touch of Dradevai's hands.

Delri's jaw slackened. "Oh, shit, you weren't kidding about Eroan."

"Delri, don't talk like that in front of such little kids!" Pystra said.

Eroan hugged the children, and even Mysse accepted the embrace.

"Asith, I'm so sorry," Dradevai said, cupping his face in their hands. Asith savored the soft warmth of their healing magic. "Heskel did something to separate us. We were suddenly half a mile away."

Asith shook his head. "It's okay. I killed Kosor."

"You did *what?*" Delri snapped her head to Asith.

"Good," Dradevai said.

Asith gave Delri a thumbs up and caught her and Pystra up on everything, except the details of Mysse's backstory. With his arms around his middle, he mouthed a thank-you at Asith.

"That explains why these three were in attack mode," Delri said, gesturing at the kids.

"How did you two find us anyway?" Asith asked.

Pystra had been standing guard for them, but she looked over her shoulder. "Dradevai's message. We figured if you'd seen the troops in North Cairn, you were probably nearby."

"Wait, you got that message?" Dradevai's brow furrowed. "The spell focus I used exploded."

"It was muffled, as if you were speaking through a wall," Delri said, "but I caught enough."

"It's a good thing you did," Eroan said, "because Heskel got away from us. We should get out of here as quickly as possible."

"How did he even find you all?" Pystra asked.

Eroan withered, glancing at Asith. "We likely left some blood behind, which they could have used to track Asith. But I don't know for sure."

"If they have Asith's blood, we need to leave now," Pystra said.

"Could my blood lead them to the Graveyard Trees?" Asith asked shakily. Dradevai squeezed his shoulder.

"Maybe," Eroan said. "But it seems like they already know where it is. We should focus on getting back there to warn them."

Asith didn't want to argue further, but he also didn't want to risk leading them straight to the Graveyard Trees. Yarrow placed her feet on his shoulder within the armor and reminded him they likely possessed his father's and Pherrosh's blood as well. So, no matter what, they would find it. Nausea hit Asith as he realized that he and his father had arrived at the Graveyard Trees by walking, practically setting up a path an army could use to get there on foot.

"The kids can't fly," Dradevai said, helping Asith stand, "and Asith's in no shape to ride on my back."

"I'll be okay," Asith said.

"No, you won't, you complained about your legs for days after the last time we did that," Dradevai argued.

Asith's muscles were twitching, the adrenaline wearing off and the fatigue settling into his bones. Delri reached out to lend her strength as well.

"This is an emergency. It's a little different."

"Well, we only have two people to fly right?" Delri asked. "I could stay with Asith to make sure he doesn't fall off."

"It's not just two." Dradevai looked at the kids.

"Either way, we have to get out of here fast," Eroan said, then looked at Mysse. "Can you run back to get our things?"

"No!" Asith yelped.

Everyone stared at him. His reaction might have been overblown. "Sorry. Mysse, lead Delri there, but don't go back into the clearing. Promise?"

Mysse frowned at Asith, raising an eyebrow. "I've seen a dead body before, Asith, you don't have to be so protective."

Asith blinked, trying to find words, but Mysse turned tail and ran into the trees. Giving Asith a quick glance, Delri followed him into the clearing. She, at least, understood his intent.

"You tried," Eroan said. He then turned and introduced himself to Pystra.

Asith's shoulders dropped and swayed as Dradevai secured their arm around him. "He'll be okay," they said and rubbed Asith's back.

"Yeah." Asith's stomach roiled, and a weight settled on his shoulders, unlike the comforting weight of Yarrow walking on him. He had once again failed to protect the dragons, and he became more confused as to why Phela had chosen him of all people.

"I should be able to carry Asith and Mysse in my paws," Dradevai said to the group. "Eroan, if you can take Idhe, and Pystra, can you carry Delri and Cemi?"

Eroan nodded. "I can do that."

"I can as well," Pystra said, "but I think maybe we should try to get some rest somewhere safe and then leave just before the dawn of the first sun."

Pystra's eyes darted between Dradevai and Asith, and she wrung her hands together. Asith smiled, trying to present some assurance, because words were far too tiring.

"I think that's a good idea," Dradevai said, then looked at Eroan. "Is that okay with you?"

Eroan shifted, folding his arms over his stomach and hugging himself. "It is. I'm just… I still haven't heard from Uri still."

"I'm sure they're back at the Graveyard Trees. I know it's hard, but I'm sure there's a good reason they haven't contacted us yet.

"Who is Uri?" Delri's voice joined them from behind some bushes. She held aside the branches for Mysse, who was carrying most of their packs. He had likely refused to let Delri hold more than the few belongings she carried.

"My husband." Eroan took his pack from Mysse and examined the contents. "Pystra, you don't happen to have any pieces of amethyst, do you?"

"Wait, no." Delri set her hands on her hips. "You don't get to glaze over being married. Did you know about this, Asith?"

Asith gaped. "I knew about Uri. I didn't know they were married."

Eroan blinked. "I mean, none of us have really seen each other since we all left the knights."

"Well, yeah, but I saw you flirting with Asith in the library that time he and Dradevai were in the Capitol!" Delri crossed her arms and tapped her foot.

"Oh, yes, that."

Pystra offered him a small, round piece of amethyst. He didn't look too impressed but took it anyway.

"Uri knew I was trying to gather allies any way I could. They wouldn't have been bothered."

"W-What?" Delri scanned everyone's faces. "That's… allies for what?"

"We found my father in a facility," Asith said. "Eroan was working in another facility with Uri and some of the other guards there, with the intention to sneak the captive dragons out."

Delri's jaw dropped, and the realization set in as she studied Cemi, Idhe, and Mysse. With her face scrunched up, she set a hand on Mysse's shoulder, a distant look in her eyes, but he pulled away.

"I'm sorry for telling you that you had a bad attitude just a bit ago," Delri said.

Mysse frowned but accepted the apology.

"This situation is a nightmare." Dradevai rubbed their forehead, laughing darkly because it was the only way to react in a moment like that.

"It is," Pystra said and pulled another piece of amethyst from her bag. "I have news, which will only make it worse."

"Oh, good." Dradevai sat on the ground. "Okay, I'm ready."

Eroan sat as well, the kids slowly joining them. Dradevai held out a hand to help Asith down.

"We continued researching the Blues and Greens. It was much easier after Delri used her connections at the Stonegarde to help gather information, but it led us down a strange path. To a man named Elaqen Vetrish."

"We've met," Asith said. "He was the one who conscripted Kosor into this situation."

Delri rolled her eyes. "Of course, a terrible henchman for a terrible man."

Pystra continued. "His sigils kept popping up nearby areas that were recently attacked by Blues and Greens." With her finger, she drew a small diagram in the dirt. "Always hidden, hard to find unless seen from above."

Eroan leaned forward. "Those are summoning sigils."

"He's summoning the Blues and Greens?" Dradevai asked.

"Not just that, but based on the bones and scale fragments Delri helped me gather, we know the Blues and Greens are arcane in nature and were made by a mage warping their forms and commanding them to do their bidding."

Eroan's face contorted, and he pressed his fingers to his lips. "They're creating them and then unleashing them on the people of Cairn? To what end?"

"I'm not certain."

"They're selling the dragon parts," Asith said. "My father told me that."

Dradevai snapped a twig between their fingers, which held a slight tremor. "But they had plenty of dragons in those facilities to do that without using the Blues and Greens to attack their own people."

Asith put an arm around them and drew them close. "If people thought the dragons were a threat, then they wouldn't hesitate to hunt them and turn them in. They might even think treating them the way Heskel and Elaqen did was justified."

"Who would ever think that this is justified?" Dradevai bared their teeth at Asith, their eyes glowing.

"I know it's not something you'd want to believe, but there are likely people out there who would."

Asith could tell Dradevai wanted to retort, but they bit back the words in their throat. Tears stained their cheeks, glinting in the low light of the moon.

"I hate to say it, but he's right," Eroan said, putting an arm around Cemi when she pulled on his sleeve.

"No," Dradevai said. "No, I think if the people of Cairn knew, if they really knew, then they wouldn't think it was justified. Maybe some of them would, but I don't think the majority would."

Asith swallowed the lump in his throat. He wanted to believe in the people of Cairn as much as Dradevai and Farin did, but his family's story plagued his mind. He said to Dradevai, "Remember what my mother told you about her old town?"

"But that was because of that…" Dradevai waved their hands around frantically. "That story about the dragon queen who disappeared and then the dragons betrayed the people. You said it yourself, Asith, a long time ago, that story doesn't make any sense!"

"Story of the dragon queen?" Pystra asked, turning to Delri.

"I think they mean the story of Cairn's war for independence?" Delri said.

Pystra looked at Asith. "You mean the war between the king here and the people, yes?" He nodded, and she shifted. "I mean, my mother told me that the king took out the queen of dragons to try to stop the dragons from helping the people rebelling."

Dradevai's mouth fell open, and they pointed at Pystra, turning back to Asith. "See, I told you that the story didn't make sense!"

Asith had doubted the story since Dradevai had pointed out the holes in it, but to hear Pystra confirm their suspicions made Asith question everything he'd learned about Cairn's history. If the people hadn't killed the queen, then there was no reason for the dragons to turn their backs on them.

"I know your mother said that people hate the dragons, but I think that's only because they've been lied to. All so people like Heskel and Elaqen can sell dragon feathers or blood or whatever else."

Asith drew back. "Okay, I believe you. I'm sorry."

Dradevai hiccupped and took a deep breath. Their arms fell to their sides. "Sorry."

"It's okay." Asith rubbed their shoulder, feeling bad for making them feel guilty; they had only startled him a little.

Eroan said, "Then they attacked North Cairn as an excuse to move in on the Graveyard Trees, not because they actually fear the dragons living there but because they want to trap some of the dragons, correct?" His eyes were on the clouds, his breath creating plumes of steam. The outline of his silver hair wouldn't stay still. He was shaking.

"It gets worse the more we learn," Dradevai said, settling against Asith's side again.

"Sorry," Pystra said, "but if it helps, we can make it to the Graveyard Trees tomorrow and hopefully help protect them."

Asith bit his lip. "Something feels off still."

"I was just thinking that," Delri said. "Why would they weaken their own forces before getting to the Graveyard Trees?"

"Yes, that's the most confusing part." Asith furrowed his brow, chewing on his thumbnail as he remembered what Farin had told them about his father before they'd separated. The Cerulean Visage was receiving shipments of dragon parts from Cairn, so they would probably want the army and the dragon knights to possess the Graveyard Trees to gain more access to dragons.

"Asith." Eroan met his eyes. "If your gut is telling you something else, please share it. I trust you on this."

The group nodded at him with expectant eyes. Asith looked at Delri again. "I don't know." Asith rubbed the back of his head. "It just feels like they're trying to draw the dragons out or make them look like the aggressors, I just don't fully know why."

Asith's brain was so tired, and he felt like his stomach was going to eat itself if he didn't get food. He tried to put together the last bits of his thoughts, forcing the pieces of the puzzle together like the pieces of a sewing pattern. If he could just figure out how to stitch them together, it would make sense.

"This isn't really resting, is it?" Pystra asked.

Dradevai sighed and stood before heading to the trees.

"Vai, where are you going?"

They didn't stop, so Asith pushed himself up with his staff to follow.

"I just need a minute," they said tightly, like they might cry. Asith didn't want to leave them alone, so he gave the group a reassuring look so they didn't follow. They walked into the trees a short way before Dradevai stopped and rubbed their eyes.

"You didn't need to follow." Dradevai hiccupped, fresh tears running down their cheeks.

Asith slipped his arms around their shoulders and set a hand on the back of their head. "I wanted to make sure you were all right." He kissed their temple.

Dradevai set their palms on Asith's chest. "I will be. I didn't want to worry you by crying in front of you. You look so worried when I cry."

He ran his fingers through their hair, making them tingle. "That is because you cry so rarely. I know it means something is really wrong when you do it."

Dradevai looked up. "Like with the ghost in the Capitol?"

"Yes." Asith's shoulders dropped. "I was really worried about you that night." He hadn't admitted it to himself then, but he had been in love with Dradevai even as far back as that night. They had become like the second sun to him, keeping him warm in a world that had otherwise turned cold by his years in the dragon knights. He felt stupid, knowing he hadn't told them right then and there how he felt and how he wanted to keep them safe.

"Thank you." Dradevai set their head gently on his shoulder, their horns reappearing for the first time in days. "For worrying about me."

"I always will." Asith hugged them a bit tighter and ran his fingers over the ends of their horns.

Dradevai cried for a little longer, then pulled away. They had to return to their camp.

When they got back, the group had already settled into bedrolls and readied themselves to get a bit of sleep. That time, no one asked Asith to make the tent, and Pystra and Delri acted as guards instead. She lay in her larger form with her tail around the group while Delri sat up and watched the darkness. Asith and Dradevai went to a spot left open for them, and Delri apologized that there was not enough room for Dradevai to sleep in their larger form but they didn't mind.

Asith lay with Dradevai at his side, his eyes on the clouds. They looked like a single sheet of paper with a few missing pieces where the night sky poked through. The stars were difficult to see, but he found a few and counted them in an attempt to settle down. He should try to rest, but he also felt like he was so close to grasping the mages' plan. It wasn't clear how Kosor had fit in, or if he had only been a useful pawn. The connection between the Maeria Spire and the Cerulean Visage seemed the most likely and least likely explanation all at once. Nothing about keeping Pherrosh below the Maeria Spire where she could so easily be found made sense either. He wondered if he specifically had been baited or if they were trying to attract anyone to find Pherrosh.

Asith grabbed the charm, and Yarrow forewent the armor, settling on his chest. As the wind swept the clouds away, revealing the moon low on the horizon and more stars blinking down at him, Asith closed his eyes and pled to Phela to help him find the answers.

She didn't respond.

CHAPTER 27

12th of Katib

By the time the first sun had risen, Asith hadn't slept. His muscles were too sore to relax, but breathing slowly had at least helped him calm down. Neither Dradevai nor Eroan had stirred during the night, but when Dradevai woke, they didn't seem pleased with his lack of sleep. But Asith attempted to quell their fears by telling them he could sleep in their paw on their flight to the Graveyard Trees. Though, he doubted he could, and they didn't seem to believe him.

Yarrow positioned herself on his shoulder for the morning, her whiskers brushing against his neck and ear. Asith didn't understand what she was up to, but he didn't particularly want to argue. Mysse brought them fish, which Eroan and Idhe gutted, and Dradevai roasted them with their breath. That technique gave them an unusual taste, but Asith didn't say anything.

After breakfast, they slimmed down their supplies to the essentials. Asith hid Farin's pack, as the cauldron was too heavy and wouldn't feed them all, but he hoped they'd return for it eventually. Dradevai switched into their larger form and took Mysse and Asith into each paw. They practiced fluttering over the trees while Delri secured herself on Pystra's back with Cemi in her smaller form and Eroan held Idhe in his paws.

Eroan led since he knew the path to the Graveyard Trees the best. He brought them up into the clouds before spreading his wings and taking advantage of the wind to glide. Gliding required less energy and would get them to the city faster. Speed was paramount, as Asith did not want to find out what would happen if the army got there first.

The air was cold that high up, so Asith wrapped an extra doublet from Delri around himself. The group stayed close together, Dradevai hovering above Pystra and Eroan on the off chance that they accidentally dropped Asith or Mysse. Asith buried his fear of falling deep in his stomach but gripped one of Dradevai's down feathers just in case.

Asith searched the sky for Blues and Greens and for any signs that Cairn had raised an army against the dragons. Asith wondered how involved the Maeria Spire was. Many of the healing mages were trained there, and he doubted they would all ignore people suffering and refuse help. But he would figure that out later, after the Graveyard Trees was safe.

A clear section of sky gave way to a wide view of the mountains below. The massive column of grave trees wasn't far off. He scanned the paths and mountain passes and discovered the movement of marching soldiers, their helmets glinting in the sun. He remembered his father saying that path had been specifically carved to be seen from above, so that it could be followed by flying or walked on by foot. But it would lead them to the Graveyard Trees.

Asith put his hand over his brow to shade his eyes, and Yarrow shifted in his bag before popping her head out. She followed Asith's gaze to the red rocks of the mountains stark against the blue sky, the fluffy white clouds billowing over the distant snowcaps. That was when he caught an illusion, a shiver along the landscape, as if a gauzy fabric were hanging on a clothesline. The illusion was similar to the one that Dradevai had used to hide their horns, which seemed like ages ago. It was a trick of the light, a flick of the wrist, so well-placed that one wouldn't notice the sleight of hand fooling their senses.

The shivering broke, and Yarrow stepped onto his shoulder as they observed a spell circle in a clearing before the Graveyard Trees. The thick rings of the sigil were blurry, but they seemed to be in the dirt. He tried to memorize the shapes the best he could, though he had a feeling he knew what they meant. And if it was a summoning circle for Blues and Greens, the approaching army might get attacked again by what they thought were the dragons inside the Graveyard Trees. Asith ground his teeth. He wished he could have gotten ahold of Heskel the other night to confirm his suspicions, or at least asked Kosor more questions.

They eventually stopped so Eroan, Pystra, and Dradevai could take a break. While the kids played games, Asith explained what he had seen to the others. They had passed the moving army, but it still felt like they were moving too slowly. The dragons ate and rested, and Asith rubbed his leg to ease the pain. But that movement also helped him think, slowly, methodically, as he traced the fabric of his pants.

"Are you okay?" Dradevai asked, propping up an egg.

Asith studied their fingers, just a few shades darker than the shell, which was shining where Dradevai had washed it. The eggs had gotten muddy somewhere along the riverbank because they'd used the bucket for fish.

"I'm all right." Asith sighed. "I'm just trying to make sense of all the choices Heskel and Elaqen and the army are making."

Dradevai chomped down on the egg, the shell crunching softly. The sound was instantly comforting to Asith. "Maybe try to say it all out loud to me? It might help." Dradevai licked their lips and swallowed, their eyes wandering to Cemi as she stood on a log and declared something about being a princess.

"Well, we know they're making money off the sale of dragon parts," Asith said. "The Blues and Greens are a diversion to make people hate dragons, and we know that Heskel and Elaqen may have a connection with the Cerulean Visage since they're selling the parts to them."

"I've been wondering about that, why would they be selling to Wacot? Aren't there plenty of mages in Cairn?"

"It's strange because Cairn and Wacot don't get along."

"Why?"

Eroan joined the conversation. "Wacot has been expanding northwest for years, usually by force. There are fears they will eventually threaten Cairn."

Asith rubbed his jaw, remembering his conversation with his aunt among the grave trees. She had spoken about Thecoria's fears of Wacot advancing on them and had been worried since they had traded with the Graveyard Trees and thus knew the city's location.

Asith said, "If Wacot took Cairn, it would be easier for them to take the Graveyard Trees."

Eroan and Dradevai didn't respond, their eyes landing on Asith.

"Right now, the Cerulean Visage has to go through Cairn to get the dragon parts they need," Asith said, his hands shaking as he gestured. "But if Cairn was part of Wacot, they'd not only have free access to those parts but also have surrounded both the Graveyard Trees and the neighboring Thecoria."

Eroan asked, "So, you think that people like Heskel and Elaqen are actively working against Cairn?"

Dradevai looked between them with confusion. Asith would have to explain it in full later because he wasn't sacrificing his thought process that was finally stitching together.

"Yes, I know that the mages at the Maeria Spire are largely from Cairn, but I think some of the upper leaders like Elaqen are working with the Cerulean Visage."

"It's quite possible." Eroan shrugged. "It would explain why they were so willing to supply the Cerulean Visage with rather powerful magical ingredients, despite them being a foreign power."

"If Cairn's army was weak after a fight with the dragons, it's possible that Wacot could even offer aid in removing the faux threat of the Graveyard Trees."

"Maybe." Eroan grew quiet, receding into himself. Asith didn't know enough about Wacot or politics, so he might have been missing something. Wacot had a king, but he didn't know what his connection with the Cerulean Visage was. It was a theory, but Heskel and Elaqen could be summoning Blues and Greens to obliterate the entire army and have Wacot move in.

Asith took the axe charm in his hand, remembering the balance that Phela spoke of. He swiped his finger over the running rabbit, feeling for the scratch that he'd grown to find comforting. But that time, he couldn't find it. He looked down and flipped it to see if he'd forgotten which side it was on, but it was gone.

He still found Phela so difficult to understand. She had helped him in the fight with Kosor, reminded him of the axe, but the politics of the situation felt opaque. With the axe being fixed, that meant something had changed; he just didn't know what. Yarrow reminded him she was working in Viteus's shadow, so she might not be able to be clear with Asith, lest he find out what she was up to. He wished he had asked his aunt more about her, though Phela had told him to not bring her up. He could, however, ask his friends about her, which Yarrow agreed was a good idea.

"Pystra, Eroan, Dradevai. Can you tell me more about Phela? What balance does she represent?"

Pystra looked at the sky. "She is the goddess of arcana and love. I don't know much more about her."

"She was the first dragon," Dradevai added. "That's all I know."

Eroan simply nodded.

"I know what my mother told me," Delri said. "Would that help you?"

Asith perked up; he had forgotten entirely that Delri's mother had worshipped Phela.

"Please, tell me," Asith said, leaning toward Delri. The kids were paying attention, too, Idhe settling next to Delri as if he were being told a bedtime story. Though, Asith had a feeling it would not be that exciting.

"The time of Astasia was a great unbalancing of the divine and the arcane," Delri said. "According to my mother, after Viteus brought the second sun and restored Desta, he knew he could only bring divine magic to the world, but that wouldn't be enough. Arcana is necessary to maintain the balance."

On the ground, Delri drew two rabbits chasing each other in a circle. "When Sula fell in love with Phela, Viteus didn't trust her at first, as she was an accomplished mage. So much so, she had unlocked her essence fully, allowing her to become a dragon."

"What made Viteus change his mind?" Asith asked.

Delri pointed at the symbol. "She drew this for him, according to legend." She then pointed to each rabbit. "This one is divine magic, and this one is arcane magic, perfectly the same and in sync as they ran. She told him that this was the basis of her abilities as a mage, her understanding of the balance between the two, the connection they shared as two prey easily stirred by danger."

Asith spun the axe and watched the two rabbits chase each other. Phela had been so powerful, yet she still cared for the balance between the arcane and divine. Therefore, the mages of the Cerulean Visage gaining more power and more access to dragon parts was a threat not only to the dragons but also to the very fabric of Desta itself.

"I think I'm right about Heskel and Elaqen working with the Cerulean Visage," Asith said to Eroan. "I think they're trying to destroy the army and pin it on the dragons."

"Just to take Cairn?" Eroan asked.

"Not just to take Cairn. I think they want to use the dragons in the Graveyard Trees to get more powerful, maybe even expand the empire wider." Asith held up the charm. "When Phela gave me this, she told me that it was my job to bring balance between the people and the dragons."

"What exactly is off-balance, though?" Dradevai asked.

"Arcane and divine magic. The mages will eventually grow so powerful that they might tip the scales too far to one side."

"That is…" Dradevai's lip trembled. "A lot."

"If Phela gave you that symbol and told you to do it," Delri said, "then you're probably right."

Eroan frowned. "I think he is definitely correct about the first part, that the mages are making it look like the dragons have killed most of Cairn's military forces so that Wacot can sweep in. I mean, Elaqen or Heskel might be seen as heroes if they negotiate a treaty."

"So, their goal isn't the dragons at all," Dradevai said, their face twisted with disgust. "They're just a reward that will come when Wacot takes Cairn."

Asith nodded and looked at his feet. He was afraid, honestly. Preventing a single attack on the Graveyard Trees was one thing, but stopping a war and a takeover was another.

"What do we do to stop it?" Dradevai asked, their arms tightening around their middle.

"I can only think of one solution, and I'm not sure it will work. We get the dragons to protect the army from the Blues and Greens."

Eroan's eyes widened, and he reached for the side of his throat. "You're going to ask them to protect a bunch of dragon knights and soldiers who are there to invade their home?"

"We were both dragon knights." Asith shrugged. "They would defend us against them."

"I was only with the knights as a means to find out more about the Graveyard Trees."

"But you still were with us. You can't act as though we weren't all friends, that you didn't love Hamon just as dearly as Delri and I did."

"I…" Eroan bit his lip. "You're right, I can't even say that the dragon knights are doing anything wrong, just trying to protect people from the Blues and Greens. But I don't know if other dragons will see it that way."

"Then you and I have to convince them." Asith looked at the rest of the group. "We all have to."

13th of Katib

The rest of the flight to the Graveyard Trees passed by slowly, Asith having faced himself backward where he'd last seen the marching army. Eventually, they turned around a mountain and lowered themselves among the tree line. By the time the first sun was dipping behind the horizon, they crested over the ridge just south of the Graveyard Trees where Asith had called on Phela. When Yarrow slipped out of his bag, the second sun was just touching the tops of the mountains, readying to sink below the horizon as well. She thumped her back foot against his shoulder. A warning.

Asith looked at the ground and saw sparkling light near the entrance to the Graveyard Trees. The snow was cleared to make a path, similar to the way fish push through mud to return to deeper waters. The tail end of an army marched along the path, led by the blue and green helms of dragon knights. It didn't make sense how they'd caught up, since they were moving on foot, but perhaps the mages were speeding them up.

Asith's stomach fell to his knees, and he licked his dry lips, shifting to get a better look at the ground.

"Do you see that?" Dradevai called out just loud enough for Asith to hear over the wind.

Asith nodded, his throat too dry to shout a response. Eroan must have noticed, too, giving their group a large berth between them and the army. He chanted, quietly at first and then loud and booming, startling Asith. As they neared the entrance, a billow of soft clouds obscured them, and Eroan led them higher and higher, over the tops of the trees instead of through the main entrance. Asith had seen plenty of dragons take that route, but he had never experienced it himself.

Passing the graves of dragons long passed, Asith braced himself for the swift dive by gripping Dradevai's feathers and wrapping an arm around Yarrow. They zipped through the branches and bows of the enormous wall, and when they dipped, Asith's stomach lurched. But Dradevai spread their wings quickly to lower to the levels of the bridges and crisscrossing catwalks.

Asith swallowed the bout of nausea prickling his chest and abs and focused on the sparkling lights that hung around the inside walls. He saw his mother and father's home, the little house he'd been living in, and for the first time, he was seeing the city the way the dragons did. A smile spread across his face as they neared the ground level.

Several dragons with heavy orange cuffs around their ankles joined them in their descent and then changed into their smaller forms as Dradevai, Eroan, and Pystra were setting everyone down. Leaning on his staff, Asith approached Eroan, who was pressing his thumb to his pinkie and speaking to a guard.

"We need to account for all of the new people with you," the guard said. "There are quite a few of you."

"Please." Asith mimicked Eroan's gesture, the symbol of peace. "We need to speak with Lestash."

The guard put up his hand. "Hold on."

"You don't understand, there is an army approaching from Cairn," Eroan urged as he scanned the crowd slowly forming around them. "The group that came here with the Irden elves? The children? Where are they? They can verify us."

"We can try to find someone from that group," the guard said, eyeing Delri, then turned to ask a guard to check the temple for refugees. "Please, where are you from? Are you all from Cairn?"

"Some of us are," Dradevai said. "We don't have time to introduce everyone formally; there's an army coming."

"There should have been someone named Uri with the Irden elves," Eroan said.

"We need all of your names, I'm sorry. There's a process in place, and we can't just skip it."

"My name is Dradevai, Freer of Wings; this is Eroan, Walker of Shadows. Now please listen to us."

"I've never heard either of those names here." The guard addressed the other dragons with him, "Have either of you?"

Both shook their heads, one shrugging.

Tears burned in Asith's eyes. "Please get Lestash. She's my aunt."

Three more guards surrounded them, all of whom were focused on asking questions that didn't matter. Eroan's voice grew more frantic, and no one confirmed whether the group of children and guards he'd teleported had made it there. Dradevai set a hand on Asith's arm to calm him down, and Pystra guarded the kids, Mysse holding Cemi and Idhe tightly against him.

The yells of his group filled his head, and he pressed his hands over his ears to think. The size of the crowd had grown, with everyone's eyes either large and quizzical or narrow and untrusting. Seeing no one he knew, Asith needed a tether, his hand finding Dradevai's. He shoved his hand into his bag, and Yarrow pushed the glass orb into his palm. Smashing it could easily be read as a threat, but it was his only way of alerting Lestash.

Dradevai squeezed Asith's hand but furrowed their brow when they saw what Asith removed from his bag. "What is that?"

"It will call my aunt," Asith said.

Dradevai nodded, their eyes locked on his. And Asith threw the orb at the ground as hard as he could.

The sound of shattered glass startled the guards and the crowd. Blue smoke bloomed around his feet and curled into the air as the guards demanded what the object was. One covered their mouth with their sleeve, telling the crowd to get back. Then the smoke was sucked into the shards of glass all at once, and all remnants of the orb disappeared.

"What was that? What did you just do?" the guard shouted, pointing at Asith.

Asith opened his mouth to explain, but the ringing of bells interrupted him. They sounded from the top of the trees, and more bells joined in, scattering the already panicking crowd even more.

"What's happening?" Dradevai asked, scanning the treetops, and Delri gave Asith an unnerved look. In Cairn, bells like that meant Blues and Greens were on their way.

"That's the warning system for the Drake Sentry," Eroan said, then turned to the guards. "Please, the Irden elves and the children, did they make it?"

A guard nodded slowly. "I just heard. They're staying at the temple of Viteus."

Eroan inhaled sharply and looked at Asith. "What's the plan?"

Asith gaped at him as his staff vibrated in his hand, unsure what it meant. He scanned the flurry of dragons flying overhead, likely finding shelter. His aunt had to be coming; she wouldn't leave him on his own.

"Asith." Dradevai squeezed his hand. Asith turned to Dradevai, their brow knitted and their lips parted. "Asith, we trust you."

Yarrow nipped at Asith's sleeve, and he pulled her out. She began her transition into armor, wrapping around his arms and chest with bright light, then hardened into leather.

Asith addressed Dradevai, Eroan, Pystra, and Delri, "We need to convince the Drake Sentry to protect the army and dragon knights."

The distinct silver shape of Lestash's wings cut over the trees, and everyone's hair fluttered around their heads as his aunt settled on the ground, with a red band around her ankle marking her as part of the Drake Sentry. She waved the guards off as she rushed to Asith, and she pulled him into a tight hug. Their armor clattered together, and Asith saw she was wearing new scales made from the Blues and Greens, based on the technique Asith had taught the blacksmiths before he left.

"What do you need? I'm here to help," Lestash said. Her eyes landed on Dradevai, turning bright as she set a hand on their shoulder. "It's nice to meet you, finally."

"It's nice to meet you too," Dradevai said.

The bells stopped, but the city was still in a flurry. Dragons who hadn't yet flown were still gathering their belongings, their children, making their way into their homes or any nearby buildings. Asith waved for Pystra to pull the kids into the middle of the group. Mysse stuck his chin out and straightened his back, but the tremble in his lips betrayed him.

Asith quickly introduced Lestash to everyone, and she repeated each name to help her remember. Then he said to her, "Do the guards at the gate know about the approaching army yet?"

She nodded, her hand falling onto the pommel of the sword on her belt. "Our lookouts spotted them about an hour ago as they came past the illusory enchantment surrounding us. It was weakened somehow, so they were able to see through it."

"How could it have been weakened?" Dradevai asked. "An enchantment that powerful shouldn't be easy to mess with."

"We don't really know, but we suspect it's also why we've seen more Blues and Greens nearby."

Asith frowned, tuning out Dradevai's questions. Heskel and Elaqen might want more than simply bolstering Wacot's chances of taking over Cairn; if they weaken the Drake Sentry, they could gain access to the Graveyard Trees. In one fell swoop, they'd have access to hundreds of dragons to keep captive, and the people of Wacot and Cairn would probably see that as a good thing.

Asith blurted, "We need you to help us convince the Drake Sentry to fight alongside the dragon knights and army."

Lestash pulled back, her features hardening. "I'm not sure that's possible."

Dradevai leaned closer to Lestash, their hair falling into their face. "The Blues and Greens aren't going to attack the Graveyard Trees. They're going to blame the Graveyard Trees for decimating the army and the dragon knights."

Asith added, "If we can't find a way to bring the two groups together, Cairn's army will be weak, and Wacot will move in on Cairn *and* the Graveyard Trees at the same time."

"But what makes you think that Wacot is involved?" Lestash asked, rubbing her brow. "I don't understand."

Pystra said, "The Blues and Greens aren't dragons; they're made by mages. They mimic dragons on purpose to make it seem like we're attacking people."

Eroan added, "And the Cerulean Visage has the most to gain from the dragons and people of Cairn being at odds. If the army and dragon knights are destroyed by the Blues and Greens, but the people of Cairn think the Graveyard Trees did it, they'll think the dragons deserve whatever Wacot and the Cerulean Visage do to them. They'll have free rein to do whatever they want to the dragons here."

Delri, whose glossy brown skin had grown ashen, said, "Asith and I can try to work with the dragon knights to make them understand that Sterlings aren't a threat. But if the Graveyard Trees attacks them and the army, they won't believe us."

Lestash set her jaw, looking at Mysse, Cemi, and Idhe, who were shivering against Asith. But she didn't seem convinced, her brow furrowed and her head shaking slightly.

"Lestash." Asith set a hand on her shoulder. He knew what he was about to say was wrong, for a shiver ran down his spine and Yarrow begged him not to speak. But they were running out of time; he had to tell Lestash the truth.

"Before I left," Asith said, "Phela, the first dragon, asked me to bring balance back to the people of Cairn and the dragons. This is the only way to do that."

Lestash's eyes widened, and her jaw slackened. The chill running over his body deepened. He reached for the charm, but it wasn't there anymore. His stomach churned, but he could do nothing about it.

"Phela is the one who's guiding you?" Lestash asked sharply.

"She was," Asith said, feeling his hand tremble on his staff. "The people of Cairn and the dragons must unite against the Blues and Greens and the mages controlling them."

In Lestash's eyes, the second sun glowed, the yellow hiding behind the gray, changing the color ever so slightly. If Viteus hadn't found out about Phela's interference yet, he had then. His aunt's attention shifted to Delri, her forehead smoothing and her chin lifting.

"It will be easier if you convince the dragon knights first not to attack us," Lestash said. "I can try to get the Drake Sentry to help them, but we're weak right now; there are not many of us."

Asith hadn't expected the Drake Sentry to weaken that much while he was gone. Though, it made sense for Heskel and Elaqen to eliminate as much of the Sentry as possible before they attacked. He hoped he had not made a mistake by losing the charm just before aligning with the weakened army. Hopefully, Phela would forgive him. Yarrow tried to reassure him that she would, but Asith's stomach didn't calm.

"Okay, so how do we do this?" Delri said to Asith.

He took a deep breath to steady himself and scanned everyone's faces, his eyes lingering on Mysse's face.

"Pystra," he said, dreading what he was about to ask, "can you bring Mysse, Cemi, and Idhe to my parents? They live in the light blue house on the fourth level. They'll be safe there."

"What?" Mysse's voice cracked, his eyes wide and filling with tears.

Asith awkwardly bent to Mysse's level with his injured leg stretched out in front of him. Dradevai kneeled next to Asith and rubbed Cemi's arm as she cried.

"I know you don't like new people, Mysse, but the three of you won't be safe with us." Asith squeezed his shoulder, but Mysse tugged away. "And remember, my dad is Listesh. You knew him in that other facility, yes?"

Mysse hiccupped, wiping the tears away from his face, but he nodded. Asith frowned, his chest heavy and his leg aching. "Do you want me to send Yarrow with you? Would that help?"

Mysse opened and closed his mouth, then shook his head quickly. "I want to be at the fight! I can heal! What if one of you gets hurt?" The boy shook, tears streaking down his dirty face.

"That's very noble of you," Asith said. "But it's my turn to protect you and keep you safe, just like you did for me back at the cave."

"And we'll both come back safely," Dradevai said, holding Cemi in their arms. "We promise."

The bells rang again, that time at a much faster pace. Mysse twitched as the ground seemed to shake. He squeezed his eyes shut and nodded. "Okay."

Mysse pulled away for a moment, then hugged Asith around the neck tightly, nearly knocking him off balance. He hugged Dradevai while Cemi and Idhe said their goodbyes to Eroan. Having hugged everyone, they walked over to Pystra, who was embracing Delri as she cried.

"I'll come find you once the little ones are safe," Pystra said and transformed into her larger form. She picked the kids up in her front paws and took off toward the treetops.

Dradevai and Lestash helped Asith up, his injury screaming in pain. Once he was standing, he studied their little group, taking in Dradevai first, then his aunt, Delri, and Eroan. Eroan was facing toward the general direction of the temple of Viteus, fidgeting with his pouch of magical components that hung from his belt. Asith wanted to get him back to Uri safely, as soon as he could, in the same way he wanted the children to be safe and for Dradevai to be by his side.

"Delri, Eroan, come with Dradevai and me to the front gates. We'll try to speak with the dragon knights there. Lestash, can you go to the Drake Sentry, then join us at the gate once you've spoken with them?"

"Yes." Lestash pulled Asith into a tight hug and set her hand on Dradevai's shoulder, saying a short prayer Asith had heard her say before. When she finished, she stepped back, holding their gazes for a few moments before reverting to her larger form. As she launched into the air, her silver feathers rippled, then she disappeared from view.

"Ready?" Dradevai asked.

Asith nodded and turned to Delri and Eroan to confirm they were too. Eroan returned to his larger form and offered his neck for Delri to climb on. She sat on his shoulders, and Dradevai did the same for Asith. When he sat, pain radiated from his injured leg to his toes, but Asith gritted his teeth, bearing it as best as he could.

CHAPTER 29

The flight to the front gates only lasted a minute or so, with Dradevai and Eroan moving at top speed due to the clearer skies. It was strange to see the city nearly empty, with only guards fluttering through the air. Dradevai shifted and steered them with ease as Eroan followed close behind them, Delri low on his back.

They landed on an empty lookout perch, for the guards moved into the tops of the trees. Some dragons were carrying large branches and laying them behind the gate, providing extra protection from any intruders.

"This way," Eroan said, waving at them in his smaller form. They followed him onto a shaky bridge that connected to a network of guard stations.

Delri stayed close at Eroan's back, her hand on her sword as Dradevai followed. Asith brought up the rear as the slowest. When they reached the central bridge, Eroan turned down a boardwalk that led past the outer walls. Dragonborn guards were moving about with heavy crossbows, their armor made of gleaming metal from the mines.

"They're so close," Delri warned, her ponytail waving in the wind as they reached the catwalk wrapped around the front of the gate. About a mile off, hundreds of soldiers and dragon knights, or maybe thousands, marched toward the Graveyard Trees, the flags of the dragon knights displaying scorch marks. They carried torches and pushed siege weapons, and horses and mules pulled trebuchets and battering rams. The dragon knights held ladders, carried chain javelins, and pushed tall platforms that would be used to reach Blues and Greens when they flew low.

Their footsteps were timed and orderly despite the length of time that group had marched. Asith remembered when a Blue or Green had killed someone he knew, someone he cared about. He remembered that determination to stop them, could see himself in the dragon knights who pursued revenge on those they thought were the perpetrators of that attack on Old High Carin. The thought made Asith's hands shake.

Asith approached Delri, who was also shaking as guards pushed past them. He identified the commanders on horseback and swallowed, his heart pounding in his ear. His blood pooled in his feet, unable to move. How was he supposed to find the right words to convince them to listen? Even if he did, his voice wouldn't even be loud enough to address them.

Dradevai's hand found his, and they pressed their arm against Asith's. He ran his fingers over the seam of his doublet, his grip on Dradevai's hand tightening. They set their other hand on his cheek and kissed him softly.

"You can do this," Dradevai said. "Remember, Phela chose you for a reason."

"I don't know that reason, though."

But Dradevai's shoulders relaxed, a small smile coming onto their face. "It doesn't matter the reason. Just remember that we all believe in you." Dradevai looked at Delri and Eroan, and Asith turned to see them tearing their eyes away from the preparing army.

"We do," Delri said, and Eroan agreed. Delri set a hand on Asith's shoulder and forced a smile. "You, Eroan, and I were all dragon knights once. You and I trained many of the knights down there. They'll listen to us."

Asith nodded, trying to swallow so his mouth wouldn't feel so dry. Once his aunt arrived, it would be easier to convince the dragon knights to listen. They just needed to treat them as people.

"Asith!"

A familiar voice cut through the sound of marching feet and guards stomping on the boardwalk. Farin's hand was raised above his head, and just behind him was Pherrosh, her eyes bright as she waved.

"Farin!" Dradevai called out, making some guards stop and turn before they resumed their business.

"How'd you find us?" Asith asked when Farin approached and wrapped his arms around Asith's middle. He was moving all right, though thick bandages covered the spot where his hand had been severed from his arm.

"Pherrosh spotted you while she was carrying branches to the gate, so she came and got me. Are the kids all right? Where are they?"

Farin hugged Dradevai, but their eyes were locked on Pherrosh, her hand pressed to her lips. She opened her mouth and hiccupped, then took two steps toward Dradevai before gesturing a series of symbols.

"Uh, I..." Dradevai looked at Asith, brow furrowed. "Do you know what she's saying?"

"The kids are safe, and they're with Asith's parents," Eroan said. "She is also asking if she can hug you."

The color drained from Dradevai's face, their eyes stretching wide. Pherrosh tapped on Dradevai's amber necklace and pointed at herself.

Dradevai stepped toward Pherrosh and hugged her tightly. "You're my mother?"

Pherrosh smoothed their hair down and sobbed.

"You're my mother," they said and began crying. They asked some questions, which Pherrosh tried to scribble down the answers to.

Meanwhile, Asith tapped his staff on the ground, trying not to disturb Dradevai as he looked for signs of his aunt. Pherrosh reached for him, though, took Asith's hand, and tugged him close. He softened once he realized she was pulling him in for a tight hug. Dradevai sniffled and wiped tears from their face, and Pherrosh wrote something for Dradevai to read before showing Asith.

I have something important to show you. Is that okay?

"Of course," Dradevai said, their eyes sparkling.

After setting the paper and pencil down, she wrung her hands and grabbed the carved amber on Dradevai's necklace. Her eyes fluttered closed, and a familiar warmth cascaded over the area as she cast a spell, reminding Asith of sitting by the hearth on a cold winter's day. The amber glowed, and Pherrosh opened her eyes to look at Dradevai and then Asith's. She brushed her thumbs over the amber, and an arcane sigil rose to the surface. Dradevai gasped, their eyes glowing as their hair flapped around their face. When Pherrosh placed her palm over the symbol, the wind kicked up, grabbing the attention of the guards. Eroan, Farin, and Delri raised their hands to block the wind from their eyes.

Light gathered in Pherrosh's eyes, the same golden color of the amber, and she pressed her thumb into the back and forced it upward into her palm. The light flashed, and when the light had dissipated, Dradevai's horns each turned into a deeper yellow from the bottom to the tip. Their skin held a different undertone; no longer a reddish bronze but the distinct tone of gold.

Pherrosh returned the amber to Dradevai's chest, the light having drained from it. But it was browner, as if the amber and Dradevai had switched tones.

"What?" Dradevai touched the amber and found Asith's eyes.

Asith smiled as Pherrosh wrote furiously. Meanwhile, Delri moved next to Asith to get a better look, and Eroan stepped behind her and looked over her shoulder, curiosity painted on his face.

"If it is easier," Eroan said, "I can translate for you if you do not want to write it all down."

Pherrosh nodded, and Eroan examined her gestures carefully. "She is saying that she and her partner knew you would be born a Gold. So, to protect you from the hunters pursuing them, they created the necklace. It made you appear to be a Bronze instead, so you would be less of a target."

Dradevai's eyes welled with tears. "I'm a Gold?"

Pherrosh turned to them and nodded, then gestured again. "She is saying that she's so sorry that they had to do this. And that she hopes you can forgive her."

Eroan's voice cracked at the end, and tears streamed down Dradevai's face. They reached for Asith's hand, so he took it, pressing closer to Dradevai and offering himself as a pillar they could lean on, even though he was struggling to stand. Pherrosh's shoulders curled over her chest, sobs threatening to escape from her trembling lips.

"I don't think I fully understand," Dradevai said. "But I trust that you were not trying to hurt me by doing this."

Pherrosh swallowed audibly and pulled out her paper and pencil again. Farin approached her side as she showed Dradevai and Asith her writing.

That's okay. I couldn't keep it from you any longer.

Dradevai's posture relaxed, and they pulled Pherrosh into a hug. Asith kept his hand on their elbow, tears rolling down his face. He wiped them away and looked toward the sky again. Wings fluttered over the treetops, but the feathers weren't silver.

Asith squinted at the leaves, realizing the shapes speeding around the tops of the grave trees were jagged. More of them moved along the sky like a collection of bats with glinting teeth, their tongues lashed and claws stretched.

"Dradevai," Asith said. Pherrosh and Dradevai looked up at the endless stream of Blues and Greens shooting across the sky. "Dradevai, we need to go to the dragon knights now."

A group of Blues and Greens broke away from the others and sailed over the city behind them. Asith felt lightheaded, his limbs tingling as guards flew from their perches to confront them.

"No," Eroan said thinly, likely thinking of Uri in the temple.

"Eroan, we have to go." Asith grabbed his shoulder and shook him.

Eroan squeezed his eyes shut but nodded. "Delri," Eroan said, then changed into his larger form.

She moved to his side and got on his shoulders, and Asith turned back to find Dradevai doing the same. In that form, the change the spell had made was more evident. Their feathers glittered like polished gold, the tightly packed feathers down their legs and chest appeared more yellow, and their wings and tails carried a metallic shine, almost as reflective as a mirror.

"You're so beautiful," Asith said.

Dradevai turned their head toward him, their honey-colored eyes squinting as they laughed sharply. "Thank you. We need to hurry, though."

Asith shook off his awe and climbed onto their shoulders. As he gripped the soft feathers, he realized he felt safer, more secure than a rope would keep him. Pherrosh transformed as well, her golden body snapping by in a streak of light as she flew toward the Blues and Greens approaching the edge of the city. Asith tugged Farin onto Dradevai alongside him, and Farin yelped as they hopped off the boardwalk.

"Oh, fuck!" Farin's voice rang out as Dradevai flew toward the dragon knights. "Why the hell'd you bring me with you? What the hell am I going to do?"

Asith grabbed the back of Farin's shirt and adjusted him upright. "I just wanted to make sure you were safe."

"I am less safe flying hundreds of feet in the air than I was in the tree!" Farin screamed.

Asith couldn't help but laugh. Farin was consistent, at least.

The wind kicked up as Dradevai spread their wings out and slowed down so they didn't dive straight into the dragon knights. Asith gripped his staff, trying not to lose it or Farin, as they neared the people below, who were already throwing javelins at Eroan.

"Vai!" Asith called, straining his throat. Dradevai turned their head and treaded in the air. Asith smiled at the sight of their face, then removed a loose down feather from their shoulder. "I'm going down, keep Farin safe."

"What?" Farin exclaimed. "Now you're leaving? I only have one hand!"

"Dradevai will keep you safe," Asith said. "And they'll pick me up as soon as I need them to."

"I'm glad you're confident, but I hate this plan so far." After Farin secured their legs around Dradevai better, Asith let go of their feathers, already casting the spell to fall slowly, the down feather in his hand disappearing.

He landed softly on his feet just a short way from the front line of dragon knights. His eyes trained on the armor of the knights, he started toward them, some noticing Asith. He held up his palm, trying to shrink himself to look as nonthreatening as possible.

One knight drew his sword and pointed it at Asith. "Who are you?"

"My name is Asith Evourin, and I used to be a dragon knight." Asith stopped several feet from the front line and glanced up at Eroan, who had shifted away from the gathering crowd. He reverted to his small form and held on to Delri as they floated to the ground. Dradevai watched from overhead.

"What are you doing here?" The knight's eyes shot toward the Blues and Greens swarming the outside of the Graveyard Trees.

"I'm here to warn you about a trap." Asith lowered his hand and studied the faces of the knights, hoping to see someone he knew.

"A trap?" one knight shouted from farther back.

"I need to speak with a commander, please." Asith gazed at the closest knight on horseback, feeling Yarrow's feet on his shoulder. A warning.

A javelin was hurled through the air, and Asith moved just in time for it to land a few feet from him.

"Cut it out!" the first knight yelled. "He's not a dragon, don't waste your weapons."

"There's a trap set for you all. If you don't want to die, let me speak with your commanding officer!" Asith shouted more loudly, hoping to catch the attention of the nearest commander, but his eyes were focused on Dradevai.

"Why in hell would we believe you?"

Asith growled, his hands balling up into fists, but he forced himself to calm down. He took even breaths, looking over his shoulder to see Delri and Eroan jogging toward him. Behind them, the Blues and Greens faced the knights, their mouths open. They would be upon them soon.

Asith ground his teeth together. "Because I am trying to tell you that you are being set up!" He said an incantation for a shield, and it glittered around him as he stepped forward and into the line of knights. They swung at his shield, but their weapons glanced off, as he made his way to one of the tower platforms.

Asith's leg ached as he moved, the knights stepping aside to let him through but watching him with wary eyes. With shaking arms and legs, he climbed the ladder that led to the top of the tower and saw the Blues and Greens fast. Dradevai dipped down and deposited Farin on the ground before flying to intercept the mimics. He made it to the top, remembering all the times he had stood there when fighting Blues and Greens.

"Dragon knights! My name is Asith, I was one of you!"

They turned toward him with wide eyes, their jaws slack. Even the commanders, sitting high on their horses, turned toward him, the frills on their helmets swaying in the wind.

"The Sterling dragons are not a threat! They are fighting to protect you!" Asith's voice cracked and his throat was dry and sore, but he continued. "Fight with them, not against them! If we work together, we will survive!"

Asith panted and grabbed the railing as the knights stared at him, unmoving, unshaken. Just as Asith became convinced they wouldn't listen, Dradevai unleashed their fire on the Blues and Greens, the light fighting against the late evening suns and winning.

Three Greens dropped, the impact of their bodies shaking the ground in an unceremonious thud. Dradevai then flew upwards and curved back toward the dragon knights to shield them.

"See!?" Asith shouted with a struggle. "They are fighting with us!"

The dragon knights gave each other confused glances before one climbed the ladder. Asith's shield flickered and disappeared as Blues and Greens shot acid toward the knights, who were ducking under their shields. Trying to think of something to make his voice louder, Asith said a few couplets, and his magic curled around his throat. That time, when he spoke, his voice boomed over the crowd.

"It's our job to protect the people of Cairn from Blues and Greens. Not to fight a war against the Sterlings."

A Green readied to spit acid on Asith and the knight on the tower, but Dradevai crashed into it. They tumbled in the air, and Dradevai caught their balance by spreading out their wings and clasping the railing of the tower with their back paws. The knight screamed and backed up against the railing, nearly falling off, but Dradevai pushed the knight back with their front paw, all while flapping their wings to keep the tower from tipping over.

"I'm sorry!" Dradevai's startled voice came out light, as if they were just as surprised as the knight. His eyes were the size of dinner plates.

"Please, we're trying to do the right thing," Asith said.

The knight clung to the railing and said with a wobbling voice, "You're really protecting us?"

"Yes, we promise, we'll do our best," Asith said.

Dradevai scooped him up and took off into the skies, leaving the knight behind. "Has Lestash contacted you?"

"No!" Asith looked out toward the sky, and Eroan was casting a shield to protect the battalion from a Blue's fire. He still didn't see his aunt or the Drake Sentry and feared they were struggling inside of the Graveyard Trees.

That was when Pherrosh collided with a Green, the two of them spinning in the air before she let it go, and the Green collapsed to the ground, unmoving. She turned herself around to chase another three that were closing in on the army and took them out with her fire, her glittering gold wings perfectly curved as she dodged a Blue trying to bite her.

A ripple in the distance caught Asith's attention, Dradevai's golden feathers providing enough shade to see the anomaly. As Dradevai swooped down to meet Farin, a Blue and a Green emerged from behind the illusory sky, causing it to ripple like the surface of a pond after a rock had been tossed into it.

"Asith, grab Farin!" Dradevai yelled.

They lowered their paw and extended their leg so Asith could grab Farin, who was frowning. He ran toward them, yelling, "I hate this so much!"

Once Asith was close enough, Farin hopped and grabbed Asith's extended staff, making it easier for Farin to support his weight. Asith tugged him into Dradevai's partially closed paw, and they flew off.

Seeing they had changed direction toward the Graveyard Trees, Asith asked, "Dradevai, where are you going!?"

"We need to help everyone inside." Dradevai was aiming for the boardwalk, where the guards were readying their crossbows for invasion.

Asith wanted to tell them about where the mimics were coming from, but he couldn't scream anymore. Farin likely needed a break, too, for he was sweaty and his complexion was pallid. So Asith asked, "Can we stop on the boardwalk for a moment?"

Dradevai gawked but ultimately slowed themself down enough to glide onto the walkway above the gate, while the guards flew to intercept the Blues and Greens charging at the front gate. Dradevai returned to their smaller form, their brow knitted with worry. "Are you okay? Are either of you hurt?" Dradevai touched Farin's shoulder and studied him, then Asith. Farin shook his head, color returning to his face.

"No, we're not hurt." Asith cleared his throat. "I couldn't keep shouting, I'm sorry. I can see where the Blues and Greens are coming from."

Dradevai's eyes locked on Asith's. "You want to go stop Elaqen and Heskel?"

"Yes." Asith looked at Farin. "Can you try to get a message to the Drake Sentry that the mages creating the Blues and Greens are nearby? They just need to look for the illusion off the southeast side of the city."

"Southeast side of the city, look for the illusion. I can do that."

"Thank you." Asith hugged Farin, bending so Farin could get his arms around him as well. "Please, be safe."

"You too." Farin let go, hugged Dradevai, and disappeared among the guards running about and calling orders.

"What's the plan?" Dradevai asked.

Asith observed the fight. The dragon knights were not attacking Eroan, Pherrosh, and Pystra, who had just made her way out into the battle, her copper feathers flickering in the light. She raised roots from the ground to secure Blues and Greens that had fallen but were still alive. The army was holding the rest of them off, and if Asith could slow the number of Blues and Greens appearing, the Drake Sentry could join, once they'd gotten control of the city.

"I think we have to get Heskel and Elaqen on our own," Asith said. "We should try to sneak up on them if we can."

Dradevai said, "I can fly quietly."

"And fly high too," Asith added. "I think they're on the ground and the clouds will give us some cover."

"I can do that." Dradevai shifted back into their larger form and offered for Asith to climb on. He did his best to ignore the pain in his leg as Dradevai straightened and launched, his stomach lurching as they rocketed toward the treetops.

CHAPTER 30

Dradevai flew faster than they had the day they kidnapped Asith. The wind was pushing Asith back so hard that he created a shield in front of him, making it easier for him to stay upright. Once Dradevai was gliding through the clouds, Asith directed them on where to turn, both by patting their shoulder and yelling. They followed his instructions as if they'd practiced, Blues and Greens passing them by.

As they drew closer to the source, Asith saw the mimics appearing in pods, then they burst through the illusion, the night sky rippling each time.

"Vai, when we get down there, don't hold back. I think we need to do as much damage as possible."

"Don't worry, I know."

Dradevai ascended into the clouds to remain hidden, and Asith's eye caught on the movement of a ring of dark clouds, the charge of static seemingly bouncing off them and flaring into full bolts of lightning. That had to be the work of mages, as the clouds only floated over one area as if they were balloons on a string and that kind of weather pattern was unnatural. It had to belong to whatever ritual Elaqen and Heskel used to create the mimics.

"There, Vai!" Asith pointed, and Dradevai's head followed his hand. "Fly through there. I should be able to shield us from the lightning."

Asith clenched his jaw and returned to a tight grip on their feathers, his fingers tingling. But he didn't dare loosen them. The thought of relying on his magic alone to protect him and Dradevai made his stomach churn, but Yarrow pressed her feet against his back. He was right, she said, that the lightning wouldn't touch them.

"Are you sure?" Dradevai called.

Asith shouted his confirmation and pulled his staff from his belt.

"Okay, tell me when," Dradevai said and flew above the roiling mix of thunderclouds. Rain pelted them as another bolt of lightning tossed itself toward the ground like a rope from the top of a cliff. Asith chanted in Endethi and focused on his staff. It was made from the grave trees of his grandmother and sister, and his father was a Silver dragon who could breathe lightning.

His breathing quickening, he finished the chant. "Now!" He flicked his wrist and swung the staff, the end hitting the side of his breastplate. Dradevai curved like water flowing over a fall before diving through the clouds. Lightning arced off the surrounding mist and slipped off the shield Asith had created. He focused on the image of early morning dew running down the tent Dradevai and he had slept in before they'd found his father.

As they burst from the bottom of the cloud, lightning followed, colliding with the shield and darting into the trees. Dradevai opened their mouth, and fire burst from it and spread across the approaching ground. Turning their wings, they caught the wind harshly to avoid striking the dirt. Dradevai swung around the back of the massive spell circle, and the rain and lightning stopped as two charred bodies fell to the ground and dissipated into ash. In the center, hundreds of Silver and Copper dragon feathers formed a summoning circle, embedded into the very boulder that created the clearing.

Elaqen and Heskel were inside a shield just outside the circle, along with two others Asith didn't recognize. They wore deep navy clothes with cerulean sashes draped across their chests. Dradevai flew at them, as if they were trying to break the shield with their body. But they slowed in time and landed in front of the four mages, snarling, making the unknown mages flinch.

"Predictable," Elaqen drawled. "You know, you killed my favorite pet. At least, I assume it was you, given that the dragons likely would have burned or electrocuted him to death instead."

"Enough of this." Asith stepped off Dradevai's back, and Yarrow shivered in his armor. "This is over."

Elaqen folded his hands behind his back. "It will never be over."

When one of the mages shifted, Asith pointed his staff at them. The shield dropped, and Elaqen was gone. In his wake, Heskel fired bolts of condensed air at them. Asith and Dradevai dove in opposite directions, but Elaqen appeared and grabbed Asith by the neck, a chant slipping from his lips. He tore Asith from the ground and raised his hand, shadows gathering around him. They were poised to hit Asith straight on.

"Asith!" Dradevai circled the clearing, narrowly dodging Heskel's spell, while Elaqen pulled Asith farther into the air.

"Get Heskel!" Asith shouted and coughed. He tore at Elaqen's hands as Yarrow frantically moved along his back. Elaqen was finally so close, and Asith didn't want to lose his chance to best him with his sword.

Dradevai received a direct hit from Heskel, likely distracted by Asith, and they plummeted but caught themself before hitting the ground. To keep Elaqen's attention, Asith spat at his opponent, but he tightened his grip, causing Asith to choke. Growling, Elaqen rolled his eyes and used magic to clean the spit off his robe. Panic gripped Asith as Elaqen raised his hand to bring a spell down, and he kicked his feet against nothing but open air.

Then he remembered how helpless he'd felt back in the facility, with Farin bleeding out and guards surrounding him. His chest filled with anger, and he focused all his magic onto his tongue, trying to summon a command word. But he realized all at once he didn't need one. He remembered from the facility the way his father had made his chest expand, his jaw unhinging. Yarrow stood fast against his back, and Asith opened his jaw as far as he could.

As Elaqen's hand dove toward Asith's chest, static rose, and a short bolt of lightning ripped from Asith's throat. It was smaller and slower than his father's, but it was enough to startle Elaqen.

Elaqen yelped, and his spell darted over Asith's shoulder, singeing his hair. Released from his opponent's grip, Asith plummeted, realizing how high they'd climbed. He jammed his hand into his pocket for a down feather and spoke the command. It flared with warmth, and a loud gasp escaped him as the spell slowed his fall. When he hit the ground, he rolled to avoid another ball of shadows, which hit the ground next to him. The shadows burst into tentacles, trying to grab anything near it, so Asith kept rolling.

Dradevai clipped Elaqen with their wing, and the two of them entered a fray of shadows and fire, bursting across the sky with thunderclouds looming overhead. Asith cleared himself away from the shadows and pushed himself up with his staff. He found it easier with the additional brace in his armor, which Yarrow apologized for not having done sooner. He shuffled to the nearest line of the spell circle and slapped a hand onto the feathers embedded there. Scratching, pawing, and using the pommel of his sword didn't remove them.

One mage in a cerulean sash fired a spell at Dradevai, and a chant slipped through Asith's lips like second nature. A shield formed just in time, and their spell ricocheted at them, setting the mage on fire. As they dropped to the ground to put it out, Heskel's condensed air flowed over them and created a strong wind that fed the fire on their clothes. Heskel's attention turned to Asith, and a bolt of lightning formed in his hands. Asith stepped forward, and he threw lightning directly at Asith, who had already created a shield around himself. It rolled off like water on a waxed tent with two people sleeping inside.

"You both think you know so much better," Asith said and drew his sword as he closed in. "You didn't even notice there was a dragon at your side, in disguise, working against you."

Heskel whirled air around himself. "Don't come near me!"

The wind kicked up the flames engulfing the mage, and they screamed, begging Heskel to stop. But Heskel didn't even spare them a glance, his fear becoming clearer as Asith adjusted his shield spell to account for the wind, allowing him to step through Heskel's whirlwind.

"No!" Heskel raised his hands, his spell falling apart and the roiling thunderclouds disappearing. "Get away."

Heskel tripped backward and landed next to the smoldering body, which once belonged to the mage helping him. "I-I'll do anything, just spare me." He held up his hands.

What a coward.

Phela's voice filled Asith's head like temple bells. His body shook with power at her sound. He felt hands smooth over his shoulders.

It is my turn to help you, let me in.

Asith looked at his shoulders and did not see Phela's hands, but her presence radiated through his staff. He felt Raystash's head nodding as well.

So he dropped his guard for Phela, allowing her to do what she needed through him. A warmth spread over his body, and his sword was extended as his staff was lowered toward Heskel's throat. Asith's throat filled with two voices.

"You will never be able to cast magic again."

The sounds of bells filled his ears, and his hair fluttered, the band on his braid breaking. Light glowed from his eyes and illuminated Heskel's contorted face.

"You will only be able to tell the truth of what your plans were and what you have done."

Heskel's eyes widened, and confusion spread over his round face. He grabbed at Asith's staff, but golden light burst from the top, where the dragon guarded the orb, and filled the entire clearing. The illusion shattered all at once, like the sun bursting from the horizon at dawn. Asith squinted at the brightness, but saw Heskel through his lashes remain frozen, with his mouth open wide and brow furrowed in horror.

The light slowly cleared and Heskel flicked his wrist, but nothing happened. Even when he started a chant, no magic moved at his behest. He stared up at Asith, moving to his knees. He looked like nothing more than a bug, and it hardly seemed fair that the man who had hurt Raystash every day of her short life got to live on. But he trusted Phela had good reason for letting him live without his ability to control magic ever again.

With Heskel subdued, Asith searched for the fourth mage who had been in the clearing. They likely hadn't gotten that far. Dradevai was still clashing with Elaqen, trying to break down his shields. In their smaller form, they shot flames from their throat, which plowed through Elaqen's shields and forced him to dodge them.

But then a spell shot out of the trees behind Asith and hit Dradevai, knocking them off balance. Dradevai righted themself quickly and started another chant. Asith spun on his heels and knew it hadn't come from Heskel, for he was folded in on himself and silently sobbing. He scanned the bottoms of the trees near the edges of the clearing and caught a single flash of cerulean. Moving forward, he followed the line of color, his injuries preventing him from running at full speed. Before he could get even a few steps, something crashed into Asith's back.

He rolled on the grass, gasping for air while his eyes blurred. When everything cleared, he saw Dradevai's smaller form next to him, their eyes closed, blood dripping from their ears and nose and mouth. Asith grabbed them and pulled them to his chest, his hand supporting their head.

For some reason, Dradevai had crashed into him, and there was no Mysse to heal them. Pystra, Delri, and Eroan were not coming, and Asith could barely move himself, let alone carry Dradevai. His breathing quickened, his grip on Dradevai's limp body tightening as his eyes rose toward Elaqen, who floated about thirty feet above them. Elaqen's teeth shone white against the blood around his mouth, an ugly grin crawling across his lips as his nostrils flared. He drew shadows into the center of his chest, and Asith didn't chant, didn't react, didn't think as he opened his mouth and formed a shield around them.

Elaqen's shadows bounced off and landed as tendrils in the grass. The shield held strong through three more attacks, and Elaqen huffed and grimaced after the fourth. "How are you doing this!?" He threw a different spell at Asith, but the shadows burst against the shield like a bag of flour that hadn't been mended correctly and set down too hard. "I am an archmage of the Cerulean Visage!"

Asith lowered Dradevai into the grass. He pressed his fingers against their throat, their pulse slow but there. But they needed help, soon. The pain in his leg had become a dull ache, which he could easily ignore, and he ground his teeth together, his grip on his staff causing his knuckles to bloom with red and then turn solid white.

Asith shifted in front of Dradevai as the shield deflected another blow. He thought of Raystash, who didn't make it, and Dradevai, who was dying behind him. He thought of Elaqen, gone from the world. He thought of his father, who had created bursts of lightning through mere will. Asith was no longer going to just protect through defense, but through attack, through harm. As he had with Kosor, as Phela had with Heskel. He needed to bring Elaqen to his knees. And Asith could. He believed he could.

He visualized lightning like his father's, strong enough to light up the entire sky during a storm, and a bolt of lightning sprang from Asith's mouth. It arced toward Elaqen faster than light. When it hit, his scream ripped through the trees, all of them shivering in its wake. He collapsed to the ground, steaming, with his long hair singed down to his scalp.

Asith stepped forward on unsteady feet, raising his sword above his head. Elaqen was barely breathing, his eyes filled with tears. Streaks ran down his face, revealing pale skin under the scorched burns the lightning had left.

"This is pointless," Elaqen whispered through his blackened lips, his tone raspy and spiteful. "If it's not us producing dragon parts, it will be someone else."

"No, it won't." Asith bent down, feeling Yarrow move along his shoulder inside his armor, telling him not to listen. But he didn't need to be told. "It won't because I will be here to stop it."

Elaqen's eyes turned toward the night sky, and blood sprang from his lips as he tried to argue. But the words never came out because the light left Elaqen's eyes.

Asith stepped toward Dradevai, and he would have thought Dradevai was peacefully sleeping in the grass if it weren't for the blood. As he stepped again, his leg gave out, and he hit his head on the packed dirt.

Yarrow turned back into a rabbit and sniffed at him before running off into the trees. The grass and rocks scratched his knuckles as he reached for his staff, the sound of feathered wings beating the air. He hoped that meant someone on his side was coming.

Asith wanted to reach for Dradevai, but his body would no longer move. He tried keeping his eyes open, for Heskel was nearby and could still attack them. But pain coursed through his body, his leg, his stomach. He hiccupped, and tears streamed down his face as Raystash tried to comfort him. But the other dragons were still fighting the Blues and Greens, and Farin might not have made it to the Drake Sentry.

"Vai," Asith forced out, but words felt as if he were vomiting gravel.

Then the reddish pink sky turned to the purple of dusk, contrasting with the light catching a large golden shape with wings outstretched and its towering horns spiraling like an antelope's.

Perhaps it was Phela's larger form, fluttering toward him to take him away, But as it drew closer, he realized it was not ethereal. It was a very real, solid dragon whose feathers shimmered in the final light of the second sun.

Pherrosh landed at their side without a sound, her smaller form appearing in a puff of smoke, with Farin beside her. Behind her, a glimmering copper dragon carried Delri on their back, followed by two sleek Silvers. The familiar form of Lestash appeared, with Eroan directly behind her, and they ran toward them.

Asith let his eyes fall closed, and the world went dark.

CHAPTER 31

17th of Katib

"Asith."

Dradevai's voice was above him. "Asith, wake up."

Asith opened his eyes slowly, the sky filling his vision. The bright light of noon shone from above, but he couldn't see either of the suns. He turned his head, just barely, and found a woman sitting at his side, possessing familiar wavering horns on her head. Her fingers gently pulled on his hair, making a braid.

"I know you were probably hoping for someone else." She finished her braid and set it on his shoulder. "But don't worry, I just needed to speak to you first."

"Are they okay?" Asith asked.

"You'll find out soon enough." Phela's voice sounded like a warm breeze moving through the trees. "You know, you broke your promise and told your aunt about my helping you."

"Sorry." Asith's voice cracked, his throat still terribly dry.

"It's okay, Viteus is angry. But I think he will come to understand." She wrapped her arms around her knees, smiling as she looked into the distance. "He took my charm from you. I am not allowed to return it, but he did give it back to me, at least. It seems a waste, though, because I made it for you."

Asith looked at her hand, which held the small axe charm, the scratch on one side. She spun it in her fingers, making the little rabbit run.

"That's okay. I was able to manage without it." Asith shifted himself onto his elbow and followed her gaze to a person standing in the distance. They had long pointed ears and short blond hair that framed their jaw, and the visage of an owl was embroidered on their fine tunic. They smiled and waved, to which Asith waved back.

"You were." Phela smiled, her golden horns tilting as she looked at him. "I am proud of you."

Warmth spread down Asith's arms, and the wind made his hair slip off his shoulder. He smiled and thanked Phela quietly.

"You have Raystash now," Phela said. Asith blinked, and his staff was in his hand. "She will be there for you to lean on as you bring together the people of Cairn."

Asith looked at the top of his staff, the small dragon that looked like his father but wasn't. It was his sister, he realized; Raystash had been guarding him as he would have guarded her if given the chance. His heart ached, feeling as if the pressure against his ribs would break them.

"She will help me do what Dradevai thinks I should do."

Phela's lips curled upward. "What does Dradevai think you should do?"

"Act as an ambassador between Cairn and the Graveyard Trees. I think I will do that."

"I think that is a very good idea." Phela smoothed his hair down, her touch making his scalp tingle with warmth, much like his mother's always did. "I will do my best to help you when I can."

"Thank you. Am I still your champion, then?"

Phela's face split into a grin, and she looked at the person in the distance. Keeping her eyes on them, she leaned down and said in a low voice, "You will always be my champion. Whether Viteus is angry with me for it or not, I have chosen you."

Asith nodded, unsure why she would risk Viteus's ire just for him, but Yarrow nudged his stomach. It was better not to ask, to believe he deserved it, so Asith trusted her instinct.

"Will you tell your father about her?" Phela touched the staff with the tips of her fingers.

Asith pressed his lips together, a frown forming. "He deserves to know."

Phela sighed. "You are right. Your honesty is admirable, you know."

Asith thought of Raystash's small face and hands, the strands of dull silver hair hanging from her head the last time he saw her. In telling his father about his daughter, he didn't know whether he was being admirable or simply sharing his grief with someone. Regardless, she was real, and his father deserved to know.

Phela stood, and her smaller form dissipated in favor of her large golden form. Asith's eyes widened, his mouth hanging open as he took in her massive shape. Her neck was long and elegant, and she possessed four horns on her head. The first pair reminded Asith of an antelope's, and the second pair was curved backward like a ram's. She *had glimmering honey-golden eyes, a tail covered in short feathers that flared out at the ends, and paws with shivering feathers hidden among her toes.*

Asith craned his neck to see every feature, and Yarrow leaned against his leg as if to support him.

"You did well, Asith." Phela's voice boomed from her much larger chest, shaking Asith as it reverberated through the grassy field. "Now, it is time for your reward."

"Reward?"

She chuckled, the sound sweet and tinkling like the bells one would play in celebration of the harvest; smaller and less powerful than a temple bell but just as beautiful.

"Yes. You deserve it."

Phela bowed her head, and her wings beat in the air, lifting her four legs off the ground with ease despite how heavy they appeared. She fluttered over to the person in the distance, their smile brightening. They waved at Asith again before climbing onto Phela's shoulders, and the two of them disappeared.

Asith lay awake for a good few minutes trying to sort out where he was. He remembered little after seeing Dradevai injured. Someone was resting on a cot near him, propped up as if they had been hurt, and he feared who he'd discover if he looked at their face. So Asith stared at the ceiling and focused on figuring out what building he rested in.

It was only when he heard his neighbor move that he closed his eyes again. He wasn't ready for anyone to know he was awake.

"Good morning, I think."

Dradevai's voice sounded dry, as it often did when they first woke up. Asith's eyes flew open, and he shot up in his cot, making his leg scream in pain. Dradevai was startled but threw their blanket off, and they approached Asith's bed. "You're awake!"

Dradevai moved with stiffness, but they were clean, no signs of blood coming from any orifice. They fell into his arms, half on the cot and half hanging off the side. Small scabs covered their hands, and bruises ran up their arms. A loose tunic barely kept them covered, and Asith wore a similar one, though someone had put pants on him. The injuries already looked old, and Asith wished he could heal as quickly as dragons, though he probably healed faster than a normal elf or a human.

"You're okay." Asith pulled Dradevai close, wrapping his arms around their middle. He pressed his head against their chest, listening to their heart beating through the light fabric of their shirt. The position made his leg hurt more, but he didn't care; he used all his strength to hang on to Dradevai.

"I'm okay? You've been asleep for the better part of a week!" Dradevai's voice cracked, tears streaming down their face. They cupped Asith's cheeks. "Mysse and I were starting to think nothing would help."

"But you were… There was blood everywhere."

Dradevai kneeled and smoothed his hair down, adjusting his braid that was stuck to his neck. "Yes, and you passed out shortly after they found us, according to my mother."

"Pherrosh?"

Dradevai nodded. Asith strung the scattered memories together. He had the faintest memory of a golden dragon flying in the sky. Farin must have told her where they were, so he trusted that.

He looked down at the many bandages covering his hands. One was tightly wound around his head, and another was around his leg, for his wound had likely opened back up. Someone had cleaned him up some-what, but blood had dried and cracked on his skin in various places. Asith wet his lips, feeling the many splits in them, and his mouth felt dry, but not as bad as when he'd woken up to Mysse healing him. He adjusted his posture, feeling pain shift in his core, as if he had been kicked there by a Blue or Green.

Yarrow hopped onto the cot, her whiskers shivering as she apologized for not properly protecting him. Asith set a hand on her head to reassure her and looked at Dradevai.

"Where are we?"

"The temple of Viteus. They have been using it as a makeshift hospital since the battle."

Asith looked at the window and saw light illuminating the stained glass. It depicted the coming of the second sun, which warmed Desta and saved it from ruin when the first sun was dying. Nearly every temple of Viteus had that depiction, he'd heard, and for a moment, Asith got lost in the image, his thoughts foggy.

"Did we win?" Asith asked. He looked back at Dradevai, whose lips pressed into a line.

"Yes." Dradevai's voice was breathy and tired, holding an edge of disbelief. "We did, we got the dragon knights and the Drake Sentry to work together."

"And the army?" Asith's chest swelled, his back instinctively straightening but the movement hurting slightly.

Dradevai's lips curved, their eyes alight. "We did it, Asith." Dradevai took his hands. "There were losses, but once we'd stopped Elaqen from summoning more Blues and Greens, they were able to overcome them together. The army, the dragon knights, and the Drake Sentry."

Tears ran down Asith's face as he smiled. Phela had told him she was proud, but Asith hadn't realized exactly why until then. He leaned into Dradevai, even as his aching body fought him, and hugged them tightly to his chest. He sniffled, the tears hot against his skin, but his body seemed lighter.

"I'm going to bring peace," Asith said. "This is the first step."

Dradevai pulled back, their brow wrinkled. With a smile, they pressed their forehead against Asith's, their hands sliding to his chest.

"You are going to be a diplomat, then? So it doesn't just go back to how it was?"

"It won't go back to the way it was. I won't let it."

Dradevai squinted as their eyes watered at the corners. They were smiling so wide that the tears fell over fast and all their teeth shone, including the fang-like, snaggled canines Asith loved so much. He kissed the side of their head and held them for as long as they let him. Dradevai squeezed until Asith said it hurt, and then they apologized and loosened their grip.

"I need to tell Maryan you're awake," Dradevai said. They took a deep breath and wiped the tears from their face before Asith let go, but not without stopping Dradevai to kiss their lips. They melted against him, their hands falling on Asith's shoulders, and pulled away.

Dradevai opened a large wooden door, and their hair fluttered against the back of their neck. With a grin on their face, they yelled into the next room, "He's awake!"

Suddenly, Asith's mother and father were through the door, and his mother wrapped him up in a hug and kissed his hair. His father placed a hand on his shoulder as Dradevai rejoined Asith on the cot. Asith moved himself to the edge to embrace his mother and father, struggling to get his arm around Dradevai as well. They realized and tugged him in, making Dradevai laugh. His mother said something about both of them giving her a scare but pet Dradevai's head. They stayed like that for a good while.

When they finally separated, Asith reached for Dradevai's hand, and they squeezed it.

"The kids? Where are they?" Asith asked. "And Delri, are she and Pystra okay? Lestash?" He realized he had so many people to ask about. Dradevai stopped him before he started naming everyone who had helped them.

"The kids are with Eroan and Uri. I'm sure everyone wants to come see you. Some got hurt, but we're all okay, I promise." They smoothed their hand over Asith's knuckles, then brushed his hair off his forehead. "It is just like you to think of everyone else first."

"It is just like him," his mother said. "I'm so proud of you, Asith. You, too, Dradevai."

Asith cried, his shakes making his body hurt, but he smiled as his mother wiped his tears away. He set his head on his mother's shoulder and peered at Dradevai, who was smiling and crying as well, and a laugh coaxed its way from his belly, Yarrow settling between his feet.

His father pressed his hand against his back while smoothing down his mother's hair, to comfort her through her sniffles. "I think the two of you may finally have a chance to relax a little."

"Please relax for a while, my heart can't take this," his mother said.

Asith chuckled, tightening his grip on his mother. "We will, I promise. I need a chance to heal, and Dradevai deserves time with Pherrosh. But then I think it is time to help our people diplomatically, rather than through fighting."

"I should go find my mother," Dradevai said. They looked toward the door, their hand on Asith's knee.

"I'll go find Pherrosh," his father said. "And Lestash."

"Can you find the kids and everyone else too?" Asith asked. "I'm sure Delri is worried."

"I'll bring everyone." His father started toward the door. "It may just take a bit."

Asith and Dradevai thanked him and then diverted their attention to his mother, her focus entirely on asking them what happened before they returned to the Graveyard Trees.

"I was so startled when Pystra showed up with the little ones," his mother said. "Especially since the eldest was clearly trying not to sob when they first arrived."

Dradevai's shoulders dropped. "Mysse is really nervous around people he doesn't know well."

"Ah, is that what it was? He hasn't said more than a few words. Though, he calmed down once the little ones warmed up to me."

"Was Papa not there watching them with you?"

"No, he's a trained doctor, technically, so he went to help. I was going to go with him, but he asked me to stay in case you came to our house."

Asith went cold. He had thought Mysse would've been okay, at least being familiar with his father from the facility, but it hadn't turned out that way. He locked eyes with Dradevai, their brow furrowed as they were clearly figuring out the same thing.

Asith's chest tightened, and he looked at his feet. "I owe Mysse an apology."

Dradevai said, "You did what you thought was safest for him, Cemi, and Idhe." They rubbed Asith's bicep.

"You're right, but I…" Asith rubbed the back of his head.

"It's okay," his mother said, catching his eyes. "This is how things go with kids. You do your best and apologize when you make mistakes."

Asith took in her green eyes, which were so much like Mysse's. She was right.

Delri appeared at the doorway, her arm in a sling and her eyes filled with tears. His mother moved out of the way for Delri to sit beside Asith and hug him with one arm. She asked him questions he'd already answered for his mother, and soon, Pystra trailed in and sat on the cot across from them with Asith's mother. Then Delri chided him for not asking for their help sooner.

A while later, Eroan entered, his eyes meeting Dradevai's quickly. For the first time since Asith had met him, Eroan had two short horns on the top of his head. They were light brown with flecks of silver embedded into them, curving back like stately arches.

"I'm glad you're finally awake," Eroan said. "We were starting to get worried."

Asith suddenly remembered the sight of Heskel in a ball on the ground. At Asith's lack of response, Eroan tilted his head, his horns exaggerating the movement.

"Wait, Heskel," he said. "Did he get away?"

"No," Eroan said, sitting next to Pystra. "In fact, I had the pleasure of throwing him in a cell while we decide what to do with him.

Asith relaxed. "Good. Phela did something to him that will make him tell the truth."

"Phela did?"

"Through me, but she did it. We should probably try to use him to convince the people of Cairn what was happening."

Dradevai smiled. "We can figure that out soon. I think you still need to rest."

"They are right," Eroan said, "but I am interested to hear what we can do with Heskel."

Dradevai turned toward Eroan. "Where are the kids?"

"Uri has them outside." Eroan folded his hands. "I didn't want to repeat Cemi stepping on one of your wounds, so I came in here first to see how you were doing."

Asith appreciated his concern, but he wanted to see them more than he cared about getting accidentally hurt. "Bring them in, please."

Eroan retrieved Uri, who was holding Cemi and Idhe's hands, with Mysse beside them. To Asith's surprise, tears immediately sprang to Mysse's eyes, and he threw himself into Asith's arms. Delri moved next to Pystra, smiling at Asith. Asith hugged Mysse to his chest, and Dradevai rubbed his back slowly, while Idhe and Cemi leaned against his legs and told him they were happy he was okay. It didn't take them long to cling onto Eroan and Uri again.

Eventually, his aunt and Thistin took Delri and Pystra's place, keeping the conversation light and focused on Asith's condition. Farin and Pherrosh appeared last, along with Asith's father. He spoke with Lestash and Thistin in the corner while Farin sat next to Asith's mother on the cot across from Asith, while Pherrosh pressed herself against Dradevai.

Eroan and Uri announced that Idhe and Cemi needed to get some rest, but Mysse didn't go with them. Asith encouraged him to stay as the room dwindled to Dradevai and their parents.

"We want to stay for a while, spend time with you, but I also want to act as an ambassador to Cairn," Asith explained to Pherrosh.

The boy twitched when he mentioned only staying for a while. Yarrow hopped into Mysse's lap, and he petted her slowly. They would talk about it, but right then wasn't the right moment.

Pherrosh smiled, moving her hands, and Asith's father said it meant she was glad. She then shifted to writing on paper, and she showed it to them.

I want to spend time with you too. And your father and I have a lot to share with you from growing up together.

Asith replied, "I'm excited to hear it. So, then, you two did know each other before?"

His father said, "That is why I called Dradevai Pherrosh when I first saw them. They look alike, and I assumed she had come to save me somehow."

It wouldn't have been the first time.

Everyone laughed at Pherrosh's words, save for Mysse, who was shivering. Asith wrapped an arm around him and looked at his mother. She seemed to understand the cue and nudged his father's shoulder.

"Let's give them some time to breathe and rest. Come on."

Pherrosh got up as well and followed his mother and father out. Mysse stood, too, but Asith took his hand. "Mysse, you don't have to go with them."

Mysse pressed his lips into a line, his shoulders pulling in. He was wearing warm clothes that actually fit him, thanks to his mother's handiwork.

"But I'm staying with Eroan and Uri…"

Dradevai met Asith's eyes. They were on the same page, so he spoke with confidence. "You don't have to if you don't want to." Asith set his hands on Mysse's arms. "I'm fine if you want to stay with us, and I'm sure that Dradevai is too."

"I am. If you want to stay with us, then you're welcome to."

Mysse looked at his feet, his shoulders shaking as he cried again. Dradevai wiped the tears from his cheeks and leaned closer, as Asith's mother had always done with him.

"Shouldn't I want to stay with Idhe and Cemi?" Mysse hiccupped. "They love Eroan and Uri so much, but every time they get near me, I feel like I need to run."

"Hey, hey." Asith set a hand in Mysse's hair. "These things don't have to be permanent. And it's not like Eroan and Uri aren't our friends. You'll still see Cemi and Idhe if you choose to stay with us."

"Asith is right," Dradevai said, setting their hand on Mysse's shoulder. "You should stay where you feel safest. If that's with us, Cemi and Idhe will understand."

"But… I've seen Asith's home. It's so tiny."

Dradevai blinked at Mysse, then laughed. "We can move, it's okay."

"Yes, we can move," Asith added, unsure why Mysse had seen his house. But he was right. Moving wouldn't be an issue because his home was with Dradevai and Mysse.

"Then I want to stay with you."

Asith smoothed his wavy hair down. "Then you'll stay with us."

"Yes, you will," Dradevai said. "But not in Asith's tiny house. We'll find a bigger one."

Mysse laughed, and Asith snorted. They spoke with Mysse until he felt better, and then Asith had him find his parents. When he closed the door behind him, Dradevai turned to Asith. "Are we parents now?"

Asith scrunched his nose and looked at the ceiling. "I think we might be. But I think that's really up for Mysse to decide."

Dradevai leaned on his shoulder. "True."

"How are you feeling?" Asith wrapped an arm around Dradevai and kissed their hair.

Dradevai kissed Asith on the lips, keeping it soft. "Happy that you're okay." They sighed. "Sorry that I scared you so bad. I'm not even sure what Elaqen did to me."

"It's all right," Asith said, his hands shaking slightly at the thought of Elaqen, but he set them on Dradevai to ground himself. "He's dead now."

"Yes." Dradevai frowned at the floor. "Asith, how soon were you thinking of working with Cairn? Can we honestly relax for a little while?" Dradevai's tone sounded hesitant, their shoulders drawn in.

"Well…" Asith rubbed the back of his head. "I think we should take a few weeks to heal."

"Yes, I think that's necessary."

"And once we have, I think I'll start with some kind of treaty between Cairn and the Graveyard Trees. That's what a diplomat would do, right?"

Dradevai picked at the scabs on their hands for a moment or two, but then they smiled at Asith. "I was hoping you'd tell me something like that."

"Really?"

"While you were asleep," Dradevai said, "Eroan and I talked about it a lot. The dragon knights may have fought alongside the Drake Sentry, but neither of us thought it would be the end."

Asith chuckled. "Was Eroan the one who first gave you this idea about me being a diplomat?"

"No," Dradevai said curtly, avoiding Asith's eyes.

"I won't be upset if he did."

Dradevai looked at him and raised their nose. "Okay, he did, but not outright." Dradevai smiled. "He was belaying his inability to be charismatic in most situations, and I pointed out that you were very charismatic and would probably be willing to help."

"Am I charismatic?"

Dradevai rolled their eyes and laughed. "Yes, very." Dradevai wrapped an arm around him. "I mean, enough so that just a couple of words caused me to take an interest in you."

"An interest in kidnapping me seemed different from an interest in listening to what I have to say. Something you didn't do a lot of at first."

Dradevai folded their arms, a pout forming on their lips. "I listened to you! Just not about taking you home."

Asith snorted and kissed their hair. "I love you."

Dradevai's pout broke into a grin, and they kissed Asith again. "I love you too."

They decided to leave the temple that night and reside in a small house that Lestash secured for them. Mysse returned with their parents, and they all helped transport Asith to their living space. It was chosen because it was built into a lower level of the city, as Asith wouldn't be able to go up and down stairs as easily. Mysse could continue to heal the muscle and flesh there, but his leg might never go back to normal. Their new home was near the large arcane lift that moved building supplies and people up and down the levels, so Asith could reach the level where his parents lived. Eroan and Uri were given a house nearby, since Uri couldn't fly.

His mother brought food and clothes, his father gave them potions for their injuries, and Lestash and Thistin prepared two beds; one just large enough for two people and the other for one person. When they finished getting everything inside, his mother and Pherrosh made sure they all ate before they left. The last thing his mother did was give Mysse a cloth rabbit doll she'd made. Asith recognized the fabric belonged to his and Dradevai's old tunics.

That left Asith, Dradevai, and Mysse sitting on the floor near a small table, with a warm fire in the hearth started by Dradevai's breath. The floor was more comfortable for Asith to stretch out his leg, and Dradevai lay flat, complaining of pain in their back. Mysse offered some healing magic, but they both told him to rest. Yarrow settled in Asith's lap, happy to have him rubbing her ears.

As they huddled together, they discussed how they'd decorate their new home. Mysse spoke about not wanting much other than a bookshelf, and Asith peered at Dradevai over his head, the two of them silently agreeing Mysse would be receiving much more than a bookshelf. Asith reached for their hand, and a new family grew in the soft light of the flickering flames.

CHAPTER 32

Year 570 with Vitiope
21st of Katib

Asith stood next to the open gates of the Graveyard Trees, taking in the smell of the large birch trees, Yarrow cleaning her face at his feet. Many of the grave trees were budding, with the leaves perking up along the branches, which knitted together into the heavy canopy that blotted out the sky. That made the light coming from the gate feel brighter, Asith realized, as he squinted toward the Cairn army and many dragon knights collecting their things to leave.

The Graveyard Trees would bloom shortly after he, Dradevai, and Mysse left, peppering the canopy with pinks, whites, and purples, whose petals would eventually coat the boardwalks. Asith barely remembered it looking like that, as, the year before, he'd barely left his house, too lost without Dradevai to enjoy the city. He would be missing spring again, though that time, he'd be with Dradevai. They needed to turn in Heskel and appeal to the leaders of Cairn alongside the dragon knights. That was a much better reason to miss spring, and he could always share it with Dradevai the following year.

"Ready?"

Dradevai approached him with a heavy pack on their back, with Mysse plodding after them, carrying a lighter bag on his shoulders. The boy was wearing a well-fitted blue tunic with brown leggings, which were both trimmed with embroidery in the traditional style of the Graveyard Trees. But they carried his mother's obvious flair. A series of yellow tulips wrapped around his wrists and the collar of the tunic, an uncommon flower to sew for that kind of embroidery, but they suited Mysse rather well. He also wore a navy cloak made of thick wool that had tulips trickling down the front. The outfit made him look both older and younger, but perhaps that was due to the weight he'd put on since eating more frequently. Regardless, wearing clothes that fit him correctly made him look like a young teen.

Asith grinned and ruffled Mysse's hair. He chuckled and pushed Asith's hand away. Setting their pack on the ground, Dradevai grinned at them, then raised on their toes to kiss Asith.

"I'm ready," Asith said. "How are you both feeling?"

"Good," Dradevai said and turned to Mysse, knowing the question was more for him.

"I think I'm ready." Mysse shifted on his feet. "So long as I'm with you both, I'll be okay."

Asith kneeled, leaning on his staff. He looked Mysse in the eyes and smoothed the cloak down under the straps of his backpack. "We'll be with you every step of the way. But if for any reason you decide you don't want to tell your story in front of a lot of people, there's nothing wrong with that."

Mysse scanned Asith's face and nodded shallowly. Dradevai set a hand on the back of Mysse's head and squatted next to Asith. Brushing some of his hair out of his face, they said, "You have time to think while we travel. You'll stay with us regardless."

"I know," Mysse said. "I want to go with you both, no matter what."

Asith smiled at Mysse and removed a package wrapped in waxed fabric and twine from his small satchel. Mysse's eyes grew large, his lips small and round. Asith chuckled and offered it to him.

"I thought you'd like to have this on the road," Asith said.

Mysse pulled on the twine, and Asith shared a look with Dradevai. The gift had been their idea, but Asith had picked it up from his mother's early that morning.

Mysse's entire frame perked up as he cradled the brass compass and opened the vellum map of the valley. His mouth hung open, his eyes flitting across the page to study the carefully drawn curves of the mountains.

"This is really for me?" Mysse turned his head between Asith's and Dradevai's faces, as if he didn't know whom to look at.

"Yes," Dradevai said, their golden eyes bright as they gestured at the map. "We thought it would give you something to do if you could record the path we travel."

"You told me you wanted to travel and see lots of places," Asith said, starting to feel uncomfortable on his injured leg but not wanting to get up yet. He wanted to make sure Mysse understood their intentions, that he was going to work toward a world where Mysse could safely travel.

Tears filled Mysse's reddish eyelashes, and his lips wobbled. Then his mouth opened into a grin that was childish and wide, exposing his teeth and tongue as a laugh came from his throat. It was the most childish Mysse had ever looked while happy, and Asith pulled Mysse into a tight hug, with Yarrow scurrying around them.

"Thank you," Mysse said, tears falling over his eyes, and turned to hug Dradevai as well.

Dradevai kissed Mysse's hair, then supported Asith in standing, and Mysse extended his hands to spot Asith. If he was being honest, he was not looking forward to the long walk to Cairn, but he needed to go. His story, Dradevai's, Mysse's, and his father's needed to be shared with people. Asith hissed as he straightened and assured Dradevai he would be fine, and Yarrow hopped into his bag.

They walked through the front gates of the Graveyard Trees and to the dragon knights, who were nearly ready to begin their trek home. Soldiers were among that group, many of whom wore bandages to cover burns. After Asith had woken, he and Lestash had spent their days forming a plan to return to Cairn. They received some good graces from the knights and army, as the dragons had provided medical care to the injured and Asith had warned them of their safety before the battle, but some distrust was still there.

"Asith, Dradevai, over here!" Delri called with her hand up, next to a small cart with the Stonegarde's symbol emblazoned on the side. Two sturdy horses were hitched to the front, and behind her, Eroan and Pystra were loading what appeared to be tent supplies into the cart.

"Are all three of you coming?" Asith asked as Delri wrapped him in a hug.

Dradevai unceremoniously added their large pack to the cart, then bickered with Eroan about his organization of the supplies. Meanwhile, Mysse quietly set his pack inside and pulled his new map open.

"Of course," Delri said. "We can't have you running off and refusing to ask for help again."

Asith frowned, his shoulders dropping. "Haven't you lectured me enough?"

"No." Delri crossed her arms and leaned on the cart. "In fact, I think I'm going to make it my life's mission to remind you that I'm here if you need my help."

"All right, all right." Asith waved her off, smiling. "Thank you."

Delri's face softened, and she pulled Asith into another hug. "You're welcome."

"Is Farin coming?" Eroan asked, his arms crossed.

Asith shook his head. "He's staying to help my parents with Cemi and Idhe while we're gone. But I have a letter for his mother, and he might join Pherrosh when she and Lestash leave to bring Heskel."

Since his aunt and Pherrosh could fly, it didn't make sense for them to leave just yet. They were also concerned about moving a prisoner on foot, even with Heskel's inability to do magic, so they would follow later. That way, there was no risk of losing him before he told the leadership in Cairn what he and Vetrish had done.

"Hopefully, he joins Pherrosh." Eroan frowned and ran a hand through his silver hair. "I just think having as many citizens who are not dragons support our cause will be helpful."

"I know." Asith set a hand on Eroan's shoulder. "Remember, all these people with us saw everything, and we were dragon knights. People will believe us."

Delri nudged Eroan with her elbow, distracting him by asking how many tents they had and what sort of rations he'd packed. Asith joined Dradevai at the other end of the cart, smiling at Pystra, who had enlisted Mysse to help her find something in a crate.

Dradevai wrapped an arm around Asith's waist and gave him a little squeeze, letting Asith lean his weight on them. "How is your leg?"

Asith pursed his lips. "It could be better." Just thinking about it made the pain feel sharper. "But Mysse is going to keep treating it with his magic."

Dradevai hummed, eyeing Asith's waist. They positioned themself in front of Asith, then crouched and secured their arms around his waist.

Asith's brow wrinkled. "Wait, what are you—"

Dradevai hoisted Asith almost all the way over their shoulder, and he yelped, his good leg flailing, while Yarrow hopped out and circled Dradevai's feet.

"You're going in the cart," Dradevai declared, carefully stepping over Yarrow, who was giving small distressed honks.

"I would have gotten in the cart if you had just asked!" Asith gripped their shoulder, his face growing hot as Delri's and Eroan's laughter rose from behind.

Dradevai gently set him into the cart, positioning Asith's injured leg to stick out the back. "No, you would have argued for twenty minutes and tried to walk until we forced you into the cart." Dradevai crossed their arms. "The same way you insist on going up the stairs to your mother's house."

Asith froze. He didn't realize they'd noticed him doing that, but he thought using his leg would prevent it from becoming stiff. Casting his eyes down, he watched Yarrow leap into the cart.

"Looks like you're staying in the cart," Eroan said. When Asith looked up, his eyes were narrow, and a broad smirk had stretched across his face.

Asith picked up a dried bean and chucked it at him. The bean bounced off Eroan's head, and he simply laughed, Delri snorting as well.

"Asith." Dradevai set their hands on his knees, their jaw set and their hair fluttering. They looked wonderful. "Promise me you will ride in the cart."

Asith nodded. "I promise."

"Good." Dradevai got onto their toes and kissed him. Asith smiled against their lips, his hand cupping their cheek.

As they pulled away, Asith let his fingers slip through the ends of their hair, watching as Dradevai went to sit in the front of the cart and grab the reins. Asith shifted himself farther inside so Delri and Pystra could slide the back into place. Then Dradevai lifted Mysse into the seat next to them and directed the horses to join the group moving forward.

The grave trees shrank behind them, and Asith faced the valley at the end of the winding mountain pass. It reminded him of the very first time Dradevai had picked him up, the tops of the mountains flying past. That time, he wasn't being taken from his home. His staff thrummed against his palm, the warmth of the second sun at his back. The light touched Dradevai's hair and skin, and when they noticed him staring, they smiled with their slightly crooked teeth, their golden-brown skin stretching. Asith took their hand and laced their fingers together, letting himself relax. For the first time, he would keep his home safe without using his axe or sword.

Year 574 with Vitiope
30th of Mikha

Asith twirled his cane as he leaned against a wall in the Capitol building. His meeting had finished early, and Eroan was supposed to meet him there. He spun his cane over the back of his hand and caught it in his palm. It was a skill he'd gotten quite good at over the past few years. The cane was a compromise, as people didn't like when he carried his staff around the building, even though Asith assured them he would not use it to cast magic. Tensions between Cairn and the Graveyard Trees had lessened but were still waning, so Asith agreed to forgo the staff in hopes negotiations would improve.

His knees beginning to hurt, he adjusted his grip and stood straight, stretching his legs a bit. He idly locked and unlocked them, hoping the pain would mitigate. Just then, the familiar sharp steps of Eroan's shoes sounded from down the hall. He usually wore boots with a bit of a heel, because otherwise, he was sometimes shorter than his students, which, according to him, made his job more difficult.

"Sorry," Eroan said, wearing his usual soft smile. "I lost track of time doing paperwork and then a student had questions for me."

Eroan had officially assumed the position of headmaster of the Macria Spire that year, as most of the upper staff had been ousted based on their affiliation with Vetrish. Luckily, Eroan had stepped up. He wore his Maeria Spire robes, tied with a leather belt that had belonged to Hamon. Asith had trimmed some of the extra leather and made holes in it to fit Eroan, and he had hardly seen the mage without it since.

"It's no trouble. I didn't notice," Asith said. "Though it's a little more boring to wait without Delri."

"You never do, yet I always apologize." Eroan smiled. "Also, you better get used to it. She will be on maternity leave from the Stonegarde for a while."

"I know. But she'll probably get antsy and try to come back sooner, saying she needs to ensure they're properly handling the lessons about Sterlings."

Eroan rolled his eyes. "We won't let her do that."

"No, we won't." Asith shook his head, chuckling. Though, he and Delri did need to discuss the integration with the Drake Sentry. That kind of work mostly consumed his time, in addition to helping dragons reintegrate into Cairn. He also identified people from cities who needed help with specific trades and filled those positions with dragons. He liked the job but found it boring at times, and he longed for the days when he could make his living on selling armor fittings or belts. However, his favorite days were those when he watched Dradevai teach classes at the Maeria Spire. They were only a guest teacher, as they mostly spent their time teaching magic in the Graveyard Trees to the children. But when they addressed the older mages, they were so compelling to listen to.

Eroan began to cast a spell, drawing Asith out of his thoughts. He waited for the familiar stomach-turning rush that came with teleportation. As his hands came together, they stepped onto the wide boardwalk in front of Asith's front door. Eroan always delivered him there, explaining it was close to where he, Uri, Cemi, and Idhe lived anyway. But it was actually because he didn't want to make Asith walk, even though his injury had mostly healed.

"Even though you're late, I can't really complain, especially when the service is good overall," Asith said with a smile.

Eroan was already walking up the boardwalk. "Yes, actually, I've decided you're not allowed to complain about it at all."

"I will see you shortly, yes?" Asith called after him.

Eroan turned and gave him a thumbs up. Then he spun on his heels and walked home.

He opened his door, wondering if Mysse had beaten him home. Luckily, he wasn't carrying Mysse's birthday gift. Last year, Mysse had seen the caliper Asith had gotten him in the Capitol before he could wrap it. He stepped inside to the smell of stewed pork, garlic and onion overwhelming his senses. He was unsurprised to find Pherrosh in the kitchen, with Mysse next to her, and Farin waved from the table.

"Asith!" Mysse called and ran to the kitchen table. He brought over a large sheet of paper. "Look at this map Farin got for me."

"That was very nice of him," Asith said. "And happy birthday, Mysse."

Mysse hugged Asith. "Thank you."

Delighted to see Mysse happy, Asith set a hand on his head, leaning over his shoulder to look at the map. It seemed topographical, of what mountain range Asith had no idea, but Mysse rapidly filled him in. The boy wanted nothing more than to be a cartographer. His room was covered in maps large and small, marking mountains and waterways across the continent. Mysse's passion could change, but Asith and Dradevai just tried to encourage whatever he liked. And if he was being honest, the maps were neat.

"Ah, I thought I heard you come in," Dradevai said, stepping out of their bedroom, their hair tied in a short ponytail. They were wearing a tunic Asith had made after they'd complained they had no clothes to relax in, with a pair of loose leggings underneath.

Their round face split into a grin as Asith kissed their forehead, and he pulled them and Mysse into a hug. Mysse laughed.

"How were the students today?" Asith asked, letting go.

"Mischievous, all of them," Dradevai said. "I was teaching them basic fire magic, and they all wanted to see if they could light me on fire."

Asith snorted. "You didn't let them try, did you?"

Dradevai shrugged. "I did. It's not like any of them could."

"I will not mention this to their parents," Asith said. "Cemi is going to try that on Uri, you know."

"I told them not to try it on anyone else, don't worry." Dradevai giggled and kissed his cheek. "Go change, everyone will be here soon, and Mama made a big dinner."

"Hey, I helped too!" Farin called, throwing his hands in the air, one of flesh and the other a wooden prosthetic with carefully carved sigils running along it. The prosthetic didn't match his skin tone, but it used magic to help him open and close things, which seemed to be all he needed. Farin could still pick a lock faster than Asith had ever seen.

"Mama and *Farin* made a big dinner," Dradevai said. "Sorry."

Farin crossed his arms, grinning. "Thank you very much."

Pherrosh waved at Dradevai, and they told Asith to go change again. Asith ruffled Mysse's hair. "You can tell me more about the map after I change?"

Mysse nodded and went back to the table. Asith admired how patient he'd been while he and Dradevai talked.

Asith walked into his bedroom and changed into more comfortable clothes before exchanging his cane for his staff. Warmth spread over him simply by touching the only gift he would ever receive from Raystash. Telling his father about her had been the most difficult conversation he'd ever had, even though he'd been prepared for his father's denial.

Yarrow touched his leg with her front paws, so he scooped her up. Then, through the heavy wooden door, the voices of his mother and father arriving at his home carried inside the bedroom. He kissed the top of Yarrow's head, and she climbed on his shoulder before he walked out to meet his family. His father waved from where Mysse was showing him the map, and his mother crossed the room to hug him tightly. She grinned at Yarrow, patted her head, and, as she often did, gently touched the flowers running along the top of his staff, saying hello to Raystash too.

"Did you hear?" his mother asked. "Mysse is currently getting top marks at school."

"Well, it's a good thing he didn't inherit my disdain for school."

His mother laughed and swatted the shoulder Yarrow wasn't sitting on. "You're doing well." She set her hand on his cheek and kissed his other.

"Thank you, Mama." Asith pecked her cheek, and she giggled as Yarrow's whiskers tickled her skin. She took the little bunny into her hands like a precious gift and entered the kitchen to help Pherrosh. Yarrow called out for him to not worry about her despite her being held. Asith had not been concerned, but he appreciated the confirmation.

After he spent some time listening to Mysse speak about his new map, Cemi and Idhe burst through the door, with Uri and Eroan a few steps behind. Uri was holding a wrapped package, while Eroan carried two rather large bottles of wine. They didn't really need that much, but he wasn't going to argue. Cemi and Idhe asked Mysse about his new map, so Asith listened again to all the details. Eroan handed him a glass of mead and returned to a heated conversation with Dradevai and Uri about something that he hadn't caught on to. Then Delri and Pystra joined the party with their daughter, Gidi, who Delri promptly put into the arms of Asith's mother in place of Yarrow. His mother loved babies, and that had not changed even after years and years. Delri sagged into a chair next to Asith, and Pystra didn't look much better, focused on finding a glass of wine, which Eroan provided her readily.

Asith offered, "Would you like me to come over tomorrow and take care of Gidi so the two of you can nap?"

Delri laughed. "I will never say no to an offer like that." She wished Mysse a happy birthday, and he thanked his aunt Delri, which made Asith grin. He deserved to have a family of adults who cared for him properly.

Meanwhile, Pherrosh and Dradevai were moving about the kitchen, having a lively conversation in Endethi. Dradevai had become incredibly invested in learning the gestures those first two years, so they probably knew the language the best. It wasn't until after that he'd started teaching, prioritizing a relationship with Pherrosh. It made him happy to see

Dradevai be with their mother and to watch Pherrosh treat them much like his mother treated Asith.

When everything was ready, everyone crammed around the kitchen table, save for Delri, who let the baby nurse on the couch. Pherrosh served the adobo with plenty of steaming rice and piled each bowl with the melting braised pork, making sure Mysse, Cemi, and Idhe received extra vegetables, much to their dismay. Asith let Mysse sneak a few green beans onto his plate when no one was looking, but he did convince him to eat the carrots. Dradevai had caught them but simply smiled and shook their head.

Pystra left the table to feed Delri at least a few bites, and after dinner was finished, his father enlisted the kids to help clean, shooing Pherrosh, Dradevai, and Farin out of the kitchen. Not long after that, Mysse opened his gifts, excited to receive new clothes and books, two of which were about mapmaking. Since Gidi was getting fussy, Delri and Pystra moved to leave shortly after, wishing Mysse a happy birthday on their way out.

The kids played while Eroan asked to pay Asith's mother to teach Cemi how to learn dressmaking. His mother insisted she'd do it for free, but Eroan felt obligated to pay her. Asith lost track of the conversation, only to get interrupted by a soft voice.

"Do you think Pherrosh would say no if I asked her to live with me?"

Asith laughed, surprised by how silently Farin had replaced Delri's position on the couch, but he stopped when he saw the nervous quiver in his fingers, which were twirling a coin across his knuckles.

"I think she'd say yes," Asith said. "What makes you think she'd say no?"

Farin pressed his hand to his face, the coin briefly sticking to his forehead before falling into his lap. "She's so independent. She'd think I was trying to take care of her."

"Well, aren't you?"

Farin glowered. "Yes, but not like that." Farin crossed his arms, an orangey flush plastering his dark cheeks. "I want us to take care of each other, maybe take in a little dragon like you and Dradevai have."

"Or have a little baby like Delri and Pystra just did?" Asith suggested.

Farin's eyes widened, and he looked at Pherrosh, who was preparing dessert with Dradevai. "Stop trying to tease me. Anyway, do you think it would bother Dradevai?"

"I don't think it would. They want their mother to be happy, whatever that means to her."

Farin hummed softly. Asith rubbed Yarrow's head, and her eyes slowly squinted closed. He moved his thumb to the very tip of her nose as she relaxed completely. He looked over at Dradevai and Pherrosh dusting little purple cakes with powdered sugar. Dradevai said something that made their mother's shoulders shake, and she silently laughed.

"Plus," Asith added, "all of our families look a little unusual at this point. I think Dradevai would welcome it."

"I guess that's true." Farin rubbed the back of his head, glancing at Eroan, who was trying to convince his mother to at least let him pay for the dressmaking materials. "'Cept for Eroan and Uri. Those two with Idhe and Cemi are so normal."

Asith chuckled. "I know. I'm happy for them."

"Me too."

With Pherrosh's help, Dradevai brought over the little cakes. Mysse's eyes widened, for they were his favorite. Somehow, he hadn't expected it despite it being his birthday.

His mother and father left the party with a large amount of leftover rice and adobo for themselves and another portion to give to Delri and Pystra on their way home. Cemi and Idhe had nodded off next to the couches while listening to Mysse read from one of his new books, so Eroan and Uri carried them away with a quiet goodbye. On Farin's way out, he ruffled Mysse's hair and wished him a happy birthday.

Pherrosh left last. She hugged Dradevai and promised to teach them how to prepare her green bean recipe. With all the guests gone, Dradevai flopped onto the couch next to him and laced their fingers with his. They kissed his knuckles, and he leaned in and kissed them softly, remaining there after deciding with Dradevai to clean up in the morning.

When they got up for bed, Mysse was already curled up in his bed with a book. He would read for an hour or so each night before sleeping, and they had gotten into a routine of kissing him on the head before going to their own room.

"Do you ever feel as though we spoil Mysse with attention?" Dradevai asked.

Asith had already removed his leggings and crawled into the cool sheets. "I don't think there is such a thing," Asith said, falling into the pillows.

Dradevai slipped their leggings and tunic off, as they preferred to sleep in nothing but their underthings, and set a glass of water on the bedside bookshelf, which held some of their many romance books, the rest on a shelf behind the couch; they had been slowly collecting them since everything had settled.

"I guess it's hard for me to gauge, given everything." Dradevai lay next to Asith, pressing in close to kiss his shoulder before their face plopped into their pillow. But the very edge of their jaw revealed a smile. Asith ran his fingers over the back of their neck.

"You know…" Dradevai turned their head toward Asith, half their face hidden by the pillow. "I never miss my hoard. I thought I would, but I don't."

Asith remembered the many pillows and books Dradevai had collected. They had returned a little over a year ago to salvage some, but a lot had been left behind. At the time, Asith had worried Dradevai was trying to be selfless, but he realized they genuinely hadn't wanted much more from there.

"I miss those self-warming pillows," Asith said.

"I will make you a few when it's fall." Dradevai kissed him, and Asith wrapped his arms around Dradevai's middle.

"You know," Asith said, "I think I have finally thought of something that will make me forgive you for kidnapping me."

Dradevai narrowed their eyes. "And what would that be?"

Asith grinned, and Dradevai raised an eyebrow, their lip pulling back to reveal their cute snaggled teeth.

"We could get married," Asith said. "Finally."

Dradevai laughed, their head flying back, and they pressed their hands to Asith's chest, clinging to his tunic.

Asith laughed, too, and kissed their collarbone and neck. "What do you say? We get married, I take some time off from acting as dragonborn diplomat hiring manager, and maybe Mysse could stay with my parents while we go on a honeymoon somewhere."

"That sounds wonderful." Dradevai cupped Asith's face, their warm thumbs rubbing the apples of his cheeks. "Let's get married."

Asith rolled them onto their back, putting all his weight on them. "Let's get married."

THE END.

AUTHOR | GAME MASTER |CONTENT CREATOR

Hi there! My name is Jess Galaxie and I write books, create videos, and all around enjoy being a nerd. During the day, I work as a content marketing manager for a large enterprise, and by night I write, play Dungeons & Dragons, make costumes, and much more. You may have seen me on either my Tik Tok or my YouTube channel, where I tend to talk about my passions and create movie-length video essays about characters I love.

Beyond my hobbies, I am a member of the LGBTQIA+ community, and care deeply about advocating for, and representing my community in my writing.